REBEL OF ROSS

Mary Lancaster

ISBN: 1-910245-15-1
ISBN-13: 978-1-910245-15-6

DEDICATION

To my husband, for the gift which set this story in motion.

And to Linda and Toni, without whom it would never have been published.

Map of 12ᵗʰ Century Scotland

Royal Kindreds of Scotland

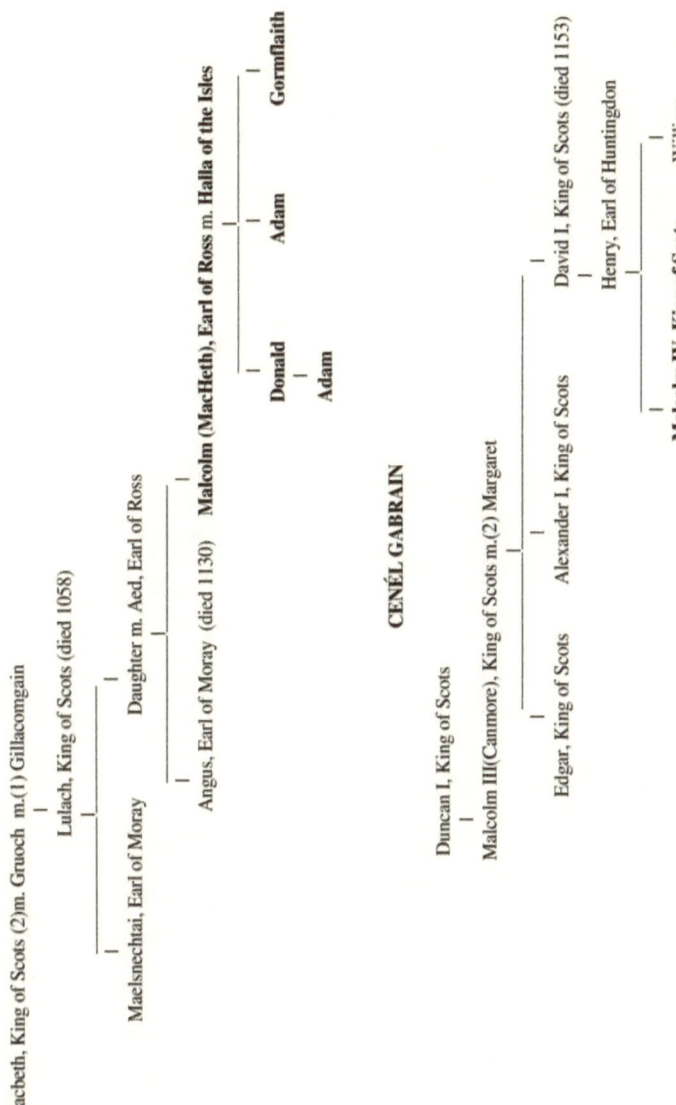

CHAPTER ONE

MacHeth.

All day, the sharp east wind had seemed to hiss that strange name as it sped past Christian's ears—reminding her that in this country, the elements themselves, the very ground she stood on, belonged to *him*, Malcolm MacHeth, more properly Malcolm mac Aed, the one-time Earl of Ross. Imprisoning him far south in Roxburgh didn't change that. And she still harboured the suspicion that every man, woman, and child in Ross, especially the turbulent sons of Malcolm MacHeth, knew that her husband was here to take at least some of it from him.

Christian lifted her face into the wind, letting it blow her hair and veil out behind her in a long stream. With one hand, she held on to the embroidered linen mask that covered the left side of her face and closed her eyes because, just for a moment, she didn't want to see the land William had come to take. She couldn't quite rid herself of the idea that she was betraying someone or something, that a hundred unseen eyes watched her with accusation.

But, already glimpsed, the view seemed to cling to the backs of her eyelids. Rugged, wooded slopes rose up under a lowering grey sky, with vast swathes of moorland between. Shallow valleys disappeared into the distant mist, and, half-hidden among them, winked the faint sparkle of silver-grey water, hinting at lochs and rivers and hillside streams.

So far, the journey north from Perth, though arduous, had

1

been surprisingly uneventful, any hopeful bandits presumably being dissuaded from attack by the size and quality of Sir William's armed force. Inverness had seemed to be a peaceful town, and entering the territory that was once the earldom of Ross had been accomplished without opposition.

She was going home. Home to Tirebeck, to the land and the hall of her father, where she'd lived the first three years of her life.

In light of that wonder, anything seemed possible. William wanted to be an earl, now that the King of Scots had dangled the possibility before him. Christian wanted peace. It wasn't inconceivable that here in Ross, they could grasp both.

Opening her eyes, she walked back down the hill towards her people, resisting the wind that tried to hurry her on in an undignified scamper. The camp, hidden from most of the country by a ring of hills, was mostly packed up and ready to move on. Apart from the women's tent.

Some of Christian's escort—left to guard her and the baggage while her husband took his main company to ambush the recalcitrant MacHeths—stood in clumps, grumbling together, quite unaware of her approach.

"If there's one thing more stupid than not actually *hiding* from the MacHeths, it's chasing them into their own country," one complained. "Trust me, this will end badly for all of us."

Henry snorted. "Well, just remember when it does that you're here to protect the lady, not your own arse."

"If you ask me, Lanson only brought her to get her killed."

Henry, catching sight of Christian just a little too late, kicked his underling roughly, and the soldier, inclined at first to protest at such treatment, followed his significant gaze and blanched. Christian smiled serenely and walked on.

So she'd become the butt of soldiers' jests and gossip. Most of her didn't care.

Besides, she was fairly sure her pessimistic soldiers were wrong twice over. William had no intention of letting her die, or, at least, not yet. Nor, whatever else he might be, was he a fool in war. Christian would happily have wagered everything she owned on her husband's ability to defeat and capture any number of wild outlaws. In fact, she already had. And while William baited the trap, she was content, for now, to hide here among the hills.

Unfortunately, William's prey was not.

****

They called him a prophet, said he was "simple," like his ancestor Lulach, King of Scots. That he spoke to the dead and saw his future in waking dreams. According to some, this gave him the advantage in battle, but right now, he didn't fill Cailean mac Gilleon with confidence. He seemed, in fact, totally indifferent to the mounted soldiers who, bristling with arms, crossed the moorland below their hilly vantage point. He didn't even look at them.

Adam mac Malcolm, sometimes surnamed MacAed—or MacHeth, since it was easier to say—for his grandfather, gazed everywhere else: up at the sky, then miles behind the column of soldiers to the rough marshland, or miles ahead into the higher hills. Sometimes he even seemed absorbed in the cold, damp grass on which he lay on his stomach. While the bulk of the men stayed well out of sight, Cailean and Findlaech mac Gillechrist sprawled on either side of Adam.

"We were right," Findlaech said.

"About what?" Cailean demanded with impatience. His first battle was finally in sight, and these supposedly seasoned warriors were lying around *talking*. "Who *are* they?"

"That," said Findlaech, lifting one finger from the ground to point to the head of the column, "is Sir William de Lanson, landless Norman knight and mercenary adventurer. The King of Scots presented him with the lands of Tirebeck, over on the Cromarty Firth. Looks like he's come to take possession. Come on, let's tickle him, Adam. We're all spoiling for a fight."

At last! Cailean's heart beat with a heady mixture of longing and fear. At all of eighteen years old, he was still untried in real battle. He'd brought his men all the way from Ross to Adam in Argyll for the purpose, only to meet Adam heading through the Great Glen for Ross and home. Retracing his steps with some frustration, Cailean still yearned for battle, to prove himself to the oddly detached young man he'd sworn to die for, and yet...now that the fight was finally proposed, he took in the reality of what they were up against. Although the Norman force below didn't outnumber Adam's men, they wore full armour. It would be a hard fight…and victory all the sweeter.

Everyone looked expectantly at Adam, who still stared into the distance.

"Adam?" Findlaech urged. "Do we attack?"

Adam said, "Where is the lady?"

Simple? Cailean began to think that Adam was merely stupid. Or actually insane. No wonder he'd been sent away to Somerled of the Isles.

Findlaech groaned. "Adam, will you concentrate on the matter in hand?"

And then, with a jolt—and not a little relief—Cailean understood. "He *is* concentrating. There's no baggage wain with Lanson, no women."

It won him a glance from Adam's strange, intense eyes, and a curt nod that warmed him as extravagant praise would not.

Findlaech grasped it at last. "This is only part of his force. The rest are with the baggage. And his lady, who's meant to be his claim to Tirebeck. Which we all know is *your* family's."

"By default. He had a daughter," Adam said, slithering back from the brow of the hill.

"Who did?" Findlaech demanded, as they crawled backward with their leader.

"The late Rhuadri mac Crinan," Adam said, "of Tirebeck."

"I won't fight you over that," Findlaech said wryly. Adam was famous for remembering everyone's genealogy back to the mists of time. In fact, some said that he remembered everything he'd ever seen or heard or read.

"Of course, it may not be true." Adam sprang up in one swift, efficient movement that Cailean, scrambling untidily upright, wished he could imitate.

Even covered in mud and riding rough for several days, there was something physically impressive about Adam MacHeth. Tall and strong, he was also handsome under the tangle of black hair and beard. Or at least if he wasn't actually good-looking, the fact got lost in the sheer, arresting drama of his face—a thin, longish nose, broad, ridiculously defined cheekbones, an incongruous hint of dimples, and beneath straight, black brows, those dark, tempestuous eyes that never seemed to be still, even when he gazed without blinking.

He looked fierce, and the men who'd been with him in

Argyll and the Isles never questioned his orders. Cailean, since meeting up with him, had wavered wildly between something akin to hero worship and a terrible fear that his hero had not just feet of clay, but brains of some similar substance. Some said it was why, lacking a father figure, he'd been sent to his uncle, Somerled of Argyll. And Cailean had harboured the suspicion that it was why he'd been sent home again.

Certainly, there was no doubting that Adam was odd. His boiling eyes would sometimes glaze over for several moments at a time, and sometimes he appeared to laugh or groan or mutter words no one else understood.

Now he said thoughtfully, "Lanson's wife may be someone else entirely."

Findlaech jumped to his feet. "He hasn't come for Tirebeck," he exclaimed with scorn. "The King of Scots made him ridiculous promises, and now he imagines he can defeat us and make himself Earl of Ross! Let's squash *that* pretension at the outset."

Adam shrugged with impatience. "Lanson will never be Earl of Ross. Findlaech, ride with all speed to Donald, warn him Lanson's looking for him. With luck, we can trap him between us."

Donald, Adam's elder brother, had been the one who'd sent Cailean to Adam in the first place. Their uncle, Somerled, lord of Argyll and the Hebrides, was their chief ally in harrying the King of Scots, but the Isles were constant distractions to Somerled, and Donald had wanted to give his uncle extra help to sort out his other problems as quickly as possible so they could all return to the main task of taking Scotland. Cailean, foolishly proud that he and his few men could make such a difference as Donald implied, had set out intent on glory.

Adam, however, had already left his uncle and was returning to the province of Ross when Cailean had found him. And now they were here, ready to face a force sent against them by the King of Scots.

Adam appeared to know his brother's location fairly exactly. Perhaps he did. Messengers caught up with them all the time, in unlikely places and from improbable directions. Since everyone else appeared to take this in their stride, Cailean had never dared to ask what was going on. Their silent trust in Adam alternately appalled and comforted him.

Findlaech scowled, unhappy with his orders for the first time since Cailean had joined them. But before he could open his mouth, Adam simply pushed him towards his horse. "Lanson obviously knows where Donald is—he's riding directly for him. Go."

With an angry huff, Findlaech leapt onto his waiting horse. "And what exactly will *you* be doing while I'm warning Donald about Lanson?"

Adam threw himself into the saddle of his own, larger, grey horse. "I'll be taking Lanson's lady."

****

When the attack came, sudden, ferocious, and at first terrifyingly silent, Christian had no doubt who was responsible. There was something inevitable about it. These were the MacHeths' men.

Christian stood well back, almost in the doorway of the collapsing tent, and adjusted the embroidered linen mask so that it fitted perfectly around her left eye and didn't impede her vision. Desperately, she looked for a way out.

The bare-legged warriors had swarmed down the hills surrounding the camp, taking her own lounging escort by complete surprise. Brutal, merciless, they fought in bloody tunics, with only a scattering of armour among them, just a few bright, ragged wrappings around their pounding legs and slashing arms. Pale skin under grey skies.

One of them caught her particular attention. One who, although in the thick of the fighting, seemed to look directly at her. He was a grubby specimen, no better dressed than the rest of them. Long, badly tangled black hair flailed about his face and shoulders. Two combatants lunged in front of him, blocking her view as well as his, but instantly his shield came up, knocking the obstacles aside indiscriminately. At the same time, he felled his own opponent with less attention than he apparently gave to the huddle of women around Christian. He wrenched his sword free, scarlet with Gavin's blood.

This was real. Men were dying for her. Men she knew by name.

"He's their leader," Alys hissed, as if afraid of being heard over the din of battle. She stood with the other women around Christian at the tent entrance. "And he's seen us! If he knows who we are…"

Christian said, "I think we can assume that."

"Show no fear," Alys commanded, drawing herself up to her full height. "We must not let Sir William down. Remember who we are!"

Christian had grown used to ignoring her pronouncements. With foreboding, she watched the enemy leader. He shouted something in his own language, running into the midst of another affray, hacking ferociously with sword and shield, kicking out with his foot to bring Henry down. Christian winced.

No longer even glancing at the women, the barbarian appeared to give his full attention to finishing what he'd begun.

Several of Christian's men lay dead, their throats slit as they'd lounged at ease in the lee of the wind. Others had been cut down as they'd reached for their weapons. Most hadn't even been wearing armour. Only minutes could have passed since the first enemy men had poured over the hills that should have protected the camp, but already it was over.

Christian raised her eyes from the slaughter, scanning the other low, wooded slopes which ringed the camp. In the end, they'd provided more cover for the attackers than for the women, but at the time, this had seemed the perfect place to camp, to wait safely for Sir William's main party to attack and defeat the sons of Malcolm MacHeth.

MacHeth…

There was no sign of her husband's soldiers looming over the hills to rescue them, to turn the tables at the last possible moment. Christian's ears rang only with the clashing of steel, the barbarous war cries of the natives, and the screaming of the wounded soldiers. Those of them still left alive.

Turning, Christian glanced up at the hill behind her. There too they had left it too late to escape. The women had been seen, and their only possible escape route was being cut off. Two men loped along the ridge from either side.

"We should run, escape," Alys said. Her voice shook.

"No point," Christian replied.

"You would say that." Even now, the contempt dripped from her lips like sour milk. "In the name of Christ, don't disgrace

7

him any further. They mustn't take you, remember? Sir William says *I* should pretend…"

Even in her terror, Alys remembered that. Christian felt vaguely irritated by the fact. William hadn't truly bargained for this and neither had she.

So it was over. Slowly, Christian turned back to face reality. The mask she'd taken to wearing at the king's court to hide the disfigurement of one side of her face hadn't brought her much luck after all.

Those of her husband's men left alive, swords drawn but wavering, were herded inexorably back into the huddle of fearful women outside the now fully collapsed tent. Their attackers advanced menacingly.

One man moved faster, pushing his way through to the enemy's front. Their leader, the man who'd observed them so closely from the thick of battle. At his gesture, everyone halted. He strode on alone, giving an impression of a young, incongruously calm face streaked with dirt and yet of dark eyes, even at that distance, not calm at all but deeply troubled, swirling like whirlpools.

"Drop your weapons," he said in passable French. "Or we'll kill all of you."

It might have been worth it to die, just to spite William, who had still no real idea how useful, not to say necessary, Christian was to him in this venture. However, luck seemed to have sent her the local berserker. Judging by those violent eyes, he was too unstable to rely on his mercy for her people.

She opened her mouth to command the men, but before she could speak, she heard the thud of weapons hitting the ground, the clash of steel as others landed on top, and she closed her lips again in silence. The MacHeth legend had won.

As if those wild, unworldly eyes had caught her tiny gestures, the berserker glanced at her, then almost immediately away as Henry formally offered him the hilt of his sword.

His mouth twisted slightly. Christian's stomach gave a sudden wrench as he took the sword. Almost, she expected him to cut Henry down with it. Instead, he inclined his head rather graciously, like a knight accepting victory at a tournament.

Maybe he could be reasoned with after all.

His men began collecting the surrendered weapons.

Others were already stripping the armour from the fallen.

The berserker stepped through the chaos towards the women. This time he had no need to push. The men left standing parted for him without a quibble.

"Which of you," he asked in the same soft, casual voice, "is the lady de Lanson?"

Close-to, he was no more comforting. Different shades of blood stained his clothes and forearms, his hands and face. Remote yet wild dark brown eyes scanned everyone impartially and still somehow gave the alarming impression of seeing something else entirely—no doubt his recent kills or his plans for the next ones.

Beside Christian, Alys cleared her throat. Christian could feel the other woman's tension, the failing of her courage, and yet Alys still meant to do it. Her loyalty would have humbled most women. Christian, it angered.

She would not let William do this. These people were in *her* charge, her care.

She caught Alys's arm, roughly enough to surprise her into silence. And to disguise her own trembling. "I am Christian de Lanson."

His gaze crashed into hers. Now that she had his full attention at last, she'd have welcomed the remoteness back with enthusiasm. Dear God, unstable was an understatement. They were the most dangerous eyes she had ever encountered: the eyes of a man who has seen and done terrible things and not yet learned how to live with them.

If he noticed the oddity of her mask, his gaze didn't linger on it. Turning away, he spoke only three words in the same quiet voice he had used before. "Come with me."

"No, thank you," Christian said clearly, and he paused without turning. Now Alys clutched *her* arm, convulsively. The other women drew back into the wreckage of the tent again, as if afraid his wrath would consume them as well. "There's no point," Christian said brazenly. "I am a useless hostage, being worth nothing to my husband."

"You are William de Lanson's wife?" The young berserker turned back to her abruptly, impatience clear in his face for the first time.

"I am. But disgraced and barren, my value is not high."

She actually laughed at his shock. "Ask them," she added,

nodding at her husband's soldiers. The one whose unflattering opinion she'd overheard earlier stood bleeding among them.

The young barbarian before her looked as if he had no idea what she was talking about. Without warning, he reached out and seized her wrist. His touch shocked her; perhaps it was the rough strength of his bare fingers or their unexpected warmth. But before she could properly register it, let alone object, he dropped her wrist as if it had burned him.

He actually spun away from her so that she couldn't see his face. It struck her that he was wounded or ill, and the watchful way a few of his men regarded him seemed to bear this out. And yet they never moved to enquire or to help him. In any case, the moment passed before it was properly begun.

He glanced back at her. "Let's talk," he invited. This time he didn't touch her, merely gestured with his arm in a fashion almost courtly. She couldn't hesitate; she could only pray he wouldn't perceive the shaking of her legs. She stepped forward, and Alys, reluctantly, released her arm.

"I am Adam," he said, "son of Malcolm."

Of course he was. Christian closed her eyes. "MacHeth."

CHAPTER TWO

Without meaning to, she let out a funny little laugh and began to walk briskly. It made the trembling easier to control.

"MacHeth or MacAed," he said. "Some call us by that name." He had fallen into easy step beside her, his stride long and swinging as they brushed through his men and what was left of hers. She wished he'd chosen her other side, where the mask allowed her at least the illusion of protection.

"My husband is looking for you," Christian said, trying to keep the desperation out of her voice. "He will return shortly—with rather more men than you."

"I doubt that," said Adam MacHeth. If anything, he sounded amused.

Christian glanced at him, only to find his disturbing gaze already on her face. Curious. Some instinct made her abandon the subtler approach. Instead she said bluntly, "What is it you intend to do with us? I have already told you my value to my husband—"

"I know what it cost you to say the words."

She stumbled over some rough tussock. He made no move to catch her, but nor did his gaze leave her naked face. She could feel it burning her clammy skin, wondered what he thought of as he looked.

She muttered, "Hardly. My people are well aware how the land lies. It makes no difference. Holding me will give you no advantage over my husband. You should let us go and ride off before he returns."

11

"I think you may misunderstand the nature of the advantage. You assume I will try to give you back to him."

Her heart thudded. Panic tried to batter its way up. "For a price. He will not pay. So what gain could there be in holding me?"

Adam MacHeth smiled. Briefly, his eyes saw only her. "Annoying him."

The sheer childishness of that took her breath away. "On the contrary, you'd be doing him a favour!"

"Oh no. Someone else has taken what is his. He'll come after you."

The wild, dark eyes left her at last. They'd come to the top of the rise that should have protected them from his sight. On the other side of the hill, a group of saddled horses of various sizes chomped contentedly on the coarse grass. One, a large, handsome grey, raised its head, sniffing the air, and immediately began to canter toward Christian and her companion.

Beyond the horses, the country of Ross spread out to the misty horizon, beyond which lay higher hills and wester Ross. A large, untamed land stretching from coast to coast. Malcolm MacHeth's land. Slamming him in prison for over twenty years hadn't taken it from him. The man beside her now held it for him, as he held her...

Catching the horse by the bridle, Adam MacHeth turned it, stirrup facing her. "If you please."

Although not quite the war horse favoured by Norman knights, the grey was not a pony. It was not even a lady's mount.

"*If I please?*" Incensed, she let the words spill out of her mouth before she could prevent them, but fortunately, they didn't appear to anger the berserker. Instead, he actually smiled faintly, a disarming lightening of those troubled dark eyes.

She swallowed. "If I go with you, will you release my people unharmed?"

Stupid. They both knew, everyone knew, that she had no choice and certainly no way to enforce such a condition.

Adam MacHeth nodded once, still waiting for her to mount as if blind to the impossibility of her ever reaching her foot so high unaided.

One of his men brushed past him, muttering something in his own tongue, clearly meaning to boost Christian into the saddle since his master was being so discourteous. Perversely, she chose to ignore him, and since there was at least a saddle on the beast, she leapt upwards, catching the horse's mane and the back of the saddle and hauling herself the rest of the way onto its back.

It was undignified and must have flashed an embarrassing amount of bare flesh as she threw her leg over—she could only hope the men were too stunned to notice. She was fairly well stunned herself—for just a moment, it had been fun. Then reality closed down once more.

Adam MacHeth landed behind her. His bloodstained arms, naked from the elbow down, thick, sinewy, and brown, closed in around her from either side, gathering in the reins, settling the protesting horse. She turned her head, watching his face.

But he looked neither at her nor the animal. His attention was on Henry, who had been dragged before them, looking alarmed but resigned.

"Go find your captain," Adam mac Malcolm commanded. He smiled deliberately. "Tell him what happened here. Tell him Adam MacHeth has taken his lady."

Add him to the list, William would snarl with contempt. She could almost hear him doing it. Such disrespect no longer hurt or even concerned her. Familiarity had seen to that. What bothered her more was the intention of her captor.

Leaving behind what was left of Christian's household and possessions, he rode in silence at the head of his men, not even touching her with his enclosing arms. He didn't need to; he had already declared that he had taken Lanson's lady. And despite the instability that she feared amounted to insanity, she was sure he had picked his words carefully. To annoy William? Or because he actually intended rape?

The MacHeths were beyond the law of the king and the Church. Since their raiding began to be talked of two years ago, the sons of Malcolm MacHeth had made themselves infamous for violence and rapine throughout Scotland. Besides, on the fringes of the country, in the parts not under the full control of the King of Scots, barbarous irregular unions prevailed. What did a marriage before God matter if by ignoring it, you could annoy your enemy?

As she had done since setting out from Perth, she observed the country they passed through, although now, perhaps, her watching had an air of desperation because she had to know her enemy.

And so she watched the people come out of their mud hovels to give Adam MacHeth oatcakes and eggs, not with fear but with acceptance. Some of the older people smiled at him. Some of the younger ones—the women—blushed if he looked at them. Christian supposed there couldn't be much competition.

MacHeth...

Shutting out the wind, she said abruptly, "Where are we going?"

There was a pause, long enough to make her think he hadn't heard or had chosen not to answer. Then: "Home."

Instinctively, she twisted round to look at him. His eyes were fixed straight ahead, open and gleaming in the lowering light, but she could have sworn they didn't see the muddy track or the woods spreading out beneath the hill. The man was unequivocally scary. But she noticed something else. Even in his distracted state—to call it nothing worse—he moved when she did, shifting his arm and his leg and even his shoulder to avoid all possibility of physical contact. The truth hit her like a revelation.

He can't bear to touch me...

She wanted to laugh. After all, it wasn't an unusual response to her person, as her husband would have affirmed. Hastily facing front once more, she remembered Adam MacHeth's reaction when he'd grabbed her at the camp. He'd dropped her wrist as if it was the business end of a branding iron. And he'd had no intention of helping her into this impossibly high saddle. For whatever reason, she was physically abhorrent to him. Perhaps he'd been listening to the men after all.

It might well save her from rape, she concluded judiciously—although there were still his men and at least one unknown brother to worry about. Either way, she wasn't inclined to wait that long to learn her fate. Now she knew her own advantage. And by now, Henry would have got the women and his surviving men far enough away; perhaps they were already with William.

She waited until the ground sloped downwards sharply on their left, falling away into thick wood. She'd never get a better chance.

So she shifted her leg back, as if it pained her, and stretched her elbows behind her. When he moved his limbs back to give her room, she hurled herself downwards, meaning to slide under his arm and roll down the hill into the woods whatever the hurt.

The breath thudded from her body. But not because she'd landed on the ground. Like a clamp, his arms had closed in on her before she could fall as much as an inch, winding her. She gasped with pain and rage but still he didn't let go. Twisting, wrenching in his hold, she caught sight of his face—and froze.

He looked...rapt. Yet his expression of wonder was at complete odds with his bruising grip. And more terrifying than fury.

The horse, completely unconcerned, walked on.

With new fear, she watched his eyes come slowly back into focus, felt his arms relax, although they didn't release her. Whatever his hatred of touching her meant, it was clearly under control.

He smiled at her. Not the slightly twisted, ironic smile she had already seen, but a dazzling one that caught at her breath. As if the sun had come out and blinded her. And then, it faded into quick suspicion and something that might actually have been embarrassment.

He frowned. "What?"

"You're not quite sane, are you?" she blurted unwisely.

Her captor, however, seemed neither surprised nor angry. If anything, his boiling eyes looked slightly calmer. "Who is? Why do you cover your face?"

Her stomach tightened at the reminder. She straightened in front of him. "Everyone likes it better this way. You knew we were coming, didn't you?"

He didn't trouble to deny it. He and his people had been one step ahead of William the whole way. Probably no one got in or out of Ross without the knowledge of the MacHeths.

Someone on foot broke through the trees on their left, one of Adam's men, by the look of him. He spoke rapidly, calling his leader by name, although Christian couldn't make out the rest of his speech.

Adam twisted in the saddle. The sudden warmth of his muscled thigh against hers shocked her. This time, *she* would have shifted to avoid the contact, only there was nowhere to go.

He lifted his arm, leaving her free on the right-hand side. Her heart lunged. She even began to throw herself to the right before his left hand, still holding the reins, closed around her waist. He didn't even speak or scold. Then his right hand came down, pointing forward, his legs moved in a sudden brisk kick to the horse's sides, and the animal leapt forward at an instant gallop.

****

Donald mac Malcolm, frequently surnamed MacHeth, had almost hacked his way through the fight to Lanson himself, and allowed himself to hope the matter was dealt with as perfectly as it could be. Lanson humiliated, defeated, and preferably killed by Donald; his wife taken by Adam. Whether or not she was who the King of Scots claimed, Donald's family would continue to hold her lands and the message would be thoroughly reinforced that it was not possible to take any of Ross from the MacHeths.

He had to admit, though, that Lanson fought well. He was a seasoned soldier: strong, efficient, brutal, the embodiment of the fight Donald needed. And finally, shoving one of the Normans off the rock on which they fought, Donald faced him.

"Sir William," he said in French, grinning. "Just the man I was looking for."

Lanson parried his vicious sword swipe. "Speaking French won't save you." He was strong, if not quick, and Donald had to balance well to avoid being pushed off the rock. At first Lanson drove him back. Since the men of Ross were winning, Donald let him, just to get the measure of his skill, and then he showed the Norman his. He drew blood with one swift cut, and then, taking advantage of Lanson's shock, he forced him back and back with every step, every cut and lunge. Victory was undoubtedly his.

Until the shout went up. French reinforcements arriving behind his own men, who now fought on two sides.

Donald seized a speedy, sweeping glance of the battle behind him and knew they could still do it. It would just be harder, and they'd lose more men.

"Fall back!" Lanson yelled, presumably coming to the same conclusion.

And then Donald was buffeted from behind, sending him crashing into the wall of rock at Lanson's back, and when he whirled around, his vision blurred, he faced not Lanson's sword but many. A row of men separated him from his own force.

"Take him," Lanson said, "and fall back."

"Yield," a young Norman panted, his sword to Donald's throat.

"Oh, for God's sake," Lanson fumed, wrenching Donald's sword from his hand. "Let's go. Now. Tell them if they follow, we'll kill this…who are you?"

Donald, infuriated by his mistake and his helplessness, his sheer idiocy in managing to turn almost certain victory into defeat, raised his head and laughed in the Norman's face.

"He's Donald MacHeth," the young Norman said grimly. "And what I've been trying to tell you since I got here is, his brother Adam fell on our camp three hours ago. Half the guard are dead, and he's taken the lady."

In fury, Lanson struck the rock with his mailed fist as they backed off down the stony path. The men of Ross stood still, staring after the soldiers they'd defeated. A few seemed to be arguing for attack anyway, but they wouldn't do it. Donald was the heir to Ross. And Adam had Lanson's lady. At least one of them had done something right, Donald thought bitterly. No one had to like it, least of all himself or Lanson, but there would be an exchange.

****

Christian clung to the horse's mane, at first in sheer terror that she'd fall off or crash into a tree, but both horse and rider seemed to be used to the country and to flying at speed through it. The forest echoed to the thundering of hooves, and after the first few moments of fear, exhilaration swept through her. They swerved past trees, crashing through undergrowth until they broke free of the woods. Then it was a mad dash over open moorland, the horse leaping over streams, taking the uneven ground in its smooth, unbroken stride.

Hills rose up on either side, narrowing into a glen and at last, by a rushing stream, Christian's captor slowed his horse and again lifted his right hand. She wasn't stupid enough even to try to escape this time. There was nowhere to go, and the chances were she'd just have been run down by a still-galloping horse.

"Rest and eat," Adam MacHeth said to his men.

Understanding the sudden swirl of Gaelic around her took

Christian by surprise. The men's words were often crude, and yet the very sound of them, the lilt of the language, threatened to deluge her with memory. She was barely aware of Adam MacHeth's leg swinging away from hers or the faint thud as he landed on the grass. Only when he grasped her waist did she jerk back to the present, grabbing at his bare forearms in instinctive defence. She could feel the sinewy strength beneath her fingers as he pulled her from the saddle and set her on the ground.

And then, almost as shocking, she was freed, stumbling backwards to land on her bottom on a grassy tussock. Since that seemed as good a place as any, she stayed put as if she'd always intended to sit there. No one, least of all Adam MacHeth, paid her any attention. They were all engaged in caring for their horses, letting them drink from the stream and munch the coarse grass while they discussed the likely location of people Christian had never heard of. Only the name Donald meant anything to her. He could have been Adam's brother.

Standing or sprawling in a shapeless huddle, the men ate the supplies earlier donated by the villagers, although two of them were climbing the hills on either side, presumably to watch for friends or enemies.

Adam MacHeth sat among his men, mostly silent. Although neither he nor his people looked at her, Christian didn't make the mistake of imagining she was actually unobserved. In fact, in much the same manner, *she* watched *them* from the corner of her eye while looking directly towards the hill climbers.

After several minutes, Adam's lips moved in speech she couldn't hear. One of the men rose and walked towards her. She dragged her gaze from the summit of the hill to find a very young, brown-haired man holding out a none too clean napkin with an oatcake and a chunk of something that might have been a rather scrawny chicken leg.

"Adam mac Malcolm bids you eat," the youth said in Gaelic. Although his meaning was obvious without words, he spoke clearly and she understood him. She even knew the correct response. It might have been an advantage, so she hid it, contenting herself with a mere inclination of the head by way of acknowledgment before taking the napkin from him. He set a leather flask down beside her tussock and then nodded, much as she'd done to him. Suspecting mockery, she looked straight into his eyes. But if he was poking fun, he hid it well.

He turned and left her.

In truth, she was too churned up for hunger, but since she was sure she'd need all the strength she could muster, she forced herself to eat the rough oatcake and a mouthful of the meat. There wasn't time for much more, for their break was short. Before long, the men returned to their horses—most of which were considerably smaller than their leader's. Christian would rather have ridden one of them alone, but clearly she would never be trusted to that degree.

Adam MacHeth stood in front of her. "If you please," he said in French.

None of this pleased her, but they both knew that she still had little choice. As she stood, he was already walking away. The youth who'd given her the food stood by the horse to boost her into the saddle, while Adam stroked the beast's head and gazed up at the hills. Only when she was mounted did he speak a brief word of thanks to the youth, whom he called Cailean, and then sprang up behind her. Even then he kept his distance as much as possible, again avoiding contact. It seemed that despite the familiarity, not to say intimacy, of their earlier ride together, he'd returned to physical repulsion. She might have been tired of that, depressingly tired, but he was an enemy, right now her greatest enemy, and it hardly mattered.

They rode at a brisk pace through a pleasant glen, and Christian began to imagine she could smell the sea. She lifted her face, sniffing the air, and the back of her head touched her captor's shoulder. For an instant, he stared down at her, his wild eyes swirling with darkness, his hair falling forward to cast shadow over one hollowed cheek. Her stomach clenched, churning with fear and with something else that had no name but felt a little like the exhilaration of racing through the trees. Awareness. Then his gaze moved and his eyes seemed to glaze.

Christian straightened her neck, and they rode on. Now, instead of the stillness she'd almost grown used to, her captor seemed to be constantly moving, twisting in the saddle, turning his head. She tried to ignore it.

Eventually, he held up one hand, and the horses came to a halt. Adam MacHeth wheeled his horse around, and the sound of pounding hooves heralded a solitary figure on horseback careering through the glen in their wake.

"Findlaech," one of the men said laconically.

Adam pushed through the column of his men to meet the newcomer, who eventually slowed. His horse blew and snorted for breath. So did the rider, a harsh-featured man with strands of grey in his black hair.

"Donald," the man panted. "Donald is captured."

Donald MacHeth? Adam's brother? Had William won his first battle in Ross?

Adam swore under his breath, although for some reason it struck Christian that he wasn't surprised. "Lanson?" he asked.

The man nodded. "He'd divided. While we watched one lot, another came up behind us. Good fight. We'd have beaten him soundly, only he retreated."

"With Donald."

"With Donald."

Adam nodded. "It's what he came for. Does Donald know we have the lady?"

The man nodded. "I told him you'd gone for her. What will we do now?"

"Exchange," Adam said impatiently, as if it was a foregone conclusion.

Christian couldn't help it. She laughed.

The man, Findlaech, blinked at her several times, as if, despite his apparent knowledge, he was surprised to find her there. Adam ignored her. She twisted her head to look up at him and although her laughter must already have given away some understanding of Gaelic, she spoke in French, openly mocking.

"Are you jesting? The great Donald MacHeth for *me*? Even I wouldn't be so foolish, and I'm biased. You might as well let me go. I told you at the outset. William holds all the cards. You have none."

His gaze flickered to her and away. "I have Ross." He wheeled around again. "And you. On," he commanded. "We'll make camp by the burn."

Fear, which had settled with familiarity, now surged up once more, clawing at her stomach. This was exactly what she'd hoped to avoid. A night spent with MacHeth. At least now that William held Donald, they might hesitate to harm her?

She wished she could be certain of it. William had made

sure the world already considered her damaged merchandise, so what difference would rape make?

I could take off my mask....

For some reason, that seemed a last resort. Right now, she had to concentrate on hiding her fear.

CHAPTER THREE

Cailean, despite Donald's capture, couldn't squash the elation of his first battle. He knew he'd acquitted himself well and bravely. Not that anyone had told him so, but the approving thumps on his back from the older, more experienced men meant more than any words.

When, night watches set, they sat around several campfires, Cailean ate in something of a blissful trance. He had to stop his mouth from smiling, even as his brain mulled over the problem of Donald's capture.

Of course, it wasn't really a problem. They'd just have to exchange the lady for him instead of for whatever Adam had originally intended. Cailean glanced at her. She sat alone, some distance from the nearest fire. Though she gave no sign of it, she must have been cold. From her posture, she could have been the hostess of some gathering in her own home. Cailean only knew her ankles were tied because he'd done it himself on Adam's orders—with apologies. The lady had only lifted her chin and gazed at the sky while he bound her. She'd probably feared worse than this humiliation.

Exactly what *had* Adam intended for her? Had he known all along that Donald would be taken and he'd need a hostage of his own to bargain with? Some of the men thought so. Cailean had no idea what went on in the young lord's strange head, although he had an inkling life was probably more bearable that way. For the lady, he couldn't help feeling just a little sorry. He wasn't blind to her position. Women were nearly always pawns. Few could rise above that, however well-born; the lady of Ross was the only exception he knew. But this woman, this girl, had struggled to make them believe she was a pawn no one wanted. And Adam was right about one thing: the admission had cost her, but she'd made it anyway in the hope of saving her husband and her people. Cailean admired that. He also tended to believe her. If she'd been lying, it wouldn't have hurt her.

The masked side of her face was towards him. He could only see her in profile, but that was…pleasing. The unhidden portion of her face was, he remembered, intriguing, even beautiful, if one could judge from half a face. Her skin was young and flawless, if pale from her experiences. A high forehead, a fine, straight nose, and pointed chin seemed to speak of intelligence and determination. Yet the curve of her cheek, the set of her lips, which she tried to hold firm, gave her a look of vulnerability that cried out to his chivalrous instincts. And she had spirit. She'd tried to escape, and she'd stood up to Adam, even laughed at him.

She was alone, the only woman in a camp of enemy soldiers…

"What are you thinking?"

Cailean almost jumped at the soft yet abrupt voice above him. Embarrassed to have been caught staring at the lady, he jerked his gaze to Adam, who was gazing down at him with the intensity he brought to everything. Adam rarely looked directly at you, but when he did, you had his full attention. It was…disconcerting.

"That she must be cold," Cailean managed, unwilling to examine the rest of his confused feelings. "And terrified."

Adam nodded. "She bears it well."

"That's no excuse," Cailean blurted.

"No," Adam agreed unexpectedly. "What would you do?"

Give her back.

And risk losing Donald? Insanity.

Cailean drew in his breath. "Bring her into the warmth, at least."

Adam's gaze drifted away and around to the lady, who still gazed a little too determinedly up at the sky, as if she knew they were watching her, discussing her. "I doubt she wants to be that close to us. Besides, she understands at least some of what the men say."

Cailean shifted uncomfortably. He wouldn't willingly expose her to the rough talk of soldiers. He felt annoyed at his own suggestion, and astonished all over again at the little things Adam noticed and acted on.

"If you'd make her easier," Adam suggested, "you could build her a fire of her own. I have a spare blanket in my bedroll."

Cailean's mouth fell open before he could stop it, but Adam had already moved away towards Findlaech, who was hailing him. As Cailean began to rise, almost numbly, Adam paused and turned back.

"You fought well in their camp. I saw." A quick, flickering smile and then his retreating back. And Cailean, his heart bursting, would have died for him there and then.

****

The boy who'd shown her small kindnesses before—Cailean—brought her a blanket and dumped a pile of firewood a couple of feet from where she sat. Her spirits soared pathetically at the thought of some warmth, before she began to wonder what reason there could be.

This was the one who'd bound her ankles. She knew that to have been on Adam's orders, and to give him his due, Cailean had been both embarrassed and as gentle as such abuse of her person allowed. She'd ignored him, fearing worse violence to come. Was the violence then to be done in the comfort of warmth? Or was this merely the kindness it appeared?

The boy did look rather pleased with himself, and in the flickering light of the sparking fire, he appeared to flush when she looked at him. She'd no idea what this meant, although she refused to let herself relax. Her body ached from the rigidity with which she'd held herself for hours now, to try to hide her trembling. She could no longer tell if it was due to ongoing fear or cold. But God help her, she was pathetically grateful for the blanket and the fire.

He stood at last, gesturing her closer to the blaze. She shook her head. She preferred her fires at a safe distance. There had been a time when, whatever the cold, she couldn't bear even to see flames.

"More food?" he asked her in stumbling French, making eating gestures with his hand and mouth. "Water?"

She shook her head. "No, thank you."

A moment longer he hesitated, then simply nodded and trotted back off to join the men, who were beginning to bed down for the night on bedrolls and blankets, some simply loosening their rough woollen clothing and wrapping themselves in it like caterpillars in cocoons.

Surreptitiously, she moved an inch or two farther back from the fire. She could still wallow in its warmth.

Adam MacHeth, she noticed—and she noticed him a good deal from both fear and fascination, inextricably bound together—prowled the perimeter of the camp. He'd set watches, so she doubted there would be any sudden midnight rescue attempts. Supposing William could find them. Supposing he tried.

She drew the blanket around her shoulders and hugged herself tight. All would be well. They were preserving their asset intact for exchange. She hoped William was doing the same with Donald MacHeth.

What if William simply killed him?

Then she'd die, and that would be that. Only it would be a shame so close to her goal…

She'd wait until Adam passed her in his circuit of the camp, and then lie down, try to sleep and revive her strength and her courage.

She expected him to ignore her, as he mostly did whenever she wasn't the direct object of his attention. As he moved around the camp, occasionally exchanging a word with one or another of his men, he scoured the land and hills, sometimes nodding at things she couldn't see—perhaps his lookouts, perhaps illusions of his disordered mind. And yet, although she'd watched quite carefully since her capture, she'd detected no disrespect in the attitude of his men. Perhaps they were used to his oddness, even proud of it in a perverse kind of way, like others were proud of a leader's cruelty, although one or two of them did seem to watch him with a care that seemed almost fatherly.

For whose sake did the people of Ross adhere to the MacHeths, rise and fight for them against the lawful king, die for them? For the absent Malcolm? Or the turbulent sons?

Christian might rail against their cause as one already lost, for the MacHeths' royal line would never claim back the throne now. The descendants of King Malcolm III and Queen Margaret had held it for too long. The old customs of varying the kingship between royal kindreds had long passed in favour of direct descent, son to son to grandson as was done in the rest of Europe. To themselves, and even to some others, the MacHeths might be royalty with a rightful claim to be kings of Scots. From the outside, they were disruptive and troublesome outlaws, and their recent fearful attacks only emphasised the fact. But here in Ross, the rest of the world didn't matter.

Had she really imagined she and William could carve out a niche for themselves in the teeth of the MacHeths? Her right, her diplomacy, and William's military skills...

In England, even in Perth, it had seemed such a good idea. Here in Ross, both she and William had been found wanting. And the strange, rough-looking man with the wild eyes, now walking towards her, was all that stood between her and oblivion. Or worse.

Something sharp clawed the inside of her stomach. Who else would Cailean have built a fire for but his leader?

The blood sang in her ears as Adam MacHeth closed the distance between them. Without looking at her, he passed behind her and every hair on her nape stood up in shrieking alarm. She held her spine rigid.

He was going to pass her, surely, continue his patrol...

He walked around the fire and sat down several feet from her. "You should sleep. We leave again at first light."

She stared at him. "How can I sleep like this?"

His gaze slewed around from the hill behind to her face. "I had to tie you. You'd run if you got the opportunity."

"You could have asked for my word," she said with dignity.

His lip quirked. "Would you have given it?"

She sighed. "No. Maybe. I don't know." She drew in her breath and looked him in the eye. "What do you want?" she asked with conscious bravery.

Surprise overlaid his guarded expression. "Nothing. I'm going to sleep."

"Not here!"

"Here."

"In case I bite through my ropes in the night?"

His breath hissed. "That I would like to see. But I certainly don't discount the likelihood of you trying to untie yourself when you think no one will see your immodesty."

"I've no idea where I am or where to go. I know you'd find me by daylight."

"Before," he said, shifting position, as if the light from the fire bothered him. "Besides, you could hurt yourself in these hills."

"And I could be eaten by a wolf," she said dryly. "I understand."

With what she hoped was cold dignity, she lowered her shoulder to the ground with her head away from him and, shrouded in the blanket, stared into the fire. From the corner of her eye, she could just make out his still figure continuing to sit there, gazing not at the fire but in the vague direction of her bundled feet. She doubted he saw them.

She'd spent most of the day far too close to him. Right now, he was the most familiar thing in her new, unknown world. Perhaps that was why, with his unlooked-for and dreaded presence, she finally relaxed and felt her eyes begin to close. For whatever reason, Adam MacHeth wouldn't touch her, wouldn't hurt her. At least not yet. As exhaustion took hold and the fuzziness of sleep began to invade her bones and her mind, she was aware of a bizarre and surely misleading sense of protection.

Must be the blanket, warm and comforting...

Her eyes flew open again. The blanket smelled of Adam MacHeth.

She should know. She'd been in his saddle, practically in his arms all day. Although she couldn't quite place it, his scent was distinctive, something clean and herbal beneath the usual male smells of horse and leather and sweat. The heat of embarrassment spread through her body, barely noticed because it seemed suddenly important that the blanket hadn't come from Cailean after all, but from his lord.

She shifted, as if in her sleep, trying to watch him unobserved. Slowly, his face turned towards the fire. The flames leapt, casting an orange glow across his skin, reflecting fire in his strange, unquiet eyes. They didn't blink but seemed to glaze. He smiled, almost as he had once before when they were riding, the sort of smile that eclipsed the glow of the fire.

Her stomach twisted. Prophets were said to read the future in flames. What did *he* see there? She listened to the relentless beat of her own heart until her eyes gradually, reluctantly closed once more, and she slept.

****

She couldn't breathe. Acrid smoke filled her nostrils, her throat. There was roaring in her ears, unbearable heat everywhere, pain she barely noticed for her terrifying lack of breath. Through the swirling, smoky darkness was a blaze she knew shone brighter than the sun. Fire.

No; dreaming of fire. Again. She opened her eyes to the campfire, now burned away to a faint glow in the darkness, and scrambled to sit up, her heart still drumming with the old fear. At once a hand closed around her bound ankle.

She froze, stunned. Beyond her feet, Adam MacHeth's arm stretched out from under his covering blanket. Either someone had covered him in the night or he'd fetched his own bedding; somewhere it chilled her that she'd slept through either happening. His fingers burned through her stocking, depriving her of breath. She was afraid to move.

Without releasing her, he pulled himself forward and sat up. It brought him face-to-face with her, only inches between them. His eyes seemed to boil.

Oh dear God, help me…

His eyelids swept down, covering the blinding gaze. He took something from his belt. A dagger. Fear surged afresh, but he moved too fast even for verbal reaction. He leaned downward, his wild hair falling across his face. The hand on her ankle moved to the binding rope, which suddenly loosened and fell.

He rose to his feet without looking at her and walked away.

"Awake, gentlemen," he said without raising his voice. The men began to stir at once, a movement that seemed to spread across the camp like a large, gentle wave. "Let's go and get Donald."

****

Christian's thoughts were so busy with her situation, concentrating so much on hiding her fear of the day, that she stopped paying the attention she should have to her surroundings.

The MacHeth men had prepared with dizzying speed, rising, rolling their belongings into saddle packs on their strong little horses, and mounting for departure as the first grey light began to shade the sky.

Cailean had appeared at her side, handing her an oatcake in return for her blanket—Adam MacHeth's blanket—though he gave her no peace to eat it, instead urging her toward the front of the gathering, snorting horses.

Cold without her blanket in the chill of the not quite breaking dawn, she'd been boosted once more into the saddle of the same horse and felt the physical arrival of Adam behind her.

It said much, she thought wryly, that she'd actually been pathetically grateful for the surrounding warmth of his arms and body as the horse plodded on over paths she couldn't see through passes between low, dark hills.

Without warning, Adam MacHeth said, "Why did you describe yourself as disgraced?"

Christian blinked. "Because the world does."

"What did you do?"

A soothing friendship, foolishly overvalued through loneliness and made ugly by accusation, violence, and death. And guilt. For although her mind knew she'd done nothing wrong, her heart agreed with William that it was all her fault.

Her lips twisted. "Nothing."

She felt him nod, as if that actually made sense to him. He said, "It doesn't always matter what you do but what the world thinks you do. Sometimes that works for you, sometimes against."

She twisted around to stare at him. No one in the months since the incident in Perth had voiced any belief in her innocence whatsoever. Including those who doubted her attractions, even masked. Perhaps it was this which made her blurt, "Is it true, then, what the world says of the MacHeths?"

His face was unreadable. "I don't know. I don't hear much of what the world says." He shrugged, as if emphasising the fact that he didn't much care either, and lifted his gaze from hers to scan the landscape on either side. "But probably."

She shivered, straightening in the saddle between his arms to face the way ahead. Daylight had broken on rough, green country that seemed to have the same strange familiarity as her captor. Small goats and sheep grazed on the green hillsides on either side of her, watching the cavalcade without interest.

Knowledge seeped in slowly, insidiously. She wouldn't even let herself suspect until they rounded the curve of the hill and came in sight of the house, and the salt sea air blew against her face.

A huge span of gently rolling, green land spread down to the sea, its distinctive earth ridges declaring its cultivation. More sheep and a few small bullocks were scattered on the two hills behind. But for Christian, the scene was dominated by a big, wooden hall behind a stockade. The gates stood wide open. Several smaller buildings surrounded the hall. Chickens clucked around the enclosure. Cattle lowed close by.

Recognition numbed her. She couldn't ask, couldn't speak. As the horse slowed beneath her, she stared and stared, deluged by a thousand forgotten memories. She didn't notice when the horse stopped. She barely felt herself being lifted to the ground. She stood alone and spun around, letting in the hills and the house, the smell of the sea and the animals and baking bread…and remembered.

Playing just *there*, with a boy about her own size, and a dog. Swinging high on the shoulders of a man she trusted. Not her father, though he was there too. And her mother, smiling, laughing at something Christian had said just to make her smile. To make them all smile.

The child she'd been choked her. She remembered the faces, the people, but what destroyed her was the *feeling*. She remembered happiness.

Her knees gave way. She knelt on the earth that had once been her home. She thought it was raining until she realised the dampness was trickling under her mask as well as over her cold, bare cheek.

She gasped, unable to control anything at all. Somewhere, she was aware of shame, of being seen by her captors in so much weakness, and yet, just for a moment, she could do nothing about it.

Home. She'd come home.

Adam MacHeth's dark face swam before her. Fingertips touched her wet cheek like the passing skim of a butterfly wing.

"*Cairistiona ingen Rhuadri,*" he said.

The name of her birth. Christian, daughter of Roderick.

He'd said they were going home, and she hadn't understood. But he had.

Some report had reached him of her supposed claim to Tirebeck. He'd been finding out the truth without asking, plunging her without warning into her childhood home to see what, if any, recognition she might betray. And Christian had given away far more than she'd ever meant to. Instead of returning as the gracious lady of Tirebeck, she'd come home a snivelling captive. Adam MacHeth at least, would guess the unhappiness of her life. Her pride and her plans were in ruins.

"I'll never forgive you for this," she whispered.

His lips quirked. "There will be more to forgive."

CHAPTER FOUR

He rose to his feet. Only then did Christian fully realise he'd crouched on the ground in front of her. He was the strangest man she'd ever met.

They were surrounded on all sides, the MacHeth men on the outside and people emerging from the main house behind her.

Adam MacHeth said in Gaelic, "We'll give them Tirebeck and Lanson's lady. It will seem like a victory."

"It *will* be a victory!" exclaimed a woman close to Christian. She didn't sound pleased. Presumably she lived here.

"We need Donald back," Adam said with a shrug. "I sent word to the foreigners to bring him here, where Lanson will find his lady. And so we live to fight another day."

Christian brushed her sleeve across her face. It didn't make her skin feel much drier, but at least it gave her the illusion of recovery.

She rose to her feet, staring straight ahead.

Adam MacHeth said, "I'll be back for you."

She turned her head, regarding him with hostility. "Is that meant to frighten me?"

His black eyebrows rose. "No."

For some reason, she wanted to laugh. It caught in her throat, fighting its way up until she swallowed it back with a sound halfway between a gasp and a gurgle.

Adam MacHeth strode to his horse, issuing rapid orders Christian couldn't quite grasp. At one point, he called someone's name. Eua. The woman from the house went to him. Christian couldn't be sure of her status. She was neatly dressed, her hair covered with a simple veil. She was still young and comely. The braids peeking from under her veil were pale yellow. She didn't look like a servant, but neither did she appear noble.

But then, neither did Adam MacHeth, and his grandfather had been the Earl of Ross. His great-great-grandfather had been King of Scots. The woman glanced at Christian, frowned, appeared to argue, and then, sighing, she nodded.

The men rode off without a backward glance. Baffled, Christian wondered how Adam meant to make the exchange. Finding his wife here would hardly compel William to release his captive. He was more likely to kill him or at least retain him for the extraction of further advantage.

The woman, Eua, walked slowly toward Christian. Her eyes were cold, and she didn't look friendly. Christian didn't blame her.

We'll give them Tirebeck, Adam had said. Against all the odds, perhaps because he knew now she was Rhuadri's daughter, he was letting her and William stay here. Providing, presumably, Donald was released. And yet he'd gone without waiting for his brother. She couldn't believe he'd trust a stranger to that degree... But in the mean time, she had to gather the shreds of her dignity and deal, first of all, with the hostile Eua.

"You live here," Christian observed in Gaelic. The first words she'd spoken in the old tongue felt difficult on her lips.

Eua's eyes widened slightly. "I did. Now, apparently, you do."

Christian nodded. It was the way of the world. If Adam MacHeth hadn't put her here, William would.

Eua said, "He told me you lived here before. In Rhuadri's time."

Christian took a step closer to her. "You remember my father?"

"No. We lived farther west then. My husband, Loegaire, and I are stewards here."

"For Adam MacHeth?"

She shrugged. "For his father the earl."

His father wasn't the earl, but Christian let that pass. "Men make plans without considering the domestic practicalities," she observed. "What will you do?"

Eua shrugged. "Go back to the lady of Ross. She won't let us starve."

The lady of Ross. Adam's mother, surely. Malcolm MacHeth's wife who hadn't seen her husband, to Christian's knowledge, for more than twenty years.

Christian considered the other woman. She didn't know anything about her except that she was loyal to Christian's enemies. But this whole country was loyal to her enemies, and she had to start somewhere. Besides, she rather liked Eua's honesty, hostile as it was.

"The King of Scots gave this land to my husband," Christian observed. "Whatever right you think he has to do so, it's done."

Eua's eyes flashed. "I heard what Adam said."

"I have brought a few attendants," Christian observed, "none of whom have experience running a household. My husband brought soldiers, not farmers. As far as I'm concerned, you're free to go where you like, but if you wish to stay, you could run things for me. Much as before, except the lady will not be absent."

Eua stared at her, her mouth slack with astonishment. "You have a right," she acknowledged at last. "But does your husband agree to this plan?"

It didn't matter. Christian would find a way to make him. "I can't see why he wouldn't. Uninterrupted stewardship has to be an advantage."

Eua lifted her chin. "We may not like to work for you."

"We may not like you either," Christian agreed. "We can call it a trial. For a month, if you wish."

"We'll never renounce the Earl of Ross or his sons."

"I know." Never was a long time.

Eua stared at Christian a moment longer, then nodded once. "Very well. I'll speak to my husband. And then, when he comes, you had better speak to yours." She glanced at the sky. "It's going to rain. Come inside and see what the King of Scots gave you."

****

In contrast to the outside, the inside of the hall didn't

flood Christian with familiarity. It was a gracious enough hall, but not old or rich with memories.

"You won't remember this part," Eua said. "The old hall burned down."

Bright orange and red flames, shooting through the roof; thick, acrid smoke choking her throat; pain and terror.

Christian grasped the corner of the big, plainly carved table, forcing back memory. Some things weren't good to remember.

Eua walked past her. "They built the new hall immediately, I'm told, in the same place, and the same size as the old."

Near the entrance to the hall was a wooden staircase, little more than a ladder, leading to a loft. Christian didn't go up, merely followed Eua through the hall, past the main table to a chamber behind, partitioned from the main part of the hall. It contained little more than a big bedframe, comfortably made up with a mattress covered by linen and blankets, and a plain wooden chest out of which spilled a few unidentifiable pieces of clothing. A child's wooden doll lay discarded on the floor.

"I'll move our things," Eua said tonelessly.

Clearly, she and her husband had occupied this chamber. Their children, Eua said, had slept in the loft.

She showed Christian the outhouses: the kitchen, the dairy, a brewery, and finally, as the light began to fade, a guesthouse which seemed to be used primarily as a storeroom. Here at last Christian found old wood and a sliver of familiarity. She'd loved someone who'd lived here. A wizened old lady. Her grandmother.

This building had a loft too: a bed space...

In spite of everything, excitement stirred. This could be home again. It could.

Christian drew in her breath. "The main loft has good space. If you wish, you could live there, partition it to suit yourself. This is too small for your family, I think."

"There is another, slightly bigger house. We could live there, if you'd rather have your women closer, in the main loft."

"They wouldn't be closer there," Christian said firmly. "I shall sleep here."

Eua frowned with incomprehension, but before she could ask the questions so clearly hovering on her lips, shouts went up from the yard, followed by the distant drumming of hooves.

William.

Christian had to stop him killing Donald MacHeth. If he did that, especially when his wife had been returned to him, the whole country would rise against him and the adventure would be over before it had begun. As one, Eua and Christian hurried from the guesthouse and into the yard before the main hall.

William rode in the open gates at the head of his men. Behind him came Henry, mounted and leading a horse on which a tall figure rode with his hands tied behind his back. Presumably Donald MacHeth. Christian's anxious eyes picked out her women in the centre of the cavalcade. Alys and the others looked pale but alive and unhurt.

William's eyes lashed her, accusing as ever. He'd won a victory and in his eyes was losing it again by having to return Donald for his own wife. That would be Christian's fault by now, not his for leaving the women with too little protection. She wondered, vaguely, what he'd have done if they'd lied as he'd told them to, if she'd let Adam take Alys instead of her. For the first time, she wondered about Alys's actual value to him. Oh, she was decorative and adoring, and she clearly made excellent bed sport. He'd humiliate Christian for her. But only up to a point. She doubted he actually loved Alys either. He wasn't capable of it. Her husband was a mean human being.

Adam MacHeth, knowing neither of them, had been right. William regarded Christian as his and was quite definitely annoyed at having his possession taken from him.

That didn't make him pleased by its return.

As the cavalcade came to a halt, he scowled at Christian, as though offended by her well-being, and then barked at Henry, who dismounted and pulled his prisoner from his horse.

Donald MacHeth was tall and dark like his brother, but any further similarity was hard to see. His face was bruised and swollen, and blood stained his arm and his shoulder. Beneath the blood, his clothing seemed finer and cleaner, as if he'd worn armour of some kind which had since been removed.

"So this is the hovel your brother gives me in return for you?" William sneered.

"Be grateful," Donald retorted in equally good French. "It's more than you'd have got from me."

"It will do for now," William said grandly. "Very well.

36

There's no sign of the brother's men still lurking in the vicinity. Presumably he knows better! The house is ours. My wife is returned. Cut off the captive's right hand and free him."

Henry, who was nothing if not honourable, blanched and fell back in protest. Christian hastened forward, but William's men were in a hurry. Cutting Donald's bonds, one wrestled his left hand behind his back while two others stretched out his right arm and held on grimly despite his struggles. A fourth man raised his sword high.

"William!" Christian cried out, but he'd never listened to her before and he wasn't about to start when she was in disgrace twice over. Donald might not die of this, but from William's point of view and hers, it would be as good as killing him. She saw exactly how hopeless it was before the swordsman even began his downward swipe.

And then something thudded into the back of the swordsman's shoulder with enough force to make him stumble forward. He crumpled to the ground, twitching, an axe head and thick wooden handle sticking out of his back.

"Where the...?" William wheeled his horse, but before anyone else could move, a voice spoke from above.

"Nobody should move. There are weapons trained on you, Sir William, and on several of your men."

Christian's spine tingled. That was Adam MacHeth's soft, casual voice, so at odds with the violence of his eyes. And his hands.

She turned, following his voice to the roof of the hall where he stood with his bow stretched and aimed at her husband.

"How did he get up there?" she wondered aloud. "He *left*."

"Of course he didn't," Eua said with contempt. "He just moved the horses out of sight to see what kind of a man he was dealing with. Now he knows."

And he'd placed his men in cover around the stables and the hills, from where several more were loping closer.

William, it seemed, hadn't looked hard enough for his elusive enemy. He seemed stunned. If he or any of his men so much as reached for a weapon, he risked an arrow in the heart.

Donald, suddenly freed from everyone's hold, gazed up at the roof. "Where in hell have you been?" he asked.

"Oh, around. The islands, Argyll, wester Ross, you know.

Somerled sends avuncular love." With one speedy, somehow shocking movement, he jumped from his perch on the roof and landed with surprising lightness beside his brother. "It seems I came home just in time."

"Apparently so. I hope you treated your hostage rather better than Sir William treated his."

Every eye turned on Christian. She froze.

"Of course he did," called someone—the man called Findlaech, she thought, who'd brought the news of Donald's capture to his brother. "But then, she's much prettier than you are."

A gale of laughter rushed around the MacHeth men, including Donald, who bowed to Christian with not disrespectful irony. Uncomfortable, she looked for the joke, which was probably that Donald's beauty had been at least temporarily spoiled in the fight, or by its aftermath, judging by Donald's words. Of the Gaels, only Adam didn't smile.

"My brother Donald mac Malcolm," he said, as if introducing him to Christian, although he didn't so much as glance her way. His chin lifted, and he raised his voice. "This is Cairistiona, daughter of Rhuadri, the lady of Tirebeck."

Christian frowned with incomprehension. He spoke in Gaelic, to his own people, those he'd brought with him and those who, like Eua, had already been here. It was almost as if he was according Christian his protection. What she couldn't understand was why.

Neither could Donald, judging by his slightly bemused expression as he gazed at his brother. Without another word, Adam strode forward. Donald kept pace, although the men who'd come out of cover from around the outbuildings and surrounding hills didn't yet lower their weapons.

As he passed William, Donald said in French, "Pray we never meet again."

At that, a ferocious grin split Adam's face and vanished. As they drew alongside Eua and Christian, Donald murmured, "Do you know something I don't?"

"Many, many things," Adam replied, his watchful, erratic gaze coming to rest on Christian for a moment. She glared back. He nodded once and passed on.

The brothers walked out of the enclosure, apparently

talking together as if they were at some social gathering, while their men trained their weapons on Christian's husband and his soldiers. Her heart seemed to slide up into her mouth when she realised they could still kill everyone.

The MacHeth brothers could easily have intended it. William had broken the agreement, tried to cut off Donald's fighting hand when he'd imagined he was safe to do so. This was their land. All of it was theirs, and de Lanson's alien invaders had taken a slice. The King of Scots had told William he could be Earl of Ross if he could subdue the natives. They had no reason to let him live, to let any of his people live.

The men of Ross began to back away, bows and spears still raised. Every few steps, a few lowered their weapons and loped off, until they'd all faded beyond the enclosure and the whole troop vanished in a rush of mud splatters.

Christian's shoulders sagged. "What a very strange day," she remarked, then took a deep breath and walked forward to meet her husband. She knew what was coming, and it wouldn't be good.

****

"Can you ride?" Adam's words came out in little more than a breath once they were clear of the gates.

Donald nodded. In truth, he ached all over from battle wounds, particularly the one in his side, and from Lanson's furious beating once he'd realised he'd have to give up his prize. But none of that, not even the humiliation of the position he'd so stupidly got himself into, seemed to matter right now. His heart sang because he was free. He wanted to laugh because Adam was back.

One of young Cailean's men was running towards them, leading Adam's big grey horse which, it seemed, he hadn't managed to kill in the last eighteen months. Well, most of his fighting with Somerled had been from the sea. The other, smaller horses trotted after the grey, as if they knew their place.

"It was nicely done," Donald allowed, trying not to wince as he hauled himself into the saddle of the other beast presented to him. Even so, he noted and approved the caution of Adam's men, many of whom still stood facing the gate, bows and spears at the ready. "Only, flattered as I am, why did you throw in Tirebeck?"

"Tirebeck is hers," Adam said from the saddle. He was

scanning the horizon, still eternally watchful, because he never knew when the visions would show him something that wasn't there. He kicked forward, not at a gallop but a mere canter, which allowed Donald to just about hold on and ride beside him as they spoke through the rushing wind.

"Then she *is* Rhuadri's daughter?" Donald asked.

"Her name is Cairistiona."

"Is that significant?"

"It's what Rhuadri named his daughter."

Donald gazed at him, half-annoyed, half-impressed, a mixed emotion he'd got used to, growing up with Adam. "How do you even know that?"

"It was talked about," Adam said vaguely, "when Rhuadri died."

Donald blinked. "You were six years old."

Adam didn't respond. The wind blew his black hair out behind him. Unkempt as he was, his whole person covered in mud and blood, he looked more like a low-born bandit than royalty.

Donald, remembering all the frustrations of living with his brother, said, "Legality is a luxury we can't afford. We don't want Lanson at Tirebeck."

Adam nodded, in perfect agreement. "In the short term, we'll move the galleys. In the long term, we'll set up watch on Tirebeck and I'll kill Lanson."

Donald let out a shout of laughter. "Is that a vision or just desire?"

"Both," Adam said.

"For what it's worth, he's not an easy man to kill. I suspect he doesn't fight unless the odds are in his favour. Even so, I'll insist on elder-brother privileges and kill him myself."

Adam appeared to consider this. "Maybe. Look." He veered left off the track, heading for a shepherd's hut. "We'll stop here and let your wounds be tended. I'll get the men to sail what galleys they can to the inlet south of Rosemarkie. We'll take the rest overland with us."

Donald stared at him, slowing his horse in front of the hut as the shepherd emerged. "You don't have enough men for that."

"You do. They'll be along any time. Besides, the men of Tirebeck will do the sailing."

"Under the Norman's nose?" Donald slid out of the

saddle, staggering slightly.

"If they do it tonight." To Donald's surprise, Adam threw one arm around his shoulder, a gesture of camaraderie that covered the fact it was his arm that held Donald upright as they walked into the hut, past the bent shepherd and his straight, tall son, and greeted the shepherd's wife. For a man so isolated from the world, Adam could be astonishingly perceptive. Not to say discreet.

Away from the men, Adam laid him on the bed made up on clean straw and unerringly found the most troublesome sword cut in his side. Without the need to pretend, Donald's hold on consciousness began to fade. He heard the shepherd's wife cluck with disapproval, felt her gentle hands on his flesh, and stupidly missed the firmer, rougher touch of his brother.

He flung open his eyes again, peering wildly into the darkness for him, but it seemed he'd already vanished into the night.

****

Sigurd, the shepherd's son, had only ever seen the earl's sons from a distance as they rode past on their way to upset some other people in some other land. He tried to be grateful for the peace and relative prosperity of his parents and his community, but Sigurd had been brought up to think for himself. As his father's only son, he'd never been intended for war, and unlike most of his contemporaries, he had no desire to follow the young lords to whatever glory—or, more likely, death—that God had in store for them. He had even less desire to have them barge their way into his home, especially when, so rumour said, they'd just installed some Norman warrior at the hall. Which seemed bizarre behaviour, even for a MacHeth.

So, while his mother tended the wounded one, Sigurd scowled at them both. Some ancient and idiotic tradition meant they would pretend to their men that Donald was uninjured, as if the weapons of mere ordinary mortals could not touch the great lords of Ross.

The wounded one, Donald, kept his gaze firmly on his brother, who at first looked back with such intensity that Sigurd actually began to wonder if the ridiculous rumours were true and Adam really could see a man's soul and his future just from looking in his eyes.

Noblemen's sons, he'd imagined from old stories, always hated each other and wanted what the other had because each wanted to be heir to their father. But staring at them without sympathy, Sigurd could see no hatred in the heirs of Malcolm MacHeth's turbulence. Donald flailed until Adam touched his hand, and then was still. And Sigurd, who enjoyed the character of men as well as of his flock, could see that Adam wanted his brother to live.

He'd only just made the discovery when Adam lifted his head and caught Sigurd staring. In spite of himself, Sigurd flushed, but he lifted his chin to show that he was no servile nonentity just waiting for his lord's instruction. If Adam noticed the gesture of defiance, he gave no sign of it.

"What is your name?" he asked abruptly.

"Sigurd. My father is—"

"I know your father. And your mother tended my broken arm when I was six. I'm Adam, son of Malcolm."

Sigurd blinked. "I know that."

"I need to go down to the shore. The foreigners shouldn't bother you today, and we'll be gone by nightfall. Will you look after my brother until then, and send to me if he needs me? Or if the soldiers move from the hall enclosure."

Perhaps it was the fact that Adam didn't order. Or perhaps it was the genuine anxiety for the wounded man that Sigurd read in Adam's eyes. Whatever, Sigurd found himself nodding. And when his mother looked up from her gory work, a smile flickered across Adam's face and he actually touched her shoulder in a gesture of gratitude.

Adam left without a word, an incivility Sigurd barely noticed until later. The young lord was not at all as he'd expected. Maybe his father was right and he didn't yet know everything of the world.

****

So long as he was comfortable, William didn't care about domestic arrangements. He didn't object to anything Christian organised that night. Until Alys told him to.

When the household had eaten and Christian began to

make her weary way to bed at last, he followed her out of the main hall into the rain.

"Christian. Alys should have a chamber of her own."

Christian didn't even slow down. "Why? You have one."

"Yes, but—" He broke off. Alys couldn't enter his chamber without stepping over all the sleeping soldiers in the hall to get to him. "Just see to it."

Christian laughed. "William, if she wants to play at being your wife, let her, but I won't upset my own comfort any further just to make it easier for her. Let her have the courage of her convictions or sleep somewhere else. If you've tired of her whining, send her back to Perth. Or London. Or Rouen. I really don't care."

And the truly satisfying thing was, she didn't.

When she shut the door of the guesthouse, he still stood there staring.

"The alternative is to send *you* back!" he railed through the door.

Christian laughed with derision. Alys couldn't have organised a drinking contest in a brewery. With her devastating new clarity, Christian knew Alys would make a terrible wife for William. Besides, like most men, he wanted a virtuous lady and that, Alys no longer was —thanks to him, of course, but the injustice of that would escape him along with that of Christian's own intolerable position over the last three years.

She bolted the door and climbed the ladder to her little loft bed, hurriedly made up but more welcome right now than the finest mattress.

****

As good as his word, Adam came back before nightfall with four men and a stretcher made of an old sail and two wooden poles.

"I'm not travelling in that," Donald said weakly.

"Just for tonight," Adam said. "No one will see, and you'll be back on horseback by morning. We can't wait any longer for you to recover."

Brutal honesty, thought Sigurd, but it silenced Donald's objections. The men laid him on the stretcher, covered him with a cloak and blanket, and carried him out. Following them, Adam paused at the door and turned.

"The lady of Tirebeck is back," he said abruptly.

"So we hear," Sigurd's mother said noncommittally.

"Her husband wishes to be Earl of Ross."

Sigurd's father sniggered. So did Sigurd, though for different reasons.

"It suits us," Adam said, "to have him here right now. But I need eyes and ears I can trust at the hall. I'm sure the lady will want more staff."

"Sigurd will offer his services," said his father.

Sigurd stared at him. "I'm a shepherd, not a lackey."

"Sigurd!" snapped his father.

But a smile flickered across Adam's face. He didn't appear to be offended. "I don't need you to do any actual work, just become a familiar face and report any oddities to Cailean mac Gilleon. This," he added, reaching out and dragging a young man about Sigurd's age back into the hut, "is Cailean mac Gilleon."

And again, the young lord left without a word.

Sigurd stared at the closed door. "What exactly does he mean by oddities?"

"Military oddities," said Cailean mac Gilleon. "And shepherds who imagine they're smarter than he is."

"I may be stupid," Sigurd retorted, "but I'm not a spy."

"We both are," Cailean said wryly. "Sort of. But mainly, in case you haven't guessed, we're here to protect the people from the lady's husband."

CHAPTER FIVE

Christian woke with the astonishing knowledge that she was home. And somehow, the opposite of a flower that thrives only in southern sunshine, she felt as if she were blooming in this northern land. In the last two days, despite her own fear and the fighting and death that she'd witnessed, she'd felt more...*alive* than she had in years. Her whole being seemed to thrum with excitement, with hope.

The scenes of yesterday's adventures played out again in her mind. Adam MacHeth glowered through too many of them, smiled in one or two. Yes, he was strange, and dangerous, and he'd used Christian for his own ends quite shamelessly. Yet for some reason, he didn't seem to mean her ill.

Or did he? *"I'll come back for you..."*

Even his meeting with his brother had been odd. Their conversation had implied a fairly long parting, and yet Christian was sure the attacks on her and on William had been undertaken in partnership, and their manner to each other had given nothing away, no joyful reunion or bitter reproaches, just a vaguely friendly banter as if they'd parted earlier that morning.

Donald hadn't even been surprised to find his brother on the roof. Although perhaps briefly distracted by the understandable fear of losing his fighting hand and bleeding to death, he'd expected it. There was no disunity there to be exploited.

Disunity was *their* weakness, hers and William's. Their sole joint aim was land of their own. Christian's task now was to foster that, to make it work. To keep it. To stop William from destroying it. Against the odds, the MacHeths had allowed them in, but if yesterday had proved anything, it was that the MacHeths could eject them again whenever they chose. That wasn't comfortable, and in any case, William's ambition would not be satisfied for long with this tiny estate. He wanted the earldom, but he needed men to take it from the MacHeths, who held it de facto, whatever the law said.

Christian rose from bed, too excited to shiver, and opened her clothes chest to find a less mud- and blood-stained gown than yesterday's. Dressed and masked—she'd grown to like the tool she'd made to defy her husband, because it made her feel like someone else, like anyone she wanted to be—she sallied forth to explore in the rain.

Servants scurried around the yard, giving the yawning soldiers wandering out of the main hall a wide berth. They cast Christian long, curious looks as she walked past them. Most gazes seemed to be directed at the region of her mask, which pleased her. It really was an excellent distraction. She wished she'd thought of it years before.

The gates were closed and guarded, but although the men there anxiously offered her an escort—which she refused—without orders to the contrary, they obediently let her through when bidden.

The sea was closer than she remembered. Her heart lifted all over again as she walked down the hill past the field where oats were just beginning to grow in the warmth of spring, and over a well-worn path to the sea.

Tirebeck, on the widest part of the Cromarty Firth, was shielded by two curving headlands, the sheltered little bay well hidden from casual attention. The Norsemen had found it, of course, long before living memory. And the King of Scots could find it too, if he chose.

As she strode along the sandy beach, gazing across the firth to the land they called the Black Isle—so strange what she could remember now—and at the fishing boats making their way back into the shore, half-formed memories flashed and hovered in Christian's mind, a background to her growing realisation of the strategic importance of the place. Ships could land here, attack from the sea, bring thousands of soldiers to force the MacHeths to the pitched battles they avoided because the royal forces would always be superior. In loyal hands, Tirebeck was a useful asset to the King of Scots. In MacHeth hands, it had made secret landings impossible.

So why had they let William have it? Just because he'd taken Donald? If that hadn't happened, if Donald had won, if William had died, what then would have happened to Christian? Would she still have been accepted as lady here, just because of her birth?

In truth, she wasn't quite sure of how her father had come to leave. Flames flared in Christian's memory, as they often did. Her hand lifted involuntarily to the left side of her face, rubbed the ugly skin through her mask.

Had they been burned out? It was hardly an unusual form of attack, only who would have done such a thing? Her mother had never spoken of it and until after she'd died, Christian had never thought to ask.

And why would her father have fled south with his family rather than seek revenge? Perhaps he'd sought redress from David, King of Scots, since Malcolm MacHeth must already have been in prison and his sons too young to rule in Ross.

Whatever, it hadn't worked. She was sure her father had died early in their exile. He must have, for she couldn't really remember him anywhere but here. Her mother had then married Ranulf, a Norman knight in King David's service who'd returned south to England when he'd inherited better lands there. He'd cared for Christian when her mother had died. She'd loved him well enough, but he had too many daughters of his own to provide for, and Christian, disfigured and virtually landless, had been sold to the first knight who showed any interest.

Only after her wedding had she discovered that Ranulf had made her claim to Tirebeck sound far more real than it actually was. Almost worse, William had only seen her in profile, first through a window, and then across a crowded hall. A poor and ambitious man, he'd seized the bait, and they were both still paying the price.

She must have been looking grim, because a group of women passing her with nets of fish across their backs cast her wary glances.

Smoothing her brow, she greeted them in Gaelic and got

polite if reserved responses. The oldest of the women paused as if she wanted to speak further, so Christian stopped too and waited.

"Are we safe here, lady?" the old woman asked bluntly.

"I believe so," Christian replied. "I pray so."

Though hardly a ringing assertion, it seemed to be enough. Safety was never guaranteed. The old woman nodded with a toothless smile and passed on. Christian turned and walked with them for a little, asked them their names and where they lived. They answered willingly enough, without the hostility Eua had shown—but then Christian wasn't displacing them from their homes.

When she introduced herself, they all smiled. The old woman, whose name was Eta, actually cackled. "Bless you, lady, we know that. I remember you as a tiny baby."

Christian gave a half smile. "Do you?" A hundred questions that she'd failed to ask of her mother, about how and why they'd left, surged up. But she couldn't ask those. She had to be the all-powerful lady, with all the answers for these people, not the vulnerable child seeking help. She contented herself with, "You must remember the fire at the hall, then."

"I remember them both," old Eta said.

Christian couldn't stop her gaze flying to the old woman's face, although at least she managed not to exclaim *Two fires?* aloud. She remembered one fire, huge, all-encompassing. She'd been three years old. When had the other fire happened?

By then, they had reached the path leading back up to the hall, and she had no reason to cling any longer to her new companions. Her search for the truth would have to be slow, gradual, a few different questions asked of different people over time.

So, ignoring her own curiosity, she said, "You've been treated well? By the MacHeth stewardship?"

"Wild boys," Eta pronounced. "More interested in war than farming. Loegaire the steward has never wronged us." She adjusted the sack on her shoulder and cast Christian a sideways glance. "The simple lord brought you here?"

"*Simple?*" Christian stared at her. "I wouldn't have said there's anything simple about Adam MacHeth at all!"

Eta let out a cackle of laughter. It sounded like genuine pleasure.

"Not that kind of simple. Or even mad-simple," one of the younger women explained. "Simple as in…fey. He has the sight."

Superstition. Fortunately, she was watching her tongue so carefully that she didn't speak the word. Her companions might well have taken it as an insult, either to themselves or to their simple lord. And in fact, if she shut out her more sane and sensible southern self, she could almost imagine the weird glazing of his eyes, his strange aloofness to be part of that impossible gift of foresight and prophecy. Almost. As it was, curiosity surged afresh.

Again, Christian had questions, and again she felt all the frustration of feeling unable to ask them. In silence, she gazed along the shoreline at the scattering of wooden huts, big and small, that lined it. Winter covering for boats, perhaps, and large enough for ships.

Maybe Eta had given her the clue. *"Wild boys. More interested in war than farming."*

Christian's lips parted with sudden suspicion. Were there war galleys hidden in those huts? On her land? The MacHeths would use them against the king. If William found them—and he would—did she want that either? His men were not sailors.

"My husband is a soldier too," she said clearly. "But war is a way of life I don't want brought here."

Their eyes flickered to her and away. Not in disagreement, she thought, but in understanding. Like women the world over, they didn't want war either. They just got dragged into the consequences.

Having made her point, Christian nodded to them. "If you need anything, you can find me at the hall. Anyone can." And she left them to walk back up the rough-hewn steps from the beach and on up the hill towards the house.

As she neared the hall, a small troop of soldiers advanced towards the woods with a horse-drawn wagon. William, on horseback at the head of some other mounted men, waited by the gate, observing. He would explore today, decide how to make Tirebeck as safe as it could be—from a military perspective. To William, it would be all about fortifications, not about the people who lived here, who could and should be friends.

Not for the first time, she wondered if she'd done a terrible thing bringing William here. With all the diplomacy of a battering ram, he was bound to antagonise the people. And if it came to war with the MacHeths, as it surely must, the people would suffer at least as much as the soldiers. By MacHeth laws, Tirebeck and everyone in it were already fair game. Since she and William held Tirebeck for the king, the MacHeths would feel quite entitled to carry off cattle and raid crops. And worse. After all, they thought nothing about raiding south into the king's estates in Moray, or even deep into what was regarded as the king's own territories of Angus, Fife, Lothian, Strathclyde, and more...

Loegaire, Eua's husband, the steward, was with William, mounted on a small, agile horse. He didn't look comfortable.

"The women are quarrelling," William said to Christian by way of greeting. "Sort it out or send the lot of them packing."

What, even Alys? She contented herself with a sardonic smile and passed inside the gates. Who knew? If Alys was being difficult about her new home, William's answer might well have been yes.

Two years ago, Christian would have rejoiced at Alys's departure. Now, she found the other woman a useful buffer, a means of avoiding her husband. Although he didn't like Christian and she'd been pronounced barren, with William's physical needs, and Alys gone, she could well become the personification of any port in a storm. Providing it was dark.

With a slightly twisted smile, she crossed the yard and entered the main hall to find all three of her women looming over Eua. Cecily had her by the arm while Alys and Felicia screamed at her.

A couple of the men lounged against the folded-up trestle tables, watching the theatre and grinning. Christian dealt with them first.

"I'm sure Sir William didn't leave you here to prop up the walls. Attend to your duties."

As they sloped off, not without a few glances over their shoulders, the women stopped screaming, although Cecily didn't release Eua's arm. Eua herself stood rigid in the younger girl's hold, fury spitting from her eyes and thinning her mouth to a hard line.

"Cecily," Christian snapped, and Cecily dropped Eua's arm like a hot coal—more through surprise than actual fear, Christian was sure. Providing they kept her few clothes clean and mended, and helped her to dress when necessary, Christian had more or less ignored them all for months, if not years. But now she had a household to run, her home, and in the midst of continual threat of war, she *would* have peace here.

She walked up to them, more irritated than truly angry. "Why are you screaming at Eua?"

"She refused to make our beds and wash our linen!" Alys exclaimed.

"You'll make your own beds and take care of your own linen until Eua has organised more servants to take care of a household this size. Eua is not your maidservant. She runs the household under me. Your first concern will be for *my* linen, and my travelling dress, which is in dire need of cleaning."

All four of them stared at Christian. Eua clearly had not expected her support either. Alys's mouth actually dropped open.

"Now," Christian said gently and turned to Eua. "We need to talk about meals. For how long can we feed everyone?"

Alys interrupted. "My lady, it is not fitting that I—"

Christian couldn't help it. She laughed. "*What* is not fitting?"

Alys's face flamed.

Christian said, "I'll keep no one here against their will. If you are unhappy, you may leave. With any escort Sir William can spare for the purpose. Now, Eua."

Ignoring the others, Christian sat down at the big table and prepared to consult Eua, who sat beside her, eyes bright with delight, although whether in having her enemies bested or in seeing her lady's unexpected mettle wasn't clear.

The Norman women shuffled from the hall, although Alys's muttered "Sir William shall hear of this!" told her the matter was not closed.

CHAPTER SIX

Gormflaith, daughter of Malcolm MacHeth, hated waiting, and yet it seemed to be how she spent most of her life. Waiting for her father—whom she'd never met—to come home. Waiting to be married, waiting for another woman to die so that she could marry Harald Madaddson of Orkney, whom she loved with a passion despite having met him only twice in her life. She felt a little guilty about this, since she'd no personal reasons to hate the current lady of Orkney—nor love her either—so she simply waited.

Sprawling alone in the tall grass half a mile from her mother's favourite hall, she lost herself in contemplation of the surrounding hills and glens, soaking up the rare spring sunshine. Idly, she chewed a blade of moist grass and waited, more immediately, for her brothers to come home. Donald had gone to meet Adam, returning from fighting beside their uncle, Somerled of Argyll and the Isles. They should have been back two days ago, or at least sent word if their plans had changed. Donald was reliable that way. Adam was not, of course. He was much more erratic, and he could easily have swayed Donald, or got them both into some terrible trouble...

Which they *would* have heard of. There was no point in conjuring up dangers for them just to pass the time because she was bored with waiting. It had been more than a year, nearly two, since she'd seen Adam, who was never boring. She missed his massive smile and his odd, forthright speech. And his even odder pronouncements although he'd learned to keep those to himself since childhood. She wanted the warmth of her whole family back around her, even her father, who sometimes seemed more legend than reality.

Through the long grass, some movement caught her eye. There, in the distant woods, light shimmered and moved between the trees. She caught the odd flash, as if the sun reflected on armour or a sword.

Slowly, she drew the blade of grass from her mouth and sat up. Her heart began to drum. Could the King of Scots' army really have come so close without warning? For a moment, she was torn between running to raise the alarm at the hall and the curiosity which urged her to wait and see who emerged from the woods.

The moving light in the trees formed into shadows. Men on horseback...

A horse moved into the light. It was grey, and its rider wore no armour. And right behind him, came another rider, and another. They carried no banner, but in Ross they didn't need to. Surely, Gormflaith knew that grey horse, the easy, apparently careless seat of its rider, as if he was one with the animal... Adam. And beside him, definitely, Donald.

From all over the woods now, men emerged into the open. And some of the horses pulled something behind them, something huge...mounted on a cart? Or no, just on rough wheels.

A ship.

Laughter bubbled up in Gormflaith. Leaping to her feet, she grasped her skirts in one hand and flew towards the hall.

"They're back, they're back!" she called to everyone she saw on her way, and to the men and maids busy in the hall's yard, before she burst through the doors and yelled the same to her mother.

The lady of Ross was with her women at the big high table, sorting clothing into piles for mending or giving away. Still fair and slender, with no grey visible in the golden braids which occasionally peeped under her veil, Halla, daughter of Gillebride, always looked every inch the great lady.

"Who is back?" she enquired calmly.

"Adam and Donald, and they've brought a galley!" Gormflaith laughed. "Why would they bring a galley inland? To convince the king the land is ours? Like Magnus Barelegs tricking his predecessor in Kintyre?"

Her mother stilled. Something in her eyes lightened. Her shoulders lowered a fraction of an inch, the only sign that she'd ever been worried. "No one else would," she said wryly. "But then we *are* talking about your brothers." She dropped the woollen gown on the table. "Have them open the gates. Make refreshments ready."

The lady of Ross never needed to raise her voice. Men and women scuttled to obey her. Just for an instant, Gormflaith envied her such effortless authority. Only it couldn't always have been effortless.

Halla, the sister of Somerled of the Isles, had come here as a young girl from Argyll, had borne three children in four years to her turbulent lord, and reared them alone as their father languished in prison for raising rebellion against the King of Scots. For more than twenty years, she'd managed the affairs of the earldom in the teeth of the king's denial of her right, had worked for her husband's freedom, and held the whole province behind him even in his absence. As they grew older, Donald and Adam had taken some of the burden, but these particular wild grown-up sons must have brought her as much trouble as respite.

Gormflaith wished for strength like that. For Harald of Orkney, she would be a rock, his right hand. Only she didn't think she could be these things if he wasn't actually *there*. Not for *twenty years*.

Gormflaith almost skipped back outside. Only at the door, she waited for her more regal mother. The lady never leaned on anyone. Gormflaith knew in her heart that wasn't good or right, and so she slipped her hand inside her mother's as she'd done as a child, and as then, her mother's fingers closed around hers.

But Gormflaith was no longer a child, and now the comfort was mutual. Although Adam and Donald were home, no one knew in what state or at what cost. And Adam... Who could tell what two seasons' fighting with the ferocious islesmen had done to his strange soul.

Most of the household had already spilled outside from whatever task or leisure was theirs, including the house guards and most of the maidservants, Father Patrick, her mother's chaplain, and Muiredach the harpist. Added to which, people had run in from the fields, from workshops and kitchens, to welcome them home. By the time the crowd spilled through the gates, Findlaech was lying in the galley with his arms folded across his chest and his mouth open to receive the ale being poured into it by one of his welcoming brothers. Adam's head was turned to watch the antics, a faint smile curving the side of his mouth that was visible to Gormflaith. Donald seemed a little more focused on his forward journey. Gormflaith's anxiety had all been for Adam, but now she saw that Donald, who'd only been gone a week, rode with an odd stiffness. The frown pulling at his brow, the thin line of his lips, told of pain.

Instinctively, Gormflaith tightened her fingers. Her mother, who would see at least as much as she did, drew her hand free. There would be no anxiety shown to the world, no hint that Malcolm mac Aed's heir was anything other than hale and hearty. But the tension was back in the lady's shoulders, a new fear. There were always new fears.

At least the men seemed entirely unconcerned. And Donald managed a smile. "My lady mother," he called in jovial tones. "Adam's brought you a galley."

"How useful," the lady responded. "Does it come with the drunk?"

Like an arrow, Findlaech shot upright and leapt out of the galley, amidst a hail of laughter. While this drew the eyes of most, only a few feet in front of her, Gormflaith saw her brothers dismount together, Adam from the less usual side so that they both landed between their two horses. There was a little clumsy stumbling, since their horses were so close together, and it may have been that Adam supported Donald for the merest instant. Gormflaith's heart tightened with dread. But when they emerged from between their horses, they both walked upright with several inches of space between them.

There was sweat and blood on their clothes, but at least none of the latter looked wet or new. And whatever was wrong with him, Donald was coping. And Adam... Beneath the wild beard, he looked as he always had—unfocused, unquiet, and yet curiously intense.

Appearances lied, of course. Adam was one of the most focused people she'd ever encountered, although one could never be quite sure exactly what he focused on. He could also be remarkably peaceful or devote himself entirely to fun. Bombarded by a thousand childhood memories, Gormflaith let her mother attend to precedence and threw herself into Adam's arms.

He seemed slightly taken aback, and in truth he often avoided physical contact. Probably because it frequently set off the waking dreams which had sometimes scared him as a child. Now, however, after the barest instant, his arms closed around her in a hug, and when he drew back to look at her, his eyes smiled with pleasure. Adam was glad to be home.

Until the relief flooded her, she hadn't understood how anxious she'd been on this point. He could so easily have preferred the freedom of plundering with Somerled. He'd always seemed to be looking for something.

"You're well?" she breathed, grasping his rough face between her hands to keep his attention. It was an old trick from childhood. "And Donald?"

He nodded once and stepped out of her reach, his gaze tugging leftwards to their mother. Donald, formally embraced in the intervening moments, stood aside, walking around his brother's back toward Gormflaith.

The lady of Ross extended her hand to Adam, who took it in his large, unclean fingers. He moved as if to kneel, but almost convulsively, his mother drew him to her. His eyes closed as his head bent and he held his cheek to his mother's.

"He's well," Donald murmured in Gormflaith's ear as he gave her one brief, careless hug, which was all that a week's parting merited.

"And you?" she breathed.

Unobtrusively, he touched his side. "Healing." He turned to his mother. "Shall we go in? We've had many unlikely adventures, which include putting the king's man in Tirebeck—"

"And capturing a galley," the lady interrupted.

"No, no, the galley's ours," Donald said. "We just didn't know what else to do with it."

"Oh dear," said his mother with a sigh. "Come inside, then, and tell us the worst."

****

"Why?" the lady of Ross said, as baffled, apparently, as Gormflaith. "Cairistiona certainly has a right to Tirebeck, but to allow the king's soldiers there is lunacy! Once you and Donald had united your forces, you should have taken it back before they got the chance to settle in. He'll build a castle there now."

While the men drank and feasted among the rest of the household, the family sat at the big front table as usual. Now the storytelling was done, amidst much joking and laughter, and Muiredach had taken to his harp, making the strings dance with joy, it was time for the more serious business of explanations and plans.

Adam shrugged. "Maybe," he agreed without obvious interest. "Castles can be taken too."

"With greater losses," the lady pointed out, frowning her disapproval.

"Then you do plan to take Tirebeck back?" Gormflaith asked, looking from one brother to the other.

"Of course," Donald said.

Their mother shoved her cup across the table in a gesture that would have been petulant in anyone else. "Then why in God's name did you give them it in the first place? A straight exchange, Donald for the young lady, would have sufficed!"

Donald, who seemed more comfortable now he was sitting still, waved one hand towards Adam, who gazed into his cup as if it held the truth of all philosophies. In the expectant silence, he raised his eyes, glancing from Donald to their mother, perhaps reconstructing the recent conversation.

"It prevents Lanson from raiding around the country for a home."

"Destroying his army, killing him, would have done that job equally well," their mother retorted. She was not Somerled's sister for nothing. "It's not like either of you to avoid a fight."

There was a pause. Adam may have been waiting for Donald to answer. When he didn't, Adam said, "The King of Scots sent him to see what he could do against us. He has a reputation, well earned by all accounts. Perhaps the king thought Cairistiona would win allies for him, enough to build a force that could defeat us. The king doesn't want to mount a major attack against us if he can avoid it. Particularly not if that leaves the western coasts open to Somerled."

Adam paused again, raised his cup, and drank, almost absently. Beside him, Donald was looking tense again. Taken together, they were a warning of bad news.

Adam said, "Somerled won't attack the west coast this year. The King of Scots is as free as he'll ever be to send the whole royal army against us."

The lady stared at him, her lips open to ask no doubt sharp questions. Then she closed her eyes. "How did you alienate my brother?"

Adam reached for the last leg of grouse. "Donald asked me the same question," he observed. Gormflaith couldn't tell whether or not the accusations hurt him, just that they weren't true. At least in Adam's eyes. "The Manxmen invited Somerled into Man. You know he wants to be King of Man, King of all the Isles, not just Argyll and the Hebrides. That comes first for him, and he needs it for his own security and ours. Once that's done, he'll be in a better position to help us. But right now, we're on our own. Once the King of Scots works this out—as he probably has already— he'll send his army to defeat us. Unless he thinks Lanson has a chance of doing it for him. While Lanson's in Tirebeck, there's still that chance."

"So you bought us time," their mother said slowly. "That was well done."

Adam's eyes fell. One of his many oddities was that he seemed less comfortable with praise than accusation. Which didn't mean he wasn't pleased.

"So what can we do with this time?" Gormflaith demanded.

"Make other alliances," Donald said. "Fergus of Galloway, perhaps. And I think it might be time to speak to our cousins in Moray again. Perhaps Gormflaith could marry Donald mac William."

"You marry him," Gormflaith said rudely. "I'll stick with Harald Madaddson."

Donald said, "We talked before about *my* marriage to a cousin of Moray. It would unite our forces *and* our separate claims to the throne of Scotland."

"No point," Adam said casually. "No one of the Moray line will ever be King of Scots again."

Into the silence, Donald said intensely, "And *our* line...?"

"Sometimes," Gormflaith interrupted furiously, "I wonder what in God's name we are fighting and dying for!"

"Ross and Scotland," Adam said, as though surprised.

"And my father's freedom." His eyes locked with their mother's. "Isn't that enough?"

For a moment, the lady's ice-blue eyes looked almost frightened. It was hard to doubt Adam's visions now. On the strength of them, they'd taken up arms against the King of Scots, secure in Adam's knowledge that it wouldn't adversely affect the position of Malcolm mac Aed, the prisoner of Roxburgh. And it was true the king had neither killed nor mutilated Malcolm. Everything depended, of course, on whether Adam's pronouncements came from God or were Adam's mere opinion. And it seemed their mother didn't want to test that.

She said, "That was never up to me. Our first aim has always been to free your father. Without that, the rest is meaningless."

"So we'll sound out the lord of Galloway and our cousins in Moray," Donald said, "and keep watch on events in Tirebeck."

"Is this Lanson the sort of man who might just settle down there? Maybe even join us in time?" Gormflaith asked.

Adam and Donald shook their heads in perfect time. Donald said, "We're quarrelling over who gets to kill him."

"And Cairistiona," their mother said, frowning. "She must be taken care of. Her father was a good man. What sort of a woman is she?"

Again, Donald looked to Adam, who had, after all, stolen the woman and forced his company on her, if nothing worse. Adam shifted in his seat, apparently considering.

"Strong," he said at last. "Brave. Unhappy. And she takes responsibility for her people."

Something in his neutral tone made Gormflaith ask, "Is she pretty?"

Adam, who never lied, said, "Beautiful."

At the same time, speaking through him, Donald said, "Hard to tell. She wears a mask over one side of her face."

"Not, then," Gormflaith answered herself, slightly disappointed.

"The child was burned in a fire," their mother said repressively.

"Well, that explains the mask," Donald said. "Pretty or not, I approve. I approve of anyone who tries to stop so-called knights cutting my hands off."

"Thank you for the praise," Adam said sardonically, and Donald raised his cup to him, only to discover it was empty. One raised finger from the lady was enough to bring the serving girl scurrying to pour more ale.

Donald caught her eye and smiled brightly, almost as if he'd forgotten her existence and was pleasantly surprised.

"Adam," he exclaimed. "You have to meet the newest member of the family."

"Shall I bring him?" the girl, Eithine, asked eagerly.

The lady nodded, and the girl scurried off. Gormflaith's brothers gazed at each other expectantly until Eithine returned bearing a bundle, which she placed in Donald's arms.

Gormflaith was a great admirer of her first little nephew, but right now, she anticipated greater entertainment from Adam's reaction to him. So, clearly, did Donald.

Adam's lips twitched. A breath of something that might have been laughter hissed between them. "White Christ, is he yours?" he demanded. "You have a child?"

"What's his name?" Gormflaith asked, to tease him.

Adam hesitated, but only for a moment, before he reached over and touched the baby's fat little cheek and tickled him under the chin. The baby made a grab for his finger and held it, gazing up at him. He smiled at his uncle.

Adam blinked. His breath caught. "Adam," he said. "You called him Adam."

God, he was good. Eerie, not to say terrifying. But he was good.

"His mother wanted to pretend he was yours," Donald said.

A smile flickered across Adam's face. "Liar," he said, without taking his eyes off the baby.

Eithine, the baby's mother, had her gaze fixed on Adam's face. "What do you see for him, my lord?" she whispered.

The lady's hand jerked and was still. Donald scowled. The family never asked him questions like that. They were too liable to upset Adam and everyone else.

Adam dragged his gaze from the child to his mother. "Happiness," he said. "And strength."

"And a long life?" Eithine asked eagerly.

Adam's eyes didn't move. "Of course."

Eithine's face split into smiles. So did Donald's.

Gormflaith wanted to weep. Because the man who always told the truth had lied.

****

They'd extended this, his mother's most favoured hall, before Adam had left, giving his mother a private chamber, and a chamber each for himself and Donald and Gormflaith. After months of sleeping among men, Adam was grateful for the peace. Home had always been where his mother was, and this was a good, secure location, off the beaten tracks around the coast and almost hidden among the hills. Lanson, without native help, would struggle to find it. And if the king came with a massive army, the family could retreat over the mountains into wester Ross while he and Donald harried the royal troops in land they'd known intimately all their lives.

Scrubbed clean, with his beard trimmed, Adam decided not to shave it off just yet. Instead, he wrapped himself in a linen sheet and sprawled on the bed, resting his back against the solid headboard and thinking of Donald's baby.

He was glad to be home among his family again. Being with Somerled had been both educational and fun—in between the fighting and the slaughter, which were more or less the same the world over. By the time he'd left his uncle, he'd known he would die for Somerled. He supposed he must love him. But there was a warmth that only came from *them*.

A knock on his door interrupted his thoughts.

"Come," he called, and a girl came in with a tray on which was a flask of ale and a cup, a bowl of dried fruit, and a loaf.

"From the lady," she said, setting down the tray.

"Thank you."

The girl hesitated, fidgeting. Now that he looked at her properly, Adam remembered she'd warmed his bed the night before he left for Argyll. Unfortunately, her name escaped him, but the memory of what they'd done together remained strong enough to tempt him.

He said, "Is there anything else from the lady?"

The girl shook her head and blushed. But she didn't leave.

Adam, who rather liked the cyclical nature of events, rose

from his sheet and walked naked towards her. She didn't flee in horror. Women didn't, as a rule. In fact, her eyes widened, scanning him from head to toe. By the time she'd returned halfway up, her breath caught.

"Oh my," she whispered.

The girl was willing and eager. Touching her hadn't plagued him before with distracting visions, so there was absolutely no reason not to slake his lust in her charming body. It was his own fault that he thought unexpectedly about Cairistiona, the lady de Lanson, whom he'd held in his arms for several hours. It was imagination, not involuntary vision, that placed her secretive, half-masked, half-beautiful face on the girl before him.

He remembered the flashing images, the dreams which had assailed him through Cairistiona's touch and later in the fire while she slept. He closed his eyes against the burning temptation, the pain of longing, and turned away from the comfort.

CHAPTER SEVEN

The rain of the early morning had dried up and left an unexpectedly warm, pleasant spring day. Enjoying the sun on her skin, the gentle bobbing of the ship, and the rhythmic splash of oars, Christian felt an urge to remove her mask for the first time since she'd donned it at court last year. It was an easy temptation to resist. For some reason, she felt stronger with the mask on. And people seemed to regard her differently too. It was as if, being unsure what lay beneath the mask, they were prepared to give her the benefit of the doubt and accord respect. Which amused Christian in a detached, dispassionate kind of way.

She smiled at the white, wispy clouds drifting across the blue sky and inhaled the fresh, salt scent of the sea, which seemed more intense after the rain. With an escort of Henry and five men-at-arms, she was travelling to the cathedral church of Rosemarkie at the invitation of the Bishop of Ross himself, who had also offered to accommodate her party for the night.

Christian was excited by the expedition. As well as confessing and hearing mass— William kept no chaplain and there was no church in Tirebeck—she looked forward to discussing with the bishop the spiritual needs of her people. And the possibility of some kind of detente between Tirebeck and the rest of Ross. The bishop would be a powerful ally.

Attending Christian were Felicia and Eua. She hoped in this way to discourage the "them and us" attitude of her women. She'd wanted to travel merely with a couple of Tirebeck men as escort, but William had insisted she take six of his own soldiers instead. He didn't trust the men of Ross after the recent brush with the MacHeths. Christian herself didn't fear any attack. Adam MacHeth had called her the lady of Tirebeck.

So they'd begun their journey before it was light, with a wizened old fisherman called Kertill supplying the ship and guidance, and William's soldiers rowing them across the Cromarty Firth to the Black Isle, which you could see from Tirebeck on a clear day.

"Why do they call it the Black Isle?" Christian wondered aloud. "It looks very green to me."

Eua smiled faintly, turning her face into the sun as though she'd missed it. "It looks black in winter when the snow covers everywhere else. Snow never lies on the isle."

They were hugging the coast around the isle, just past the village of Cromarty, when the old fisherman, Kertill, shouted in Gaelic, pointing outward towards the deeper water.

"Dolphins," Eua said with pleasure, and Christian found herself on her feet between Felicia and Henry, watching the amazing creatures jump in and out of the water in perfect arches.

"How beautiful," Christian said in awe. "I've never seen them before."

"They might come right up to us," Kertill said. "They're curious creatures, but they'll not harm us. They seem to like people."

Christian, desperate to see them up close, was disappointed when, although they followed their ship for a little, they didn't come any closer. It might have been too noisy for them, for several ships and smaller boats seemed to be heading towards Rosemarkie for the market. Henry watched very carefully any vessel that came close to them.

A few children, taking advantage of the warmer weather, played along the shore, splashing and laughing. They called and waved to the ship, staring wide-eyed at the men-at-arms.

Christian enjoyed watching the boats in the firth, no doubt bringing supplies to the small communities scattered along the coast. It came to her that this was not unprosperous country. When gaps between wars allowed.

While Henry and the men scowled repellingly towards a curious and rather leaky-looking boat approaching from the Moray side of the firth, Christian turned her head back towards the shore. There were no villages that she could make out just here, and she almost missed the unobtrusive little cove, until the sound of splashing and laughter drew her closer attention.

In fact, several grown men appeared to be frolicking in the sea around a large vessel that resembled a galley. Christian paused, gazing at the ship. Galleys could be used for trading as well as for war. William had found no trace of warships, not even tracks in the sand, in Tirebeck. She knew because she'd asked discreetly about the large huts along the shore.

In any case, the raucous, good-natured calls of these seamen were not so different from those of the children they'd just passed. But the children had splashed about in the shallows. The galley men were swimming like fish in much deeper water, over and under the oars in some kind of race. They took it in turns while the others chanted a beat, perhaps timing the swimmers.

A cheer went up, making Christian smile. Then one of the swimmers hauled himself out of the water and up the side of the boat, stark naked. Stretched and honed with muscle, water streaming off him like rain, his body looked golden, almost godlike.

After years of occasionally amusing and comforting herself by imagining people without their clothes on, Christian discovered there wasn't necessarily anything silly or laughable about a naked man. Instead, even over this distance, the sight of this one brought warmth tingling through her, taking her by surprise, reminding her of her youthful reactions to handsome—if fully clothed—young men, in the days before her marriage. Marriage was a great cure for lusts of the flesh.

The naked swimmer hauled himself to a sitting position on the side of the boat, from where he called something down to those still in the river. As they laughed and called back, he turned his dark head and looked towards Christian's party. For an instant, he stilled, shocked, perhaps, to be discovered naked by passing strangers, several of whom were obviously women. Then he swung his legs inside the ship, and Eua moved alongside Christian, blocking her view.

"Men," she said tolerantly.

"Men," Christian agreed, walking forward. The pit of her stomach still churned and tingled, because just for a moment, she'd imagined the dark, naked young god to be Adam MacHeth.

****

"That," Findlaech said, balancing on an oar as he gazed after the vanishing vessel top-heavy with men-at-arms, "had to be the lady of Tirebeck. I thought she'd have been too frightened to leave without Lanson's whole army."

Not she... Adam shrugged. "They'll be going to Rosemarkie—church and market, no doubt, catering for both spiritual and material needs. Eua is with her." A creature of instinct, he had to force himself to weigh up the advantages and disadvantages of the plan forming in his head.

"They didn't turn Loegaire out?" Findlaech asked, surprised.

Adam shook his head. "The lady kept Eua to look after the house, and Loegaire is still running the estate. According to Cailean." He'd left Cailean in hiding at Tirebeck to observe and report on any threats. But beyond cutting down trees and building a mound for a castle behind the main house, and suspiciously patrolling the immediate environs, Lanson didn't appear to have made many changes.

Adam began pulling on his clothes. "They've seen this galley. Keep the others well out of sight." And with luck, Eua would lead them well away from the boat-building camps now set up in the deep inlet on the isle's coast beyond Fortrose.

While Findlaech summoned the men back on board, Adam stamped his feet into his boots and grabbed his tunic before leaping into the small boat on the shore side of the galley and beginning to row himself towards the beach.

"Hey!" Findlaech yelled after him. "Where are *you* going?"

"Rosemarkie," Adam said, loping off along the bank of the river while struggling into his tunic.

****

Perhaps foolishly, Christian had expected a distinguished town to match the honour of the cathedral. But Rosemarkie was little more than a village. What first caught and held her eye was the church, rising up from the surrounding buildings with pride and elegance. And whatever its size, Rosemarkie was certainly bustling.

The little market was crowded, filling the square outside the cathedral gates. A cross was nailed to one of the wooden buildings next to it, proclaiming this the marketplace, and a balance for weighing stood underneath it for common use. Although small by the standards of Perth or Edinburgh, let alone those of England, the market at Rosemarkie seemed to have everything necessary. As they approached the cathedral gates, Christian glimpsed pots and pans, fresh meat, a few small pigs and sheep, bright-coloured silk threads.

"I hadn't realised this was the king's burgh," she said, presuming it had been so since before the current rebellion, for only the royal burghs had the rights to hold markets.

"It isn't," Eua said drily. "It's the earl's. The lady introduced the market unofficially, giving the merchants much the same rights—and obligations—as in the king's. It's good for the local people, farmers, and tradesmen. And we get goods coming in from the north as well as the south, even from the east."

Christian glanced over her shoulder again. Most of the throng looked like ordinary people, but here and there, a flash of bright-coloured cloth proclaimed buyers of higher standing, both men and women. Excitement twinged once more. This would be a good day, an interesting day, a day for meeting people and making things better. Beginning, she told herself firmly, turning back to the church, with the spiritual.

The cathedral gates were not locked. Walking inside the grounds, following the path to the arched entrance, she gazed around her in amazement. The gardens were well tended, with spring flowers adding colour and beauty. But it was the standing stones that amazed Christian, the kind she associated with the relentlessly pagan.

When she stepped off the path to examine the biggest, she saw that, of course, it was not pagan. Hundreds of years old, perhaps, but bearing the symbols of Christianity. Mostly. Exquisitely carved into the stone were decorated crosses as well as the animal heads, combs and mirrors common on other stones, including one at Tirebeck. Stones like these surrounded the cathedral, proclaiming what she'd only vaguely understood. There had been churches here long, long before this stone cathedral.

She'd have wandered farther in the grounds except that the sudden soaring of voices from inside the church distracted her attention once more. Raised in song, they were beautifully harmonised and drew her on with a shiver of pleasure.

Henry, ever watchful, opened the door but did not let her pass first. Hand on his sword hilt, he entered, presumably in expectation of the barbarian natives ignoring the sanctity of the place in favour of indiscriminate slaughter. Christian followed him, and, fortunately, he stood aside almost at once before she needed to say the impatient words forming on her tongue.

The cathedral wasn't magnificent by the standards of others she'd seen, but it was a gracious building with wonderful stone and wood carvings everywhere. A tapestry graced the wall behind the main altar, and several religious paintings hung in fine frames. The smells of stone and incense surrounded her, old and comforting. There was always peace to be found in the house of God. Well, nearly always.

The singing stopped abruptly. A man's voice murmured something, and one young boy, perhaps ten years old, broke away from the group in the choir who had clearly been responsible for the beautiful singing, and bolted across the church. The song master, a young man, smiled and bowed, and spoke words of welcome in Gaelic as he walked towards them. Christian went forward to meet him, but just as they got within speaking distance, a door opened and closed somewhere, and at the sound of hurrying footsteps, the master stopped and stood respectfully aside.

A middle-aged man with a beard in shades of grey, wearing plain white robes, strode around the left of the choir and beamed as he approached.

"I'm Symeon, son of Macbethad," he greeted her. "Welcome to Rosemarkie and the cathedral church. You must be the lady of Tirebeck."

Since Symeon was the name of the Bishop of Ross, she could only assume this was the great man himself. She answered him accordingly, with his title, and introduced the women and Henry, who also received the friendly episcopal greeting before the bishop deprived her of breath by introducing the "song master" as his son Gregor.

Behind her, Felicia gasped audibly. Christian hoped she maintained a calm smile, but the bishop's kind eyes gleamed with amusement. "You are shocked," he observed. "In many things, our church maintains the old ways, when no one in a distant land told us we couldn't marry or have children for the glory of God. My father was bishop here before me, and we hope that Gregor will follow."

Christian regarded him with fascination. "Does His Holiness the Pope know?"

"I have his blessing as Bishop of Ross. I've no idea what he knows of my family background. I've never hidden it. Come, shall we have refreshment before we begin?"

****

Having retrieved his horse and more suitable attire from the camp, Adam rode back into the growing town of Rosemarkie, keeping his eyes peeled for the Tirebeck party. As expected, he found them at the church. Or at least, he glimpsed a few Norman soldiers and Eua in the cathedral grounds. Of the lady herself, there was no sign.

Leaving his horse at the gate, Adam strolled up the path. Eua, who must have recognised him from the boat and been keeping watch, saw him at once. A Norman woman kept her distance, which made it easy for Eua to move casually away. The men-at-arms lounging against the building paid her no attention.

She greeted him nervously, adding that the lady was inside with the Bishop.

Adam nodded with impatience. That much he'd worked out already. "How are things at the house?" he asked.

"Bearable," Eua said. "The lady I could grow used to. Her women are foul and so is her husband."

Adam frowned. He didn't like to think of her with a foul husband. Although killing him would be that much more pleasant. "Did she say anything about the ship?"

"No, but she saw it. She saw you too."

Adam glanced at her. "She recognised me?"

Eua raised one eyebrow. "I doubt it was your face she was looking at. What happened to your famous observation, that you didn't see or even hear us coming?"

Adam didn't answer. In fact, he had seen them, although he hadn't let their presence change his mind about the right time to come out of the water. Besides, some unamiable part of him had wanted to shock the superior lady who'd said, *"MacHeth"* on their first meeting as she might have said, *"Pig shit."* And there were the dreams.

Over Eua's shoulder, he saw Cairistiona emerge from the church. When she smiled, her upper lip seemed to have a double curve that was curiously endearing, adding to the mystery caused by the mask.

Eua muttered, "I'd better go. And you should stay away from the men. Trust me, they'll remember you. Even if you do look more like a lord than before."

For the moment, Adam elected for discretion. The bishop would not be pleased by a brawl in his churchyard. As Eua walked back to meet the lady, Adam backed up behind a willow's branches and paced the perimeter of the cathedral grounds until he found the unguarded side door to the church.

The boys from the song school almost knocked him over by bursting out just as he entered. He stood in the shadows and watched them go before closing the door behind them and walking into the main body of the church.

The bishop stood in front of the altar, quite still and alone. He often stood so, gazing inward, deep in thought of one kind or another while his eyes seemed to be fixed on the carved crucifix before him. Adam felt a smile flicker across his lips. Symeon didn't move as he approached and rested his hip on the corner of the altar table, so Adam let his gaze wander over the priest's familiar face, gauging his mood and his health and happiness.

"Whatever possessed you to abduct a woman, a girl, like that?" Symeon enquired. He'd never needed to raise his voice to make his hearer aware of disapproval or anger. He didn't even look at Adam as he spoke.

"Political advantage," Adam said.

"Quickly nullified," Symeon pointed out. At last he turned his head, his clear blue eyes piercing straight into Adam's brown ones. "Did you hurt her, Adam mac Malcolm?"

"No. I never touched her. Well," he amended, "I made her ride with me."

"Well, considering the other ruffians who follow you, I suppose that was a kindness. Why did you give her Tirebeck? To make amends?"

"No," Adam said again, and when Symeon frowned at him, he added, "Tirebeck is hers."

A moment longer, the all-seeing blue eyes that had caught out nearly every mischief he or Donald had ever perpetrated seemed to dig into his brain to his soul. Then the bishop's face softened.

"You still don't lie, do you, Adam?"

Adam smiled faintly and bent to take Symeon's hand. The bishop forestalled him, embracing him instead. "I'm glad you're home. Your mother misses you, and so do I, God help me. But you haven't given up this wild road you and your brother have set out on."

"No." Since they were on uncomfortable ground, Adam changed the subject, leaning back on the altar table. "Did she tell you off for your heresy?"

"Your lady of Tirebeck? No, although I'm sure she'd reform me if she could. She wants to build a church in Tirebeck, though she can't yet pay for it."

Adam shrugged. "If they build it, we'll endow it. Can you supply a priest?"

Symeon blinked. "Has she spoken to you about this already?"

Adam raised his eyebrows. "No. She doesn't speak to me about anything. I'm an outlaw to her, not the son of a great lord."

"She has troubles to bear."

"Then you'll be a friend to her?" Adam wasn't quite sure why that should be so important, and judging by the bishop's shrewd glance, neither was Symeon.

"I will, of course. She and her people will stay with me tonight. If you're good, I'll invite you to dinner."

Adam looked at his old teacher. He wasn't sure why the offer was made. He just knew he wanted to accept too much. He shook his head. "I wouldn't add to her comfort."

"Maybe you should. Her position in Ross is…impossible."

"Maybe," Adam said noncommittally. He stirred. "How is your lady?"

****

In the cathedral church, Christian had confessed her sins, with the emphasis on pride, and received absolution. After mass, she felt both cleansed and ready for the next fight—or at least for her first serious conversation with the very odd but charming Bishop of Ross.

"We'll talk more over dinner," he said. "I can take you to my wife now, if you'd like, or perhaps you have things to buy at the market?"

"I do," Christian acknowledged while wondering what kind of woman would marry a priest. But even as the thought entered her head, she recognised it as stupid prejudice. Without following all the rules of the Church in Rome, the bishop was, surely, a good man, as well as an educated and intelligent one. As was his son. The wife and mother was likely to be good too.

When she emerged from the church, Christian invited the waiting women and her escort to take care of their own spiritual well-being. But no one, not even Eua, took her up on her suggestion. She suspected the Normans didn't regard Symeon as a true priest. However, instead of confession, they all repaired to the market.

There was certainly enough variety there to attract the attention of Christian and Felicia, who'd been either travelling or trapped in rural security since leaving Perth. One booth carried some decent linen, so Christian ordered a bolt and some embroidery silks and left Felicia poring over rather coarse wool in bright colours. Eua was still at the stall opposite, buying salt and other dull household necessities. At least William had disgorged silver for the purpose.

The next booth was surrounded by barrels. The owner, a slight, sallow man, very neatly dressed in a dark tunic, called to her in Gaelic. "Wines of quality, my lady," he insisted. "From France. If you please…" He offered her a cup.

She was about to shake her head in refusal when the scent of the wine hit her nostrils. Raising her eyebrows, she inclined her head and accepted the cup. She took a sip.

"Is there much call," she asked curiously, "for wine of this quality around here?"

"You'd be surprised," said another soft, casual voice beside her.

She froze. Because it sounded like Adam MacHeth.

CHAPTER EIGHT

Slowly, she turned her head and looked up, and her heart turned over in fear. Surely in fear.

Undeniably, her captor of only a week ago, Adam MacHeth. But he stood before her now, at the curtained doorway of the market booth, in a red-brown cloak fastened with a silver brooch and flung back over one shoulder to reveal a long, dark green tunic. A silver-and-enamel buckle adorned his belt. His hair, cut and combed, no longer looked unkempt, and his beard had been trimmed back almost to the skin, so that the lean, angular shape of his face was apparent. He was not, she told herself, a handsome man, but the black hair, the wild eyes, and the unexpectedly refined features did make him dramatic. He was not a man one would easily overlook. Whatever his dress.

His eyes held hers without blinking.

"I will come back for you..." She said, "I have six men-at-arms within calling distance."

"Five. One of them is guarding the boat. You don't need to be afraid of me."

She lifted her chin. "I'm not."

Although he must have perceived the obvious lie, his eyes didn't mock her. They looked serious as they gazed at the visible side of her face. She darted a quick look up to left and right, trying to see past the people to her men-at-arms. She thought she glimpsed their armour at either end of the market. To her right, Eua and Felicia seemed to have joined forces in admiration of some jewellery. Perhaps her plan was working.

"So, you're here to buy wine?" she said with derision, meeting his gaze once more.

"I probably will. Have another taste. It's good." He took the cup from her numb fingers, passing it to the merchant, who needed no further urging to fill it to the brim from the barrel inside and bring it back to her.

She thought of hurling it at Adam MacHeth—pointlessly rude and far from ladylike in these surroundings. She thought of turning up her nose and refusing, or instructing the merchant to give it to Adam instead. But for some reason, this situation seemed stranger and harder to deal with than being forced to ride captive across the country with this man and his band of outlaws.

So, trying to look haughty, she took the cup and let the wine touch her lips. In truth, it was good, so she allowed a tiny trickle into her mouth.

"Two casks for your hall, lady?" the merchant suggested. "Just to let your lord try it. I'm sure he'll want to order more next time I'm passing."

In truth, there was no money for wine. From frugal necessity, all her household would drink ale brewed at home. Guests of wine-drinking station were highly unlikely.

"I'll think about it," she said distantly. Then, since the man's face fell, she added, "It's an excellent wine."

Instantly, he was wreathed in smiles once more. Adam MacHeth regarded her with a strange quirk of his lips. She couldn't work out whether or not he was laughing at her, but from nowhere, she realised that he was the one she could question about her past without losing dignity or face. Although not quite sure why, she needed to understand her broken connection to Tirebeck, to know what had driven her parents from here. Perhaps it would help her to stay.

Her breath caught. "A word, sir, if you please." Before she could change her mind, she turned and walked into the booth.

Inside, an upturned cask had become a table between two rough stools. The booth was plunged into gloom as the curtain closed out the sunshine. Setting down her cup, she sat on one stool as if perfectly at ease and lifted her gaze to Adam MacHeth.

He stood just inside the curtain, watching her with a curious, wary expression that told her she'd surprised him.

"I congratulate myself," she said sardonically. "I understand it isn't easy to surprise a man with second sight."

He stirred, walked past her to the back of the booth. "Who told you that?" He reached up to a shelf, taking down a flagon and a cup.

"Is it true?" Christian asked.

"Is what true?" He set down the cup and poured wine from the flagon.

"That you have second sight. Or are you just a berserker like the old Vikings?"

He eased his large body down onto the stool. His knee brushed against her skirts. "A lady of your education knows there's no such thing as second sight."

She smiled deprecatingly. "And you despise ladies of such education."

His eyebrows flew up. "I don't despise you."

For some reason, that brought colour seeping into her face. To cover it, she lifted her chin in challenge. "Then you're a berserker after all?"

"Why should you think that?"

She shivered, seeing again the men she knew cut down by his sword, trampled beneath his merciless boots. "The way you fight."

His eyebrows twitched. "That." One dismissive hand seemed to wave her accusation out through the closed curtain. "It's a mask. Not unlike yours."

She stared at him, wondering what on earth he'd ever had in his life to hide from on the battlefield. She had to press her lips together to stop herself asking. She hadn't come in here to discover such things. Giving herself time to regroup, she raised her cup and sipped.

"Why did you let us have Tirebeck?" she asked abruptly.

He stirred. "For my brother."

"You'd have got your brother back just for me."

"That's not what you said at the time. According to you, I wouldn't have got a chicken for you, never mind the Earl of Ross's heir."

"But you didn't believe me. Why then give us Tirebeck?"

"Tirebeck is yours."

She set down her cup, meeting his whirlpool gaze. For

some reason, that wasn't so difficult now. "To keep us contented. To keep the king unsuspicious and unaware of whatever it is you truly intend."

A smile flickered across his face. He didn't look afraid.

"Galleys," she said.

Neither of them blinked. Without looking at it, he swirled the wine in his cup. "I apologise for exposing myself. What is it you really want to ask me?"

The heat of embarrassment surged through her body at the memory of his. He *had* seen her in the boat. But, determined not to back down, she hung on to his dark gaze. "How did the old hall at Tirebeck burn down?"

His gaze dropped to his wine. His hand stilled, then raised the cup to his lips. He drank and lowered the cup before he looked at her again. "Rhuadri burned it. The day you left."

Her father had burned it himself? She frowned in the effort of memory. After all, she'd only been three years old. "The day we left? Why did we leave?"

Adam shrugged.

"You don't want to tell me," Christian discovered.

"You don't want to know. It wasn't that fire that injured you."

Before she could prevent it, her hand flew up to her mask. Old Eta, the fisherman's wife, had mentioned another fire too.

He said steadily, "You were knocked into the hearth fire during a fight. When you were a baby. More than two years before you left."

Her ears seemed to sing. All the blood which had rushed into her face drained away. She'd always assumed it was the fire she remembered which had injured her. The memory was associated with such fear and pain. No one had told her otherwise until now. She lifted the cup to her mouth and lowered it again untouched.

"Who?" she whispered. "Who was fighting?"

"Your father and a Norman knight sent by the king to take my father after Stracathro." Stracathro... The battle by which King David had defeated the rebellious young Earls of Moray and Ross. The Earl of Moray had died in battle, but his brother, Malcolm MacHeth, Earl of Ross, had escaped and eluded capture for another two years. The king had deprived him and his sons of the earldom, outlawed the family, and when Malcolm was finally captured, he was imprisoned in Roxburgh Castle, almost as far away from Ross as you could get without leaving the kingdom.

"So I was injured by my father defending yours," she said a little shakily. "No wonder my mother never told that story. It wouldn't have looked good to the King of Scots."

His eyes fell. He had very long lashes. "It's past. It shouldn't affect your future."

She straightened her shoulders, regarding him with a touch of mockery. "So you do have second sight."

"That was only common sense."

She wasn't sure what made her do it. Mere curiosity, perhaps, or pique. Her gaze lit on his big, scarred hand, abstractly swirling his cup. She reached out and seized his hand as if to still it.

It jerked, slopping the wine over the barrel, but that wasn't enough to dislodge her fingers, and she hung on.

"You don't like to be touched, do you?" she said, holding his startled gaze.

"By some." His stormy eyes darkened further. "I like your touch."

Which wasn't quite what she'd intended, although she'd brought it on herself. Flushing, but forcing herself not to snatch her hand back, she asked, "Do you see things?"

His breath rushed out on what might have been a laugh, quite at odds with the burning of his eyes. Without warning, his hand twisted, curling his fingers around hers. "Many things."

His eyes seemed to swallow her. His fingers burned into her skin, and she couldn't breathe.

From beyond the curtain came a sudden fit of coughing. Adam MacHeth blinked and released her. Relief flooded her. It must have been relief, although she couldn't account for the curious coldness of her fingers. As the curtain swung back, he stood, blocking her view of the doorway.

"She isn't here," he said.

The curtain swished back.

"Eua," he said, even as her lips parted to ask. "We'd better go. She won't be the only one who saw you come in here."

Under her bemused gaze, he strode to the back of the booth, loosening his cloak, and dropped to the packed mud ground. The wall didn't quite meet it. In fact, there was a dip in the earth, almost designed, one would have imagined, for alternative exit. Adam MacHeth grinned at her, for all the world like a mischievous boy, and threw her his cloak, which she caught from instinct, before he rolled onto his stomach and wriggled through the gap.

It was happening again. Like climbing onto the massive horse all by herself, like riding with him at breakneck speed...Wicked fun surged up inside her. Wrapping herself speedily in his cloak, she dropped and imitated his wriggle under the wall.

His boots were planted right in front of her. She could feel heat, hear loud voices and clatter, and then she was yanked to her feet in an open booth which seemed to be selling hot broth or stew. So far as she could tell, no one paid them a blind bit of attention, but then, Adam was blocking her view again. Or protecting her from curious eyes.

His hands rested on her waist, strong and heavy. His face, alight with fun, bent closer. Sudden butterflies in her stomach dived. And his eyes weren't laughing any more. His breath hitched. Without warning, he closed his mouth on hers.

She gasped in shock. Swiftly, he dragged his mouth the length of her lips, reaching even under the linen of her mask, before releasing her.

"I *will* come back for you," he muttered, and before she could even think what he meant, let alone speak, one of his hands fell away, and he whisked her out of the open booth, spinning her away from him, whipping the dirty cloak away from her as she went. She caught a glimpse of busy strangers in the alley backing onto the one she'd left. A glint of armour flickered in the crowd.

Her stomach tightened. Stupidly worried for him now, since he didn't seem to have his men with him, and hers would have been happy to kill him if they only recognised him, she turned back to warn him. He wasn't there.

She walked into the middle of the alley, peering between two plump women in bright-coloured shawls drawn up over their heads. She might have seen a black head and a muddy red-brown cloak vaulting over the jewellery stall, but she couldn't be sure.

Slipping among the crowd, still slightly stunned, she resisted the temptation to touch her lips. She supposed kissing her must have been some kind of cover that she couldn't quite understand. Or so she told herself, but as she walked around the market, waiting to be discovered by Eua or Felicia or one of the men-at-arms, the ridiculous thought that clung in her mind was that, although she had been a wife for four years, Adam MacHeth was the first man who had ever kissed her lips since she was a tiny child. And that even though it had been a pretence, for some reason, she was glad.

****

The next day, on the sail home, despite the language barrier, Felicia and Eua still shared their gleeful triumph. Between them, they'd tricked the jewellery merchant into bringing down his price and were now the proud owners of pretty, pewter, carved rings, which Christian duly admired. Felicia claimed to have seen similar rings on the fingers of great ladies in the south, although made from gold and silver. Christian assured them the pewter was just as pretty and the craftsmanship equally good. Gratified, Felicia and Eua gabbled together in an odd mixture of French, English, and Gaelic, which, together with a certain amount of gesticulating, seemed to create enough understanding.

Away from Alys and Cecily, Felicia seemed to show more character. She was certainly more appealing, and Christian was not the only one who noticed. Henry, who up until now had more or less ignored her women beyond basic civility, turned his head toward Felicia several times during their return journey. In fact, at one point, he sat beside her. And Eua, perhaps feeling like a gooseberry, moved to the bench beside Christian instead.

"What did he want?" she asked, low.

"I think he's discovered there's more to Felicia than he thought."

Eua scowled at her, "Not Henry. Adam mac Malcolm."

It brought Christian up short. Since Eua hadn't mentioned him until now, Christian had reassured herself that she hadn't been seen with Adam MacHeth. She'd used the unexpected encounter to learn what she could about his plans and her own past, but somehow in those discoveries and their improper parting, she'd lost of sight of his reason for being there in the first place.

She couldn't help the frown that flickered across her brow. "I don't actually know. It was I who wished to speak to him. Why? Do you consider him dangerous?"

"The MacAeds are all dangerous. They're good lords, but everything takes second place to their family's position."

"I never met a lord for whom that wasn't true." All the same, she understood that the MacHeths took such ambition to the extreme. They'd plunged the whole of Scotland and the Isles into war—three times—because they thought they had the right to be Kings of Scots and wanted to be. "I know he imagines he's using me, giving us Tirebeck."

Eua glanced at her quickly and away. "Perhaps. We're all being used."

Eua had brought the subject up. Perhaps Christian stood too much on her dignity. "*Does* he have second sight?" she asked.

Eua shrugged. "So they say. *He* never has, or not to me."

"You know him well?"

Eua shook her head. "No one does." She took a deep breath. "But don't be fooled, lady. His manner might be…odd, but he's sharper than all of them. It's not really Donald who rules Ross, it's Adam. Even while he was in Argyll with his uncle."

Christian's frown deepened. The conversation had gone beyond wary gossip. "In what way?"

Eua shrugged with impatience. "In the way of everything. Administering the land, justice, tribute, raising the men for war. *Fighting* the war, for all I know."

"Interesting," Christian murmured. The man had already confessed to wearing a mask in war. A mask of ferocity. Was his…*peculiarity* a mask too? To lull people into false security, to hide the sharpness of his mind? Did that give him the edge over all the other warlords in Scotland? And yet he was so young, younger than she'd first thought when he'd been covered in beard and dirt and blood. Cleaned and tidied up, he'd revealed himself as no more, surely, than twenty-three or twenty-four years old. How long could he have been wearing this mask?

She looked at Eua. "You're saying we're not safe at Tirebeck."

"You know that," Eua said. "The lord de Lanson didn't come to be safe, did he?"

"Eventually," Christian said, determinedly. But until then, they'd all pay the price. She could only try to ensure it didn't rise too high.

****

When Christian entered the hall after finally arriving home, she found her husband and Henry drinking wine. A cask perched on the table.

"You know, this isn't bad," William said, swirling the wine in his cup and taking another sip. "It isn't bad at all."

"I like it," Henry said. He cast a smile and a bow in Christian's direction. "It seems the merchant who gave you the wine to taste yesterday has made you the gift of a cask."

"A whole cask?" Christian said, frowning. "There must be a mistake."

"His message was clear," William said. "A gift to the lady de Lanson of Tirebeck. Of course, he's hoping for a large order out of his generosity. Damn it, I might just give him one too, once things are in order here. Didn't expect such decent wine so far out in the wilderness." Ironically, he raised his cup in a silent toast to her. "Felicitations, Christian. You've done something right."

Christian made him an exaggerated bow, which he ignored, and carried on towards the table of cold dishes set out for the late homecoming. But her stomach churned because she was sure the wine hadn't been given by the merchant. The gift was Adam MacHeth's.

CHAPTER NINE

"While the villagers build a church, *he*'s built a bloody great castle," Cailean said in disgust, staring through the trees and the relentless rain which had been pouring down for hours.

Beside him, Adam MacHeth didn't seem impressed or even terribly surprised. "He's built a little wooden tower."

Cailean snorted. "Good enough to control nearly all the land around him and to observe any attack from the sea."

Adam nodded. "Wood burns," he said.

"I thought of that," Cailean said ruefully, "but it's very close to the hall. Eua's children live in there."

Adam turned his head and looked at him. It might have been approval or impatience. "Wind," he said.

Cailean wasn't quite sure what to make of that either, but before he could ask for confirmation, something moved at the top of the wooden structure, distracting his attention. The man-at-arms stepped back from the opening, and a veiled woman took his place. Veiled and covered on one side of her face.

"It's the lady," Cailean said.

Adam didn't reply, but then his eyes were at least as good as Cailean's.

She divided her attention between the view and something inside that might have been at her feet. She seemed to laugh, causing an unexpected wish in Cailean to see the effect close up. He'd only seen her determined not to be frightened, her fine half face stiff with a different kind of mask.

She bent and lifted a child in her arms so that he could see over the wooden rampart. The boy crowed with delight. He was Loegaire and Eua's son, but clearly the lady had a kindness for him. She set him down, let him run out of sight, presumably to one of the three other sides of the tower.

Something in the lady's tolerant smile as she turned away to follow him reminded Cailean of his own childhood, his own mother who'd died giving birth to his youngest sister. Memory tugged at his heart, half pleasure, half pain. The lady would have made a good mother.

"She has no children of her own," he said aloud.

"She will do," Adam said, his voice still vague.

When Cailean glanced at him, the lord's eyes were glazed in that disconcerting way that made Cailean wonder if anyone was at home behind them. Or if so, who.

He shivered. "She said she was barren."

Adam blinked, dragged one hand through his hair, and turned away. "She also said Lanson would give nothing to get her back."

"Lanson doesn't lie with her," Cailean volunteered, catching up with Adam as he strode through the wood back the way they'd come. "He lies with one of her women."

"Who has no children either." Adam swiped his hand across his forehead and nose, scattering the raindrops which had gathered there. "You'll be wanting to get home to your people."

Cailean blinked, forcing himself to catch up with the change of subject. For a while, he'd agonised that being left here to observe was merely to get him out of the way with an unimportant task. But Adam had come twice in person to hear what he'd learned, and in between those visits, there had been messengers. And now Cailean was reluctant to give up his post. "I'd rather be here when the action starts."

Adam cast him a quick sardonic smile. "We won't leave you out. I'll send one of the men to relieve you, probably by tomorrow morning. It's not a punishment. Thought you might prefer to join an attack on some royal demesnes—double pronged, from land and sea."

Cailean flushed. His greatest fear had been that he wouldn't be considered a worthy enough captain, that the young lords would want a more experienced man in this position when the action began. He never doubted that when the time came, they would take back Tirebeck. But his heart swelled with pride that Adam wanted him in the coming action first.

Considering all the doubts and sheer bafflement that suffused his feelings about Adam, he couldn't quite understand his desire to strive and succeed for him, personally. Not any more for the MacHeths in general or the legendary earl, or the lady of Ross, or even the woolly concepts of fame or justice. For Adam, who barely noticed his existence beyond the intelligence he could provide.

Or so he'd thought until this moment.

Adam gave a low whistle, and there came a responsive whinny from his horse, who seemed to behave much like a dog with his master. In a moment, the big grey came trotting through the trees, and Adam caught the reins before swinging up into the saddle, enviably quick and agile, and rode off without a further word or even a backward glance.

The normal courtesies of greeting and farewell simply passed by Adam MacHeth. He arrived, said or did what he came for, and departed. None of the men took it amiss or even seemed to notice. Maybe that was why it had become Cailean's ambition to make the young lord notice him above the others, even with one word.

It might even have been why he made the unforgivable mistake of walking out of the wood at the foot of the hill, lost in thought—and straight into one of Lanson's mounted patrols.

Clear of the trees and the large dollops of water they occasionally released onto his head and shoulders, he shook himself like a dog before he glanced up, and only then saw the column of armoured men coming straight for him.

There was nothing for it but to keep walking as if he had every right to be there. At least he wasn't wearing a cloak. To blend in, he'd wrapped himself in a rough wool shawl borrowed from the shepherd. Now, he kept his head turned away, veering to the right to avoid the soldiers in as natural a way as he could manage. He might even have got away with it, for the sword on his back wouldn't have been visible to them until they rode past and then happened to glance back, which they were surely unlikely to do for so unimportant and solitary a figure.

Only, as bad luck would have it, the knight at the head of

the troop was the same captain who'd commanded Cairistiona's escort when they'd taken her.

"Wait, there!" the man shouted in English.

Pretending not to understand, Cailean kept walking, his heart thudding. He could brazen this out, he could… But a word from the knight brought two mounted soldiers into his path, and he looked up, trying to appear both surprised and vacant.

And then the knight himself was there, staring down at him.

Perhaps it was inevitable that the knight's failure in letting his lady be taken had burned the faces of each of his attackers on his memory. But it was damned bad luck.

"I know you," the knight said grimly.

Cailean leapt backwards, reaching for his sword, but the sound of it scraping from its scabbard already screeched in his ears. The knight had seen it and seized it as he moved. With his left hand, Cailean grabbed for the dagger at his belt.

"Take him," the knight said.

There were times to fight, and times to live. Cailean spun around and legged it. A foolish attempt when attacked by mounted men, but he at least had a chance if he could make the cover of the forest.

He couldn't. His feet slid out of control in the mud, slowing him as he sought to keep both balance and speed. Inevitably, horses thundered past him, wheeling around to block his path.

Panting, Cailean slowed, spinning to take in the men encircling him. They dismounted, advancing on him. He swiped his dagger through the air in a wide arc, by his suddenness catching one man across the throat and forcing the others back. But he had to keep turning, keep sweeping his dagger—which was a poor weapon against swords and armour in any case. He ended by dropping it and using his feet and fists instead, but the outcome had never really been in doubt since the knight had seen his face.

Hot with exertion, fury, and shame, he found himself bound and led by a rope, staggering after one of the horses along the edges of the wood. The patrol was returning home with its prize. He wished he'd just paid attention, been aware. He wished he were faster, stronger. He wished he were dead.

He fell more than once, dragged through the mud by the

horse before he could find his feet and pound faster. The ridicule of the soldiers, the pain of his abraded skin, was nothing compared to his own self-disgust.

And then, without any warning, a massive tree branch crashed outward and downward, landing square on the rope that joined him to the soldier in front. The soldier was dragged from his horse, landing heavily on the ground with an astonished cry.

Cailean, who'd barely been able to keep to his feet as the rope suddenly dipped, made a frantic effort to tug the whole rope free of the branch. Someone landed in front of him, sword plunging downward. For an instant, in the midst of his sudden, desperate hope, Cailean thought he was dead.

Adam MacHeth cut the rope cleanly. At almost the same time, a dagger in his left hand cut the bindings between Cailean's wrists.

"Run," Adam said.

Cailean obeyed from pure instinct. Adam had come back for him. Adam was risking himself *massively*, for *him*. After the first, staggering pace, he glanced anxiously over his shoulder.

"I'm right behind you," Adam said. His sword sliced into the nearest attacking soldier, who cried out and fell. Adam's flying boot sent another crashing into a third, and then he was pounding after Cailean into the cover of the wood.

Cailean laughed with pure joy, caught the answering grin on his lord's face. Here in the forest, their feet had more grip on the ground, which made little sound as they ran. They could play hide-and-seek for hours here with the heavily armed, blundering soldiers.

Not so blundering. The whine of an arrow made Cailean duck behind a tree. Something thudded on the ground behind him. Already running again, Cailean glanced back and pulled up short.

Adam was on his knees by a puddle, an arrow through his shoulder. The world tilted and stilled.

"Go on," Adam shouted, yanking the arrow free. Blood gushed from the wound, splashing over his tunic. To Cailean's further amazement, he hurled himself, good shoulder first, the rest of the way to the ground and rolled in the mud. "I'll catch you," he said, splattering his face and hands with it.

Would he? Like that? Cailean doubted it. So did Adam, or he wouldn't be disguising his distinctive looks. Cailean stumbled on.

"*Run.*" If Adam couldn't escape, then running was the only way to save him, surely, to find the men, to tell Donald and get him back...

In deeper cover, Cailean halted and peered back through the trees. The rain had finally gone off, and during the forest chase, the sky had begun to lighten. Steel glinted in the dappled, very watery sunlight, even before the clash of sword on sword. Adam was fighting. Already injured, he was fighting, surely for his life, and Cailean couldn't see how the hell he could win. Neither Donald nor his men could change that now.

He, Cailean mac Gilleon, was the only one who stood a chance of it.

A damnably faint chance.

With a roar, he surged back through the forest. Taking the nearest soldier by surprise, he leapt on him, snatching his sword by the hilt and booting him hard. The man flew across the ground into undergrowth, and Cailean entered the fray with the sword of his victim.

Adam was hard-pressed. His back to a thick tree trunk, he wore what Cailean thought of as his battle face, the reason, he suspected, some called him a berserker. It was almost as if he went to another place, and Cailean began to understand why. Neither compassion nor pain could touch him there. And right now, defending against three armoured soldiers, he needed to fight through agony.

Cailean took out one with a clean thrust straight through his armour.

"Damn it, *go!*" Adam snarled.

Cailean didn't answer. He was too busy defending himself from the furious attack of the second swordsman. They needed to end this fast and tend Adam's wound. Perhaps, if they could just get back to the shepherd's wife...

Burning pain seared his chest. Perhaps it was just the sinking of his heart, caused by the close neighing of horses, the crashing of hooves and feet in the undergrowth. They had no time to do this. The world felt shaky, sore.

I'm wounded too. I didn't save him. Now I'll die knowing I've caused his death as well...

Horses broke through the trees, spreading out,

surrounding them once more.

"Enough!" the knight commanded, piercing Cailean's fading consciousness. "Yield."

Adam kicked out, sending his opponent staggering backward, perhaps to prevent any possibility of treachery, for at the same time, he lowered his sword and swung his ferocious gaze on Cailean, who understood.

Cailean said hoarsely, "We yield."

****

Sigurd the shepherd's son was crossing the yard towards the kitchen, a chicken in either hand, when the soldiers rode in with their captives drawn along beside them by a rope. Sigurd, his heart sinking at the unnecessary cruelty which had been brought to this land, paused to gape. He doubted he could have prevented his anxious stares, but at least he made them as foolish as possible, opening his mouth like an idiot as the cavalcade approached.

There were two prisoners. One, a filthy, gangly fellow almost entirely covered in mud and blood, carried the other on his back. Over the big man's shoulder, Sigurd saw a shaggy brown head and a young face he'd come to know well recently.

Cailean mac Gilleon. Damn. The young lord needed to be told. Sigurd hoped he wasn't dead. He looked dead...

Sigurd lifted his gaze to the dirty, unfamiliar man who carried Cailean mac Gilleon. He wore no cloak, no weapons, no signs of rank. Another man of Ross, a soldier, probably, one of Cailean's. For the tiniest instant, their eyes met, and Sigurd's heart lurched impossibly. No two men in the world had eyes like that.

Sigurd turned away and clumped on to the kitchen with his dead chickens. The men of Ross here in the hall would know. He had to make sure they all knew also to keep their mouths shut, because at all costs, this must be kept from the foreigners.

Sigurd dumped his chickens in front of the frightened kitchen maid to be plucked. "Not a word," he breathed, and grabbed a bucket and cloth from the shelf before plodding back out to the well. Having collected his clean water, he went straight to the main hall. If Lanson or the captain were there, he'd clean tables until they left.

It could have been worse. He knew the foreigner who

skulked at the front of the hall, flirting with the girl who was removing cobwebs with a brush on a pole. He wasn't a cruel man, for a soldier, and Sigurd was pretty sure he'd have no complaint about someone tending the captives' wounds.

The captives were chained by the ankles to rings already fixed to the hall's stout wooden wall for the purpose of punishing peasants who denied tribute to the new lord of Tirebeck, usually because they had none to give. At least the straw on the floor was clean and their hands were free. The large, muddy man sat propped against the wall with Cailean mac Gilleon lying beside him. Both had their eyes closed. Sigurd dropped to his knees in front of them and pulled back the mud- and blood-soaked layers of fabric from the young lord's shoulder.

A hand closed around his wrist. Sigurd's gaze flew at once to the young lord's face. Adam mac Malcolm's eyes were open, and though perhaps he hid it from everyone else, Sigurd could see his physical pain.

Low-voiced, Adam said, "Him," and moved his gaze to the youth beside him.

And perhaps he was right. Though he couldn't see Adam's injury for the mud, at least he was conscious. Obediently, Sigurd shifted closer to Cailean, who also, suddenly, opened his eyes.

"Make it fast," Cailean breathed. "He needs help, and no one must know—"

"I know," Sigurd said. The trouble was, he didn't have his mother's skills, and he'd no real idea what to do about such awful wounds.

****

Cailean had been in agony in the short, terrible journey to the hall. Not so much from his wound as from the horror of being carried by a more severely injured comrade who happened also to be his captain and the son of the earl. But Adam was right. It was the only way to carry this off with any hope.

And so he suffered the shepherd's son to hastily bind his wound before turning his attention to Adam. The young lord held himself rigid as Sigurd bound the wound with his own shirt and helped Adam pull his tunic back on, still anxiously observing him.

"You understand *he* is *my* man?" Cailean muttered urgently.

"He understands everything," Adam said, and for the first time, the shepherd's son smiled, before leaping to his feet and running off with his bloody bucket.

Adam's eyes looked glazed, although whether with pain or foresight, or whatever else went on behind there, Cailean had no idea. As if he forced them, Adam's eyes refocused, meeting Cailean's worried gaze.

"I told you to go," Adam said clearly, the first time he'd spoken directly to him since he gave his sword to the Norman captain. "You came back."

"It seemed a good idea at the time," Cailean muttered, dropping his gaze. "Only now we're both captive, and no one knows we're here. Will Sigurd be able to get word—"

Adam's hand jerked dismissively. "That doesn't matter."

Annoyed, Cailean opened his mouth to explain exactly how much it mattered, and how much he'd wanted to help Adam, who'd risked his life for surely the least significant of his men. Then the faint gleam in the dark, pained eyes gave him the hint of a reason of Adam's acceptance of his situation, and he let out a half laugh. "Don't tell me you have a plan for this too."

"I always have a plan," Adam said mildly. "This was hardly an impossible outcome. The secret is to make the most of every situation."

"And how do we do that, injured as we are, and chained here like dogs?"

"Learn." Adam closed his eyes.

****

Of course, the main difficulty about learning from his surroundings right now was to stay conscious for long enough to observe anything, let alone to escape to do anything about it. Pain devoured Adam. His ears sang with it. Inside, his whole body shook. He knew that if he relaxed, he'd tremble outwardly too, and yet darkness beckoned, promising at least a temporary respite from pain.

He forced his eyes open again. But already Cailean was calling out for a drink, his voice both frightened and determined.

Adam liked Cailean. Behind his youthful desire for glory lay a sound mind and a perception lacking in many of his lieutenants. Adam would probably have attempted to rescue him whoever he was, and even if the idea of observing from within hadn't come to him. But he hadn't bargained on Cailean returning the favour. Being Malcolm MacHeth's son should preserve Adam from execution, but that wouldn't help Cailean, who, of lesser value, could be slain as unnecessary. And so Cailean, already recognised, had to be the important hostage, and Adam too *un*important even to kill.

Although he might die anyway, despite the visions which denied it. Why the devil had the boy come back? Now he had to get both of them out of this, and he wasn't sure he could, not like this...

Something hard and cold touched his lips. Someone held a cup for him. Wine trickled over his lips and down his throat, strong and reviving. More than that, he recognised the taste. He smiled as he took some more. He was in Cairistiona's home, drinking the wine he'd given her, had even tasted on her lips one sunny market day in Rosemarkie. He knew that had been real.

He could manage the pain now. And the shaking. He might even be able to think through the fuzziness.

He opened his eyes on Cailean's worried face and grasped another truth. It wasn't just duty or the loyalty he'd been born with that had brought Cailean back to defend Adam. Adam understood such loyalty, but for the first time ever, it struck him there might be more. Bonds like those that tied him to Donald. And to Somerled. They had always been there. But others, those forced upon one by birth, could become genuine. That was why Findlaech and the others looked out for him, even covered for him when his mind slipped too far from the present. It might even have been why he'd jumped in to rescue Cailean in the first place.

Interesting, but it didn't matter. Loyalty was absolute.

Uncomfortably, he shifted his gaze from Cailean's pale face to take in the servant who'd brought the wine. Not Sigurd this time, but another local man with real, personal fear behind his concern.

Adam nodded by way of thanks, jerked his eyes to Cailean, who seemed about to protest, and then, under Adam's gaze, drank anyway before returning the cup to Adam. This time, Adam could hold it for himself. No one was watching. The soldier who was meant to be their guard was gazing at the breasts of the girl cleaning cobwebs away. She'd been doing this for a very long time. She must like the soldier, Adam thought. It got complicated, living with your enemies...

Male voices, hurried thudding footsteps, a word in French drifted through the nearby door. Terror flared harder in the servant's face. Adam shoved the cup into his hands, and he fled. He was well away from them before the door opened and Sir William de Lanson strode through with their captor, whose name, Adam remembered, was Henry.

Adam rested his head back against the wall as Lanson halted inside the door and stared at the prisoners.

"Are you sure he's one of the MacHeths?" Lanson said doubtfully.

Beside Adam, Cailean stiffened, but they weren't looking at Adam. To them, MacHeths were everyone associated with the family.

"He looks different to me," Lanson said.

"Better dressed, sir," Henry answered. "But it's the same man. I'd know him anywhere."

"Having sat back and watched him and his captain take my wife," Lanson snapped.

Shame coloured Henry's face. Adam felt an urge to defend the quality of the knight he'd defeated that day, though it was an impulse easily squashed. Adam's approbation was unlikely to help either of them.

Lanson didn't so much as glance at Henry. He was still staring at Cailean. He scowled. "What the hell are you doing on my land?"

"Visiting," Cailean replied, also in French.

"Visiting whom?"

Cailean smiled. "You."

Lanson's slightly puffy eyes narrowed. "I hope you're enjoying my hospitality."

"I've known worse," Cailean lied.

Lanson shifted his body, as if suddenly impatient. "Where are your men?" he demanded.

"All over Ross," Cailean replied. He glanced at Henry and around the men-at-arms who'd followed their lord into the hall. "Except here," he allowed.

Lanson smiled thinly. "Well, the pleasure of your company

is unexpected, if not unwelcome. All I have to decide now is what to do with you."

Adam could almost see the slow, brutal brain turning over his options. Keeping Cailean prisoner, he risked attack from without and possibly treachery from within. Several local people were employed here, and more came to the hall to speak to the lady, according to Cailean. Lanson could only guess at how important Cailean might be to the earl's sons. But killing him would not end the MacHeth rebellion. In the short term, it might bring them all down on Lanson, who surely understood now that if it wasn't for the MacHeths' favour to his wife, he would never have held this land at all.

"Or," Lanson said, "there may be more personal advantage. Advantage there undoubtedly is. Please, enjoy your stay." Bellowing with laughter, Lanson walked away.

Cailean spoke an obscene word under his breath, adding, "I pity his lady."

Adam wasn't sure it was pity, but something roiled in his stomach, intense and bitter, at the thought of her with such a man. At least it concentrated his mind.

****

Word of his presence at Tirebeck would be all over Ross by morning. The servants who set up the tables in the hall for dinner, most of them local, knew he was there. They cast him long, surreptitious glances and one maid even brought them a flagon of water under his guard's nose. The guard didn't care, so long as they stayed sitting down and chained. Eua, who supervised the setting of the tables, looked worried.

By nightfall, Donald would be mounting a rescue. He'd be here, probably, by first light. Adam doubted he'd even try to buy Lanson off—capturing MacHeths had become far too frequent a pastime.

Perhaps it was time to retake Tirebeck. It would, probably, bring the royal army at last, but Donald mac William in Moray was offering at least passive support, and Fergus, the powerful lord of Galloway, had expressed veiled interest in talking. With Fergus threatening in the south and Somerled at least hostile in the west, in their own country the MacAeds could surely win a good enough position to negotiate...

On the other hand, Somerled wasn't yet sure of the Isle of Man, and Fergus of Galloway was hardly a certainty. Adam preferred to stick with the original plan and lose as few men as possible until it was necessary. Which meant getting out of here before Donald arrived at dawn.

The hall door slammed open to admit Lanson once more. He ignored his prisoners beyond a smirk in their direction as he strode through the tables and servants to the back of the hall from where a door led, presumably to his bedchamber. A little later, a woman entered the hall—the fair, pretty thing who'd tried to tell Cairistiona what to do when Adam had first captured them. Now, as then, she was dressed, so it seemed to Adam's perceptive gaze, in a finer gown than her lady's. The ribbons in her golden fair hair were shimmering silk. She flitted along the length of the hall and disappeared into Lanson's bedchamber.

"Blatant," Cailean observed with contempt. "His lady is due more respect than that. The man is a pig."

Adam stirred and swallowed a wince. "Pigs are loyal creatures. Tell them we need to piss."

Obediently, Cailean called the message out in French to their new, more careful guard.

"Be my guest," the guard invited.

"Outside," Cailean said. "The chain doesn't stretch."

The man grinned. "Neither it does."

Cailean swore at him in Gaelic. Adam merely heaved himself to his feet. They'd had the same argument before and lost, but right now, he only wanted the excuse to stand up. The table at the head of the hall was set for four, but despite the gathering household, including Cairistiona's other women, there was no sign of the lady. At least she wasn't obliged to see her woman go in and out of her husband's chamber. He wondered how much it hurt her. Or if it relieved her to have his attentions elsewhere.

"I have little value as a wife." She ignored it, he guessed, never appeared to see it, never deigned to comment or even scold. But it had hurt her to speak the words to him. It had taken the last of her pride.

He turned his back on the company, although he had neither the need nor the intention of relieving himself. But no one else came through the hall door. Instead, the door at the other end opened. Adam turned in time to see Lanson and the woman emerge from the private chamber and take their seats side by side at the high table.

"Begin!" Lanson roared impatiently.

"Sir, the lady is not yet arrived," Henry pointed out into the sudden silence.

"Then we'll begin without her."

From her seat with the other women, Eua waved the servants to bring in the meal. From the tight set of her lips, she didn't approve either. Which was also interesting. As he'd guessed from their brief conversation in Rosemarkie, Eua had taken sides among her enemies.

From what Adam could make out, the food was plentiful enough, but not over luxurious. There was ample bread and fish, and poultry with spring vegetables.

Beside him, Cailean's stomach rumbled. "Do you suppose they'll give us any?"

"Unlikely," Adam replied. Although he wasn't hungry, he needed food for strength. And Cailean, still growing, must have been ravenous.

The hall door swung open, and someone swept inside.

Adam's gaze stuck to her. Cairistiona. Wearing a grey cloak spattered with mud. Clearly, she'd been out somewhere on the land. Every face in the hall turned towards her. Talk fell away to a murmur. Cairistiona's feet faltered, then almost immediately carried on, making her way through the tables without looking to right or left.

Henry pushed back his chair and stood, glaring at the men-at-arms until they also stood.

"Please. Sit," Cairistiona said clearly. Her head was high. As she allowed Henry to take her cloak and took her seat between him and Lanson, there was no sign that she perceived any insult. Her husband ignored her. Talk started up again.

As Henry civilly passed her food—what was left on the serving plates—Adam continued to watch her half-masked face. She looked serene. And yet she held her body as stiffly as she had in the beginning of their first encounter, when she was afraid of him. But not later, and not in Rosemarkie. She'd been more comfortable with strangers, abductors, and outlaws than here in her own hall.

No wonder. This was her daily torture, her ritual humiliation, taking second place to her attendant. How long had it been like this for her? Women were forced to suffer in ways men never even thought of.

His gut twisted. A woman already humiliated and belittled was unlikely to have enjoyed the added insult of a stranger's rough embrace, and yet he'd put her through that too. There had been no need. He'd just wanted to kiss her. Had wanted it since he'd held her before him in his saddle, and dreamed. Maybe before that when he'd first seen her half face held together with determination and desperate humour. Her taste still seemed to linger on his lips. Like the wine…

He was growing wandered, delirious, losing control of his mouth and his thoughts. Pursing the former, he reined in the latter and waited for her to notice him.

CHAPTER TEN

Christian had mistimed her entry to the hall. After visiting a struggling family on the other side of the hill, she imagined, by the height of the sun only just visible through the universally grey sky, that she was just late enough to avoid pretending not to see William and Alys emerging from his bedchamber.

But it seemed that either he'd foregone his tumble for the day or he'd got it over with faster than usual and it had made him hungry. She didn't mind the rudeness, or the lack of respect. She hated the public nature of it. How was she to win her people over, be their lady, if they learned her worth from William? Or worse, pitied her.

It undermined everything she was doing here.

"Forgive our rudeness, lady," Henry said when things had settled back down.

"Hungry men must eat," she replied lightly. "Thank you," she added, for the food he helped her to. A servant ran up and poured her wine, then refilled William's cup while he was there.

She found she didn't really want to eat. The poverty of the family she'd just visited, who'd asked her to intercede for them against William's tribute demands, combined with the petty humiliation to turn her stomach. So she picked at the food while she finally took the time to observe her surroundings and her people. Felicia and Eua seemed to be continuing their slightly guarded friendship, as a result of which Cecily too had reined in her hostility. The local servants gave none of their feelings away. At the back of the hall, one of the men-at-arms was flirting with a maid, seemed to be trying to repeat her words. Learning the language, perhaps. With time, she reminded herself, harmony was not impossible.

Her gaze drifted, for the first time taking in the men chained at the back of the hall. Frowning, she swung around on William, who'd agreed not to imprison any more peasants for nonpayment of his tax, but before she could speak, Henry's words stayed her.

"You see we have prisoners. None other than your late abductor."

Her heart, her stomach, her whole body seemed to jolt. Her gaze flew once more to the back of the hall, but she didn't want to peer too obviously around tables and people.

"Adam MacHeth?" she managed. "How did that come about?"

"No, sadly not Adam himself," Henry said. "Just one of his men wandering out of the wood. I recognised the boy—I'm sure he's well-born, by their standards at least—and he bolted. Stupid, considering we were mounted and he was on foot, but before we could catch him, his servant dropped a tree on us and freed his master. We pursued and, after a brief fight, captured them both."

"What in God's name were they doing here?" she wondered. But she already knew. Adam had given her Tirebeck publicly, but he still regarded it as his.

Henry shrugged, taking the second to last piece of fowl from the plate. "Spying, probably, or retaxing the people. Whatever, I doubt it was worth his wounds and several days' discomfort here while Sir William decides what to do with him."

Damn him. She tilted her chin and finally saw more than simply legs on the floor. The boy was the one who'd given her food during her capture and helped her to mount Adam's huge horse. Cailean. He'd been kind to her, even blushed when she looked at him. His attention seemed to be divided now between herself and his large, filthy soldier, who leaned his head back against the wall as if not so far from death.

Although it was impossible to tell over this distance and in the poor light of the prisoners' corner, she was sure there was blood on them, much blood. She had the oddest feeling too, that the slumped servant was looking right at her. There was something familiar about his shape and posture, the unblinking stare from the filthy face.

Oh blessed mother of God, no... She glanced at Cailean, and her suspicion sharpened. No wonder the boy was so anxious for his man... But no, she must be wrong. Someone surely would have recognised that Adam MacHeth himself, however hidden in grime and blood, graced the hall and the chains?

Dear God, what if he died?

"*Will* they die?" she blurted.

"Hope not," Henry said ruefully. "Not sure either the MacHeths or the lesser natives would take that too well."

"Who tended his wound?"

"His man, I suppose."

She drew in her breath. She knew her duty, and right now it attracted and repelled her in almost equal measure. She didn't know if compassion or sheer curiosity was responsible, but she beckoned the maid who stood to the side of the high table. "Have the prisoners eaten?"

"No, my lady," the girl replied.

"Then see to it now, if you please."

A smile that looked very like relief split the girl's face. They would have fed the prisoners anyway as soon as they were unobserved. Now they had sanction.

But William, of course, had to be ungracious. Leaving off whatever entertaining conversation he might have been conducting with Alys, he turned to Christian for the first time since she'd arrived.

"They're *my* servants," he said loudly. "None of them will serve a MacHeth and expect to live."

Damn him, did he have to provoke a confrontation over this? Slowly, she turned her head and met his glare. Ranulf, her stepfather, had given her to a strong warrior he'd imagined would protect her. But William was a bully, a vindictive, selfish, arrogant, and, in many ways, stupid man. She could obey her husband publicly, stick to the merely passive resistance that she'd indulged in since their arrival, working, in effect, as if he wasn't there.

Or she could be the lady of Tirebeck.

She met his gaze until, pleased with his spiteful little victory, he smiled and turned back to Alys. Christian sighed, reaching for the almost empty serving plate in front of her. To it, she added from the meagre remains of the other dishes, including some bread, and stood up, grasping her wine cup at the last moment.

She kept her passage down the length of the hall as unobtrusive as she could. If William had any sense, he would leave it that way. She could almost feel the stunned silence behind her, prickling at her neck until a crack of what sounded like genuine laughter issued from William.

"Fitting," he said contemptuously. "More wine here!"

Christian kept walking. Although talk in the hall didn't generally die down, she was aware of the several curious glances cast at her. They didn't bother her. She was more concerned with the state of her prisoners, whom she didn't feel able to look directly at until she'd passed the farthest table.

When they realised she was approaching them rather than the hall door, the big servant made a sudden movement to stand. The youth's arm went round the waist of his lord, though whether to help or prevent or seek help of his own was impossible to tell. Christian didn't care. Her stomach twisted as if an unseen hand was wringing it out.

Adam MacHeth's wild, glazed eyes met hers and seemed to calm. A tiny smile flickered across his lips. *Will you betray me?* he seemed to ask.

She ignored him. "Don't get up," she instructed Cailean, quickening her pace and hastily crouching down in the straw before them. With relief, they dropped back to sitting positions. Christian placed the plate and the cup between them. "Eat it quickly before the dogs get a scent of it," she advised.

"Bless you, lady," the youth said in passable French. "I hope your kindness won't rebound against you."

"Of course not. And you may speak in your own tongue if you prefer. I find it's come back to me. Mostly." At last, feeling as if she took some reckless leap into the dangerous unknown, she turned her gaze up to Adam MacHeth. "How is your wound?"

Although his breathing was too rapid, perhaps from the exertion of trying to stand, his attention was entirely focused on her, his eyes a little too bright but quite steady. "Better."

"The arrow is out and the bleeding is less," the youth added.

"I'll tend it for you when you've eaten."

"There is no need," Adam said. "One of your servants already did."

Of course. While her husband and Henry weren't looking.

"On the contrary," Christian returned tartly, "I choose that you don't die in my house. I won't risk the wound becoming corrupted."

Unexpectedly, a smile flickered across his lips. "Assertiveness suits you."

"I'm always assertive," Christian said. "Other people just don't always notice. I'm afraid you'll have to share this offering."

"Thank you," Adam said. His intense, troubling gaze held hers. "Will you tell your husband?"

She didn't pretend to misunderstand. On the other hand, she chose not to answer. Instead, she asked, "How close are your men? Will they attack us?"

The youth went very still, his eyes wide. Adam said, "They won't attack *you*."

A hundred more questions struggled to get out, but with an effort, she forced them back, saying only, "Eat. I'll come back when you've finished."

She rose and returned to her own dinner. On the way, she spoke to Felicia, asking her to bring the medicine box from her chamber in the old guesthouse. As she sat down, her husband ignored her.

Henry, however, who had all of the young man's belief in chivalry, smiled at her with approval. "You were born to be a great lady," he said warmly.

"I was born with basic compassion," she corrected with a faint twist of her lips. "I suppose we are prepared for an attack?"

"Always," Henry said reassuringly. "Since we took him, we've been doubly alert."

There was no need to ask. William was the consummate soldier.

Henry said, "Then you think I'm right, that the young man is important to the MacHeths?"

She nodded. "I believe he is. We must make sure they survive." Which was by no means certain. Her stomach churned at the possibility of them dying at Tirebeck. And yet, she couldn't get out of her head that, injured or not, Adam MacHeth was up to something.

"I'll come back for you." Had he? The idea made her heart beat so hard, she couldn't think, and yet she didn't even know what his words meant. All she knew was that he couldn't die here. Too many tragedies would result from that, and she wouldn't allow it.

She began to eat without paying much attention to what was in her mouth. When her husband drew breath from boring Alys—or flirting with her, she rarely noticed which, since Alys's reaction to both was much the same smile and admiring glances from beneath her lashes—Christian said, "Will you ransom your captive?"

"When I've decided what I want for him," William said, wiping his sleeve across his mouth and reaching for his cup.

"Our supplies are short," she observed. "Silver would be useful." She turned her gaze on him. "So would the land of Knockalsh that adjoins Tirebeck."

William turned his head and stared at her. The inevitable disparaging comment formed on his lips but never sounded. His eyes narrowed. "Knockalsh would improve our security here... You think we'd get both land and silver? Just for the MacHeth's boy?"

"I don't know," Christian said honestly. "But we should keep him alive in the hope of it. The alternative is an attack we can't hold off for long."

William nodded thoughtfully before he remembered who was talking to him and scowled at her instead. "Of course we can hold off a few savages!" He turned back to Alys.

When Christian had forced down the food before her, she rose from the table, bade her husband and anyone who was listening a polite good night, and left the high table once more. Alys tripped after her as she always did, and the other women joined them from their own table as they passed, Felicia clutching the medicine box.

"Thank you," Christian said, taking it from her. "Good night."

"We would stay and help," Felicia said in a rush. Behind her, Alys wrinkled her nose.

Christian smiled at the other two. "Thank you. But it won't take long." She nodded dismissal and walked across to the captives, sinking to her knees in the straw by Adam's shoulder.

There was a wary set to his face. "Don't look so worried," she said lightly. "I've spent most of my life dressing the wounds of injured soldiers."

"Did they live?" Adam enquired.

"Some of them," Christian replied. "The ones who didn't give me any trouble."

"Then please, Cailean first. Since you haven't given us away."

"Yet," Christian said, watching Cailean unwind the bandages from over his torn tunic and shirt.

Adam's breath hissed in what might have been laughter. For some reason, that lightened her spirits, as if mirth made his death less likely.

Although close in position to his heart, Cailean's wound was minor, shallow, and clean, so she merely applied some ointment and rebound it. He thanked her humbly, blushing slightly when she patted his arm.

Adam MacHeth was a different matter. He tried to untie his own bandage, and Christian was forced to catch his hand. He didn't withdraw it as he had that first time. It didn't even jump in hers, and his eyes never left her face. The combination unnerved her before she began.

"Be still," she snapped, although he already was. She snatched her hand from his, and, trying very hard not to think of the body beneath, she removed his tunic and untied the bandages for him. Beneath the mud and moss he must have rolled in, the gore caught at her breath. She'd seen men die of lesser wounds. But at least whoever had dealt with it had cleansed it well. A good beginning.

Laying aside the bandages—a roughly torn shirt—she poured a poppy tincture into the empty wine cup.

"Drink this," she instructed Cailean first. "For the pain."

"What is it?"

"Opium tears."

Cailean took a couple of mouthfuls and passed the rest to his "servant."

Adam hesitated. "Will it make me sleep?"

"It will *let* you sleep," she retorted. "Why do you care? Do you have an urgent appointment?"

"You have a sharp tongue for a ministering angel."

"I have a sharp tongue for anyone. And I've had a tiring day." She stared at him, at the half smile forming and dying on his lips, until he raised the cup and drank it all. Then she set about closing and anointing the ugly wound to prevent corruption. She didn't know if the torn muscles beneath would repair themselves.

He never winced under her ministrations, although his flesh occasionally flinched, an involuntary reaction he seemed unable to prevent. For the rest, although he had whitened under his mud and there was a certain tightness around the corners of his eyes, his face showed few signs of pain or distress. He seemed to distract himself by watching her face as she worked.

She wondered what he saw there and came to the conclusion that he simply had to look at something. He'd learned well the first lesson of a leader, to show no weakness.

She took a clean dressing from her box and used old linen strips to bind them around his body. This brought her too close to him. He smelled too warm, too male, reminding her of his embrace in Rosemarkie. Beneath her suddenly clumsy hands, his back and chest were hard with muscle. Worse, his hair brushed against her cheek, and she could have sworn he actually dipped his head closer rather than leaning back to avoid her.

But then, he was weak with loss of blood.

The hall began to empty while she worked, the men-at-arms sent back to their duties since the MacHeth presence presented an added danger. Her heart twisted with guilt. If only they knew how much danger. But she couldn't risk William knowing he had Adam MacHeth in his power. He could, and probably would, ruin everything.

When she finished and drew back, Adam's gaze still rested on her face.

"What?" she demanded tartly.

He stirred. "I'm wondering."

"Wondering what?"

"Many things. For one, why you haven't told Lanson who I am."

"I'm considering what's best."

His head dropped back against the wall, a smile flickering and vanishing on his lips. No wonder. They both knew she couldn't give him away now. If she'd been going to, she'd have done it as soon as she recognised him.

He said, "What will Lanson ask for Cailean?"

"Silver and the village of Knockalsh."

Adam blinked. "Is that what you told him?"

"What makes you think I'd presume?"

"The fact that he wouldn't acknowledge it was in Donald's power to give land. We're outlaws to the King of Scots."

"William is a realist," Christian said, closing her box. "He must work with matters as they are, not as how they should be."

"Yes, he must," Adam said gravely. "So he should know that is too much to ask for Cailean mac Gilleon here. Donald will pay a silver penny for him. The lady my mother will double that since she has a kindness for him."

"And for the villainous servant?" she enquired, rising to her feet. She wanted to smile because, despite his wound, he was joking, and because beside him, the appalled Cailean clearly hadn't yet realised it.

Adam tipped his head farther back, following her with his gaze. "They might send you a cake now and then, just to keep him here. Thank you."

For some reason, his thanks, or perhaps just his sudden seriousness, disturbed her. She could no longer meet his gaze.

"My people will bring you blankets," she muttered. "Do you need anything else?"

He shifted his foot, making the chain rattle. "The key?"

She didn't grace that with an answer.

****

Like his captain, Cailean watched the lady of Tirebeck leave the hall in something of a daze. He rather thought he'd made a discovery that explained so many of Adam's odd actions concerning her. There may have been his sense of justice, maybe even compassion for her intolerable position, but mostly, Adam just liked her.

Perhaps the poppy juice had loosened Cailean's tongue or given him false courage, for he said, "I'd sing you mournful love songs, if only I had a lute."

"I might not kill you, if only you could play it. If you sleep, Cailean, be ready to wake on the instant and move quickly."

Appalled, Cailean stared at him. "You can't leave tonight. You're in no state to go anywhere, even without a fight."

105

"On the contrary, it has to be tonight," he said grimly. "While the poppy is working."

"She'll give you more in the morning," Cailean argued.

"Tomorrow will be too late."

Sigurd the shepherd's son came in with an armful of blankets, enough to make their night's captivity almost comfortable. Cailean found himself longing just to give in to that comfort, just for tonight. Just to see the lady again. He liked her in her own hall, in her own home, managing her pig of a husband and her people with dignity. Once her husband was dead, she would be considered a pretty suitable wife for a man of Cailean's birth and position. Much more suitable for him than for Adam mac Malcolm...

Cailean watched Adam exchanging hurried speech with Sigurd as they arranged the blankets. The sons of Malcolm MacHeth, Cailean knew, would look for wives among the great families of the land. It was pointless being jealous of Adam. God knew what his "liking" her meant anyway. He never behaved like other men, probably didn't *feel* like other men, either...

"Are you listening, Cailean?" The young lord's impatient voice cut through his stupid, rambling thoughts, dragging him back to the reality of huddling in chains and blankets with the friendly shepherd's son taking Adam's orders for their escape.

"Sorry," Cailean muttered. Lanson's soldiers, having completed their last duties, were drifting back into the hall where they would sleep. One or two were helping the servants move tables and benches to make space. Cailean gave himself a little shake. "I was drifting off. How are we to manage this?"

****

No one slept near the prisoners. No one guarded the hall door on either the inside or the outside—why should they when the men on watch in the castle tower could see that too? Adam quietly rubbed his chafed ankles, and with the key Sigurd had wrapped in one of the blankets, unlocked the chains. Loegaire, the ever resourceful, must always have had a copy of the one on Henry's belt.

It would take several supposedly sleeping movements to draw their limbs free without rousing suspicion in anyone who might be awake. But he had to time this right, and it was damned hard when his mind roamed all over the place, into dark corners and massive open fields of light, and he was terrified of slipping completely out of reality.

It was the damned poppy juice. It wasn't good for him, although at least it dulled the pain. And at least he was aware that if anyone but Cailean spoke to him, and that in no more than a low whisper, then it wasn't real.

By the time the owl called, they were free of the chains and could both slither silently through the darkness to the hall door. From there Adam rose openly, as if he was a soldier stumbling outside to relieve himself in the darkness. Which, in fact, was what he did, in the densest shadows, waiting for Cailean to follow, focusing desperately on the silence of night, straining for the sound he needed to hear: Sigurd's voice.

It came a little quicker than he expected, before Cailean had even emerged from the hall. But as the door began to open and a voice from the castle answered Sigurd's, Adam slipped through the shadows of the hall, using those of the outer buildings too as he gradually made his silent way around the enclosure towards the closed gates. Only, when he looked back, someone who wasn't Cailean was pissing against the wall of the hall. Damnation. From outside the enclosure, Sigurd would run out of things to say. The guards would let him in the back gate and return to their posts, the distraction over before he and Cailean were even out the front gates, let alone in the cover of the forest.

Trees filled his mind as he flew over their branches in bright sunlight, soaring, flapping... *No, no, stay here, feet on the ground...*

Without warning, the door behind him opened. Adam reacted quickly, spinning himself into the emerging figure to launch them both back inside the building. There he kicked the door shut and pushed his victim against it so that he could slam his hand over the mouth already open and ready to shout.

Only, his fingers found linen as well as soft, warm lips. The body he pressed into the door was small and fragile and smelled of Cairistiona.

Real or not real? He could still be in the yard waiting for the bloody soldier to stop pissing and go back inside so Cailean could slip out to join him. His mind preferred to be with her, gazing down at her wide beautiful eyes in the dim glow of the tiny lamp she still held clamped in one hand. A nice detail, pointing at reality. He took the lamp from her clutching fingers, placing it on the table beside the door before he risked loosening his hand on her lips.

She stared at him, her eyes shining with startled anxiety. No fear, no anger, which surely meant unreality. Unless she couldn't see who he was by the dim glow from the little lamp.

Focus on the sound of Sigurd's voice—faint but still audible—*on the door of the hall*... No chance. Not while her heart galloped against him, not while her body was so soft and his so hard as he held her against the door. Not while she looked at him like *that*.

He slid his hand fully away from her mouth and kissed her, because he wanted to, and because if he didn't, he wouldn't be able to think of anything else.

Stupid reasoning. Stupid. Because all he could think of now was the feel of her crushed lips, parting in shock, or to shout at him which he couldn't allow, so he deepened the kiss, opening her mouth wider, sweeping his tongue greedily inside.

Her hands clutched his forearms, his good shoulder. *Don't hurt her, don't hurt her.* Even in dreams, he could never let himself do that. But before he could force himself back, her fingers touched his cheek. Not to scratch and fight. It felt like a caress, a kind of wonder.

Surely not real, then, but sweet, so sweet. He let himself prolong it, absorbing her yielding softness, losing himself in his need, heavy and urgent...

Urgent. He forced his lips to stillness. All his urgency should be focused on escaping, not abusing the kindness of his hostess and ruining the only plan they'd have in this mess. Cailean. Sigurd. The gate. Bloody poppy. The pain wasn't in his shoulder. But he wasn't dreaming either.

Slowly, softly, hoping she'd understand that as apology, he released her mouth and her person. Her breasts rose and fell as if she couldn't breathe without difficulty. But her glowing eyes still showed no fear. In spite of himself, he knew he smiled at that as he reached for the door latch. She stepped aside, as if from instinct, and he slid out into the cold, dark shadows. He hoped she wouldn't scream.

A quick glance at the looming tower showed him the back

of two heads at the far side. They were still calling to Sigurd in low voices, half in annoyance, half in ridicule.

For the smallest instant, Adam rested the back of his head against her door. He wanted to go back inside, see where she lived apart from her husband, where she slept, alone, all the little details and comforts that made up her life. When he opened his eyes, a shadow was flitting towards him. He clenched his fist, ready to fight if his numb shoulder would let him.

But it was Cailean, at last. A short burst of laughter came from the castle. Only one head was visible now. The other guard had gone down to open the back gate while the first one watched.

As one, Adam and Cailean ran silently towards the front gate. From nowhere, another man materialised in the darkness, pulling back the bolts.

"I'll fasten it behind you," breathed Loegaire.

CHAPTER ELEVEN

Christian stood where he'd left her, just to one side of the door. She seemed unable to move, apart from to close one hand over her heart as if she could slow down its beating.

There were no guards on the gate. He might get outside the enclosure before the shout went up from the castle. But the more she strained her ears, the less she seemed to hear. No footsteps. No shouts. No clattering of horses' hooves across the yard.

How could he—*they*, for surely Cailean was with him—not be seen from the castle? From the tower, you could see all over Tirebeck, right down to the sea. There was no way anyone could reach the cover of the forest or the hills without being observed.

Surely the men on watch couldn't be asleep? William commanded a much more efficient force than that. Distracted? She'd heard voices, faint, without urgency or threat, when she'd opened her door, but surely none of the Tirebeck people could hold the guards' attention as long as this without raising suspicion?

With every beat of her heart, they could be farther away. Or an instant closer to recapture. And anyone caught aiding them...

I'm aiding them. By keeping silent, I'm aiding them. Have I picked my side in this war?

No, she was still picking her way between, trying to keep Tirebeck safe and her loyalty to the king intact. But something still kept her rooted where she stood. Guilt. She closed her eyes, leaned her head back against the wall.

She'd never undressed for bed since leaving the hall, merely paced her own tiny house, mulling over what should be done about Adam MacHeth's presence here. Anxiety for his health, fear of discovery, guilt over her own silence and divided loyalties all seemed to take second place to a kind of delighted excitement. As if she liked the danger. Or this unexpected new reunion with her erstwhile captor.

Adam MacHeth was like no other man she'd ever encountered; he was strange, unpredictable, and she couldn't help liking that. And his odd, almost expressionless humour. And his rare, elusive smile. But these were not reasons to let him kiss her…

She slid her hand higher from her breast, letting her forearm take the job of slowing her heart while her fingertips touched her lips. He followed his instincts, did Adam MacHeth, not convention. So he'd kissed her in the dark. No one would kiss her in the light. And besides, his head was fuzzed with poppy juice.

Her danger here was dwelling on the trivial and forgetting the surrounding importance. Adam MacHeth was escaping. She'd been about to help him do it when she'd discovered, by being bundled back inside her house, that he'd already done it for himself. With, she was sure, the aid of her people. And with or without their aid, he seemed to be succeeding.

All Christian could do now was retire to bed and wait for others to discover the escape.

She would never be lady of Tirebeck while the MacHeths lived. That Adam was fuelled only by opium right now and just as likely as not to die by morning did not make her feel better.

****

Henry woke before dawn, very conscious that with their MacHeth prisoner, the watch had to be fresh. Rank provided him with the sleeping space of his choice, close to the fire and with an illusion of privacy provided by the main table. He sat up and lit the lamp he kept by him for the purpose. He hated tripping over bodies in the dark—especially bodies which swore at him without realising who he was. Rising, shivering, he made his way to the man nominated for the next watch and shook him.

"Thomas. It's your watch."

The soldier groaned but hauled himself upright, rubbing his eyes. The glow from the lamp spread over his erstwhile pillow, a rather luxuriant, if muddy, fur-lined cloak.

"Found it in the forest," Thomas said sheepishly. "Must be the prisoner's. Can I keep it?"

Henry shrugged. "You found it." He was about to stand and return to his own space to pack up his things, when the lamp caught a glint amid the cloak's fabric. Henry blinked, then paused, frowning, and reached down to touch the brooch which had been used as a fastening. Rather fine for a man of Cailean's standing, it must have been a gift from his lord, for it had an ornate letter "A" picked out in inlaid gem stones.

"A" for Aed, the ancestor for whom they were named. There was, Henry had discovered, some prophecy about him which lent mystical support to the MacHeths' claims to the Scottish throne. Or it could be "A" for Adam.

Something tugged at his memory, twisting his stomach.

"He wasn't wearing a cloak," Henry said.

Thomas stared at him. "Well, it's not the servant's!"

Henry closed his eyes in the effort of memory. "When the servant cut Cailean's bonds, what was he wearing?"

"I didn't see. It happened so fast..."

"I think we've been duped," Henry said grimly. "Get a bucket of water and throw it over the servant. We'll ask the lady to identify him with his mud scraped off." He stood, holding the lamp high to the annoyance of several sleeping soldiers, and gazed over the recumbent forms to the two at the back, a huddle of chains and blankets.

If the servant really was Adam MacHeth, then an attack was surely inevitable. The men had to be roused. As Thomas scuttled off to the well, Henry went directly to the prisoners. If he just heard the man talk, he'd know...

If the man *could* talk. There had been copious amounts of blood, and although he'd carried Cailean on his back, everyone had known his wounds were severe, much more so than Cailean's. No one had cared much because he was only a servant. But if he *died*...

At least the lady, in her kindness, had tended the servant's wounds too, though even she hadn't seen through the mud and blood and silence to her erstwhile captor. *If* it was he.

Henry bent at the first body and hauled back the blanket.

Oh teeth of God! "Awake!" Henry yelled. "Everyone rouse! Now!"

****

Donald MacHeth dismounted, unable to speak, and walked with dread towards the still figure in the shelter of the trees, and the familiar grey horse that stood beside him, occasionally bending to nudge his head.

Behind Donald, the men were silent, perhaps with dread, like him. Or grief.

Oh no...

Cailean mac Gilleon gazed at him, wide-eyed, ashamed of something. That he'd let Donald's brother die?

"Is he dead?" Donald asked harshly. There was no other way he could speak.

Cailean shook his head. "Asleep." It was no more than a whisper, but the relief seemed to unhinge Donald's knees, and he fell rather than knelt by his brother. There was blood all over him, and an impossible caking of mud.

He took a handful of the mucky hair and tugged. "Adam, you bloody idiot, wake up." Fear, only just relieved, galloped back. "Why isn't he waking? Cailean, for God's sake, how badly is he hurt?"

Cailean swallowed, sitting back on his heels. "I don't think it's the wound. I think it's sheer exhaustion. The lady gave him poppy tears for the pain, and he wouldn't sleep. He insisted on escaping in the night before you turned up and fired the place."

Donald held the younger man's gaze, aware he'd already made too much of this in front of the men. Fear of losing Adam had made him stupid, careless. Silly when Adam had faced worse danger every day, surely, with Somerled. He'd seen the scars on his brother's body.

"My brother is asleep," he announced. "I suppose we'd better carry the lazy bastard home. Until he wakes up, when *he* can carry *me*."

The men laughed, surging forward to help. Findlaech was first, his fierce eyes almost weeping with fear. He didn't believe a word of Donald's nonsense, but he knew what to do and how to play the game. A stream of rough, obscene idiocy fell from his lips as he lifted Adam with the tenderness, almost, of a mother.

"What happened?" Donald asked Cailean, drawing the boy to his feet.

Cailean turned his face into the wind, away from the men, and told him.

****

"I don't care," the lady of Ross said adamantly. "I will not risk him so soon. Donald must take the galleys. One of the other captains can lead the land attack."

Adam had been home for three days and sat now in the private corner of the hall leading to his mother's bedchamber, which she had turned into a snug little area with a couple of chairs and benches. In the sunshine, she'd opened the shutter to let the fresh air and warmth in. It was very comfortable and pleasant, and Adam was glad to be alive.

It didn't stop him feeling caged, not just by the care of his mother and sister. And brother. And Findlaech. And the maidservants. The hazy memories of his escape from Tirebeck made him restless, frustrated, unsure what had been dream and what reality, and whether or not he should be ashamed or glad or neither. He needed peace and action at the same time. At sea, he could lose himself in the illusion of being alone in the ocean's vastness. And plan his part in the triple attack which would heap pressure on the King of Scots.

And then he could fight. Once, he'd taught himself to *bear* battle; now, it seemed, he sought it with longing, needed it. Another oddity of life.

"Donald lead the galleys?" he said to his mother. "Donald couldn't sail down the river."

"Wrong and insulting as he is," Donald said, "he has a point. It's Adam and the men who fought with Somerled who have to be in the galleys. Plus…the men need to see him fighting, Mother."

Her gaze fell. She knew Donald was right in that, but she was a mother before anything else. "*You* are your father's heir, Donald. The heir to Ross and to our claims to Scotland."

"Only if we allow ourselves to follow the modern obsession with primogeniture," Donald said wryly, "which would be ironic since our claim to Scotland is through the old traditions."

His mother curled her haughty lip. "Don't try to outsmart me with such babble."

"I'm not," Donald assured her. "But in the absence of my father, our claim, our fame, has always stood together. We are the sons of Malcolm MacHeth. 'Donald MacHeth is here' just doesn't strike the same terrible note as 'The MacHeths are coming!'"

"I'm almost healed," Adam said abruptly. "I can rest another day and night at sea, and then I'll just wave my sword around and let Findlaech do my killing for me."

His mother looked at him, and his heart curled up at causing her pain. He looked away. "I won't die. There are things still to happen."

"To you?" his mother almost whispered. Her hand caught his, drawing him back to her. He allowed it because he loved her.

He nodded. "To me. To all of us."

She swallowed, blinking rapidly. "I suppose she has a healing touch, your lady of Tirebeck."

Adam took that as permission. He was glad of it, although he'd have gone anyway. He lifted her hand, brushed it against his cheek as he had when he was a child. "Thank you," he said and left her.

****

Although it was almost pitch-black when they sailed past the Cromarty Firth, with a tiny moon and only a few stars visible behind the clouds and rain, Adam imagined he could see down the coastline as far as the Tirebeck inlet. He painted the new tower against the blackness for himself, all the time knowing that even in daylight he wouldn't see them. He doubted they could have seen him either from the castle tower, but taking no chances, he'd doused the lights on his ship—the same galley the men had carried overland from Tirebeck when he'd first come home—and used the darkness to sail by unseen to meet the rest of his force on the other side of the Black Isle.

Not that any warning from Tirebeck would have reached his targets before he did, but he thought the mystery and speed of MacHeth raids helped their legend and their cause, just like their use of the prophetic name of Aed. No one expected a sea attack on the east, certainly not while Somerled was in the west, subduing Man. The king of the Isles wouldn't let any of his fleet move so far from his main objective, although he might be willing enough to harry the west coast when he could spare the time and the men.

Adam turned his face away from the coast, as if by doing so he could stop himself thinking about *her*. He wanted to. But staring into the rippling blackness of the sea below, he saw her still, illuminated by the soft glow from a lamp or stars. This was how he wanted her, of course, naked and loving, her black hair, which he'd never seen in reality, tumbling loose around her pale, delicate shoulders. He couldn't bear the intensity of emotion battering him.

A sound of distress jerked him back to reality. A hand—Findlaech's—on his shoulder reminded him that the noise was his, and he bit down on it as the darkness of night at sea and the rhythm of the oars filled his senses once more.

His fist was clenched on the side of the ship. Another vision, surely born of desire rather than prophecy. Only…why should he dream so much of her when all logic dictated that because of who she was, she should belong to Donald? Donald, his brother in blood and birth and friendship, probably the being closest to him in the world. Especially when taken with the much more certain foreknowledge that he, Adam, would kill Lanson. He couldn't recall any other dream ever conflicting so entirely with common sense that it *hurt*.

Findlaech's casual hand fell away, and a fine spray from the oars moistened Adam's face. The delightful fantasy he had indulged in his mind after taking Cairistiona and restoring her to Tirebeck had turned into a clawing in his gut.

Adam was no stranger to desire. But he'd never known it to be so married with care and anxiety. Or denial. He wasn't used to denying himself. And whether or not he'd *actually* held her in his arms and kissed her at Tirebeck, pressing her into the door like a plundering soldier in a hurry, the memory tore at him. Because he wished he had done it and much more besides, and he wished she didn't hate him for it.

He wondered if Donald would hate him. Surely Donald, the older brother who'd taught and protected him in their early years and had always stood by him, would know that Adam would never betray him either?

It was just that wanting to interfered with his plans.

So he'd concentrate on the immediate.

"Has anyone," he asked, "ever been to Banff?"

****

When, on impulse, she invited Felicia and Cecily to accompany her to the shore after dark, they were clearly baffled. So was Christian. But they came anyway, following her across the sand and standing by her side as she gazed over the gently rippling sea as the breeze whipped at her veil.

Restlessness and something suspiciously like loneliness had consumed Christian each night since Adam MacHeth's capture and escape. In the daytime, she was too busy to dwell on things she couldn't change, but as darkness fell and she sat alone as she had chosen, she'd begun to wish for companionship—Eua's, perhaps, or Loegaire, whom she scarcely knew, or even her women, whom she'd always more or less ignored because William had thrust them upon her, and because they'd come at the same time as Alys.

Because of her husband's relationship with Alys, she'd imagined they were all his mistresses, or had been at some point. Now, she doubted it. They were all just women of indeterminate origin but a smattering of education to whom life had been unkind. They had no means of supporting themselves and so they were willing to serve Christian for her husband's protection and their keep. Christian had been too concerned with her own unhappiness and her own plans to care for them as she should. And now she'd isolated them in Ross, where her husband was the enemy of everyone.

Maybe she should visit the bishop again, she mused. His wife was a kind woman of good family, who might agree to find decent husbands for her women…although Christian couldn't really countenance them marrying priests! Maybe, just maybe, she should visit the lady of Ross…

Christian had been ridiculed for failing to recognise her own captor when she'd been so close to him, but oddly enough, even William didn't seem to think less of her for it. After all, he and Henry and several of the men had also been up close to him. It seemed to be an understandable mistake to ignore anyone who behaved like a mere servant—a lesson to them all.

The soft tumbling of the waves filled her ears. The women

had stopped whispering and giggling. They almost provided the illusion of companions. Would she miss them if she married them off?

She smiled into the breeze as she imagined turning up with them at the lady of Ross's hall. She didn't even know where that was. William had enquired, of course, but the only answer seemed to be that she moved around the province constantly, as did her sons. It was probably true, and yet Adam had said "Home" to her once, as if he understood the concept. Where was home to him?

She could almost imagine something moved out there in the gently rolling blackness. A fishing boat, perhaps. Or several. She could imagine women watching in the past, from the hill behind her, perhaps, as a fleet of Norse longships sailed by on its way to pillage along the coast. Until one day they'd discovered the enclosed bay and Tirebeck. Like most of the coastal communities, the people here were a mixture of Gael and Norse. As were the MacHeths themselves.

Is he alive or dead?

There was no one she could ask. In the absence of any obvious grief among the Ross people, she could only assume he still lived. So why did she still ache? She willed her pain into the imaginary fishing boats as they sailed on into the distance and only then recognised it as longing.

CHAPTER TWELVE

Mairead, daughter of Dufoter and lady of Kingowan, spent so much time riding across the country at breakneck speed that she found it almost restful to travel in a carriage. Her husband's summons had reached her almost as soon as she'd returned from Roxburgh to her old home in Strathclyde to visit her ageing parents.

Entertaining the king at her husband's stone house at Kingowan in Angus was an honour she couldn't and shouldn't miss, and she was aware that her secret trip to Roxburgh had put her journey a couple of days behind schedule. The king was probably there already, but there were many excuses for delayed messages, especially with the MacHeths active, and Mairead foresaw no real trouble.

Although it was dark, she was almost there, on the familiar road, planning her greetings and apologies as well as suitable menus for the next few days, when the carriage suddenly veered, rocking wildly as it came to a shuddering halt amid the neighing of horses and shouting of men.

"Oh Lady, save us!" wailed Grizel, Mairead's woman. "Brigands!"

"Nonsense," Mairead said crossly, "And even if they were, we have men-at-arms. More likely we've lost a wheel."

Leaning forward, she opened the carriage door and found herself gazing into the grinning face of a strange man armed to the teeth. Several strange men, some on foot, all armed to the teeth.

They surrounded her carriage and were in the process of disarming her own men, who seemed to have given up without much of a struggle. It seemed her woman was right.

The first man had Mairead by the elbow while he peered inside. The light from the lamp clamped to the carriage's side played over Grizel's terrified face and the brigand's ferociously amused one.

"You'll be the lady of Kingowan?" the first one said, distracting Mairead from the safety of her woman.

Mairead chose to step down gracefully rather than be dragged from the carriage. Then she shook herself free. "I am, and you will pay for robbing me so close to my husband and my soldiers!"

Perhaps it wasn't so clever to threaten them in the circumstances, but it didn't have any of the effects she might have expected.

"It's her!" the man called, and someone else loped out of the darkness through the ring of men surrounding the carriage. The dim light from inside the carriage fell across a tall figure with wild black hair and eyes that had once made her bones melt just by giving her their full attention.

He smiled at her. "I've come to steal your jewels."

"Bastard," Mairead said, most improperly, and lifted her face to his. After all, her own servants were well bribed to loyalty, or at least to discretion.

Before his grinning men, Adam MacHeth kissed her with enthusiasm if excusable distraction.

"Is the king at Kingowan?" he asked, releasing her more quickly than she might have liked, even though she was no longer utterly besotted with him. For a while now, he had lain in her memory like a shadow, an echo of his father, although up close once more, there was nothing shadowy or remotely insubstantial about Adam MacHeth. There were new lines around his eyes, a rigid set to his mouth that she didn't remember seeing before.

"I'm not sure," she answered. "He's expected. I'm only just arriving. But, Adam, you can't take the house—especially not the king—with ten men!"

"I have more," Adam said. "I just have to wait for them to catch up. Besides, I only want to talk to him. Stuff whatever knickknacks you love somewhere in your clothing. I'm afraid we do have to steal the rest to keep your cover. Rush into the castle and bewail your robbery as you normally would."

Anxiety warred with the old surge of excitement she always seemed to feel around him. She didn't know whether to laugh or shoo him back to sea. "Adam, this is madness! We have archers who'll shoot you!"

"Arrows are like lightning. They don't strike twice."

"Rubbish. Are you hurt already?" It would explain that odd rigidity around his mouth and eyes.

He shrugged. "No. Only an old wound. They've got your chest, I'm afraid."

"Of course they have," Mairead said resignedly. "If I didn't love you, Adam mac Malcolm, I'd kill you."

Adam grinned—it wasn't the first time she'd said this—and handed her back into the carriage, where Grizel was almost fainting from fear. "Bless you, Mairead," he said, and reached for the bridle of the grey horse, which had appeared through the darkness to stand at his shoulder.

Judging by the speed with which Mairead's horses leapt forward, someone had hit them on their rumps.

****

Fergus of Galloway always had mixed feelings when he visited the court of the King of Scots. On the one hand, he had to pretend he didn't mind that the king—a mere child—regarded him as one of his nobles and never accorded him his title of King of Galloway. On the other hand, there was nowhere better to collect interesting news and make sure Galloway was always represented by the important men he regarded as his allies.

Whoever owned the land around it, Galloway was always regarded as a border region. Since King David had acquired Cumbria and Northumbria during the support of his niece Matilda in her wars with the English King Stephen, Galloway was becoming squeezed, and Fergus was aware he had to push back. Without, of course, waging any wars he couldn't win.

Having made a stately progress through the country called Alba in his native tongue, Fergus finally caught up with the King of Scots between Dundee and Aberdeen, where the lord of Kingowan was ruining himself by entertaining his royal visitor and his court of followers, advisers, and hangers-on.

The young king and his host both received him graciously, and Fergus enjoyed a most satisfying meal. Here, he learned the latest news, that the MacHeths, no doubt while their cousins and allies in Moray conveniently looked the other way, had attacked the king's lands and burghs there.

"By all accounts, the ships appeared out of nowhere!" the king exclaimed. Which Fergus translated as the man whose duty it was to notice such things hadn't been paying attention and had explained the matter away to the young king as something more akin to magic. The MacHeth reputation helped here. Fergus rather admired that. "They plundered Banff and beyond, driving off cattle indiscriminately, and when the local militias streamed out to give battle, another lot attacked from the sea farther south! Fortunately, the galleymen ran off with their loot back to sea, and the militia were free to chase the others back into Ross."

"Fortunately indeed," Fergus said, gazing intently at the king. "So...we were successful against the MacHeths in the end?"

"In the end," King Malcolm said. At least he had the sense to look glum about it. "But we lost much land to fire, and many animals. To say nothing of the men and the revenues."

"What will you do, my lord?" Fergus asked. "Send the royal army against them at last?"

"It would leave me weak in the west, with their uncle Somerled waiting to pounce. He'll leave Man in a trice if he thinks Scotland itself is weak."

"Perhaps," Fergus allowed, reaching for his cup. "But surely we can't allow this rebellion to go on any longer?"

King Malcolm's eyes sparkled as he laid down his knife. "We're crushing it by stealth. I have a man in Ross with a small force, still holding the land I gave him there. The MacHeths cannot shift him. From small seeds..."

"Indeed," Fergus agreed. "And at worst, he will be there on the inside to aid any invading royal army."

"Exactly," young Malcolm said, clearly pleased by Fergus's quick understanding.

"This would be Sir William de Lanson?" Fergus asked, as if he'd just heard the name. "Who's already fought for the King of England?"

"And in the Holy Land," Malcolm said proudly. "And

killed the traitor Arthur for us in single combat."

"I'm sorry I missed Sir William during his stay with you," Fergus said. "And his lady sounds most interesting too."

As he'd hoped, he was able to stop asking questions as the dangerously political turned into the merely personal gossip concerning Christian de Lanson, daughter of Rhuadri of Tirebeck. The court was amused by her disgrace, although the king himself was inclined to believe her more victim than actual adulteress. The king, of course, was intrigued because the girl wore a mask over one side of her face and was, apparently, rather charming and unusual.

In more ways than one, although no one here seemed to be aware of that.

The lady of Strathearn said, "The funny thing is, she fell straight into the arms of the MacHeths. Fortunately, Lanson captured Donald MacHeth and exchanged him for both his lady and Tirebeck. Or so I heard."

"I would have thought Lanson would just leave her with the MacHeths," murmured an older woman. "He has a much prettier mistress."

"I suppose in the eyes of the people, the lady de Lanson is the one with the right to Tirebeck," Fergus said mildly. "And Lanson has the ability to hold it. And maybe even the whole of Ross, who knows?"

The king nodded enthusiastically.

Keeping one ear open to the continuing discussion among some of the women, Fergus moved on to enquire about the king's next meeting with King Henry II of England.

Malcolm's face lit up like the sun. In spite of their disputes, King Henry was something of a hero to the Scottish king and had promised him knighthood at the earliest opportunity. A romantic, young Malcolm was far too desperate to win his spurs from a man no Scot should trust. But judging from the scowling faces around the table, he'd been well warned about this without Fergus adding to it. Fergus didn't care for too strong an alliance between Scotland and England. It constricted Galloway.

"My nephew is a great soldier," Fergus allowed. Being the husband of Henry the First of England's late daughter, illegitimate though she was, remained a useful tool to boost his standing. And, hopefully, gave him a position from which to *subtly* wean Malcolm off his hero worship. "His power—" Fergus broke off as someone burst suddenly into the hall like a blast of wind on a calm, sunny day.

Before the shocked silence could properly fall, the whirlwind exclaimed, "My lords, the MacHeths are coming! They can only be a mile distant!"

It was a woman, a beautiful, clearly agitated woman, wearing an elegant travelling cloak and a frantic expression. Presumably the lady of Kingowan herself.

Close behind her came a soldier. "They landed not four miles from here," he said heavily. "We've only just had word, and they robbed the lady!"

"I thought they'd returned to Ross," Fergus said innocently, while the women all rushed to comfort the distraught lady. Her husband looked furious, dividing his attention helplessly between his abused wife and his threatened king. Fergus's mischievous soul was delighted.

"One lot left," the soldier growled. "The galleys must have doubled back." And again, nobody saw. "Sir, we must evacuate."

King Malcolm sprang to his feet. "Evacuate? Nonsense! Gather the men! Bring my sword!"

He had courage, the little king. Fergus allowed him that. But of course the king could not be risked. The Earl of Strathearn took him in hand, letting him give orders for the defence of Kingowan while bundling him out and rushing him south.

From curiosity, Fergus stayed with the defenders rather than accompany the king, and waited with interest for the notorious MacHeths to arrive.

It was, Fergus reflected with even greater interest, alarmingly close. Another few minutes and the king could have been besieged in here. Who knew? By the time the royal army arrived in enough force to relieve him, the attackers could have negotiated the release of Malcolm MacHeth himself.

Malcolm MacHeth. Now there was a man. Not for the first time, Fergus wondered how that untamed spirit coped with more than twenty years' imprisonment. And now, here was at least one of the wild sons, worthy successors, riding like the wind from the coast road. From the wooden rampart built around the top of the house, Fergus watched beside the lord of Kingowan. The lady, seemingly recovered from her ordeal, lurked behind them, apparently more curious than afraid. Fergus liked that, felt his erratic interest stir.

The MacHeths couldn't easily have brought the horses on the ships—already loaded with plunder, by all accounts—so either they stole them en route from the coast, or they had help. Either way, it spoke of careful planning.

Perhaps not so wild.

The tall young man on the big grey horse—presumably the young MacHeth—who moved forward in front of his men on the other side of the moat, wore a breastplate and helmet. So did many of the others. Hardly full armour, but protection against most stray arrows. And, in their leader's case, against assassination. Although they carried merrily burning torches to light their way through the darkness and provide more than enough light to shoot by.

"Am I addressing the lord of Kingowan?" the tall young man called, mildly enough.

"You are," the lord replied loudly. "And without my permission. Who are you and your rabble?"

"I'm Adam, son of Malcolm, son of Aed," the young man replied. "And my rabble are the men of Ross. Largely. I hope you'll forgive my rudeness when I explain I came to speak to King Malcolm."

Fergus shifted position to get a closer look. So this was Adam MacHeth, the younger son, the one rumoured to be mad, simple, or a prophet, depending on whom you spoke to. No one ever said he wasn't ruthless or brutal. Over this distance, all Fergus could tell was that he was big, sat a horse well, and spoke polite English.

"The King of Scots is not here," the lord of Kingowan sneered.

There was a pause, then, "Are you sure?" Adam MacHeth enquired. "Because if it transpired he could meet me, I'd be happy to leave with you the cattle which ran into us and the fripperies your wife and your people have generously thrown our way since we landed."

Laughter hissed between Fergus's teeth. He was an insolent lad, and Fergus rather liked him. God, when he turned his head into the light, he even looked like his father. Something twisted inside Fergus, a memory of youth, perhaps, or a new excitement. There were always more games to play...

Some of the Ross men roared with more obvious amusement. Of greater interest to Fergus was the breath of laughter, quickly disguised as a sob that came from the lady Mairead behind him.

Her lord scowled into the night. "The king does not meet with thieves. He hangs them. So do I."

"Then I trust you won't hang each other," Adam MacHeth said. His attention appeared to be distracted, and Fergus immediately saw why. A horse and rider galloped rapidly up from the road so recently taken by the king.

The rider yelled something in Gaelic. It sounded like "Flown!"

The lord of Kingowan caught his breath, muttering, "What if he pursues the king?"

Fergus raised his eyebrows. "And risk being caught between your men and the king's, who must already be closing in from the other side? Unlikely."

"But not impossible. This is the mad MacHeth, is it not?"

"According to some. But no one's ever caught him yet to find out."

Adam MacHeth said, "I'll leave you a cow and a bullock for your honesty. As for the king, I thought I might just miss him. Perhaps you'd be so good as to tell him we'll catch up with him on our next visit, when we'll be coming for my father. Good night, my lord!"

Adam MacHeth wheeled around and rode through the parting line of his men, who prepared to fall into line behind him.

"Shoot me that puppy," Kingowan snarled to his archers.

"I wouldn't," Fergus said. "They've closed in behind him, and he's wearing armour. You won't get him now, though we could have a damned good fight if you're game. I'd be honoured to join you in a little harrying."

Fergus's sword hand itched. He loved a good brawl, and he wanted to see the son of Malcolm MacHeth fighting. Kingowan stared at him, then grinned ferociously.

"After them!" he commanded.

So Fergus had the pleasure of an unexpected gallop across country to the beach in pursuit of the raiders, though he only managed to enjoy a tiny skirmish that got him nowhere near Adam MacHeth. Sometime before midnight, he found himself shooting arrows into the sea, while a little fleet of six galleys sailed north. Some animals lowed from the ships. And from the beach, a sad-looking cow and a bullock answered back.

****

It rained during Christian's next trip to the market at Rosemarkie. She'd sold a huge load of timber to the seafarers of Caithness, just in time to replenish dwindling food stocks at Tirebeck. William, who was finally realising the costs of maintaining so many soldiers without regular pay, just from his own land, was heartily pleased with her for once, bade her buy some new fripperies for herself and her women, and bring home two casks of the excellent wine they'd been gifted the last time.

Despite the drizzling rain, Christian's spirits lifted on the journey. Even Alys's presence couldn't quell her excitement. Alys sat mostly with Cecily, reasserting her domination there, although Felicia seemed to have slipped permanently from Aly's grasp into Henry's. The dynamic threw Christian mostly into Eua's company, which was pleasant enough, although she had to keep biting her tongue to prevent herself asking the question still burning inside her: *Does he live?*

And if she was honest, she knew most of her excitement had to do with the possibility of seeing him again at the market. She had to force her eyes not to dart around in search of his disturbing presence, especially when, with Eua, she finally approached the wine merchant.

He had several customers already standing outside his sheltered booth in the blink of sunshine between showers, listening with intent delight to whatever story he was telling.

"...but then came the clever part!" said the merchant, one finger lifting to keep their attention. Clearly, he was a born storyteller. "The two forces met up, Donald took *both* lots of plunder, and drove *all* the cattle both had taken north, while Adam actually sailed south and almost captured the king himself at Kingowan!"

Christian's heart gave a funny little lurch. Dear God, she'd been worrying about his health.

Unreasonable anger, with herself as much as him, choked her, and she missed the next part of the merchant's speech before his words penetrated once more, "…the lord of Kingowan chased him into the sea itself, but he took with him every last animal from the estate, leaving behind only one cow and one bullock, presumably to allow his lordship to start again."

The listening men guffawed with delight.

Beside Christian, Eua smiled faintly. "They're just stories," she said. "We hear them all the time."

"I thought he was probably dead," Christian said carelessly.

"I believe the lady of Ross gives you the credit that he isn't."

Christian moved quickly to meet the wine merchant, who was approaching her with a friendly greeting. She didn't want to think about Adam anymore. Despite the killing of her men and her own abduction, which had somehow faded into the warmer memories of their later encounters, the half story of the MacHeth raid somehow made their violence more real than ever before. Their dispute with the king, their cause, wasn't just a point of law or tradition. It was a war of pillaging, stealing, *killing*.

If he had captured the king, what would he have done with the boy?

Her blood ran cold. Stupidly. He would have exchanged him, of course, for Malcolm MacHeth.

Returning from market, their boat loaded with supplies, they were greeted by the Ross servants on the shore with some delight and excitement. Apparently several cattle had appeared onto Tirebeck land. The general view was they'd wandered off from Donald MacHeth's train of plundered beasts.

Christian's first, haughty instinct to send them back to the MacHeths was hardly sensible. Who knew where they'd come from originally? Besides, William actually smiled sourly when he heard the tale and made it clear he regarded the animals as legitimate plunder from the outlawed MacHeths. If nothing else, the extra cattle could feed them over the winter.

****

When they'd unloaded the galleys, Adam sent Findlaech home with the men and the plunder.

Inevitably, Findlaech objected. "The lady will want to see

you, make sure you're still well."

"You can reassure her," Adam said patiently. His wound ached, and he wanted to be alone to heal in his own way.

"They'll want to hear what really happened too, not just the tall tales. And the drinking, Adam! Think of the drinking."

"I *am* thinking of the drinking."

Findlaech grinned but lowered his voice. "The men like it when you're there. It doesn't seem right going home and celebrating without you."

Adam turned away. "Findlaech, just go. Donald will be there. And I'll be back in a day or so."

"It'll be worse when you do," Findlaech warned, not without sympathy.

"I know."

And it was, although after two days and nights alone in a snug fisherman's hut, doing nothing but sleeping and eating, he was capable of dealing with it, even his mother's anxiety, all the more intense for being unspoken.

CHAPTER THIRTEEN

The prisoner of Roxburgh Castle paced his cell.

Beyond the walls surrounding him, the wind howled, sometimes whistling through the slit window high above his head. He strained his ears for footsteps on the stairs, but all he could hear was the rain lashing against the outer walls of his prison, hurled there by the gale.

She wouldn't come in such weather.

He paused, tilting his head towards the door. Footsteps on the stairs, two sets, one heavy, the other light. The prisoner smiled with relief and stood still, listening to the scrape and clunk of the key, and then the door opened.

The soldier grinned. "Visitor, my lord," he said, and stood aside for the woman.

She was a mess. He didn't think he'd ever seen anyone so bedraggled. The wind had played havoc with her bright red hair, which had lost whatever flimsy covering she might have used. The rain had plastered it to her head, soaked her thin, garish clothes through to her skin, and made the paint on her face run. Tall and willowy, she normally came to him looking like a whore with a difference, full of life and character and a peculiar elegance which easily explained why he asked for her by name.

His lips twitched.

"Beggars can't be choosers, my lord," she said cheerfully, barging past him. "You got a fire in here?"

The soldier snorted with laughter and closed the door on

them, locking it with the same unrelenting clank as he'd opened it. They listened to his laughter and his footsteps fading downstairs to the dry warmth below.

"Take off your clothes," the prisoner said, "and get into bed. Quickly."

"I like an impatient client," the girl said, beginning to obey.

Laughter shook the prisoner's shoulder as he turned his back on her. "Lady Mairead, you are outrageous. Thank you for coming in the storm. I thought you might not be able."

"I only have tonight. I have to rejoin the court at Edinburgh before my husband notices I've gone."

The girl huddled under the blankets with a sigh, and he turned and strode to the chair, which he placed facing her. This girl, a lady recruited by his brother-in-law and his son, was his only link with the outside world, with his wife and his family and the events that affected them. His guards, with the constable's tacit permission, were happy to grant him this occasional pleasure, and though he never touched her, he was surprised by how much pleasure he actually got from her simple company. Not just for her news and the letters she occasionally brought him, but for her wit and her courage and her sheer vitality. She'd become more real to him than his own wife, whom he hadn't laid eyes on for twenty-two years.

"What news?" he asked Mairead, as he always did.

"There's a letter from your lady in the bodice of my dress. I hope the rain hasn't spoiled it."

Impatiently, Malcolm, son of Aed, rummaged in the discarded dress until he found the parchment. Opening it with one hand, he distractedly hung the dress to dry on the back of his chair with the other.

"Did your guards tell you the latest exploits of your sons?" Mairead asked, and proceeded to regale him with the details of a story he'd already heard in part. He laughed out loud when she told him about being robbed by Adam and having to feign such fear and distress when she reached home. "Though to own the truth, I was more than a little scared when I first opened the carriage door. I knew all those ruffians in the isles, but somehow they seem much scarier in the dark."

"Including my son? Somehow, I imagined you were used to seeing him in the dark." Malcolm wasn't sure how he felt about that. Jealous of both of them, he suspected ruefully. Captivity did twisted things to one. This magnificent girl was his son's age, and part of him was proud of Adam for winning such a conquest.

"That was a year ago and more," Mairead said without embarrassment. "I suspect we've both grown up. I met another interesting character for the first time while I was in Kingowan. The lord of Galloway."

"Fergus," Malcolm said with a quick smile of reminiscence. "He was a wild lad. I imagine he still is. What was he doing at Kingowan?"

"I think he'd been commanded to follow the king there. Do you trust him?"

"Up to a point," Malcolm said cautiously. "He'd do us a good turn if it wasn't bad for him. Like the rest of us, he looks after his own. But he's...slippery. Or was. Why do you ask?"

"I don't know. I just thought he was very observant. I caught him watching me a couple of times."

"I imagine men must watch you a great deal."

"I assure you, I'm less noticeable in real life."

"I doubt that."

She blushed a little. He hadn't known she could blush; he rather liked the effect.

"I've seen admiration in men's eyes," she admitted in a rush. "And I've used it to my own advantage. In Fergus's case, I was afraid he'd guessed that my robbery wasn't real, suspected somehow that I was in league with your sons. What would he do?"

"I don't know," Malcolm said slowly. "He needs the King of Scots' friendship, but he values his independence over everything. It would depend, but I'd suggest you be very careful. Stay away from here for a while."

"I'll ask Adam."

Malcolm blinked. "Has Adam met him?"

"Not to my knowledge, but he might have seen him. In his waking dreams."

Malcolm shifted uncomfortably. "Does he really...*see*?" He didn't actually want to hear or even think about this rumoured aspect to his son, as if it diminished him, opened him to ridicule.

"Oh yes," Mairead said blithely. "He has waking dreams, and sleeping ones. Your people only rose up because Adam saw that the king would not kill you, that you *will* go home to Ross."

Malcolm hadn't laid eyes on Adam since he was two years old. He'd been a funny, curious child then. Mischievous, daring. But sometimes he hadn't seemed to hear when you spoke to him; he'd gazed at nothing. At other times, he'd listened so attentively to what you said that even at two years old, he could repeat it back to you word for word. In any language. It broke Malcolm's heart that he'd no idea what sort of man this boy had grown into, that he had to ask a stranger.

"Do the men follow him?" he asked bluntly.

"Oh yes," Mairead said. "Into hell, if necessary."

****

A wet spring had lightened into a much sunnier summer than normal when Adam returned from one of the remoter regions of Ross to find that someone with a following, mounted on horses far larger than was commonplace in the north, had broken cover from the woods close to the gates of his mother's hall.

Discovering the tracks, Adam was conscious of anxiety tightening his shoulders and stomach. That there was no blood, no sign of a fight on either side of the gate only partially reassured him. Isolated as they were in Ross by their current status, they received few visitors save those that gave warning, like Somerled, or the minor lords from the south who didn't travel with huge retinues.

Strangers hung around the yard, a few in slightly wary conversation with his own people. They all spoke in Gaelic. Adam didn't wait for those hurrying across the yard to speak to him, but simply brushed everyone aside and all but ran into the hall.

His mother sat at the high table with Donald on one side of her and a stranger on the other. Donald's pose, upright and alert but not rigid, spoke of excitement rather than danger. And there were no other strangers in the hall.

Relaxing at last, Adam slowed to a mere stride.

"Here is my other son," his mother said calmly.

The stranger rose to his feet. Not a large man, but a big, overwhelming presence. Adam steeled himself and observed the fierce, almost black little eyes, the grey-streaked beard, the lined, harsh face of a man who'd lived and aged hard. There was curiosity in the rugged stranger. And if not quite derision, a readiness to deride. Adam encountered that in many new people. Sometimes it never went away.

"The famous Adam MacHeth!" the stranger said jovially, leaning across the table and thrusting out his hand. "Honoured to meet you at last."

Adam looked at the outstretched hand. Smallish for a man's. Clean. Hard. Leathery as a saddle. He lifted his gaze to the man's face and felt reality begin to slip.

"We welcome the king of Galloway to our hall," his mother said. Although she didn't raise her voice, it definitely had an edge, a hint of warning, in case Adam would avoid the physical contact. Well, one wouldn't want to offend so powerful a potential ally, who didn't look the most patient of men, however amiable his smile.

Adam drew in his breath. With resignation, he took the hand of Fergus of Galloway.

The world didn't just slide. It catapulted into chaos as he'd known it would. Blood and battle. A tonsured monk looking on with curled lip and the fierce eyes of the king of Galloway. Young men were tied to Fergus by long ropes which suddenly whipped free, coiling round and round yet another young man. Fergus of Galloway held the ends, drawing them tight. His captive threw back his head. Donald.

But the scene had changed. Heavy, solid iron gates were opening under blazing sun, and a man strode through. Although his face was hidden by the blinding sunlight, he seemed to drag happiness in his wake, along with a tail of dancing, laughing children.

"That's a firm grip you have, Adam mac Malcolm," Fergus said, no longer jovial, breaking through the dream, which only partially faded as Adam stared at him. "I'll be needing my hand if I've to wield a sword in your family's cause."

The hall and Fergus of Galloway swung back into focus, merging with the dream, slowly drowning it. Fergus's not quite amused eyes seemed to flash. Beside him, Donald and his mother stared at Adam as though willing him fully back to this world.

Adam dropped Fergus's hand, "Is that why you've come?"

"I'm sure we can do each other a few favours. And Roxburgh's not so far from my own country."

Adam blinked. "You plan to lay siege to Roxburgh

Castle?"

Fergus laughed and sat down, accepting his refilled cup from the serving girl. "That would be a long and costly business. I'm sure there are faster ways to free the Earl of Ross, your father."

"I hope you'll tell us what they are," the earl's wife said tartly.

"Well, that's what we must discuss."

"You have no quarrel with the King of Scots that I ever heard of," Adam observed, taking his own cup from the girl and perching his hip on the table. It was Eithine, the mother of his nephew. He smiled at her.

"Well, he is a little cosy with my nephew, the King of England," Fergus said carelessly. "Galloway is squashed between. A little more...acknowledgment of my country and my position would please us. You understand the old ways."

"By which you mean," the lady of Ross suggested, "that were the kingdom of Scots in our hands, we would guarantee your own country's total independence?"

"I walk a narrow path, lady, between my powerful neighbours."

"And your sons," Adam observed, "are not conciliatory."

Something flickered in Fergus's eyes and vanished. "My sons are warriors," he said with pride. But Adam knew he was right. In some not quite clear way, Fergus's visit had something to do with his sons, who were, generally, at each other's throats. Adam, who'd met them more than once during his sojourn with Somerled, doubted their ability to walk the same narrow ridge as Fergus. Under whichever feuding son succeeded their father, it seemed likely Galloway would vanish into the great maws of Scotland or England. Or both.

Fergus set down his cup and leaned forward, his fierce eyes open and frank as he gazed from Adam to Donald and their mother.

"Let us speak plainly as friends," he said, low. "I will do everything in my power to put Earl Malcolm on the Scottish throne, in return for his"—his gaze flickered over Donald—"and your guarantee of Galloway's sovereign independence."

Donald stirred. "That is a most generous and welcome offer. Though you must know we can't speak for my father the earl, and it is his freedom we must accomplish first."

Fergus smiled. "Well, I have a few ideas there. I'll say no more than that I have friends in many useful places."

****

While the lord—who preferred the title king—of Galloway was shown to the best guest quarters and offered every hospitality before dinner, Adam went to his own chamber to wash and change his travelling clothes.

As he pulled on a fresh tunic, Donald entered and closed the door. "What do you think of him?" he demanded. Excitement sparkled in Donald's wide eyes. It was clear what *he* thought.

"I think he's a wily old fox, and we can't trust him or his sons."

Donald frowned at him. "I thought you were all for such an alliance! It was your idea!"

"For the *right* alliance." Adam considered. "But yes, we have to ally with Fergus. It leads to…"

"To what?" Donald demanded with a fresh scowl of impatience.

Adam shrugged. "To what we want."

Donald looked at him. "What did you see? When you touched him?"

"Chaos," Adam said vaguely. "And open gates."

Donald drew in his breath. "Father's prison gates? He will be freed with this alliance?"

"Someone will be. I think it's him."

Grinning from ear to ear, Donald spun around and headed for the door. But Adam was remembering the rest of the dream, which didn't yet make much sense. Sometimes, visions were more metaphorical than real. Either that or he was as insane as people used to whisper. Still whispered, probably, though he no longer cared enough to listen.

"You're not quite sane, are you?"

Out of my head Cairistiona de Lanson.

"Donald?" he said aloud.

His brother paused, his hand on the still-closed door, and glanced back over his shoulder.

"*You* shouldn't have anything to do with him. Or his sons."

"Why not? We're together in this, always."

"Together is good," Adam said feeling his way. "Separately, not so much."

Donald winked. "It's all right. I'll hold your hand."

****

Guests of the importance of Fergus of Galloway were rare enough to ensure that Gormflaith attended dinner in her best gown. Not that she wished to attach Fergus, who was old and whose sons were appalling, but, bored with her constant waiting, she was happy to flirt.

And Fergus, clearly, liked to look. On the other hand, his attention frequently wandered to her mother, who seemed to fascinate him.

Well, the years of care and hard work had not dimmed her mother's beauty. Several years ago now, when her uncle Somerled had come here with his following, Gormflaith had begun to see her mother through the eyes of others, mainly the tall, fighting men in Somerled's train, and most of them had not been old, even to her youthful eyes.

Her mother was calm, regal, easily commanding. She had presence without stridence. More than that, she held all the attractions of unswerving loyalty and faithfulness to her incarcerated husband. Most men dreamed of loyalty like that. And in her thirties, she was still beautiful. Steady blue eyes and soft, flawless, firm skin. Somerled's men had been dazzled. The bolder among them, who tried to pay court to her, were discouraged with amiable but firm reminders of her status—and perhaps a growl from her brother.

Fergus too was caught in the unconscious, invisible web of the lady of Ross. At least, Gormflaith *thought* it was unconscious. At any rate, with the attentions of both women, Fergus looked inordinately pleased with himself.

Not that he neglected Gormflaith's brothers, asking Donald sensible questions and appearing no more than amused by Adam's odd mixture of bluntness and vagueness. They talked about marriage alliances. Fergus, apparently, had an unmarried daughter he would be happy to bestow upon Donald.

Adam frowned at that and seemed about to speak,

although he shut his mouth upon the words. Donald and the lady both welcomed the offer, after which they talked about the possibility of Gormflaith's marriage to Fergus's son Gilbert as an alternative. Gormflaith bit her tongue to prevent herself from protesting. There was no point if the alliance never happened. She would just have annoyed everyone for nothing. She even left the more obvious objections to her mother.

"Gilbert is not your heir," the lady of Ross pointed out.

"But Uhtred is already married. I suppose," Fergus said thoughtfully, "that if we chose that road, we could set aside his present wife. I doubt he'd object."

Then I wouldn't marry him for a crown, Gormflaith thought, appalled by such hateful disloyalty. Although it wasn't an uncommon occurrence that wives were set aside for new alliances. Women were merely pawns in the games of men. Wise women played the game well and made the best of it. Gormflaith had long understood that she was not a wise woman. She wondered how her father regarded her mother. After more than twenty years apart, years during which the lady had brought up his children alone and worked tirelessly for his release, would he set her aside, say, for the chance of freedom and marriage to Fergus's daughter?

Unlikely, since that would offend Somerled. Would he care that it offended the mother of his children? Gormflaith hoped so. But she'd never even met her father. He'd been imprisoned before she was born.

"Talking of wives," Fergus said, sitting back and reaching for his cup. "What is this I hear about your installing some Norman's wife on your doorstep? On valuable land, by all accounts."

Adam's distant eyes flickered upward, but he didn't answer. He looked to be miles away. He might have been.

Donald said, "The girl is the rightful heir."

"And brings an uncomfortable military enemy into your heartland. Seems me the girl should be a widow."

Adam was very still. He'd taken the girl, exchanged her for Donald, and installed her at Tirebeck as if it was always what he'd intended. Gormflaith understood that the Norman presence there kept the king's army out of Ross in the short term. But for the first time, she began to wonder if there were other reasons. Was it the wife or the husband who was important?

And why had Fergus even mentioned her?

****

"You are a healer," Eua observed.

It was dark, and, with a silent soldier behind them, they were walking home from the fishermen's huts that lined the shore. The wife of one of the young fishermen had given birth a couple of days ago and was struggling with a fever. Christian had taken her an infusion that morning and returned with Eua in the evening to see how she did, and found her well enough to inspire Eua's statement, which almost sounded like an accusation.

"No more than most women," Christian returned. "I've just spent a good deal of time around fevers." She gave a deprecating shrug. "In any case, it's quite possible she'd have got better without my intervention."

Christian swerved a little. The path they'd come up meant the old Pictish standing stone she remembered from childhood was clearly visible in the moonlight, and Christian elected to walk to it before heading along the side of the enclosure to the gate.

Eua's gaze fixed on Christian's face. "You're good at this," she said with apparent reluctance.

"I've lived much of my life among soldiers, who were always contracting fevers from battle wounds and marsh sickness. My stepfather—"

Eua interrupted with an impatient flap of her hand. "I don't just mean sickness. I mean…being the lady. You *were* born to this."

Christian, warmed if a trifle uncomfortable at the praise, said, "I will make mistakes. I thought I'd make more, but looking after one's people seems to be much the same wherever your location."

"Your stepfather," Eua repeated, returning unexpectedly to the part of the conversation she'd interrupted. "You travelled with Ranulf?"

"Some of the time. Before my marriage." She stared through the darkness at Eua's averted face. "You *know* Ranulf?"

"I know *of* him. From when he was here."

Christian trailed her fingers along the ancient stone and kept walking in silence, which she struggled not to break. It was odd, but the longer she was here, the more questions she seemed to think of.

CHAPTER FOURTEEN

Still and straight on the back of his big, restive grey horse, Adam mac Malcolm gazed from the shepherd's hut to the top of the hill and the sky beyond. "No one suspected you played any part in our escape?" he asked at last.

Sigurd shook his head. "Too many others to blame for not recognising you in the first place. Besides, I played a good drunk." In fact, the soldiers on watch had come in for all the reproach. No one seemed to ascribe any importance to a native drunk. Sigurd began to explain it, but Adam, clearly had moved on.

"Fergus of Galloway is here in secret, at my mother's hall," he interrupted. "He has our safe conduct out of Ross."

Sigurd nodded, unsure why he was being told. In another man, he might have assumed mere small talk or passing on of news. But he'd discovered that Adam rarely said anything, however odd, without a purpose. Once you knew the purpose, his words didn't seem odd at all.

"He has no reason to pass this way," Adam observed, dragging his gaze from the darkening sky down to Sigurd. "His plan is to head south to Inverness, and then west through the Great Glen to where his own ships await him."

And yet if he wasn't coming here, why did Adam bring the subject up? Because Fergus of Galloway hadn't lived so long by necessarily doing what he told the world he was doing. He was a creature of cunning, by all accounts. And Adam mac Malcolm clearly didn't trust him.

"When does he leave your mother?" Sigurd asked.

"Tomorrow morning."

"And if he does happen to come to Tirebeck, you want us to watch out for your ally?" Sigurd allowed a hint of a question into his voice.

Adam nodded. "Though it won't be necessary. I'll escort him into the Glen myself." He dug in his heels and rode off.

****

Riding hard and, some might have considered, dangerously, by the shortest route, Adam made it home by nightfall. He found the hall quiet. Fergus of Galloway and his followers had left unexpectedly early, while he and Donald had both been too busy on other matters to escort him.

"South to Inverness," Adam said intently. Although he didn't yet pause to sit, he was careful not to make it a question.

From the men's tables, Findlaech said, "Aye. Just the way they should. Of course, he knows the way."

Adam was barely aware of the laughter as he sank down into his own place and grabbed blindly at the food in front of him, uncaring what it was, just that he was hungry. Leaning forward, he checked again who sat at the table.

"I sent an escort with him," his mother said.

"We can do things properly without you, Adam," Donald added irritably.

Adam nodded. And his mother did things properly without either of them. He was worrying about nothing. Only…

"Why did he leave early?"

His mother laid down her knife. "He got a message from home this morning. Something in Galloway required his urgent attention. So he made his thanks and farewells, accepted the safe conducts, and departed. You and Donald will go to Galloway in the autumn and confirm the alliance, perhaps with a joint attack after Gormflaith's marriage."

The juxtaposition of the acts amused Adam, but only briefly.

Gormflaith, who, being still set on an Orcadian marriage, was sulking, said suddenly, "The messenger can't have come from Galloway. I was on the hill, and I saw him ride in from the coast road."

Adam stopped chewing. Every nerve in his body tingled with alarm he barely understood.

"Why does that matter?" his mother asked sharply. "We all have messengers who report from all directions. Fergus will not betray us. He genuinely wants this alliance, at least as much as we do. I believe him to be a man of honour."

Adam nodded and stood, stuffing food into his pockets without discrimination. "He'll help us *and* himself."

Donald, watching his actions with a mixture of amusement and irritation, said, "And that is a problem for us, why?"

"Because he knows who Cairistiona is."

****

Fergus of Galloway was enjoying himself hugely. The freedom of youth seemed to have recaptured his spirit as he'd ridden away from his men as soon as they were free of the MacHeth escort, and doubled back alone, travelling instead towards the east coast.

Everything was wonderful with his world right now. He had made an exciting alliance, soon to be cemented through marriage. And just in case they were inclined to change their minds before the autumn, he was about to present them with an extra gift, by way of proof of his value.

He looked forward to their gratitude and to seeing them again. Over the years, the lady of Ross had grown from a lovely, impetuous girl into a mature woman of overwhelming presence and beauty. She dazzled him. As he was sure her daughter would dazzle his son. Gormflaith, like her brothers, seemed to be a child of nature.

As for Malcolm MacHeth's sons, they were rather more than the wild, insolent raiders he'd more than half expected. Each in his own way had his father's thoughtfulness and intelligence, though they used it very differently. Adam was the biggest surprise. The meticulously planning, if mischievous, outlaw he'd chased from Kingowan had seemed at first, close to, peculiarly unfocused and unworldly. But he'd followed every conversation, as his few interjections had shown. And what he'd said, though sometimes strangely expressed, always had a good point. Neither his brother nor his mother ever derided him with look or word. Neither had the servants or the fighting men and those, Fergus had discovered over the years, were generally the best guide to the man beneath the surface he showed the world.

Oh yes, exciting allies, exciting times. And a legacy, please God, that would long outlive him and his turbulent sons...

In their own way, although untamed, the MacHeths were too honourable. He was more than happy to help them, and snatch a little prize for himself.

There were no guards around the illuminated hall enclosure at Tirebeck. There didn't need to be, for the Normans had built one of their favourite castle towers, from which they could see over the whole of the surrounding countryside. Apart from the wooded area, from where Fergus watched in the gathering dusk. Even there, they would have observed the movement of several men. One alone was neither obvious nor threatening.

As he peered through the tree branches, a woman hurried across the yard towards the hall. She wore a cloak and walked with odd reluctance but definite grace. She paused at the hall door, as if taking a deep breath. The Norman, it seemed, did not run a pleasant hall. The woman glanced up at the sky and the light from the torch above the door showed Fergus not just a comely face—at least over this distance—but one that seemed to be partially covered.

So it was all true. This must be the lady of Tirebeck. Fergus smiled and turned his attention back to the tower.

****

Again, Christian had mistimed her entry to the hall. It was almost dark as she hurried across the yard, and she knew that at William's bidding, they'd be eating without her. It would never enter his head to send someone to fetch her, and that her women didn't come for her was her own fault. She'd made it clear she didn't need them to dress and direct her.

And yet, in spite of everything, Eua had said she was good at being the lady. In her heart, she'd known she would be, in the ways that truly mattered. She'd looked after Ranulf's soldiers and their families, and then William's, although there was never much in the way of family there. His men were largely rootless mercenaries like himself, employed for particular tasks. But here, they could take root. They all could. If she could negotiate some kind of peace with the MacHeths and curtail William's ambition.

Of course, she mused as she picked at her food, it could all come to nothing if and when the king invaded, as he would have to do if William couldn't defeat the MacHeths. And he couldn't. She knew that now. He would have to come to terms, and then the royal army would invade. It would benefit William, perhaps, but destroy the relationships she was building. It came to her, with a pang of guilt, that she didn't much care anymore whether they gave loyalty to the King of Scots or to the MacHeths, so long as they were united in peace.

However, in the long term, surely only the King of Scots could guarantee that peace. While the MacHeths raised rebellion, only turmoil could ensue. She didn't want them to die.

She didn't want the strange but vital force that was Adam MacHeth to die.

Her nostrils twitched. Smoke. Inevitably, her stomach twisted. But it was dinnertime. The kitchen fires would be burning full tilt. There was nothing in that to worry her, to make the damaged side of her face twitch with a distress she couldn't control. Her body seemed to remember more than her mind, infecting both with her irrational fear of fire.

She even imagined she could hear shouting outside, over the general hum of noise in the hall. Chattering voices, odd bursts of laughter, the clattering of knives and serving dishes on the tabletops, the scraping of a bench as someone left the hall to relieve himself.

Surely the smell of smoke was stronger? Surely that shout *was* from outside, not in? Her heartbeat quickened as she watched the soldier open the hall door and go out.

Henry spoke to her. She smiled without hearing his words. This was stupid. What was she imagining here? If there was uncontrolled fire in the kitchen, they would either deal with it or leave. The kitchen was far enough separated from the hall not to be a problem. And no one could attack unseen because of the new "castle" built right beside the hall.

Her stomach twisted. If the MacHeths burned the castle, the servants wouldn't warn them. They'd cheer. They might even have done it themselves on MacHeth instructions. So much for her being their lady...

A trickle of sweat ran down her forehead; another dripped between her breasts. She was too hot. Fear? Or...

The hall door burst back open. "Fire!" yelled the soldier who'd only just left. "The castle's on fire!"

William leapt to his feet. "The wind will blow it right into the hall," he said grimly. Grabbing Alys by the arm, he strode across the floor, knocking tables aside.

It didn't even surprise Christian that he ignored her. Only by Henry's tight-lipped expression as he urged her to hurry did she realise the insult. The rest of her was far too occupied with fear. Which was no way to be a great lady. Her women were standing, wringing their hands in the chaos.

Christian shooed them forward behind Henry, who forced a passage for them through the men.

"The buckets are in place," she shouted. "Use them!"

She knew they'd all derided her insistence on fire precautions. But in this country of wooden buildings, fire was a vicious and frequent weapon.

In front of her, by the door, she saw Henry spinning, dementedly looking for her, expecting her to be right behind him.

"Go!" she yelled, dragging a serving girl in front of her and pushing her on. Smoke was seeping through the roof and through the walls. Panic threatened her. Memory. Of thick smoke choking her; a man glimpsed through the hot, impenetrable fog, surrounded by flames. But there wasn't time to remember or imagine; present reality was too vital.

Her gaze swept the hall which was beginning to fill with smoke. She counted Eua's children, stumbling out in a chain behind their mother. The youngest wasn't there.

Christian turned, sprinting up the rickety wooden staircase to the loft. The little girl, slumbering happily through the noise below, looked ridiculously contented in her little cot by her parents' bed. Christian didn't even try to wake her, simply grabbed her up and stumbled downstairs again, clutching her.

Once more, the smell of fire threatened to fill her nostrils, her whole being, with mindless panic. At the hall door, two soldiers were trying to prevent a demented Eua from coming back inside, presumably for her daughter.

"I'll fetch her," one of the harassed soldiers promised. "But you have to—"

"No need," Christian interrupted, thrusting the child into Eua's arms and shoving them both out the door. Beyond it was fresh air.

"Is everyone out?" she gasped to the soldiers.

"All but you, lady," came the reply, and she was more than happy to be pulled outside and breathe... Sort of. There was smoke everywhere, but at least everyone was safe and the men could concentrate on putting the fire out.

She pushed through the throng, trying not to gasp in air, her only concern, now that she no longer had to think about her people, to hide the terror consuming her. She pushed past them, rushing beyond the gates.

Instinct made her want to run to the sea. But she couldn't be quite that cowardly. She could still have distance and fresh air and see what harm the fire had done and was likely to do. With purpose once more, she strode around the side of the enclosure, where the wind blew the fire away from her.

The wooden tower was burning merrily, little more than a bonfire. The top had collapsed, but from the lack of screams, the guards had probably jumped out of it rather than burned to death. She hoped their injuries weren't too severe. That would be her next task...

She found herself by the standing stone, and sagged against it. The flames seemed to crackle with their own terrifying voice, saying a name she knew all too well.

MacHeth.

"MacHeth," she repeated with despair. She'd almost liked him and he'd done such a thing. With his own hand or someone else's. They had an ambition, a goal which burned everyone and everything in its path. "MacHeth..."

She swung away from the hall, her vision still misty. Or perhaps a particularly thick cloud of smoke had blown in front of her. She could remember the same thing happening before. A burning building, the old hall of Tirebeck, seen, surely from here... And another memory, inside—falling wood, impossible heat, roaring flames, screaming and pain in her chest...and a gust of smoke billowing towards her, drifting upwards to reveal the figure of a man engulfed by flame.

Christian blinked away the half memory. Perhaps as people discussed this fire, they'd drop information about the old one that she could never quite remember.

From nowhere, it seemed, the figure of a man seemed to have formed in front of her. She blinked away wetness from her eyes, trying to make out the stranger's features by the flames of the castle fire.

In a confused mixture of embarrassment in case he'd heard her speak the infamous name, and secret pleasure that someone had noticed her at last, despite her desperation to escape all eyes in her moments of weakness, she took a step closer to him, opened her mouth to ask his identity. She didn't even see his arm move before his fist struck her chin. Pain exploded through her head and neck, and utter blackness rose up and swallowed her.

****

What in hell is going on?

Sigurd the shepherd's son watched the guards in the burning tower leap, still yelling, into the arms of their comrades below, though God knew with what injuries. Only just in time, for the structure was collapsing entirely, throwing planks of burning wood at the back wall of the hall.

At least by now, both soldiers and servants had formed a chain with remarkable speed, passing buckets of water from the yard well to the back of the hall most at risk. Of course, the lady had organised this from the beginning of her stay. Not surprising she was so aware of fire, given her history; and how useful her derided insistence had turned out to be.

Everyone was far too busy or preoccupied to notice Sigurd, standing stock-still and alone behind the backs of the watching household.

He saw Eua with her children, the youngest clutched in her arms. And at last, he saw the lady stumbling through the gates. She looked alone and lost, and Sigurd's throat closed up in sudden pity. He couldn't go to her. He was a shepherd pretending to be a servant. What comfort could she possibly find in his sympathy?

He should go and help with the fire. Only, Adam mac Malcolm had placed him here for a reason.

Sigurd backed away, melting, he hoped, into the shadows

before anyone noticed him. The lady broke away from the crowd, perhaps for privacy. It didn't matter. She was safe. And now it was time to find the arsonist. This was no mad scheme of the young lords, whatever wild ideas had entered his head at first.

Sigurd had started back toward the woods before the whinny of a horse caught his attention. Because it hadn't come from the stables within the hall enclosure. It had come from the foot of the hills to the left of the hall.

His blood ran suddenly cold. Were there more of these people? If so, surely this had to be Fergus of Galloway's men, a day earlier than Adam had warned of.

But it made sense in the bizarre, careless manner of the nobility. Fergus would imagine he was giving the MacHeths a present without understanding the implications. For one thing, Adam mac Malcolm had given his protection to the lady of Tirebeck. For another, the young lords weren't yet ready to defeat Lanson and risk a royal invasion this summer. Their plan was to take the war to the king. This burning could be nothing more than a gesture of bravado, for William would simply rebuild the castle, and again the MacHeths would let him.

Sigurd's main concern was that Fergus's men intended more mischief: cattle stealing, plunder, murder on this, the only piece of land in Ross held in the name of the king. It would be blamed on the MacHeths, which didn't matter much. It was all food for the legend. But Adam would want to know. And in grim fury, Sigurd refused to allow his family, friends, and neighbours to be harmed or killed for such foolishness.

Sigurd changed direction, following the whinnying of the horse. It snorted a little later, thumped one hoof as he approached. But it was one horse and still, it seemed, one man, which explained, perhaps, how he'd got past Lanson's and Sigurd's own observations.

Sigurd could see him now, gazing toward the left side of the hall—where the lady had gone. Even though she would surely be in full sight of most of her people, alarm slid up and down Sigurd's spine.

He approached the stranger obliquely, which turned out to be a mistake, for without warning, Galloway's man, if such he was, began to move, hurrying with his horse down the slope towards the lady, who stood by the standing stone, gazing up at the hills and quite unaware of the danger.

The stranger released the horse's reins and strode the last few feet toward the lady. Sigurd ran faster, lightly, silently, determined to take the man by surprise if he could. It was his only hope of defeating a seasoned fighter.

The lady turned, at last looking directly at the danger. There was no start of fear as he approached her. She even took a step nearer him. And then, the stranger simply hit her.

Sigurd couldn't breathe as he pounded over the ground. He'd never get there in time. The stranger simply caught the lady in his arms, sprinted back to the horse, and threw her over the saddle. After which, he mounted behind her and rode off around the foot of the hill.

"Teeth of God," Sigurd whispered in despair, dragging both fists down the sides of his head. He had to get a horse and follow them. And he had to get a message to Adam mac Malcolm.

****

The acrid smell of smoke left behind in the hall was unpleasant but harmless, so as everyone trooped back inside, Eua made plans to air it from first thing in the morning until dinnertime. The straw and rushes on the floor would all be changed, and she'd beat all her family's bedding in the open until it regained its freshness.

So, the fire had given her extra work, but at least it had brought down Lanson's castle. Perhaps Sigurd the shepherd's son had done it on Adam's orders. She knew Sigurd only worked here at the hall—sometimes—on Adam's orders, and since Cailean's capture and escape, he'd become the eyes and ears of the military-minded MacHeths in Tirebeck.

Lanson was furious at the loss of his tower. As he yelled bad-tempered orders for the placing of guards around the perimeter, Eua left him to it and took her children back to the loft that was their home. From Lanson's side, Loegaire caught her eye as she climbed the stairs, and winked. Eua hid a smile. She just hoped her husband had had nothing to do with the fire, for Lanson was vindictive.

But no, Loegaire would never have so risked his children, leaving their baby in the loft to be rescued by the lady! Besides, it would have been someone outside of the Norman's reach. Which excluded Sigurd too. Perhaps the MacHeths had finally decided to take Tirebeck back. Like everyone else, Eua knew it was only a matter of time. She supposed things would just go on as before the Lansons came.

Or would they? Adam had emphasised Cairistiona's claim. And in truth, even before she'd rescued her child tonight, Eua had rather liked the lady who was both compassionate and efficient and went about her business as if she was above all the petty insults and humiliations offered daily—and nightly—by her pig of a husband.

Men weren't faithful creatures by nature, of course. They strayed, from circumstance or impulse. But even where affections were truly engaged elsewhere, an honourable man knew what respect was due to his wife.

From the top of the loft steps, Eua glanced over her shoulder, still holding back the hanging which gave her family sanctuary its privacy. She saw Lanson push Alys impatiently towards his bedchamber at the back of the hall. She'd stay there until halfway through tomorrow morning, long after William was abroad, still pretending she wasn't a whore. While the lady...

Eua paused, frowning, until her younger son tugged anxiously at her hand, as if worried he'd done something to make her angry. She smiled to reassure him, bade them all prepare for bed.

Her eldest wrinkled her nose. "It stinks. And everything's damp."

"I know, but we'll have to live with it for tonight. I'll be back shortly, and I want you all asleep by that time."

She passed through the hanging once more, dropped it behind her, and descended the steps, searching the hall as she went. The soldiers and the servants, exhausted by their efforts to put out the fire before it consumed the hall as well, were preparing to bed down for the night. The tables were being piled more haphazardly than usual at the side of the hall with the benches. Lanson was conferring irritably with Henry. Of the lady, there was no sign, although her women were disappearing through the hall door for their own quarters.

Eua followed them to their little outhouse. Cecily, about to close the door, saw her coming and paused.

"Where is the lady?" Eua asked abruptly.

Cecily shrugged, glanced back over her shoulder, where Felicia appeared, opening the door wider.

"She'll be in her own house," Felicia said, nodding towards it.

"Did you see her go there?" Eua demanded.

"No, but she always does," Cecily said impatiently, about to close the door with enough force to make Felicia jump back.

Eua seized the edge and threw her foot in the doorway. "Have you seen her since she left the hall during the fire?" she asked urgently.

The other women exchanged glances. "Actually, no," Felicia admitted. "But she's afraid of fire. They say that's what damaged her face. She'll just have kept out of the way."

At least she had the grace to look ashamed. Cecily still didn't seem to recognise the issue.

Eua decided to make it clear. "She's afraid of fire for such a reason, and you just left her? You haven't been to see if she needs anything or even if she's inside the enclosure? For God's sake, what is your *purpose*?"

She didn't wait to see their reaction but turned on her heel and hurried across the yard to the other guesthouse, where she knocked loudly on the door. "Lady? Are you there? It's Eua."

There was no answer. Eua put her ear to the door, and hearing no movement at all, she lifted the latch and pushed. The door opened at once to reveal the house in darkness. Eua quickly lit the lamp by the door and picked it up. No frightened woman huddled inside the comfortable space Cairistiona had made for herself.

Eua walked to the loft ladder, calling her name. She knew before she looked that the lady wasn't in her loft bed. By the time she came back down, Felicia stood in the doorway, Cecily at her shoulder.

Felicia swallowed. "Who's going to tell Sir William?"

****

Lanson, discovered at the back of the hall about to reenter his own bedchamber after some other interruption, predictably exploded at this fresh annoyance. As if the world conspired to upset his comfortable night's sleep. Or his sport with Alys.

"There's nothing we can do tonight," he growled at last, hitting his fist against the wall. "Henry! Warn the watch to look out for her. We'll send out patrols at first light. If the bloody MacHeths don't attack us."

"Yes, sir," Henry said expressionlessly. He turned, ushering the women in front of him.

Felicia said, "He can't just leave her out there all night."

"Well, he's right. We can't do much in the dark," Henry said grimly. "Especially not while we're expecting an attack. But I'll take a few men and scour the immediate surroundings as best we can. The lady is no fool. She won't have gone far. I'm sure we'll bring her back."

Felicia nodded gratefully, satisfied with Henry's action.

Eua was not satisfied at all. She slipped out the gates behind Henry's men and sent word out among her own people to find the lady.

CHAPTER FIFTEEN

Christian came to staring at leather and fur and heaving ground full of stones and mud and grass. Something jolted her rhythmically. Her head and her jaw ached, and she was freezing. Memory flooded her. Fire and a stranger's sudden violence. Someone had captured her. Again. And they weren't as kind as Adam MacHeth had been.

But this wasn't right. No one did anything here without MacHeth permission. Had they suddenly withdrawn their protection? Had William committed some unforgivable crime without her knowledge? Had they fired the castle and then taken her when they realised neither she nor William had died?

Would Adam really do that to her? Somehow, it was easier to blame Donald, whom she didn't know. Or the mysterious lady of Ross, whose tentacles stretched right across the province. Despite her supposed gratitude to Christian for saving her son's life.

She tried to lift her head, and the world went sick and dizzy. She must have let out some kind of involuntary groan, for her captor patted her shoulder, not unkindly.

"There, girl," he said in English. "Awake now, are you? We're far enough away, so I'll let you down now for a moment until you feel better."

The bumping stopped. Whatever had been digging into her side—her captor's knee, perhaps—vanished. Hands took hold of her waist and tugged, and she was dragged backwards off the horse until her feet hit the rough ground. Her head swam alarmingly before it began to clear.

Still dark. Open country, surrounded by low hills. It might have been familiar. Right now, she couldn't tell. Her captor was a stocky man with a neat beard. Perhaps in his forties or early fifties. He wore a fur-trimmed cloak. He could have stolen that, of course, but something about him told her he was no brigand.

She became aware that the gloved hands on her waist seemed to be pushing her towards the ground, and in sudden panic, she slapped at them, trying to twist away.

The hands tightened. "Don't be so skittish, lass," her captor said irritably. "Sit until your head clears. I'm not going to hurt you."

She glared at him. "You hit me!"

"Aye. Well, you'd have screamed if I'd let you."

Unarguable. She let it go, even allowed herself be eased down to sit on the tussock. He threw a blanket over her shoulders, and she clutched it around her with gratitude. She couldn't escape if she froze to death.

"Who are you?" she demanded. "What do you want with me? Are you one of the MacHeths?"

"My name is Fergus. I am the king of Galloway and a *friend* of the MacHeths. And I want you for my son's wife."

****

It wasn't hard for Sigurd to catch up with the lady and her abductor. Once he'd persuaded his best childhood friend to fetch Adam with all speed, he ran in the same direction as the abductor and soon picked up his trail. It sometimes involved knocking on doors in the middle of the night, which didn't make him popular, but did mean that within a couple of hours, he had them in sight.

After the first rush of escape from the environs of Tirebeck, his quarry had slowed, perhaps to save the strength of his horse, which allowed Sigurd, on foot, to catch up. Besides, because the miscreant was riding and it was dark, he was forced to follow the well-beaten tracks, although he seemed to know where he was going—skirting the forested land south toward the Great Glen to rejoin his men, Sigurd guessed.

As if he remembered the way. If this was truly Fergus of

Galloway, he'd been in Ross before, apparently, for Earl Malcolm's marriage.

Sigurd's task was impossible. By the morning, if everyone rode flat out, Adam could have sent men to help, but Sigurd rather thought he was expected to rescue the lady tonight in order to keep both her person and her reputation safe. All without harming Fergus of Galloway, if that was truly who had taken her.

Sigurd groaned inwardly. He was a shepherd. He wasn't up to this kind of work. For the moment, all he could do was keep them in view without being observed.

He had no idea why Fergus would take Cairistiona of Tirebeck, but at the first hint of further violence, whoever the abductor was, Sigurd would have to intervene. In fact, while she was still slung over the saddle like a sack of grain, he wasn't sure he shouldn't intervene at once to make certain her injury wasn't severe.

His blood boiled in fury when he remembered the man striking her. But if this was Fergus of Galloway himself, Sigurd was by no means sure he stood a chance in any fight with such a seasoned warrior. Ambush was his only hope. Although somehow, Adam would expect him to accomplish this without harming his ally.

And then he'd have to get her away to safety—quickly. All on his own, since there was no way Adam could send help before morning.

He was anxiously making and discarding increasingly ridiculous plans when he became aware that his quarry had halted close to a thin ribbon of water which glinted in the moonlight. Sigurd crept silently over the spongy, wet ground into the trees at the forest's edge.

The man had dismounted and now heaved the lady off the horse too. Sigurd closed his fingers over the dagger he'd taken to carrying, but the man seemed to handle her gently enough, lowering her to a sitting position, covering her with a blanket, giving her his flask to drink from.

Sigurd allowed himself to relax just a little. This, surely, was the place and the time for his ambush. If only he could think how to do it without actually killing the abductor, just in case he was the lord of Galloway…

A breath, a soft thud behind him, gave him an instant's

warning. He spun around, dagger in hand, and found his wrist clamped in an iron grip.

"Don't." Adam MacHeth's soft voice had never been more welcome.

Sigurd all but sagged in gratitude and relief. Especially when he saw that Cailean mac Gilleon was right behind him, his normally good-natured eyes glittering with righteous fury.

Sigurd knew what was expected of him. "He hit her cold at Tirebeck, but she's conscious again. He hasn't harmed her further. They're resting just ahead by the burn."

Adam nodded in the darkness as if he already knew. Which, possibly, he did.

"Is it Fergus? How did you get here so fast?" Sigurd blurted. At least he kept his voice low.

"Oh yes. And I was already on the way back when I met your messenger. Cailean came with me. Come on. Let's go and fetch her."

"How many men do we have?"

"Just us," Adam said.

Ahead, bathed in moonlight, Cairistiona and her abductor sat side by side and appeared to be talking together in friendly enough fashion.

What the hell was going on now? Sigurd glanced at Adam to ask, but the words dried in his throat.

Adam looked as he'd never seen him, cold and grim, with thinned lips and curiously vacant eyes. He picked up a large stone.

****

"My name is Fergus. I am the king of Galloway and a friend of the MacHeths. And I want you for my son's wife."

Perhaps, Christian thought with odd detachment, she was still dreaming.

"You've taken the wrong woman," she said firmly. "Even if I wanted to, I couldn't marry your son. I have a husband."

Fergus sat down beside her and offered her his water flask. "Not for much longer."

Christian frowned, accepting the skin flask. "What do you mean?" She lifted the flask to her lips and swallowed the fresh, reviving water.

Fergus shrugged. "Without you, the MacHeths have no need to let him live."

She lowered the flask slowly, staring at him. "You're saying the MacHeths will murder my husband so that I can marry your son?"

"It won't be their motive," Fergus allowed, "but the outcome will be the same."

"That makes no sense! You have a huge lordship—a kingdom, if you prefer. What do you want with a tiny piece of land at the other end of Scotland?"

"Oh, the MacHeths can have the land back. Or you can keep it. I don't care. It's you that I want."

Her heart quickened, seemed to tug painfully at her stomach. She pressed her palm against it, trying to calm it.

"So," she said, "I would get to be lady of Galloway one day. I can see that it's a promotion. But what, in God's name, is the prize for you?"

"You." He peered at her, searching her eyes, her face. His breath caught. "You don't know, do you? You genuinely don't know."

"I know who my father was," she said dryly. "He was a good man, and a gentleman, but hardly worthy of a marriage alliance with the lord—the *king*—of Galloway!"

Fergus guffawed into his beard as he reclaimed the flask.

"You do know," she said carefully, "that I am Christian de Lanson?"

Fergus turned his sharp, black eyes upon her. "I know exactly who you are. Why do you wear the mask? Are you disfigured?"

"Yes."

"Badly?"

"Yes!"

"A defect from birth or an accident?"

She shrugged, grabbing every opportunity to repel that she could. "I don't remember life without disfigurement."

His lips curved, as if he guessed what she was doing, "You wear the mask with a certain style," he allowed. "At least in the dark. Take it off."

Instinctively, she leapt to her feet and out of his reach, delighted the movement no longer fuzzed her head. "Why? You'll see nothing in the da—"

Before she could finish the word, there was a thud. Something dropped to the grass beside Fergus. Fergus stared at it, frozen, and then crumpled to the ground.

Three large shadows bounded silently out of the darkness. Large men, daggers drawn.

"Oh, in the name of—" Christian had had enough of men forcing her to this place or that by threat or violence. No one even gave her time anymore to argue. The truly strange thing was that, despite that, she didn't seem to be afraid yet.

Instead of trying to run, she dived at Fergus's prone figure and snatched the glinting dagger from his belt. Armed with the wickedly sharp blade, she faced the newcomers. "Not one step nearer," she snapped.

A half laugh that wasn't unfamiliar spilled from one of them. Under her scowl, he dropped beside Fergus's head, feeling for the pulse at his throat. One of the others caught the reins of Fergus's restive horse and soothed the animal with caresses and murmured words in Gaelic. Though not quite the response Christian expected to her command—she'd been prepared for lunges, derision, or even, if her luck had finally changed, their obedience—her anger deflated into a rush of something she couldn't name.

"It's you, isn't it?" she said to the kneeling man.

"Anyone would have to answer that in the affirmative." He rose to his feet as the third man joined him beside the prone Fergus. It looked like Cailean mac Gilleon. "You sound unharmed."

Paying no attention to the dagger she still held out in front of her, he walked the few steps to her and took her chin in his fingers, turning her face up to the moonlight. Oh yes, definitely Adam MacHeth's large person, his intense countenance with its hollowed cheeks almost cadaverous, his unblinking eyes darker than the surrounding night. Something twisted deep inside her, churning over and over. She didn't move. She couldn't.

His breath caught.

"I told you he hit her," the man soothing Fergus's horse pointed out. He reminded her of someone, though in the darkness, she couldn't tell who. She was sure she'd heard his voice in Tirebeck. "You should have used a bigger stone."

Adam nodded once. His fingers glided over her bruised chin. "Is there blood in your mouth?"

Baffled, she shook her head, and his hand fell away, though only to take hers and tug her forward. "We have to leave now."

"You're leaving *him* here?" she demanded, resisting his pressure, waving her free hand at the still figure on the ground.

"Cailean will take him back to his followers in the Glen."

Cailean, still kneeling by Fergus, glanced up at her. "I will."

"You've recovered," Christian blurted. "You both recovered."

Cailean said, "Thanks to you."

She had no idea how to answer that, not when the still figure of Adam MacHeth loomed beside her, his rough hand gripping hers as once it had held her face as he kissed her. *Oh no, I will not remember that now. They're all going to pretend* this *never happened.*

"Is that it?" she demanded. "Is there no punishment for violence and abduction in Ross?"

"Not when the perpetrator's Fergus of Galloway and you need his friendship," muttered the Tirebeck man. Sigurd. His name was Sigurd.

Remembering Fergus's words, Christian gazed at Adam MacHeth with foreboding. "Please tell me you haven't killed my husband for that friendship?"

There was a pause. "I'm sure it was expected of us, though not from friendship." And this time, there was no resisting the tug of his hand. "Come," Adam said impatiently. "I'm taking you home."

Christian gave in. After another step, however, Adam stopped again, extracted Fergus's dagger from her now careless fingers, and handed it to Cailean, who wordlessly bent to restore it to Fergus's belt.

Adam pulled her on. And there in the trees, another horse snuffled. Not the big grey she remembered, but another animal, just as big. This time, he more or less threw her into the saddle and leapt up behind her. Before she could draw breath, they were plunging through the night at full gallop.

****

Cailean gazed after the vanishing horse and riders with, he suspected, his mouth open. "So that's it," he murmured.

"What is it?" Sigurd asked impatiently, looking in the same direction.

"Nothing," Cailean said hastily.

But Sigurd wasn't stupid. Adam rarely picked stupid people to help him. "You think he wants her for himself," Sigurd said.

"Don't you?"

Sigurd shrugged. "He could have Tirebeck without marrying her."

Cailean gave a lopsided smile. "That's the thing, my friend. I don't think it's about Tirebeck. I don't know that it ever was."

Sigurd stared back at him. "He just wants *her*?"

Cailean said wryly, "There's no 'just' about Adam mac Malcolm. Now shut up before Fergus comes round."

****

Many things about this whole adventure bothered Christian as Adam's horse carried them off the track and into the hills. For one thing, she felt far too safe and relaxed, considering whose company she was in and whose arms held her in the heaving saddle. She tried to keep her mind on the practicalities.

"Won't Fergus suspect the others, punish them when he wakes up?" she asked.

She felt Adam shake his head. "Cailean will be tending his wound and know nothing of any girl. Honour and alliance will be preserved."

"Oh good."

Something brushed her hair. It might have been his mouth, smiling, but he didn't otherwise respond.

She looked into the wind, clinging to the horse's mane. "How did you find me?"

She wasn't even sure that she meant to speak the words aloud, or that he'd hear her.

"Sigurd saw him take you and sent a messenger to me. He found Cailean and me already on the road in search of Fergus. We knew which way he'd come. And we know shortcuts."

Christian didn't understand any of this—not why Fergus

had abducted her nor why Adam had put himself out to rescue her. But right now, it didn't seem to matter. Though her head still ached, she felt warm, and, wrapped in Fergus's blanket and the odd familiarity of Adam MacHeth's arms, she felt suddenly very sleepy.

****

Fergus woke with a stinging pain in his head. Not the dull ache of overindulgence, but the sharp discomfort of a wound. The senses born of a lifetime of battle and difficult situations told him he wasn't alone.

That was good. The girl should still be here. He'd no time to worry now about what had hit him. A fire had been lit close by. He could smell it, hear its crackles, feel the faint comfort of its heat. His head was pillowed on something soft—a blanket or a cloak maybe. And someone began to bathe the side of his head.

Fergus released the dagger hilt he was clutching and opened his eyes.

Not the girl.

In the light of flickering flames, he beheld the concerned face of a young man. With a struggle, he even remembered him. One of the MacHeth followers. He'd seen him in the hall, been in his company hunting and drinking. Cailean? Close by, another man stood holding two horses, Fergus's and another.

Fergus swore under his breath. "Where's the girl?" he demanded, throwing off the lad's hand and sitting up.

"What girl?" Cailean asked. "What happened?"

Fergus was now in a tricky situation. He could anger his allies by admitting to stealing a woman officially under their protection. Or he could pretend she was someone else, although he was pretty sure he wouldn't fool Cailean that way once they found her. He could kill Cailean, of course, but it would come back on him, for the lad did seem to be important to the MacHeths.

"I'm not quite sure," Fergus said, touching the side of his head. "There was a girl beside me and then something hit me on the head...and when I woke up, you were bending over me. How come you're here?"

"I could ask you the same question," Cailean said evenly. Clearly, he wasn't intimidated by Fergus's status or reputation. In other circumstances, Fergus might have admired that. Right now, it was annoying.

He shrugged. "Impulse. I spent a summer up here with Earl Malcolm when we were young. Before Stracathro. I wanted to see if I could find some of the places I'd been with him. Wish I hadn't bothered," he added, rubbing his head. "Your natives hit first and don't bother with the questioning."

"They probably took you for a king's spy. They know all the noblemen of Ross, and you'll have stood out like a sore thumb. Especially in the middle of the night."

"*Probably?* You mean you didn't catch them? Why, then, do I still have my weapons and my purse?"

"They ran off when I shouted. There were only the two of us, and I chose to look to your wounds rather than pursue the culprits. They must be better trained than I'd imagined," Cailean added—slyly, Fergus thought, "if they managed to track you and take you unawares."

"Ah well, I was distracted," Fergus said with as much dignity as he could muster.

Cailean grinned. "The girl?"

With relief, Fergus saw that Cailean didn't know, that he hadn't been following him and seen who his captive was. What's more, his way out had been handed to him on a platter. He grinned back and nudged Cailean before struggling to his feet. "You've guessed. I'm not as old as you think. Though maybe I should stick to one task at a time!"

Cailean threw himself onto his own horse. "I know the lady of Ross and the young lords would want me to apologise on their behalf for what occurred," he said formally. Then he grinned again. "And we'll look out for your girl on the way. She'll have taken cover when the idiots attacked you."

"Then they didn't take her?" Fergus said. Another surge of doubt assailed him. He wasn't sure he was buying Cailean's story and yet there was no way he could doubt him publicly without admitting his own crime. Damn it. Either the fates or the MacHeths had tied him in knots.

CHAPTER SIXTEEN

In the sheltering lee of a hill, Adam MacHeth halted his horse and dismounted.

"We'll camp here," he announced, leading the animal a few steps towards a tree to which he could tether him.

"Can't we just keep going?" Christian said. "I'm sure I didn't come so very far with Fergus."

"Far enough," Adam said with odd grimness. Having tied the horse, he straightened and reached for Christian.

She caught at his hands on her waist. "I would rather go home."

"I need to sleep," he said, as if that settled the matter.

She supposed it did. But as he drew her inexorably down from the horse, she couldn't help demanding shrewishly, "Why? Aren't you tough enough to last a few hours beyond your normal bedtime?"

"Not when I didn't sleep the night before either," he replied without rancour.

Having set her on the ground, his hands loosened, but she caught at his arms with both of hers. "My people will believe you abducted me. Again. They won't believe some nonsense about a high-born stranger wanting me to marry his son."

"By people, you mean your husband."

"He'll add it to the other folly," she said impatiently. "But there are more concerns now. I..." She tailed off, trying to look away from his unblinking gaze and failing. "I thought I was

164

becoming their lady," she said in a rush. "I need respect."

He was silent a moment. Then: "You have respect. Your husband's opinion does not weigh with them. Besides…" A smile flickered across his face in the moonlight and vanished. "Spending the night with me will not damage you in Ross."

She wasn't quite sure what he meant by that, but since her whole body flushed with heat, she released his arms and pushed past him. "I need to be home. The fire could have damaged the hall."

"I believe the hall is saved." He bent, heaving some brush and bracken off a hillock, which turned out to be made of firewood. This was clearly an oft-used camping ground. Adam bent and lifted a pile of wood, carrying it a few paces before setting it down and building a fire with quick, familiar efficiency.

"It wasn't you, was it?" she said. "You didn't fire the castle."

He shook his head, concentrating still on the firewood. "Fergus did that. Partly, I suppose, he imagined he was doing us a favour. And perhaps showing us that he could so easily do what we'd failed to. And partly, he wanted to draw you out and abduct you in the confusion."

Without meaning to, Christian moved nearer. "That's what I don't understand. Who does he imagine I am?"

Adam took the tinderbox and flint from the bag at his belt. A cloud had drifted over the moon, and she could barely make him out. Patches of lighter and darker black hung together. When he'd abducted her three months ago, it had been in daylight. Maybe because she'd come to no harm then, she wasn't remotely afraid of him now in the dark.

I should be. I should be very afraid.

A sudden spark of light, the quick flare of a flame, caused her to jerk backwards. Although she'd known what he was doing, she must have been more affected than she'd realised by the fire scare at the hall.

Adam stood and walked over to the horse, removing the bedroll from the saddle pack. He set it down under the sheltering branches of the tree, close to the fire, and spread it out. "Sleep here."

With her eye on the growing flames, she said, "You're the one who wants to sleep."

"I have this," he said, sitting at one end of the bedroll and drawing a blanket around his shoulders. "It's all I need."

Her tongue stuck to the roof of her mouth. She stayed where she was.

He said, "We both need the warmth from the fire. I won't touch you."

For some reason, his words embarrassed her into motion. She lifted her chin and walked around to the bedroll.

"I'm not afraid of you," she said coldly and bent, drawing the blankets farther back from the fire.

"I know," he said. "I was giving you an excuse not to admit your fear of fire."

Something involuntary escaped her throat with a hiss. It might have been laughter. "My thanks," she said drily. She knelt in the middle of the bedroll, drawing one of the blankets up and around her shoulders. He shifted back too, turning his head to watch her. Firelight leapt over his face, warming and shadowing. His position reminded her of that other campfire and unexpectedly delivered her a weapon.

"I suppose you have sympathy with my fear," she observed, "since you possess something of the same dislike."

His brows twitched, though his eyes didn't waver. They didn't even blink. For no obvious reason, her heartbeat quickened.

She said, "You see things in the flames, don't you?"

His gaze dropped, turned towards the fire, and then swiftly away again. He nodded once and swallowed, for all the world like a boy admitting he was scared of the dark. His vulnerability struck her like sudden, cold rain, allowing her a glimpse, a possible glimpse, of his life. The son of the great Malcolm MacHeth, Earl of Ross in fact if not in title, had to be a great warrior. Adam had been covering his curse all his life; he must have known everyone recognised his strangeness, and yet he never admitted it. And he'd won. He *was* a great warrior, and strange or not, his men would have followed him through the gates of hell itself. He didn't even pay them, not as William paid his mercenaries.

"What do you see there?" It came out as little more than a whisper.

His eyes returned to hers, boiling and…warm. "I don't think you want to know."

"Is that how you knew where to find Fergus? Did you

foresee this?"

He smiled distractedly, shaking his head. "I knew he was up to something because he left early while neither Donald nor I were there to accompany him on the first stage of his journey. I'd only just got home, but I left again. Sigurd did the rest."

She frowned. That was the other question. How come Sigurd had been there to witness her abduction? It had crossed her mind he'd started the fire…

Adam said, "Don't you know that he watches your husband for me?"

Then he watched everything: the domestic as well as the military comings and goings from the hall. With the cooperation of the staff, he would know everything and must have passed it all on to Adam.

"No," she said. "No, I didn't know that. But I should have."

She lay down, curling herself into the blanket's warmth, keeping her feet closest to her companion. After a few moments, he lay down too.

She stared into the depths of the fire, thinking, wondering.

"If William hadn't captured your brother," she said aloud to the flames, "what did you mean to do with me? You said you didn't intend to give me back, because it would annoy William."

He didn't answer at once. He could have been asleep. "I hadn't made up my mind," he said at last. "Probably I'd have taken you to the lady of Ross, my mother."

For some reason, laughter bubbled up again. "Do you take all your abducted women to your mother?"

There was a pause, then: "No." He stirred close to her feet. "But to be fair, I don't abduct so very many."

She jerked her head up from the blanket, peering in his direction. It was on the tip of her outraged tongue to demand exactly *how* many, before it came to her that he was teasing. She laid her head back down. "I perceive I should be grateful for the honour. And if I was with your mother, would William have Tirebeck?"

"No."

The stark word caught at her breath. If William hadn't captured Donald and forced an exchange, the MacHeths would have fallen on his force and, probably, slaughtered everyone.

Perhaps not in one attack, but it would have been done.

Everyone, including the king, had known that when they waved William off with gifts of extra armour and weapons. They'd pinned their hopes—last-gasp hopes—on Christian winning over her own people. Even Christian had understood that when they'd set out.

But it had always been a doomed adventure. The people of Tirebeck might fight for her against the King of Scots, Fergus of Galloway, or any invader she could imagine. But they would never lift a finger against the MacHeths.

"Do you really see an end to this?" she asked. "Do you really believe you can harry the king into releasing your father?"

"Yes. One way or another."

"Is that hope or foresight?"

Another pause, then: "Both."

She wanted to ask him about the future of Tirebeck, the people there, and William. But words never came. Perhaps she didn't really want the answer. Perhaps it seemed like...cheating. She gazed silently into the flames, controlled and safe, and yet in constant motion, consuming, dying, being reborn. She could almost imagine pictures dancing there. Perhaps that was all foresight was: imagination.

History, now, she could ask him about that, although perhaps it was equally open to interpretation.

"Do you know why my parents left Tirebeck?"

He was probably asleep. Part of her hoped he was. The fire, the abduction, the casual recue, all seemed curiously unreal. There was only the fresh, stinging air on her face, the warmth from the crackling fire and the blankets in which she huddled. And Adam MacHeth's even breathing at her feet.

A faint movement disturbed her feet, as if he'd stirred. "Rhuadri, your father, never left Tirebeck."

She frowned. "No, that isn't right. I remember him being there on the journey..."

"Do you? You were three years old."

She opened her mouth to say she remembered perfectly, but the memories she carried were already flashing in front of her mind, and her father's face was hazy. Not in Tirebeck; she could remember him there, big and smiling, lifting her high. And angry; he'd been angry too, though not with her. She could see his distinctive face in those memories: bright blue eyes, a shock of thick blond hair, and a mouth with a slow, curving smile.

She couldn't see these things on the journey. It had all been too confused, but he'd been there. She knew he had, though her mother had never said.

A hall, so like the one that had so nearly burned down tonight, in flames as she'd ridden away in her father's arms, the smell of smoke still burning her nostrils.

"He was there," she repeated.

Adam shifted position again. "He can't have been. Rhuadri died in the fire. You and your mother escaped to the south."

Startlingly, he spoke almost directly above her. She jerked her head around to see him sitting up, gazing down into her face. Something twisted in her stomach and dived lower. Worryingly, she didn't recognise it as fear.

"Then why do I remember him on the journey?"

Adam shrugged. "Because you wanted him there. And there was a man with you, taking care of you and your mother."

"A servant?" she wondered.

Adam was silent a moment longer. "Ranulf."

"Oh no. We met Ranulf later. I remember..." What did she remember? A tall soldier coming to their home; her mother's happy welcome. Not a first meeting, a reunion. Things, a few things, began to make sense. "He was a good man," she said, staring up into Adam's unfathomable eyes. "Since I've come home, several people have told me that about my father. No one says anything about my mother. She left him, didn't she? She took me. And went with Ranulf."

Her breath caught. "Oh no." Without thinking, she grabbed Adam's wrist. "Please tell me Ranulf didn't burn the hall..." She couldn't believe such a thing. Ranulf had been good to her in his distant way, and in her own way, she loved her stepfather, even after he'd given her to William.

She could almost imagine flames in Adam's eyes. Her head was full of fires.

He said, "I told you. Rhuadri burned his own hall."

Her lips fell apart. There seemed to be nothing she could do about that. Adam's gaze followed them.

"Why would he do that?" she whispered.

"I don't know," Adam said. "And there's no point in

guessing."

"I saw it," she whispered. "Tonight, when I smelled the smoke, and later when I watched the tower burn, I remembered...imagined...a man in the flames. That was my father, wasn't it? In my memory."

"I don't know," Adam said again. His fingers closed around hers on his wrist, forcing her to realise how hard she gripped him, but when she tried to release him, his other hand held hers in place. "It doesn't matter now."

She tried to laugh. "It's an unhappy house. Why do I deny it?"

"Because you were happy there, maybe. Or because you will be."

"Maybe," she said. She knew her smile was twisted. "Or maybe I'm just delusional. Or plain mad."

His eyebrow seemed to quirk in the firelight, as reflected flames shot over his face. "Like me?" he said without emphasis.

She flushed, glad of the dark and the merely flickering light to hide it. He'd remembered her words. Stunningly, they appeared to have...*hurt* him.

"You killed my men and abducted me," she said gruffly. "I was trying to be rude. I don't really believe you're mad."

He stirred, though still his gaze remained on her face, his hand warm and rough over hers. "I probably am, a little. My mind is not...conventional."

"Is anyone's?"

He didn't answer that. Instead, he said, "I shouldn't have drunk your poppy tincture. It gave me more waking dreams, confused my thoughts and memories. Did I kiss you?"

A surge of embarrassment heated her skin. Thank God for darkness. "You were confused by the pain and the poppy. You were probably fevered too."

His eyes slid away from hers, then almost immediately came back as if he forced them. "Did I hurt you?"

She shook her head, searching wildly for a change of subject. But all she could think of was the deeper darkness of her house that night, save for the faint glow from the lamp that cast more shadows than light upon him. And the sudden, silent assault on her senses. He hadn't spoken one word to her.

At least her answer seemed to relieve him, for his

shoulders lowered by about an inch. In the glow of the flames, his lips stretched. "I'm glad. In my memory, you touched my face and kissed me back."

She shook her head in violent, instinctive denial, but something kept her gaze locked to his. It could have been pride or weakness. Certainly, she was very aware of her vulnerability, lying prone with her hand held between both of his, while he sat looming over her, his face almost directly above hers. Half his length separated their heads, but not their bodies.

He said, "You're no longer afraid of me."

It wasn't strictly true. The glow of his intense eyes caused a thrill, deep in her belly, that was at least partly fear. Surely. She swallowed, trying to keep her voice steady. "I am when you lower over me like that."

His fingers curled over the hand he held, lifting it from his wrist. "No, you're not," he said and kissed her palm.

She forgot to breathe. If he were to kiss her again, as he had in her house the night he escaped, there would be no one to disturb them, nothing to make him stop.

He said, "You don't flinch."

"Neither do you." It was almost a gasp.

A smile flickered over his face. "No…"

"What?" she asked unsteadily. Was he seeing now? Or just remembering, as she was… "What do you see?"

"Right now? Just you."

She couldn't move or even breathe under the force of his gaze. She had to make herself before his lips asked the question she was sure she could read in his eyes. Slowly, so as not to startle him, or, perhaps, herself, she drew her hand free and turned away from him under the blanket.

"We both need to sleep," she reminded him.

The silence deafened her. He didn't move. Then, at last, she felt him lie down in his previous position.

She was too aware of him now, far too aware to sleep. She couldn't help going over their odd conversation again in her head.

"Are you happy, Adam?" she murmured aloud before she could stop herself.

There was no response.

She smiled slightly. "You're asleep," she whispered.

"No," he said, the unexpectedness catching at her breath

all over again. "I just don't want to answer."

Some emotion that was close to laughter shook her shoulders. She listened to the beat of her own heart, trying to talk herself out of it. But she asked anyway. "Why not?"

Another pause. "Because at this moment, I *am* happy."

As his words wrapped around her, she closed her eyes and realised she was smiling. Under her blanket, which smelled of him, her heart still beat and beat; it felt full and she didn't know why.

****

The lady had not come home during the night. On the other hand, although Lanson and all of his soldiers were up and ready for it, neither had there been an attack at first light.

While Lanson bad-temperedly organised patrols to search for his absent wife, Eua walked quietly across the hill to speak to the shepherd's wife.

"Adam mac Malcolm went to get her back," the woman said laconically.

"From where?" Eua demanded. "And from whom? This stranger Sigurd saw take her?"

"Aye."

"Then I suppose we can consider her safe," Eua said slowly.

"As safe as any woman alone with a young lord who wants her."

"Don't be ridiculous," Eua snapped. "She's under his protection."

"Aye, but who's to protect her from him? Men say protection. What they mean is power."

"You're a nasty-minded old woman."

"I'm a smart woman who knows how the world works. And not so old either."

Eua waved one hand in annoyed disparagement. But she didn't leave. "There's nothing we can do, is there?"

"Not until she comes home."

"If she's spent the night with Adam mac Malcolm..."

"Maybe she shouldn't come home. Who would you rather have? Adam or Lanson?"

"Adam," Eua said impatiently. "But she should at least

have a say!"

"Why? No one else of her rank does. The rest of us do as we're bid too. Besides, who's to say she hasn't chosen?"

Eua folded her lips. Although he'd abducted her, Adam had made Cairistiona lady here. And she'd said nothing to anyone, when he'd accosted her at the market in Rosemarkie, nor when he'd been captured at Tirebeck and she'd tended his wounds.

"I thought he frightened her," Eua said.

"He frightens most folk. Doesn't stop people liking him. Or women enticing him to bed."

"*Enticing?*" Eua repeated, staring at the older woman. "Cairistiona?"

"You think she isn't?"

"Oh, she's comely enough," Eua said impatiently. "Beautiful, even, behind that mask. But she's no idea of her attractions. She has no thought of *enticing* anyone!"

The shepherd's wife smiled slyly. "And yet here you are defending her, the woman who supplanted you as lady, in fact if not in title."

"You think she was deliberately seducing Adam MacHeth?" Eua said with frank disbelief that had nothing to do with Adam's undoubted physical attractions and everything to do with the lady's character.

"I think she's very good at being a friend to everyone. And she wants to keep Tirebeck."

Eua stared at her. "I don't recognise your scheming lady."

"It isn't all scheming," the shepherd's wife allowed. "She's the natural lady of Tirebeck, and she meant to keep it in the teeth of the MacHeths. She can't have expected them to hand it over. In fact, she probably understands they haven't. But Adam mac Malcolm makes it difficult for her."

"How?" Eua asked, unsure whether to listen or tell the woman to hold her tongue on the subject of her betters.

"By being Adam mac Malcolm."

Eua let that one lie. Instead, she said, "Even if he brings her back today, Lanson will make her life unbearable. The trouble he caused in Perth over that other matter proves it." Slowly, she lifted her eyes to the wise older woman, who stopped her scrubbing. "She is a good lady for Tirebeck."

The other woman nodded. "Pray for her."

****

Unlike that other morning after she'd slept outdoors by Adam MacHeth, she woke without the feeling that cold and damp had lodged in her bones forever. The blankets bundled against her back, fitting around her hips and thighs, had kept her warm and snug and secure.

She opened her eyes to find daylight creeping over the hills. The fire had gone out, leaving nothing but the fresh smells of morning dew. The world around her was still; Adam MacHeth couldn't have wakened yet. Birds were singing their welcome to the day, although the seagulls were silent. She'd imagined they would be close enough to the coast by now to hear them. No matter. She wouldn't object to a few more hours in the company of Adam MacHeth. Now that they seemed to be friends, she wanted to know him better.

There was danger in that, in the new tenderness surrounding her heart, but she knew she mustn't let it grow. That way lay misery. Friendship with him, however, would be fun and exciting.

Smiling to herself, she justified it with its usefulness to her goal at Tirebeck. Softly, so as not to wake her companion, she eased away from the warm bundle of blankets and turned over. She gazed into the sleeping face of Adam MacHeth, and forgot to breathe.

At some point in the night, consciously or unconsciously, he'd moved. Of course it hadn't been bundled blankets against her back, it had been him. Only an idiot, or a woman unused to a sleeping companion, could have thought otherwise. *God save us, he's warm.*

Her stomach clenched.

His eyes were closed. If she rose now, he'd never know— or at least never be sure—that she'd been aware of his improper closeness. But she didn't move. In repose, as in its waking, constant movement, his face fascinated her. He had thick, straight eyebrows, half-hidden from her view by hair, and long, black lashes formed perfect half circles across his lean, stubbled cheeks. Asleep, his mouth betrayed none of the ruthless cruelty she'd attributed to him, and of which she knew him to be capable. She suspected now it was never thoughtless cruelty. Everything he did had a point, an end.

Including his kindness to her. Her stomach twisted. It didn't matter. She had a husband who was his enemy. And this young man had happily plunged an entire country into war to have his father released, to claim the throne of Scotland for his family.

Her throat constricted. Asleep, he looked so vulnerable, this wildest and scariest of the MacHeth kindred. A boy, almost, despite the whiskers on his chin and jaw. He must have shaved his beard altogether recently…

For an instant, the stillness and the birds' song closed around them, as if there was no one else in the world. An invisible thread seemed to wind around her, drawing her to the unfathomable young man she'd begun to understand. Unable to stop herself, she freed her hand from the blanket and brushed his cheek with the very tips of her fingers. Cool, rough skin with, surely, burning warmth and passion beneath.

Her blood heated. Imagination. Dangerous fantasy she didn't even comprehend. But at least he didn't wake up. She withdrew her fingers, closing them into a fist as she slithered back from him and rose.

The sun was beginning to rise, spreading spectacular pink and gold above the hills. She walked around the fire, past the horse, which stood still, half-asleep. It opened its eyes as she passed, gave a quiet snort by way of recognition, but otherwise didn't move.

The site they'd camped in was almost like an ancient Roman theatre, surrounded on three sides by hills. Christian walked towards the centre of it, stretching her arms out to greet the rising sun of the new day. The blanket flapped around her arms and legs.

It would be a difficult day. She had to face William and the rest of her people with her unlikely tale of abduction by a stranger. The natives would know very soon, if they didn't already, that she'd spent this night with Adam MacHeth. There was no point in even trying to keep his name out of it. Rescuing and returning her to her husband unharmed and unransomed might even begin to endear him slightly to William…

She smiled, lifting her face to the wind. That truly *was* fantasy. But she wouldn't think of it, not now. She still had a few hours of rare freedom that amounted to gladness. And suddenly everything rushed in on her at once: the joy of returning to her childhood home; the start she'd made on being the true lady of Tirebeck; the scare of violent abduction by a stranger; and most of all, this new warmth that somehow bound her to Adam MacHeth, in whose company she'd spend, the next couple of hours at least.

Her pace increased until she was running, spinning, almost dancing under the skies of home. The blanket fell to the ground unheeded. She'd been right to come back. This, at last, surely, was happiness.

Finally dizzy, she collapsed on the damp grass, hugging her stomach until the world stopped spinning around her. When she rose sedately and walked with decorum to pick up the blanket from the grass, Adam MacHeth stood by his horse, watching her.

She flushed with embarrassment. It must have looked as if neither of them was quite sane. However, lifting her chin, she walked towards him, noting that he'd trampled the fire and rolled the bedding back onto its place behind the saddle.

If he found her behaviour odd, he gave no sign of it. "Oatcake," he said, holding something out to her in a napkin. "It's a sparse way to break your fast, but I'm afraid I ate the rest last night before I found you."

She took the crumbling pieces with thanks and stood beside him while they ate. The silence between them was unexpectedly pleasant, even companionable. Although she didn't look at him, it came to her that first impressions to the contrary, he could be a peaceful man.

He passed the water flask to her, and she drank it almost dry. She walked to the nearby stream which bubbled through the hills, and bent to refill the skin. He watched her as she brought it back to him, his gaze focused but unreadable.

"What?" she asked with a hint of the old defiance, handing him the flask.

"Nothing," he said. "I like to look at you."

I like to look at you too. Her tongue, fortunately, seemed to have stuck to the roof of her mouth. Well, she could look. And then she would go home to face the accusations. It would be worth it.

****

The men of Tirebeck, with sly glee, saw no need to keep

the news from the Norman incomers. Henry knew the truth long before midday and had to force himself to go in search of Sir William, whom he found pacing the hall and scowling through the din from outside where the castle was being cleared and rebuilt.

"Well?" Lanson barked at him. "What news?"

There was no easy way to tell him, so Henry merely walked up to him and said, "The locals believe she was abducted by a guest of the MacHeths. Probably the same culprit as fired our castle."

"*A guest* of the MacHeths?" Lanson scoffed.

"It looks like he just seized the opportunity," Henry said. "He may not even have realised who she was. She'd wandered away from the household and he, no doubt watching his handiwork, took his chance, and grabbed her."

"And took her where?" Lanson demanded, his eyes narrowing at the prospect of a good fight.

"Not very far before she was…either rescued or reabducted by Adam MacHeth. No one seems very clear on motive. But she is undoubtedly with him."

Lanson stared at him before suddenly thumping his fist into the table. "Then his motive scarcely matters, does it?" he said savagely.

****

She wore Adam's cloak as they rode through the morning, pausing every couple of hours to allow the horse some rest. It was almost a familiar pattern after her first forced journey with him. But everything was changed now. She was too aware of him. Perhaps she always had been, but the big, blood thirsty barbarian who'd captured her and frightened her so badly had turned into a friend who fascinated her.

If they ever had been, even during her first abduction, the pressure of his thighs against hers, the feel of his chest against her back were far from unpleasant now. Sometimes his hair brushed against her cheek as he bent to speak. Sometimes, she was sure his face touched the top of her head.

Once, she asked, "How much longer?" It sounded abrupt since she had to force herself to break off before adding *do I have?*

"Another couple of hours, maybe."

She glanced at the sky. "It must be midday already. It

didn't take half so long coming the other way. We're not returning by the same route, are we?"

"No."

"Are you avoiding William's patrols?"

"They're bound to be out looking for you."

The practicalities of her return forced their way to the front of her mind again. "They have no idea you rescued me," she said anxiously. "They'll kill you without question if I don't speak to William first. So you mustn't come too close. Let me down well before Tirebeck Hill and keep out of their way."

When he didn't answer, she twisted her head around to look at him. He was smiling, the rare, full smile that lit his eyes, his whole face.

"Flattered as I am by your care," he said in clear amusement, "you don't need to organise me. I'm not really one of your people."

"It's become a habit," she admitted.

"You wear it well. But I can't be ruled."

Although he spoke with a mix of deprecation and humour, she thought it was probably true.

As they drew inexorably closer to their goal, she found herself embroiled in unexpected discussions with him. They talked of history and the MacHeths' claim to Scotland through Aed and Lulach, Macbeth's stepson.

"Do you really think that matters now?" she asked curiously.

"It matters because it's right."

"*Is* it right?" she pursued. "That all these people should die, or lose their homes and livelihoods so that your family can be kings?"

His eyes, which had been gazing ahead, dropped to meet hers. "People have always died and lost and grieved. They always will."

"As long as men make war for their own ends."

"Women make war too," he pointed out.

Not as often. She closed her mouth on the words which only sounded childish. No one knew better than she did that war was part of life. "Sometimes I wish it could be different," she said.

Unexpectedly, he nodded, as if he understood. "So do I. But it won't be. We'll always fight for something. And maybe we should."

She said, "I don't want to fight."

"And yet you defend and support the King of Scots. Rhuadri, your father, fought for mine against King David."

"I never knew that until I came here. I think my mother was always loyal to the King of Scots. Even in England, or in Normandy, she brought me up to believe in that loyalty."

"I suppose she would have," Adam said obscurely.

As they talked more, she discovered that he could read and write in Latin as well as in English, French, Gaelic, and Norse. However isolated the southern Scots imagined the MacHeths to be, his education had not been lacking. Apparently, the Bishop of Ross himself had been his teacher.

"He says we made him a better teacher by being such bad pupils," Adam said, making her laugh.

"I think you were mischievous, not bad," she guessed.

"I think the same of you."

She twisted around to peer up at him uncertainly. And yet now it seemed easy to say, "Are you talking about my disgrace?"

"The man your husband killed in Perth—was never your lover, was he? Though perhaps he wanted to be."

"I was foolish," Christian said. "He was kind, and I wanted a friend. I don't believe he meant me any dishonour. But he paid the price for kindness when William challenged and killed him."

There was no pity in Adam's eyes. "So did you."

She shrugged and straightened in the saddle. "William couldn't have proved my guilt to the world more forcefully if he'd tried. There was no point then in even trying to explain the truth. No one was interested, least of all my husband. And then I realised the strangest thing of all: I didn't care. All I wanted was to come home to Tirebeck. And for once, my wishes and William's were in accord."

But that was enough. She didn't want to speak of William to him. She didn't want to *think* of William in these stolen hours. And as if he understood—or didn't want to dwell on William either—he changed the subject. There was, it seemed, so much to talk about.

They even discussed poetry, about which Adam seemed to know a surprising amount, including spoken Gaelic and Norse traditions, and texts both ancient and modern. He didn't think much of the new fashion of love poetry from France, which he claimed was too unrealistic to believe in.

It should have given her the clue. An honourable knight loving another knight's lady from afar, setting her on a pedestal to serve her and bring her gifts to prove his love was, in his eyes, nonsense. It was a reminder to rein in her imagination, her wayward emotions. But they were discussing literature, not life.

And then, through a thinning forest, she caught glimpses of a large hall with rambling extensions and outbuildings, much more splendid than the simple house at Tirebeck.

"Where is that?" she asked him. "I've never seen it before. We must still be miles from Tirebeck."

"We are."

She frowned, the first hint of unease finally twitching in her mind. "Who lives there?"

"I do," said Adam MacHeth. "I told you we were going home."

It seemed he caught her out every time.

CHAPTER SEVENTEEN

Inevitably, Gormflaith saw them first. She all but exploded into the hall, where her mother was judging some petty dispute with more patience than Gormflaith would have known how to show.

In the light of Adam's mad start after Cairistiona of Tirebeck, Donald had ridden out with his men to check for any threatened incursions from the lady's bellicose husband. Gormflaith wished he was present to hear this, because she was fairly sure her mother would hide the best of her reactions.

As Gormflaith hurried across the hall, her mother raised her hand to silence the man ranting in front of her. It worked. The lady's ability to effortlessly master the most vocal and brutal of men always impressed Gormflaith. She sat down in the chair beside her mother, who turned to her, brows raised. She seemed displeased by the interruption, although anyone else, Gormflaith reasoned, would have been grateful.

"Adam's coming," Gormflaith said. "He has a woman with him."

Her mother's eyes closed briefly, a better reaction than Gormflaith had hoped to surprise from her. Perversely, it made her uneasy. She tried to work out why this should be so serious and failed.

"Then have them prepare a suitable welcome. I will be finished here shortly."

Gormflaith stood obediently and tripped out to the

kitchen, where they were already cooking dinner. But there were sweet cakes baked earlier, which she bade them bring to the hall when her brother arrived, together with a bowl of nuts and dried fruit, and a jug of the wine Adam had brought back from the market at Rosemarkie.

That done, she went to change her gown to one not covered in mud from the hills, and to brush and dress her hair. She did not want to be outdone by the "French" lady of Tirebeck.

By the time she was satisfied, she could hear the shouts of welcome in the yard and ran outside to welcome her brother and his strange guest.

Adam walked his horse across the yard. A woman sat in front of him, wearing his cloak, although this did not appear to denote any friendship between them. On the contrary, the lady sat straight and rigid, staring straight ahead of her. A mud-streaked mask that must have once been quite a pretty ornament covered one side of her face. The other side was cold, proud, and angry.

Oh dear. Not grateful, then.

The usual boisterous welcome of his men and the house guards was muted in honour of his guest. His captive, apparently. As Gormflaith advanced to meet them, Adam halted and dismounted, reaching at once for the woman. Although she suffered him to touch her, she stared over his head from the saddle, and when she landed on the ground, she stared at his chest. Somehow, although Gormflaith didn't see her shrug, the cloak fell from her shoulders to the muddy ground.

The proud lady didn't appear to notice, merely stepped away from the restive horse and stood rigidly two paces from him.

Findlaech had materialised by Gormflaith's side.

"Do you know, I thought she might be worth saving?" Gormflaith murmured. "I thought there was a reason he took such care of her."

"Oh, there is," Findlaech allowed, "But you and I aren't likely to fathom it."

"I thought he liked her."

"He does."

Why? She couldn't ask. Good manners urged her forward to the repellently proud lady.

"You are welcome in our hall, lady," she said as pleasantly as she could.

The cold eyes deigned to focus on her, but the woman made no response.

Adam said, "My sister. Gormflaith, Cairistiona daughter of Rhuadri, the lady of Tirebeck."

Gormflaith inclined her head, as though to an equal— which the woman wasn't, whatever she thought of herself—and at last Cairistiona's lips parted as though she would speak.

Too late. Halla, who could depress the most entrenched of pretensions with the twitch of one eyebrow, had arrived and actually took the woman's hand with a sympathetic smile.

"How delightful to meet you at last. Forgive me, I was detained in the hall, but I'm sure my daughter has bid you welcome."

"The lady of Ross, my mother," Adam said, as if she needed it spelled out. "Halla, daughter of Gillebride."

The proud young woman dropped a sudden, jerky curtsy. "Thank you," she said stiffly. "You are kind. But your son has misunderstood. I need to be at Tirebeck. There was a fire, and my people don't know where I am."

"We will take care of that," Mother said smoothly.

"That—" The woman swallowed her words back, and Gormflaith glanced at her with unexpected new interest. Had she been about to say, *That's what I'm afraid of?*

"Come inside," Mother said. "You must be in dire need of refreshment and warmth." Gently but inexorably, she drew Cairistiona with her towards the hall. The young woman had not relaxed at all.

Gormflaith glanced at her brother, who gazed after them for a moment before bending and absently picking up the fallen cloak.

"I don't like her," Gormflaith announced. Although she lowered her voice, she didn't much care if she was overheard. "Disagreeably proud and ill-mannered."

"No," Adam said without heat. "She's just afraid we'll keep her here."

Gormflaith glanced at him warily. "Will we?"

"Yes," Adam said, and as his horse was led off to be cared for, he walked on towards the hall.

****

Christian seemed to have entered a different world from any she'd encountered before. The beautiful young woman, Adam's sister, who almost shone with vitality and natural, confident grace, met her brother's unexpected captive with a civility and aplomb that somehow denied the crime.

Hurt and fury consumed Christian at Adam's betrayal. The words *How could he? How could he?* repeated over and over in her head. And then, *How could I? How could I be so gullible?*

To make everything worse, Halla, the legendary lady of Ross, was *kind* to her. Somehow, Christian hadn't expected Adam and Donald's mother to look so young. The strength, character, and regality Christian had imagined were certainly there in her high-cheekboned face, so like Adam's, but so also were sheer beauty and intelligence.

Stiffly, Christian followed the lady through a large, gracious hall. Servants were setting cakes and wine on the high table. Only when the lady spoke in Gaelic, asking them to move the refreshments, did Christian realise they'd all spoken French before. Pointing out that she was still the stranger in this country? Or merely civility?

It didn't matter. She needed to go home.

Halla led her to a space behind and to one side of the high table, like a miniature hall, where two chairs and a cushioned bench were informally arranged under a half-shuttered window, near a wooden table, on which the servants now set the refreshments.

The lady murmured a dismissal and herself poured bloodred wine into four goblets, the first of which she gave to Christian, bidding her sit in one of the two comfortable chairs. Christian thought of eating and drinking nothing in protest, but she knew she had to think through her anger, and being rude to her noble hostess would hardly endear her.

So she sat, and because she'd no idea what to say, she sipped the wine. Instantly, the smooth, spicy taste cut through her thoughts and her memory. Before she could prevent it, her glaze flew up and found Adam by the table. His lip quirked slightly, and he lifted the cup to her in a silent toast.

She'd never even ascertained that it *was* him who sent the wine cask, let alone thanked him for it. Now she knew for certain and had given the fact away.

So unimportant.

"First," Halla began pleasantly in French.

"We can speak in Gaelic," Adam interrupted. "She speaks it perfectly."

The lady of Ross inclined her head without so much as glancing at her large son. "Then let me say in our own tongue that we apologise unreservedly for the behaviour of our erstwhile guest. He misunderstood and imagined for some reason that his action would please us."

"Which act?" Christian asked wryly. "Setting fire to Tirebeck or abducting me?"

Halla paused, searching her face. Christian thought she had at least surprised her. "Both," Halla said smoothly. "I am only glad my son was able to remedy the worst of the situation."

"Certainly, I had no wish to go to Galloway or to be forcibly married to the lord of Galloway's son. I am grateful to be free of that fate."

Gormflaith sat down on the bench, frowning. "How could you marry Fergus's son when you're already married to Lanson? Was Sir William meant to set you aside in rage?"

"No, I believe your brothers were meant to murder him," Christian retorted.

Gormflaith nodded as if this was not such an unreasonable expectation. She lifted her eyebrow. "Well, I confess I never expected to be your rival in love," she said flippantly. "Only a day or so ago, there was talk of giving *me* to Gilbert of Galloway." She rose and walked to the table, slapping her brother's distracted hand off the plate of cakes before picking it up and offering it to Christian.

"That I could more easily understand," Christian said, accepting a cake before she meant to.

"Of course, he has two sons," Gormflaith remarked. "Perhaps we were to have one each. Although, like you, Uhtred is married already."

"Why is he so eager to find another wife for his already married son?" Christian wondered aloud.

Adam said, "His sons hate each other. He's looking to give one of them an interest outside of Galloway, or they'll tear it apart between them when Fergus is dead."

Christian bit into the cake, which, like the wine, was

distractingly delicious. With an effort, she hung on to the thread of her thoughts and fixed her gaze on Gormflaith, who was returning to her seat armed with a cake of her own.

"That could be," Christian said thoughtfully. "Marriage with your family would give him an eventual claim to Ross. I love Tirebeck. It's my home. But even I can't see it as much compensation for the loss of Galloway."

Gormflaith let out a gurgle of laughter that sprayed cake crumbs over her lap. Unselfconsciously, she brushed them off before glaring at her brother.

"Very well, Adam. Speak. Tirebeck has some strategic value to us and maybe, therefore, to Galloway. But we all know it wouldn't distract Gilbert or Uhtred of Galloway for more than a minute."

Adam said nothing. He'd finished a cake and was reaching for another. Gormflaith scowled at his averted face.

"*He knows who Cairistiona is*," she said with a significance Christian couldn't fathom. It almost sounded like a quotation, and it got Adam's attention at last. "*Who* is Cairistiona?"

Not everyone looked at Adam. The lady of Ross was gazing at Christian. Christian could almost feel her eyes, watchful, unblinking, rather like Adam's at times.

Adam took a long draught of wine and set down his goblet. For some reason, Christian's heart was beating and beating, as if she cared what he was going to say. He didn't look at her but at his fingers lingering on the stem of the cup.

He said, "Cairistiona is the daughter of Mary, the daughter of Ranghilda, the daughter of Devorgilla, the daughter of Malcolm."

Christian's lips parted. She couldn't remember ever hearing the ancestry of her mother. Her apparently adulterous mother, according to Adam last night. And it did make unpleasant sense. If her father had been a friend of Malcolm MacHeth, he would hardly have gone south to King David.

And now here was mention of a Malcolm in her ancestry. Obviously a different Malcolm, but a significant one judging by the way Adam paused after his name, as if his recitation was finished.

"Which Malcolm?" Christian asked drily.

"Son of Duncan," Adam said. His intent gaze lifted unexpectedly to her and held.

Christian's throat had gone dry. *Malcolm son of Duncan*...

"King of Scots, third of his name," Adam said. "You're descended from his illegitimate daughter, who was born in Lothian long before Malcolm married Queen Margaret. It was said her mother had no ambition except to keep her daughter free of the constant squabbles over the Scottish throne."

Into the silence, Christian said flatly, "I don't think I believe that."

"My son is never wrong about genealogy," the lady of Ross said thoughtfully. "He hears it once and remembers. However, in this case, I would be interested to know exactly who he heard it from."

Adam's gaze jumped from Christian to his mother. It almost seemed as if he didn't want to speak. He swallowed, much as he had before he confessed to Christian that he saw visions in the flames.

"From my father."

"Adam," Gormflaith scoffed. "Were you even three when you saw him last?"

He shrugged that off. "I found it in a letter he wrote to Rhuadri of Tirebeck, telling him the ancestry of his wife-to-be. He sent a copy to the bishop, which is where I read it when I first went to Symeon for lessons. I don't know where it is now."

He spoke as if that part of it was unimportant. Christian was still struggling with the personal significance when she was provided a glimpse of the quick, grasping intelligence that had kept Malcolm MacHeth's wife in command of turbulent Ross for twenty years.

"He's aiming at the kingship itself," Halla said with wonder. "Fergus wants Uhtred to be undisputed lord of Galloway, and Gilbert to be King of Scots. Or vice versa."

Christian stared at her. "With an illegitimate claim that even *I* couldn't prove if I wanted to?"

"I expect Symeon can. More importantly, Fergus can prove it," Adam said. "He wouldn't have abducted you if he couldn't."

"It's still nonsense. The royal line has long been secure in the *legitimate* descendants of Malcolm the Third and Queen Margaret. Fergus couldn't change that by marrying me!"

"It gives him a claim," Adam said. "One that opposes

ours."

"No, it doesn't," Christian insisted. "You might as well say he has a claim to the throne of England because he married King Henry I's illegitimate daughter!"

"England has different traditions," Adam said. "And their kings are French. They follow the eldest male line in marriage."

"So do we," Christian said.

A hiss sounded between Adam's teeth. It might have been a laugh.

The lady of Ross said, "Fergus thinks to use our help to overthrow the King of Scots and then turn on us and take the throne for his son through Cairistiona's claim."

"Maybe," Adam said. "Or just hold the possible threat over us to extract cooperation or concessions from my father."

Gormflaith sighed. "Then our promising alliance with Fergus is over."

"It most certainly is not," Halla said roundly. "Not until he has arranged the release of your father as he promised."

Gormflaith frowned with incomprehension. "He really means to try for that?"

Adam nodded. "Of course. He doesn't know we're aware whom he took on his detour from the Great Glen. Once my father is free, we can renegotiate."

One had to get up very early in the morning, Christian reflected, to beat the MacHeths.

****

Although Cairistiona appeared to forget her anxiety and her anger in the discussion about her ancestry and Fergus's plans, Adam knew she hadn't forgiven him. Which was probably for the best, although he hadn't set out to offend her. It was just that his feelings and his plans were getting muddled along the way, and he didn't really know yet how to deal with that.

When his mother sent Cairistiona off with Gormflaith to make herself comfortable for dinner, he knew he had another problem. He tried to avoid it by slipping past in the wake of the girls, but his mother stayed him with one word.

"Adam."

He could have pretended not to hear her as he'd done with

many people as a boy, although somehow blocking out his mother had never made him feel good. So he halted and turned to face her.

At least she came halfway to meet him, which meant she wasn't furious.

"Why didn't you tell us before?" she asked, mildly enough.

"About Cairistiona? I thought you knew. My father knew. And then I had no time."

She took his arm and gave it a little shake. "Adam. We *all* need *all* the facts if we're to think and plan together. Why did you bring her here? You know what the world will say."

He shrugged that off as unimportant. "It will bring Lanson out and let us defeat him. With Fergus's help, we can keep the king too busy in the south to invade Ross until my father is released. By then, more galleys will be ready, Somerled, hopefully, will be king of Man, and we can all attack the king in earnest. If that's what my father wants. If it isn't, the threat of it will surely strengthen our hand for the earldom of Ross."

His mother blinked. It was a good plan, and one she would already have grasped. It didn't deflect her. "And the girl?" she said with patience.

Adam turned away. "She unites our claim with that of Malcolm Canmore's line. I brought her for Donald."

****

Somehow, in the revelations and discussions, the awkward fact of Christian being here against her will had got lost. She found herself in a bedchamber with Gormflaith, being given water to wash in and fresh clothes to change into.

The other girl's presence was irritating. For one thing, despite the short moment of understanding in the hall, Gormflaith radiated dislike. For another, Christian found that washing her face was suddenly complicated in company. She couldn't remove the mask. She settled for wetting the drying cloth and wringing it out before scrubbing her face with that, merely pushing it flat under the mask with her fingers.

"Were you frightened?" Gormflaith threw the words at her as she drew on her fresh overgown.

"When?"

"When Fergus abducted you."

"I was unconscious when Fergus abducted me. I was certainly afraid when I woke up." She glanced at the other girl, who sat now on a chest by the wall, brushing her hair.

"I've never been abducted," Gormflaith said.

"Neither had I until I came to Ross. Now it's almost familiar."

Gormflaith bridled at the implication. "At least my brother never hit you. And he rescued you from the one that did."

Christian turned and searched the other girl's face. There was a hint of pride in her eyes, something that might have been anger in the set of her lips and the tilt of her head. She'd been right. Gormflaith really didn't like her.

Christian said coldly, "He killed my bodyguards, and took me from my people."

"He took you from your vile husband," Gormflaith snapped. "And gave you a home you'd otherwise have had to fight for. And have lost. I didn't understand it then, and I still don't." She tossed the comb on the bed and stalked out of the room.

Christian didn't have long to enjoy her solitude. She was brushing the tangles from her hair, and wondering the best way to achieve her departure, when she had another visitor—the lady of Ross herself.

Halla was hardly the bandit queen or the evil witch of court gossip. In fact, Christian knew instinctively that any salvation lay in this apparently gentle woman of implacable authority. If anyone could rule her son, she did. And Christian was sure that, for whatever reason, the lady wasn't happy about her presence here.

"We must think of the best way to inform your people," the lady said, once the civilities were past. "Without mine being killed."

"I would only trouble you for the loan of a horse, and a guide in the right direction," Christian said. "I will carry my own news."

The lady sat on the chest as Gormflaith had. "My dear," she said, gently. "Have you considered how this will appear to your husband?"

"As I'm sure you know, I came to Ross in disgrace. Yet another can make little difference either to him or to me."

Halla spelled it out. "Since coming to Ross, you have spent two nights outside your husband's protection. Both have been with my son."

"I chose neither. As my husband is aware."

Halla gave a slightly crooked little smile. It wasn't unsympathetic. "My dear. When did our choices ever enter men's heads? We just pay the price for theirs."

As she still paid the price for her husband's rebellion which she was obliged to continue for her sons? Oh no, it wasn't quite like that. The lady of Ross was a force in her own right, and one to be reckoned with.

"I am not quite such a poor creature as you think me," Christian said.

Halla's eyebrows rose. "I don't think you poor at all. Before I ever met you, my son's actions told me all I needed to know. *Most* of what I needed to know. Your care of him and Cailean mac Gilleon when they were captured told me the rest." She held Christian's carefully expressionless gaze. "We are not enemies, Cairistiona."

This was what she'd always intended. To build bridges, come to some kind of accommodation with the MacHeths that did not involve renouncing the King of Scots. The king had made that difficult by offering the earldom of Ross to William if he could subdue it. But if she could acquire more land to satisfy William's ambition for the price of peace... Would that not be the best she could do?

"I do not wish us to be enemies," Christian said honestly. "But my husband and your sons make it an unlikely friendship."

"Adam is...difficult. But he has always looked out for you."

Christian felt a flush rise to her face, hoped the lady didn't notice. "Why?" she said evenly.

Halla stood. "Because he always does what is right in his own eyes."

"Right for the MacHeths," Christian said gently.

"In Ross," the lady returned, "it amounts to the same thing. Come, let us go into the hall together. You are, of course, our guest of honour."

CHAPTER EIGHTEEN

The lady of Ross kept a large and gracious hall. Elegant decorations were carved into the walls and into the high backs of the chairs. A beautiful, ornately carved harp that Christian hadn't noticed before stood to one side of the high table. The household itself was much larger than that of Tirebeck, with people of all walks of life sitting down together, including many men-at-arms, who must have included the lady's own guard as well as some of Adam's men. And there were several more servants bustling around with washing bowls and towels, food, and wine.

But for so grand a hall, there was surprisingly little ceremony.

There was a horrible moment when she first sat between the lady and Donald—who'd arrived home just in time for dinner—when someone shouted out, "Lady Cairistiona! I knew you'd come back to us!"

And through the burst of laughter around the hall, she realised that this meal would be like all others she'd known since her marriage; merely the form of abuse would be different.

So she did what she did at home: forced a faint smile onto her lips and pretended not to hear. The man who'd spoken, however, remained standing, grinning directly at her in what looked like a friendly manner. *Findlaech*, she thought. *I remember him.*

"You're well?" he asked, so unexpectedly that she almost forgot to answer.

A slightly wild glance around the hall told her that

everyone was looking at her and waiting for an answer, even the lady of Ross beside her.

"Quite well, thank you," she managed. "As, I trust, are you."

Findlaech grinned, bowed, and sat, and the buzz of conversation rose up, granting her a reprieve.

It was a pattern for the whole meal. Although the family and Christian sat at the top table, the rest of the household seemed to see nothing wrong in addressing them during the meal. Likewise, the family, would occasionally shout questions or jocular comments down the hall.

On the other hand, like Findlaech, no one appeared to overstep the bounds of civility. The people joked but never derided or used unfit language. They seemed not remotely in awe of the MacHeths—which would have surprised the southern Scots, who, if they hadn't personally suffered under their depredations, always knew someone who had—but there was a line that no one crossed. It might have been drawn in a different place than William's, but it was there.

"You find us informal," Donald said beside her.

"Intriguingly so," Christian replied honestly.

"Different customs," Donald said, "added to three years of warfare and the absence of the earl, my father."

"It works for you." She hesitated, but here in the MacHeths' hall, bluntness seemed to be in order. "Talking of warfare, have you been fighting with my husband?"

Donald smiled. It wasn't a comforting smile. "Not since we last met," he replied, not troubling to hide his regret.

"Then you have not been to Tirebeck?"

"We came close. There are parties out searching for you. We avoided them. But apart from your absence, I believe all is well there for the moment."

"Then, when I return tomorrow, there will be no need for any more fighting."

Donald picked up his wine cup. "That would rather depend on whether or not your husband takes exception to our hospitality. It would make us—my mother and my brother and sister and me—very happy if you would stay."

As with Adam, a great deal seemed to go on behind Donald's eyes. And behind his words, both more comprehensible and less straightforward than Adam's. She sensed no enmity from Donald. But Cailean and Sigurd had been watching Tirebeck for them. Everyone knew her true status as William's wife, which was not the same as her status as lady.

"You are kind," she said, lifting her eyes to his. She felt almost as she had when she'd confessed to his brother her worthlessness as a wife. "But by staying away, I neglect my people. And I damage my position as lady of Tirebeck."

Donald only smiled again. "In the eyes of your people, it is natural that their lady should visit the lady of Ross."

They wouldn't understand. This was impossible.

Unexpectedly, the lady of Ross herself leaned forward and spoke up. "She isn't just the lady of Tirebeck. She is also the lady de Lanson. It's like walking on a slender rope across a river in flood."

"What is?" Donald asked, clearly baffled.

"Loyalty," Halla said shortly. "A woman is expected to follow her husband's."

And certainly no one could fault the lady of Ross there. But if they were speaking of honesty…

"My loyalty is not just to my husband," Christian said clearly. "It is to the King of Scots."

There was a short silence, into which a cup thudded on wood.

From his place farther along the table, Adam said. "Then we'd best hurry and change the King of Scots."

Which was greeted with a surge of laughter around the hall that told her exactly how many people had been listening.

As the laughter died away, a different sound cut through the general noise of eating—the cry of a baby, somewhere at the back of the hall. By itself, the cry would hardly have attracted Christian's interest, except that in her direct line of vision, a comely young maidservant in the act of pouring ale for Findlaech whipped her head towards the noise and froze.

Findlaech expostulated as his ale spilled over, and the girl muttered something, swinging around, her eyes seeking and finding the lady of Ross, who lifted her head in subtle and yet clear dismissal. The maid smiled, abandoning her ale, and skipped down the hall to one of the tables at the back, where she took a bundle from another woman.

Christian looked away, found Halla's eyes upon her. Hastily, she searched for something to say just to divert the conversation from babies and barrenness.

"Muiredach," the lady called. "I think it's time for some music. Something sweet and soothing."

Christian watched a lean, handsome young man in a green tunic rise from the table below and walk across the hall to the harp. It seemed the lady had her own musician.

With relief, Christian found a topic she imagined was safe. "My lady, do you remember the fire at Tirebeck when I was a child?"

"I remember seeing what it left behind. In part, at least."

"Is it why my mother and I left?"

The lady hesitated. "Not exactly. Rather, I think, the fact of you leaving made your father burn the hall."

"But I remember it happening. I saw it."

As the harp strings sounded in a ripple of music that sent shivers up Christian's spine, the lady gazed at her, not entirely comfortable. Then she nodded. "Yes, you rode away from the fire with your mother."

"And my father?"

The harp swelled into melody, as sweet and soothing as the lady had requested. Christian hoped it wouldn't make her cry.

"I suspect he was already dead," Halla said, not ungently.

"But I think I saw him. In the flames."

"You remember that? The servants said you ran back into the burning building to find your father. Your mother managed to drag you away just before the whole roof collapsed."

Christian looked at the food still in front of her. "Then my father killed himself."

"I think he did, though I'm not sure he intended to die." Halla's tone was oddly comforting: down-to-earth, factual, and yet not without sympathy. Over the years, she must have told many people about many losses, many tragedies. "He just couldn't stop your mother leaving with you. He didn't want to when she confessed to adultery with Ranulf."

"Tell me," Christian said. Her voice sounded harsh to the point of rudeness, but if the lady noticed, she ignored it, merely inclined her head.

"Ranulf came to Ross to arrest my husband. I don't know

why he went to Tirebeck, for Malcolm wasn't there; he was hiding in the hills. Perhaps Ranulf meant to force Rhuadri to give him up. I don't know. We do know they fought, and in the turmoil, you were somehow thrown into the fire. That was when your mother rescued you and managed to stop the fight. I believe both men were horrified by what had come of their actions. So Ranulf left.

"But he came back, several months, maybe a year or more later. After Malcolm mac Aed was taken. Perhaps he'd been so smitten with your mother that he came back to win her. Maybe there had been something between them before, when he'd first come. I don't know. But when your mother decided to leave with Ranulf, your father fired the house. Nobody knows why. To be sure she never came back? Just because he was so angry? Or perhaps it was a game to make her order his rescue.

"Whatever his motive, he stayed in the burning hall while they prepared the horses. He can't have expected you to run in to find him. Nor could your mother. When the servants could drag him out, he was dead."

Christian swallowed carefully. It didn't hurt as much as it might. She'd already pieced together something of the same story from the bits of memory that had come back since the fire, and from Adam's snippets.

"Well," she managed, her voice sounding only a little hollow to her own ears. "Thank you. Now I finally know."

****

Pleading tiredness, Christian retired early. Gormflaith conducted her with icy civility to the door of her own chamber once more and left her to return to her place and, possibly, a family discussion about Christian's fate.

Christian had no intention of allowing the MacHeths to decide that.

Inside the room, the same maid who'd gone to attend to the baby was making up an extra pallet. She smiled at Christian without shyness or insolence and indicated the larger bed, clearly Gormflaith's own.

"For you," the maid said.

Christian sat down on the bed. Since it was no part of her plan to alienate the servants, she said, "Thank you. I seem to have unwittingly disturbed the whole household."

The girl laughed. "Bless you, lady, this household is *always* disturbed by something. You are a welcome guest."

Christian watched her work for a few moments. She had to almost sit on her hands to prevent herself rising to help.

"What is your name?" she asked at last.

"Eithine."

"You have children?"

A huge smile swept the girl's face. "I have a baby son. You probably heard him demanding his own dinner. Little Adam won't feed from anyone else."

Understanding sang in Christian's ears, drowning the merry music from the harp in the main hall.

Adam. The baby was called Adam. The lady of Ross's indulgence to her servant was, then, easily explained. The child was her grandson. Adam's son.

What had she expected? That his peculiar gifts, his strangeness, made him celibate? His position alone would have made him hard to refuse, but the proud way Eithine said her child's name spoke of nothing but adoration. Christian could understand that. What she couldn't understand was her own reaction. Adam MacHeth, for his own reasons, had tried to forge a bond with her, a bond she refused to acknowledge now and never would.

But perhaps she'd said the name aloud, for Eithine's smile had slipped slightly. "I thought he would be Malcolm for the earl, but Donald mac Malcolm chose Adam. He missed his brother."

"Of course he did," Christian said faintly. Stupid. Adam had been with Somerled for the best part of two years. So young a baby could not have been his unless he'd brought mother and child home with him from the west. Eithine's child was Donald's. And why in God's name did she care? Whatever foolish fantasy she'd been half indulging to add excitement or romance to her dullness had always been ridiculous, whatever mistresses or children he did or did not have.

"And Adam mac Malcolm guessed his name just by touching him," Eithine informed her with pride. "He'll have a long and happy life."

An old woman at a Rouen fair once told me the same thing. Christian kept the sardonic thought to herself, and a moment later, Gormflaith entered and dismissed Eithine with not unaffectionate

197

familiarity.

Eithine would never be Gormflaith's sister, and yet she was more than a servant. Here in the north, the niceties of legitimate birth were unimportant, and Eithine's child could well be lord here one day. But when Donald married...would Eithine become to his wife what Alys was to Christian?

No, the lady of Ross would never allow it. For the first time, Christian began to see what her own pride had allowed. Hurt and humiliated, she'd chosen to pretend she cared less than William. She'd chosen to seize what comfort she could in privacy and allowed Alys to encroach the position that was hers. Even in Tirebeck where she'd deliberately set out to be the lady, she'd allowed Alys not to command, perhaps, but still to take her place in matters Christian thought unimportant. She should never have allowed Alys's feet to get so far beneath her table or her sheets. It was William who should have gone elsewhere, not Christian.

Though when she returned home, she would not be in a strong position to lay down the law with William. She doubted he'd cast her aside, though. Not until he'd defeated the MacHeths.

Her stomach tightened. She needed to plan...

****

Christian assumed she'd be far too churned up to sleep. Used now to sleeping alone in her own little loft, she was aware of every breath Gormflaith took in the pallet against the other wall. But the other woman's presence was hardly a comfort. In fact, it would be easy to be flattened, overwhelmed by the blows of the last day.

Christian was alone in the lair of the notorious MacHeths, no matter how civilised that had turned out to be. When Gormflaith blew the candle out and the household quietened for the night, Christian could still hear his deep voice among all the others leaving the hall. Her throat constricted, but she would never weep for him.

Not while his sister lay across the room.

It was her last conscious thought before she woke to daylight breaking through the gaps in the shutter.

She sat bolt upright. *Damnation.* She'd meant to have risen and dressed by now, to have borrowed a horse before most of the household was abroad and be already on the road back to Tirebeck. A quick glance showed her that Gormflaith was gone from her pallet. Christian hadn't even heard her move.

"Last up," she muttered to herself. "Good beginning, Christian."

She had nothing else to do but carry on with her plan. So she leapt up, splashed water on her face, retied her mask, and, after a fruitless search for her own gown, donned the borrowed one with her veil and sallied forth to establish how quickly she could leave.

At once, she saw the lady at the big table with Adam, Donald, and several other men whose faces she knew. They all turned toward her as one, except Adam, who took a second longer.

Well, that took care of her preferred plan of slipping away unnoticed, but perhaps that had always been overoptimistic. Blatancy would have to do.

"Forgive me," she said brightly. "I can see you are all busy. I came only to give you thanks for your kind hospitality and beg you for the loan of a horse to Tirebeck."

There was an exchange of half-annoyed, half-amused glances in which Adam didn't appear to participate. He straightened, gazing only at Christian.

"I'm afraid that's impossible. Tirebeck is coming to you, and we can spare no horses or guides."

Christian blinked. "Tirebeck is coming to me?" she repeated. Her blood chilled. "Oh, no."

"Your husband misled us. He left only a few men at Tirebeck. The rest have marched on us. And found us."

"A pity you didn't see *this* coming," Donald said grimly.

"Maybe it's as good a time as any," Adam muttered. He seemed restless, shuffling his feet as if he wanted to be off somewhere. Slaughtering her people, no doubt. "*She* is here and safe."

"I'm glad you noticed," Christian snapped. "And your problem is easily solved by returning me to my husband. There need be no bloodshed over a misunderstanding."

"I believe," the lady of Ross murmured, "that they understand each other pretty well. It was always going to come to this. But you're letting him choose the time, Adam. We—"

"It *needn't* come to this," Christian interrupted ruthlessly.

"There is no need for any fighting at all. Why should men die for nothing?"

"Not nothing," Adam said vaguely. On the words, he strode away towards the hall door, while the others went on talking with apparent openness.

"Here on our land, the advantage is all ours," Donald said. "The foreigners don't know it."

"Lanson is an experienced and famous soldier," Halla argued. "Presumably, he learns quickly."

Surreptitiously, Christian watched Adam leave. In the doorway, he crossed with a maidservant carrying a jug and a plate of oatcakes. He didn't appear to notice the girl, who smiled at him, beyond distractedly seizing an oatcake in passing, but Christian saw her gaze turn and follow him as if she couldn't help it.

Christian snapped her attention back to the important conversation. If she could learn William's exact direction, she stood more chance of succeeding.

****

Lanson, who'd begun to feel like a fly being enticed into a spider's web, made a decision.

"We'll make our stand here," he announced. From the top of the hill they'd just climbed, he commanded a good view of the surrounding country. "Any farther, and they're too likely to close in behind us. Henry, keep your detachment out of sight. Move around to come through *that* valley and fall upon their flank. It should just be mopping up for you. Once we charge them from up here, they'll be in pieces."

"Yes, sir," Henry said. On foot, he gazed down the slope to the rough ground below. "It's difficult ground for horses," he observed. "There's a reason the locals fight on foot."

Lanson curled his lip. "They don't have decent horses."

After a moment, Henry asked, "How will you draw them out?"

"I'll just sit here and wait," Lanson replied. "They'll come."

"*They* could just watch *us* and pick us off a few at a time when we forage for food. They've done such things before."

"Yes, but this is their heartland. From the number of men

we've seen and their panicked movements, we're close to the MacHeth lair, to their women, including Malcolm MacHeth's wife. And mine. They'll fight."

Henry, who had recently developed an irritating habit of questioning everything, lifted his gaze from the ground below and opened his mouth once more. Lanson had had enough and simply glared at him.

Henry closed his mouth and bowed. "Yes, sir."

He didn't sound happy about it. Lanson didn't care. He smelled victory. Although he'd been furious with Christian for falling into MacHeth hands again, he began to think now that it was working out pretty well. One mounted charge from this height could annihilate the MacHeth rabble. And somewhere in that rabble would be the son of a whore who'd escaped his clutches before. Killing him would not only give Lanson personal satisfaction, it would take the fight out of whatever MacHeth men were left. If Lanson moved quickly, he could take their stronghold, their women, mop up the brother and any other male relatives who might cause trouble later, and Ross would be his. He'd have achieved the impossible and be made an earl by the King of Scots.

Lanson rather thought he'd forgive Christian. Up here in the wilds, apart from falling constantly into the hands of their enemies, she was proving a decent asset. She could organise a household and she wasn't stupid about military matters either. He'd known for weeks it was time he sent Alys home and lived properly with his wife. Who knew? Perhaps back in her own country and more contented, she'd even conceive at last. He'd heard of such things.

It all hinged on this battle, of course, and whether or not he'd get the MacHeths to stand and fight. Despite Henry's anxieties, Lanson knew that this time, they *would* fight. They couldn't risk him getting any closer. Even if their women fled deeper into the country, the MacHeth reputation, the MacHeth legend, was at stake.

As his men formed up behind him on the plateau, Lanson felt like rubbing his hands together.

****

Adam and Donald rode out together, and men streamed

behind them, at first from the hall enclosure and then from outside it. They already had more men than William, and although most were on foot and none wore full armour, they were well armed with swords, daggers, spears, maces, and bows. They all wore helmets at least, and without cumbersome armour, they moved quickly.

Christian's throat closed up. She refused to be the excuse for men to kill each other so wantonly.

Low and intense, she spoke to the lady of Ross beside her. "Can you not see how wrong this is? How stupid? If I rode out instead of them, there would be no blood spilled."

"It's beyond that," the lady said, not without sympathy. "It always was. You're not the cause of this, Cairistiona. You may be a prize, but you're not the cause."

Christian glanced at her curiously. "Are you?"

She nodded. "I brought them up to fight for their father. So, yes."

"I may be slow-witted," Christian said, "but I fail to see how your sons fighting with my husband in a quiet corner of Ross could possibly cause your husband to be released."

The lady gave a faint, gentle smile. But Christian wasn't deceived. The lady didn't know either.

Adam MacHeth didn't look back once.

"Let's go inside," the lady said, "out of this wind."

As she followed her hostess back inside, Christian saw how it would be. In their polite, friendly, implacable way, they would never leave her alone. And even if she was rude enough to escape their grasping hands and run, there were men-at-arms in the yard who presumably had their orders to bring her back.

I hate you, Adam MacHeth...

What had he said to her when they'd first come to Tirebeck? *"There will be more to forgive."* Prescience? Or simple planning?

Eventually, in desperation, she retreated to Gormflaith's room with the excuse of needing to lie down a little. She half expected Gormflaith to come with her, but fortunately she was spared that torture. So at least she could pace and plan away from the women's distracting observation.

Closing the door firmly, she threw herself onto the bed and stared around the chamber until her gaze fell on the window shutters. They stood partially opened, a chilly breeze spilling fresh air into the room. Christian rose and walked to the shutters, investigating the hinges and the latches and the narrow view of the yard outside.

Experimenting, she touched the shutter, pushing against the catch that held it in place. Nothing creaked. She released the catch and opened both shutters wide. Grey daylight flooded the room. Outside was a useless piece of yard space between the main hall and the built-on extra chambers. No one was around. With luck, everyone was in the front yard, and she could easily reach the stables unseen.

The gates had stood open when she last saw them. If she covered her face, she could surely ride right up and through the gates unchallenged. Or at least take them by surprise. She could stop this if she got to William. She could return to Tirebeck and begin again. The MacHeths had acknowledged her right to the place; surely they wouldn't take it from her now, just for going against their wishes.

Before she could talk herself out of it, she seized her cloak, drawing both veil and hood over the mask before she climbed somewhat clumsily out of the window and closed the shutters tidily behind her. She couldn't fasten them, of course, but the wind didn't seem to be strong enough to blow them apart.

Drawing in her breath, she marched on towards the stables as if she had every right to be there. However, the stables were almost entirely deserted. The men, probably, were all at the front of the yard, waiting for news of the battle, and in any case, there was little work for them, since nearly all the horses were gone.

The black horse she and Adam had ridden here was in one of the stalls, presumably resting after its arduous journey. At least it knew her.

She laid her hand on the stall door, her heart galloping, but before she could go in or even murmur soothingly to the horse, a shiver ran down her spine. She jerked her head around, praying it was only her imagination playing tricks, and saw a girl standing alone, very still, watching her. A maidservant. The girl, surely, who'd passed Adam in the hall doorway and gazed after him as if pleading for some attention, some notice.

As calmly as she could, Christian turned back to the horse, casually lifting her hand from the door to stroke the horse's nose, as if that was all she'd ever intended. Considering her anxiety, it was only surprising the horse didn't pull away in distress. Her heartbeat counted the moments. At least the girl didn't shout. Christian hoped she was just walking away.

A shadow fell across her. "Do you imagine that hides you?" the girl said.

Christian turned her head slowly, raising her eyebrows in the haughtiest way she could manage.

But the girl didn't seem to have intended insolence. She was unwrapping the shawl from her head and shoulders. "The cloak is yours. You're clearly neither of the ladies." She stretched out her hands, offering her the shawl. "Put that over your head and body, push your mask farther aside, and you're just one of the servants, unworthy of notice."

Christian stared at her, looking for the trick, and then for the motive. The way she'd looked at Adam in the doorway. She was Adam's Eithine. Or wanted to be, only he didn't notice her. For some reason, she seemed to imagine he noticed Christian.

Slowly, she took the shawl. "A servant wouldn't ride this horse," she observed. "But I need to ride, to cover the distance."

"There's a pony by the house at the foot of the hill," the servant said, pointing to the east. "Take it. If anyone challenges you, say the lady asked for it."

Christian took off her cloak and tied it around her middle in a bundle, which would also help to alter her shape for observers, then pulled the shawl around her head and shoulders. The girl watched her, even pushed the mask aside for her. Instinctively, Christian reached up to grab it back into place, and the girl gave a faint, sardonic smile.

"It doesn't matter," she said. "It's you he sees."

Christian felt a quizzical frown forming, but the girl was already walking away, and of course her meaning didn't matter. She had greater priorities. Drawing in her breath, she hunched her shoulders a little, then followed the servant at a distance, walking away from the stables and around the outside of the hall.

No one looked at her as she hurried across the yard, and she didn't look around much either. She couldn't see the girl who'd given her the shawl.

The largest group of men had gathered by the gates. They seemed to be gazing over the hills in the same direction, as if they knew that was where their comrades had gone and that was where the battle would be. If Christian couldn't stop it.

Head down, muttering she barely knew what, she pushed through them and hurried down the hill in the direction the servant had given her.

CHAPTER NINETEEN

Gormflaith gazed around her empty bedchamber and focused on the loose, flapping shutters. Her breath caught. "She climbed out of the window. How rude."

"Send one of the men to find her," snapped her mother.

"Looking where?" Gormflaith wondered. "She must still be around the hall. She's not exactly undistinctive. She could never have left unseen."

Her mother stilled, then turned and walked back into the hall. Two maids were sweeping out the old rushes. Her mother didn't hesitate but walked straight up to the younger girl, whose head was uncovered.

The girl stopped sweeping but didn't lift her head.

"If she dies," the lady said harshly, "*you* will be to blame. Did you really imagine her presence makes any difference to you?"

Gormflaith remembered, eventually, to close her gaping mouth. She'd never imagined her mother deigned to notice which maids her sons took to their beds. She felt almost sorry for the miserable girl.

"Gormflaith," her mother said.

Gormflaith, reminded of her task, hurried on to complete it.

****

The little horse was fast and sure-footed. Although it had

no saddle, at least there had been a bridle hanging on a tree branch inside its paddock. The horse hadn't objected to her putting it on.

Before mounting, Christian had picked up a round, good-sized stone and wrapped it in the depths of her cloak, which was still tied around her middle. The weapon made her feel safer as she had guided the little horse in what she hoped was the direction the men-at-arms had been gazing. Her skin itched as if aware of a thousand staring eyes. It didn't matter, she had to remind herself. She needed to be seen.

What she didn't need was to run into the MacHeth men instead of William's, so she rode in a wide arc and searched constantly for glints of armour.

In the end, she saw them simply form up on the flat top of a hill. She could even see William at their head. She was in time. She was still in time. The fastest way to William's hill was through the wooded glen to her right. She just hoped he'd see her coming. Pushing the little horse on to a gallop over the rough ground, she let her have her head to navigate the trees as quickly as possible. Which meant Christian had to watch out for low branches and other hazards which seemed to whizz out at her. She wondered if she should shout to William, if he or his men would hear her.

Abruptly, two men leapt out in her path. The little horse reared, forcing Christian to cling to its neck. Gasping, she tried to soothe the animal. Someone seized its bridle, and with massive relief, she recognised him.

"Henry!" she exclaimed. "Thank God."

Henry spoke fervently at the same time, probably with similar sentiments. "Are you well? Unhurt?" he demanded.

"Yes, I'm fine, but I need to get to William. The MacHeths did not abduct me. On the contrary, they looked after me, and now I'm here, there's no reason to fight them. They have more men than us, and I need to go home."

It seemed perfectly plain to Christian. But Henry's lips parted in a baffled way that seemed to imply he wasn't quite sure how to tell her she was talking nonsense.

"Henry, I need to speak with him. Let go of the bridle."

"You can't go up there," Henry said. "The MacHeths could attack at any moment, and you'd be caught in the middle of God knows what violence."

"But there's no *need* for any violence! Here I am, alive and well. We are, in fact, beholden to the MacHeths for my safety! William needs to know."

"I agree," Henry said, harassed, wiping one arm across his face. "But you can't be the one to tell him. I'll send a messenger back to him, and you must get as far away from here as possible."

"If there's no battle, there's no danger," Christian pointed out.

"That is not up to you or me."

"Of course it is. Send your man to him now. I'll ride on to Tirebeck, if you'd just point me in the right direction."

Henry had actually released the bridle before the impossibility of that appeared to hit him. "But you can't go alone!"

"Then give me one man," Christian said. She had no fear she was depleting William's force. There should be no battle now. "You'll probably catch up with us, but I want to be back in Tirebeck as soon as possible."

****

Lanson blinked at the soldier. "What?"

"We ran into the lady Christian," the man repeated stolidly. "In the valley. She wants you to know she's well and unhurt, says it was the MacHeths who rescued her and were kind to her and that you have no cause to fight with them."

Lanson emitted a sharp bark of laughter. No one could deny the girl had spirit. "Where the devil is she now? With Henry?"

"No, sir. Henry sent her on with Gaston as escort. She's heading for Tirebeck."

Then she was clear of the battle. He wondered if she'd waited with Henry, would it have made any difference? No, because he planned to finish this quickly and neatly, march on the enemy lair, and take it. Holding it might be a problem, of course, but surely if he killed both the MacHeth brothers, opposition would dwindle with no focus, and the king would send him reinforcements along with his earl's belt...

"Go back to Henry and tell him the plan stands."

The words were barely out of his mouth when the first men began to slip over the brow of the smaller hill below. They came with peculiar silence, watching the armoured knights at the top of the higher hill with interest but no surprise.

From all sides of the lower hill, men swarmed and swelled the opposing numbers. It was a sizeable fighting force. But if he hadn't come so close to their lair, Lanson doubted he'd have drawn them out. Tirebeck was not enough to feed his men, let alone pay them. He needed this. And he'd have it.

But he wasn't stupid. Before he attacked, he needed to see not one but both sons of Malcolm MacHeth.

Yes, there they were. No divided forces today. The brothers pushed their way through the throng, easily distinguishable by their height and poise if not by their rich cloaks. Their heads were uncovered—fearlessness or bravado, Lanson didn't know which. But the men they passed began to stamp and beat daggers and swords against their shields in a rhythmic, swelling wall of noise that rose higher and higher until even William de Lanson's flesh crawled.

"Savages," he uttered, and, pushing down the visor of his helmet, he addressed the men on either side of him. "You know your tasks." He raised his voice and his sword. "For Scotland and the king!" he yelled. "Charge!"

Downhill cavalry charges were probably the most exhilarating experiences of Lanson's life. The sheer speed, the thundering of hooves in his ears, the rushing air against his visor, and the irresistible force with which he fell on his enemies were impossible to replicate. In this case, of course, discipline was essential so that his momentum didn't carry him or his men over the other side of the lesser hill. There wasn't a great deal of space to fight in. Many of the enemy, he knew, would flee in sheer terror from their first contact with a cavalry charge. Henry's men, pouring in from the right, would hem in the rest, and Lanson anticipated a complete rout.

He pointed his mount's nose towards the figure of, he was sure, Adam MacHeth. But if he didn't get to him, someone else would. The man who'd dared to lay hands on his wife—twice, whatever conciliatory messages her ridiculously kind heart compelled her to send to him—would pay in full, and very, very soon.

Even before he reached the bottom of the hill, the Ross men were drawing back, away from the charge, as if in awe, spilling out to the sides of the hill. And then the horse beneath Lanson leapt for flat ground at last and he spurred the beast to push him on.

But something was wrong. Mud spattered up his boots and thighs, landing even on his helmet, and the horse's speed slowed with terrifying abruptness to a mere stagger, the ground under its hooves not just spongy but soft. Horribly soft.

The rain rolls down from the hill above and settles here, he thought numbly. *It doesn't drain, or perhaps there's even an underground stream making it worse. We're in a bog.*

The nightmare of a mounted knight...and he'd no one to blame but himself. He hadn't checked the land, making a schoolboy error of judgment that could well lose him the day.

"Dismount!" he yelled. "Fight on foot! Kill me the MacHeths!"

His horse went down under him; rough hands pulled at him, and he found himself staring into the grim face of Donald MacHeth.

"To the death," Donald said. "Yours or mine."

****

Henry swore, long and grimly. They'd been led into a trap.

He'd expected to emerge from the glen to see his comrades pushing the enemy over the side of the hill with great slaughter, not floundering like clumsy infants, waiting to be picked off by the sure-footed Ross men. At least Lanson himself could still end it. Henry picked him out at once in the melee, and he was clearly fighting one of the MacHeths.

"Take off your armour," Henry commanded, already struggling out of his. "Keep only helmets and breastplates. Idiots!" he added in a yell through the swell of protest. "Can you not see your own comrades being cut down like wheat because they can't move? It's marshland, and if you want to survive this, let alone defeat the enemy, you'll do as you're bid."

He dropped the heavy armour to the ground and replaced only his helmet and breastplate. His men were silently following suit. Henry turned back to the battlefield and knew they were too late to make a difference. Unless Lanson managed to kill the MacHeths. The men had orders to that effect. Henry hadn't cared for such orders at the time, but right now, they seemed their only hope.

"Ready?" he demanded impatiently. "Advance!"

But as they emerged over the shallow brow of the hill, a ring of men suddenly closed in, blocking the battle from Henry's view. He found himself staring at someone he knew all too well and would have recognised now under any amount of grime.

"Sorry," Adam MacHeth said, sparing a glance back toward the battle. He held a bloody sword in one hand, a gory dagger in the other. "There's no room."

How the hell had he seen them? His attention should have been fully engaged in the battle. It was as if he *knew* they were coming… The stories about him were true. Henry had to suppress a shiver, but he knew his duty.

"No room? Then we'll make some," Henry said and continued his advance, his men close at his back.

Adam glanced over his shoulder again, then back to Henry. "Yield and you'll live," he said conversationally. His dark eyes, his whole face, seemed distracted, which told Henry all he needed.

"No chance," Henry said clearly and raised his sword.

Adam's dagger hand jerked. Something struck Henry hard at the joint of his thigh, and he could no longer stand. He fell like a baby. Only then did he realise Adam's dagger hand was empty. The dagger itself was in his thigh. Pain began to surge.

He lashed out with his own sword, more in desperation than hope. Someone swore, so he must have cut something before it was wrenched from his hands.

"Yield," Adam said briefly.

The men yielded. Lanson didn't pay them enough.

He doesn't pay me enough.

****

Up until the moment Donald challenged Lanson, everything had been going pretty much as Adam had planned. By judicious revealing of the men's movements, they'd drawn the foreign army to the plateau above the marshy area. Weighed down by horses and armour that sank them deeper into the bog with every step, every stagger, the foreigners not only lost their advantage, they became easy targets.

There were other hills, other traps that would have worked

as well, but the hill marsh had been Adam's preference. It made the battle familiar because this was where he'd seen it in a dream.

However, he wished he'd paid more attention to that dream. He couldn't remember from which side the others would attack, and fresh new arrivals could still turn the tide back in Lanson's favour.

He became aware of the duel between his brother and Lanson at the same time as Findlaech yelled, "South!" above the din of battle. Meaning that Lanson's missing men were arriving from the little glen to the south—which was how Adam would have arranged it.

He had no choice but to cut these men off before they could damage his own. Since it was Henry who led them, he didn't kill him. He supposed Henry would see it as a mean trick, but Adam wasn't playing games. He needed this done quickly so he could get to Lanson.

Leaving his men to disarm Henry's, he ran back to the main fray, pushing and hacking his way through the unsteady fighting to where Donald had engaged Lanson. They were no longer there. A scattering of armour, half-ground into the marsh, showed where someone had discarded his disadvantage.

Fear twisted Adam's heart. Lanson was a formidable fighter and he'd be as determined as the MacHeths to kill his enemy's leaders. If he'd killed Donald...

All the old anxieties of childhood rushed upon him. His sword came up, apparently of its own volition, to parry an attack. Adam forced the man back and cut him down. He was no longer that terrified child. He was a man with responsibilities and a task to complete. Worrying about Donald would not save his brother.

As if a mist cleared before his eyes, he suddenly saw Donald again, struggling over a fallen soldier and round a terrified, struggling horse, to reach...Lanson, who was wielding his sword with fury against several men of Ross who had difficulty getting near him. Lanson could see Donald coming back for him and waited for him with grim impatience.

Only, according to Adam's plan, it *couldn't* be Donald. Christian wouldn't forgive him. And Lanson would be just as happy with Adam.

It was like one of those dreams where whatever your efforts, you just couldn't reach your goal. Adam pushed grimly through the fighting, screaming men, hacking and cutting his way towards Lanson with maddening slowness, eventually reaching him at almost the same time as Donald.

"I'll do it," Adam yelled at Donald, buffeting Lanson to send him staggering backward. Adam stood between his brother and Lanson. "Round the rest up, make them stop."

Donald scowled under the mud and blood. "Adam—"

"It's me," Adam said, parrying Lanson's furious attack. "Please." He didn't really know what he was saying. His mind was all now on defeating his enemy. A hated enemy who'd done so much to hurt his people. To hurt Cairistiona.

Lanson was strong, with more power in his right arm than Adam had expected, even after fighting so long.

"You're an imbecile," Lanson ground out, driving him back. "Your time is up. Your father will die. Your family will all die, by my hand or another's. It makes no difference. Even if you kill me, the king's men will come."

"Not," Adam said, lashing his sword into Lanson's side and going on the attack through his opponent's astonished yell of pain, "if the king doesn't know you're dead."

Even through his agony, Lanson's eyes widened. Parrying Adam's attack, he held his own. "You'd murder me? Bury my body in a dark corner and hide?"

"Is this murder?" Adam wondered. "You're on our land."

"You have no land!" Lanson snarled, sweeping his sword inward in an attack clearly meant to cut off Adam's left arm at the elbow. "You're nothing but outlaws."

"We have land," Adam said, forcing up Lanson's sword before it could do more than break the skin. Blood ran down his forearm to his wrist. "And we're taking yours back," he added, to rile him.

Lanson laughed. "You can't hold my land. You can't even hold my wife, who is even now on her way home."

It was like a blow in the stomach, and it allowed Lanson another hit, a low cut to his thigh which could, he knew, bleed like a stuck pig.

It didn't matter, he reminded himself. When this was done, they'd find her again. Donald would take her home to Tirebeck as planned. What harm could come to her in daylight while all the ruffians in the area were beating each other's brains in on this marshy hill?

"Your wife is a loyal lady," he said, panting now with the effort as he forced Lanson back with a series of sword clashes. He wished he hadn't left his dagger in Henry's leg. "You don't deserve her."

Lanson laughed, an exhausted, laboured sound. "So what are you going to do about it, fool?" He bent suddenly and charged at Adam with a roar. His head thudded into Adam's stomach.

Adam went down under him, still clutching his sword. Lanson pushed himself up, straddling Adam's hips.

Adam said, "I'm going to marry her and give her children, heirs to my father."

Lanson, sword raised for the kill, paused and stared into his eyes, wondering, perhaps, where the words came from. Adam couldn't blame him for that. Even he wasn't sure whether he was taunting or prophesying. Taunting, surely, for it was Donald who would marry her. And yet the mists were falling over his eyes, inconvenient as ever, superimposing confused dream images over the reality of the present, which was Lanson about to kill him.

He struggled to see Lanson's face, Lanson's sword, for the other battles raging across his vision. Almost worse was the little voice in his ear wondering what it would be like if he did marry her, if he took the dreams of her as his own and made her his and not Donald's. Desire, even love, had nothing to do with marriage arrangements. He'd kept her for Donald, but Donald would never have her if he gave in to the dream and let Lanson kill him.

He flexed his fingers, grasping the hilt of his sword tighter, peering desperately through the swirling images which only grew stronger. He couldn't even see Lanson's sword anymore for the face that stood out in his dream. Lanson's face.

Someone was roaring. Dream or reality, he neither knew nor cared. With a mighty effort, he threw himself forward, sweeping up his sword in a powerful arc across the throat of his dream attacker. Something spattered on his face. The weight on his hips shifted and the mists cleared to show him his own bloodstained legs. Across one lay the headless corpse of William de Lanson.

Adam stopped roaring.

Someone, Findlaech, stood in front of him, holding up Lanson's head, yelling out the victory. Then Donald was there, grinning, pulling him to his feet.

"Overdramatic but well done. Did you have to give us such a fright first?"

"Apparently," Adam managed. "Is it over?"

"It's over."

Adam dragged his bloody left hand across his face. "She left the hall. She got to Lanson, tried to stop the battle, and now she's on her way to Tirebeck. You have to find her."

Donald glanced around him, then grasped Adam's shoulder as he began to walk off in the direction of the horses. "Adam. *You* have to find her."

Adam stared back at him, struggling to put the images and the feelings into words. "She's...important."

"I know," Donald said, too gently. He wasn't understanding.

"To the family," Adam said urgently. "To the people. To happiness. Her birth makes her yours."

Donald pushed at his shoulder, giving him a shake that hurt his wounded arm but kept his attention. "Adam. Forget your calculations for once. She was always for *you*. She's your obsession. Everyone can see that. And besides, much as I love you, and much as I admire your spirited lady, you don't get to choose my marriage alliances. I'll wait for our father's release."

Adam felt his breath catch. The visions were never written in stone. They were of possible futures, sometimes even of possible pasts that had never happened. In recent years, he'd imagined he could tell the difference, which was why he followed his head in this matter and worked towards Cairistiona's marriage to Donald, their father's heir.

But his head had never been clear around Cairistiona. Part of him was afraid of that, of being lost in her. Had there not been just a hint of relief amidst the pain in his heart when he'd decided Donald should be her husband?

It needn't be that way. He, Adam, could try for that happiness. As it had been in the dreams, which just maybe he shouldn't have discounted... He closed his eyes. He wanted this too much and wasn't even sure why.

"Find her," Donald said, releasing his shoulder at last. "I'll take the news home."

Adam dragged his eyes open again. "I killed him so she

wouldn't blame you."

"I know. To a woman like her, it's an obstacle, but not insurmountable. For you."

Adam let out a long, shuddering breath. With it, a deluge of tensions and anxieties seemed to break.

"Send Findlaech with the prisoners who're able," he said and walked away, whistling for his horse. His thigh hurt, making it hard not to limp, but his head at last was clear.

****

Christian heard the noise of the battle with despair. The MacHeths had been right. She couldn't halt this. When men truly wanted to kill each other, no one could stop it. Her stupid fantasy of building peace and understanding between the MacHeths and the king through her presence was revealed as just that. Naive, stupid, tragic.

She halted the pony and gazed around her. She couldn't see the fight, but she could still hear the screams and the clash of steel.

Gaston, the man Henry had sent with her, had stopped too. He said, "Sir William never fights unless he can win."

It was true. William was a mercenary to the core. However badly outnumbered his troops here, he could still win from the right position. A handful of mounted, armoured knights could still annihilate a much larger force of infantry. They just rode them down and slaughtered them. None of this made Christian feel better. For anyone.

Adam MacHeth's vital face with its unfocused, unworldly eyes swam into her mind. She couldn't bear him to die, couldn't bear him to win. Involuntarily, she clutched one arm across her stomach as if she could keep in the pain. But she'd no more control over that than she had over who would live and who would die today.

She should be with her own people. She couldn't imagine what this battle would mean for them. If William won, even if he killed the sons of Malcolm MacHeth, would he not face a thousand insurrections inspired by their mother, Malcolm's wife? William had never met the lady of Ross. He couldn't know her strength, her sheer implacability…

If the MacHeths won… Either way, she needed to give her people whatever protection she could. Whether they were natives or Normans, she had to care for them. Somehow. And yet the battle noise held her still, eyes closed, until it began to die away.

Christian opened her eyes. Into the growing silence came another roar, single voiced but blood curdling with fury and determination, almost inhuman. Christian's spine tingled with primeval fear. Then that noise stopped too, and the incongruous sounds of cheering echoed through the hills.

The battle was over and won. God knew by whom. Or who was left alive. Shivering uncontrollably, she urged the horse on after Gaston, whose frequent glances in the direction of the battleground told her where he would rather be. Perhaps where she *should* be. But she could do no good to anyone in the vicinity of victorious soldiers. Ranulf had made sure she understood that from an early age. Men still in blood lust were too dangerous to go near.

She hadn't gone far before the sound of horses' hooves penetrated her daze of anxiety. Because of the surrounding hills, she had difficulty gauging their direction, but she was glad of the covering forest just ahead.

"Hurry, lady," Gaston said grimly. "There is more than one horse, and I've no idea if they're ours or theirs."

"They must be ours. Henry knows which direction we took." All the same, she'd no intention of stopping until she was sure.

When they came to the thick cluster of trees, they paused. Soft hooves in the distance, probably skirting the wood. Another set, closer, but not yet close enough to worry her. And then, closer yet, a rustling… Were those hooves? Human feet? On the soft forest floor, it was hard to tell.

Gaston put his finger to his lips, and gestured with his hand for her to stay put. Then he drew his sword slowly and carefully to be as silent as possible, and urged his horse quietly in the direction of the rustling.

Christian waited, soothing her restive mount, counting the seconds. A clash of steel broke the silence, followed by a smothered cry.

More death…? Her stomach twisting, Christian urged her horse forward two paces and peered through the tree branches. A glimpse of grey and rust resolved slowly into a familiar grey horse and, surely, the battle-stained figure of Adam MacHeth.

Her heart thundered in her ears. She had to press her fingers to her throat to suppress the feelings trying to jump out through the hammering pulse there. Adam lived.

Adam lived!

What did it mean? Was he hunting William? Escaping the battle?

She couldn't wait to find out. And there was no time now for stealth. She ducked her head to avoid the low branches, yanked the reins to the right and kicked her horse into an instant gallop.

The animal bolted through the trees, swerving right and left to avoid obstacles Christian didn't even see. She let out a sob of relief when they broke free of the wood and saw no one. They bolted on through some flat land. But the beat of hooves wasn't far behind her. Adam or one of the others was pursuing. She felt at her girdle for the stone she'd picked up earlier. It was her only weapon, and she couldn't waste it.

She glanced over her shoulder, caught a glimpse of grey horse, and kicked the pony harder. Impossible to outride him, but she wouldn't make him suspicious by giving up too early. There was nothing she could do to prevent his catching her.

In the end, he catapulted beyond her and wheeled his horse around in a flurry of hooves and whinnies to block her path. She yanked on the reins to turn the little horse, but Adam simply leaned forward and seized the bridle.

Breathing hard, she lifted her gaze from his bloody hand over his muddied and bloodstained clothes to his equally bloody face. There was no way of telling whose blood it was, or what mixture. The recent violence stood out in his eyes like a vicious storm.

Life is a circle. This is where I came in.

He said, "William de Lanson is dead. I killed him."

It wasn't a boast. Or a confession. Just a simple statement of fact that tumbled hopes she had refused to harbour into the bloody mud of reality. She couldn't help it. She swept her hand from inside the cloak and hurled the stone at Adam MacHeth.

His head jerked, whether from the blow or an attempt to avoid it, she couldn't tell. She dug her heels into the horse, hauling at the reins, but the animal only snorted and stayed where it was. It had to. Adam still held it. Blood oozed from a cut in his forehead, trickling down his cheek amid all the rest. Some of the rest was probably William's.

"Give me the reins," he said steadily.

She stared at him wordlessly until he simply took the reins from her stiff fingers and led the horse forward.

Through rigid lips, she said, "Where are we going?"

"Home," said Adam MacHeth.

CHAPTER TWENTY

She refused to ask, maintained a stony silence for the whole journey, even when Findlaech and most of the men she remembered from her original abduction caught up with them, and she saw Henry and several other wounded men in their train, including Gaston. They must have found him in the wood. Some kind of parole must have been exchanged, for although some were on leading reins—probably because the rider was too injured to control the horse—the prisoners were not tied.

Relief to see those faces, at least, warred with grief that so many on both sides would never be seen again. Henry's shame and clear grief for her stood out in his open face, and she had to look away.

William was dead. She'd no idea how she felt about that. She just knew it was the worst of all possible outcomes that Adam of all people had killed him.

Her throat constricted, but she would not weep.

Not until the familiar view of Tirebeck Hill told her where "home" meant today. With the salty tang of the sea in her nostrils, in the taste of the fine misty rain now wetting her face and lips, she saw the people running inward from the fields and hills; and her silent tears escaped at last, mingling with the damp of the rain.

A few soldiers around the stockade watched their progress with drawn bows. Without a word from Adam, Christian pushed back the hood of her cloak to make sure they knew who rode beside Adam MacHeth at the head of the men of Ross. The

Norman prisoners rode among the rest, making clear aim at an obvious enemy impossible.

The gates to the hall enclosure were closed, as they had been since William had first come. For the first time, Adam released her reins and surged towards the gate, drawing his sword. Even now, Christian's heart seemed to fly into her mouth. At least he must have cleaned the blood of her husband off its blade, which glinted clear and pure in the rain. And he did nothing worse with it than bang on the wooden gate with the hilt.

"Open!" he yelled. "For the lady of Tirebeck!"

From inside, someone snarled in French, "Keep back!" Then feet scuffled on the ground. A few dull thuds and muffled groans followed. Beside Christian, Findlaech actually grinned. Adam didn't move or turn.

Then the gates opened, revealing Loegaire and Sigurd pushing them wide. They were grinning too. A Norman soldier sat on the ground, clutching his bare head and groaning.

"Welcome," Loegaire said with such obvious relief that Christian's stomach twisted to realise how awful his serving of her husband had been for him.

Adam didn't speak, merely tugged on the reins, drawing his horse aside for Christian to precede him. There was nothing else to do. The past was done and the future not yet written. But these were *her* people. Drawing the reins into her grasp, she rode slowly forward, past Adam MacHeth and through the gates.

Just for a moment, she thought that was it. That he'd returned her and was leaving, and relief rushed through her blood. She couldn't deal with this, with *him*, right now. She just wanted to be home. And alone.

But no one closed the gates behind her. Hooves clopped in after her, and although a groom hurried to meet her horse and Eua was running out of the hall door, it was Adam MacHeth who lifted her from the animal's back, who held her up when sharp pain from riding so long without a saddle shot through her body. He held her arm firmly on his. Eua pulled up short, standing aside to let them enter the hall together.

"Welcome home, lady," Eua breathed as she passed.

She managed to nod, her gaze flickering over the other woman, assessing, before she looked forward into the gloomier environs of the hall. Alys, Cecily, and Felicia sat in a huddle on the bench beside the big table.

Outside, a cry rang out and an order to yield given in Gaelic and French. Findlaech, she thought in a detached sort of a way. But William hadn't left enough men here to put up a fight, not once the heart had gone out of them by seeing Henry and the others already in captivity. And they would know William was dead. They were mercenaries, and it was time to find a new paymaster.

The women stood up. They looked petrified. Felicia took a step forward. "My lady?" she uttered, her voice husky with fright.

It was a question she couldn't formulate, and Christian, who'd done nothing to win her affection or loyalty, was grateful for it. She nodded in what she hoped was reassurance and halted. Her place right now was with her women.

But Adam drew her on, insisting when she tried to draw back, holding his other hand over hers to restrain her without either hurt or indiscretion. Christian chose not to throw a childish tantrum but to obey.

A mistake, surely a mistake, for he walked on without pause towards the bedchamber at the back of the hall. William's bedchamber.

A tiny sound escaped her lips, which made him glance at her, but didn't stop him. He threw open the bedchamber door, tugged her inside, and kicked it shut behind him. Only then did he release her, so abruptly that she stumbled.

"You are the lady of this hall," he said. "You sleep here."

"If I'm the lady of the hall, I may sleep where I wish," she retorted.

"You sleep with your husband."

"My husband is dead," she said harshly. "You killed him."

"And his hall is now mine," Adam said, throwing open a chest and beginning to drop things into it—William's comb, a perfume bottle that must have been Alys's, a shawl, a necklace, a shirt. "As is his wife."

"*What?*" She stared at him as he finished his tour of the room, pulling the trunk after him and hurling everything he found inside it, apart from a purse, which he tossed to her. She caught it from instinct and wished she'd let it fall at her feet.

That done, he turned his attention to the bed, pulling off the linen.

"Are you *actually* mad?" Christian demanded. "Or criminally deluded? You killed my husband a matter of hours ago. Were it twenty years ago, I would not marry you!"

"It's quite accepted practice," he assured her, "to marry the widow of your victim. That way, you keep control of any heirs, born or unborn."

"I have no heirs," she snapped. "You're excused."

Somewhere, some part of her was horrified that he'd turned this so suddenly and easily into banter, that she'd joined in without even noticing. Only as the faint, fugitive half smile flickered across his lips did she realise, and bit her lip with shame.

He dropped the under sheet on top of its fellow on the floor and raised his eyes to hers. "Then the heirs will be all mine."

Her mouth opened, but no words came, so she closed it again. It didn't matter, for she'd lost his attention again anyway. He strode to the door, opening it and calling for Eua and Sigurd.

Eua hurried first into the room, her wide eyes flickering warily between Adam and Christian.

Adam pointed at the linen. "Can you arrange fresh linen? The lady will sleep here from now on."

"Good," Eua managed. She fixed Christian with her eyes. "That's good."

"Sigurd, take the chest away, will you? Give the woman Alys whatever from it is hers and leave the chest in some corner of the hall. Have Findlaech divide up the rest."

Eua hurried out of the chamber with the linen and Sigurd followed, lugging the chest.

Christian stared at him. "*Who* is the lady of Tirebeck?"

Again, the smile flickered on his lips but didn't touch his eyes. "Those were my last domestic orders."

With a shuddering breath, Christian pulled herself together. "Good," she said, walking to the door. "Because I have wounded to see to and dinner to arrange."

****

She didn't see Adam again before dinner. By then, she had attended to all the wounds she was allowed to see and had treated the soldiers of Ross and those of the king, who lined up in the hall without discrimination.

223

Henry's wound was not in the most dangerous part of his thigh. Though debilitating while it healed, heal it would.

"There," she said when she'd bandaged him and covered his modesty with a blanket. "I hope that makes you more comfortable."

"Thank you, lady," he said meekly. "I'm so sorry for this…grief that's come to you."

Grief. Surely he didn't mean William? Henry of all people knew how things had stood between them. And yet William and she had been companions of a sort for almost four years. No part of her life had excluded his presence, even if only to acknowledge his absence or the consideration of his reaction. That was loss, of a sort. Perhaps that was why she felt groundless, rudderless. In her more honest moments, she'd liked to imagine a life apart from William, to go where she wanted to go, do what she wished. Coming home to Tirebeck had been a compromise of that fantasy, one in which she'd hoped to live apart and yet in partnership. It might even have happened in time.

Well, now they were irrevocably apart. And it seemed she was to have no time to enjoy her freedom. From one loveless marriage to another. Dear God, Adam had *killed* William! Despite ancient customs of war, could he really not see what a sin it would be for her to marry him?

Henry said hoarsely, "I'm sorry I failed you."

"You failed no one," she said firmly. "You must get well now, and then we'll decide what's best to do. It's a new future for all of us."

She rose quickly, summoning Felicia. "Cheer him up," she begged, and, her duty done, she walked out of the hall, still carrying her medicine box, and went to her own little house, her grandmother's house.

The chest containing her clothes had gone, as had her book of psalms and her few other personal items. She doubted they'd been stolen. So, he'd completed her move to the main hall. She felt too tired to fight about it. In any case, hadn't she realised yesterday that she should never have left the chief bedchamber to William and Alys? She'd looked to her own privacy, her own comfort before what was seemly. If she truly wanted to be lady here, she had to care.

She set her hand on the door latch and paused, flooded

suddenly with the memory of Adam's embrace in this precise spot. Out of his mind on poppy and pain and fever.

She couldn't think of that now. It made what was to follow unbearable.

She walked out of the house and closed the door behind her. As she returned to the hall, she noticed Findlaech crouched against the wall of one of the outhouses, his shirt dragged halfway down his arm while he tried to peer at the back of his left shoulder. So absorbed was he in contemplation of whatever he found there that he seemed unaware of her approach. He winced.

Christian set down her box at his feet. "You had better let me see."

Findlaech jumped to his feet. "Bless you, lady, it's no more than a scratch," he said hastily, dragging his shirt back up. It was caked in blood.

"Indulge me. I like to be useful, and I would rather you didn't die in my house."

Findlaech's frown deepened as if he was about to argue. Then his face relaxed into a crooked smile. "To be honest, my lady, I thought it was a scratch. I don't even remember it happening. Only now it hurts like—well, it hurts." He turned his back to her and dragged down his shirt once more, revealing an ugly sword cut. At least most of the blood had dried.

"I think you should sit down again so I can reach you more easily," she said calmly, and called to one of the MacHeth men lounging in the yard to bring her some fresh water from the well. It was only after the water arrived at her side with impressive speed that she realised she hadn't even been sure he'd obey her. She wondered if Findlaech had glared at him over her head while she opened her box in the light of the sinking sun.

He sat on the damp ground in silence, his head bowed while she washed and anointed his wound. Only when she faced him again to bind it did he raise his head and look at her and become aware, apparently for the first time, that she was kneeling on the ground in front of him.

"You'll have spoiled your gown."

Laughter surged up with so much force that she feared hysteria. She let it shake her for only a moment. "This gown has been through too much to care," she managed. "Besides, it will always look better than your tunic does now."

She saw his thin lips stretch in a smile as he watched her work with open curiosity. After a moment, he said abruptly, "Are you afraid of him?"

"Who?" she asked calmly. She knew, of course. There was only one "him" to Adam MacHeth's men.

"Adam mac Malcolm."

"Should I be?" she countered.

"No. But some people are." He stirred. "Some people should be, of course. You're not one of them."

She said nothing, concentrated on tying the ends of his bandage to keep it in place.

"He isn't mad," Findlaech said, "whatever anyone tells you. Strangers sometimes think he is because his manners are...different. And the lads like to exaggerate because battle madness is a traditional virtue among fighting men. But he's got a clearer mind than anyone I've ever met, including his mother."

"Despite the visions?" she said lightly, mostly to see Findlaech's reaction.

He didn't bat an eyelid. "Despite the visions. Or because of them. I don't know."

So, she should marry her husband's killer because he had a clear mind? Didn't that make it worse?

"Would it have been easier if I'd killed Sir William?" Findlaech asked, as if he read her mind. "Or if Donald mac Malcolm had done it? One way or another, in losing the battle, he was going to die. Between you and me, he was lucky to die in battle, for the man was a—"

"My husband," she interrupted. "Thank you. Look, it's getting cold out here. You should go into the hall. I'll help you."

But Findlaech refused her hand, rising on his own although he staggered slightly. "Lost a bit of blood," he explained with dignity.

"I know," she said gravely. For some reason, Findlaech seemed to wish her well, had tried to reassure her. He hadn't needed to do that. As they walked together towards the hall, she looked up at the sky, blue in the low sun with only a few drifting white clouds. "You know him well."

Forgetting his wound, Findlaech shrugged, then winced. "All his life. I was fourteen years old when Malcolm mac Aed was taken. I became a sort of foster father to his sons when my own father died. I taught them both to ride and fight and hunt. But I spent more time with Adam."

"And now you'd die for him."

Findlaech laughed. "I'd always have died for him, for his father, mother, brother. Dying's easy."

She blinked, pausing with her hand on the hall door. "Then what's difficult?"

Findlaech winked and pushed the door open for her. "Living with him. Fun, yes; exciting, mostly; but definitely not easy."

****

Every inch of Adam was aware of her at his side. Although the hall was lively and convivial with talk and laughter as they ate, he and Cairistiona barely spoke to each other. What could he say? *"Sorry I killed your husband. I did it so Donald wouldn't have to and you wouldn't feel obliged to hate him. Only then I decided to marry you myself."*

For one thing, he wasn't sorry he'd killed William de Lanson. For another, she needed time to come to terms with all that had happened in the last few days. Besides, his wounds were aching, distracting him from clarity, and he felt the importance of every word he said to her now. Best to hold his tongue, especially when his body reacted so. One brush of her clothed arm against his felt like any other woman's most intimate caress.

And so he joked with Findlaech and the men as they discussed the battle, and talked with Loegaire about the land. The Norman prisoners who could do so sat scattered among his own men, disarmed but otherwise unbound. He was aware of Cairistiona observing this as she picked at her food in silence.

She had changed into another gown. He'd seen her come into the hall with Findlaech while he talked to Loegaire and Eua. Without looking at him, she'd carried her medicine box into the bedchamber he'd forced upon her. Eua had seen that her things were already there, and when she'd emerged, she wore a clean mask and veil and a different gown. Like most of her clothes, it was respectable rather than beautiful. In fact, since she wore not the smallest ornament with it—even the mask was plain, unadorned linen—he suspected she was deliberately trying to look drab. Perhaps she was making the point that marriage to him was nothing to celebrate. Or perhaps she was trying to discourage him from the intention.

Because he truly wanted to, Adam turned his head and gazed at her. He would like to see her in bright colours one day—in crimson silk and rich greens and blues. He thought she would shine. But in truth, whatever she wore, the beauty of the half face she revealed moved him more than any other woman's more obvious charms. This, more than her birth, was the true reason he would marry her, but he'd no idea how to deal with her.

Without warning, she turned her gaze on him, frowning with curiosity. "Why are my husband's men sitting among yours? Are they not prisoners?"

It seemed a safe enough subject. "For the moment. Apart, they're less likely to conspire to cause us trouble. For one thing. For another, they're mercenaries and no one now is paying them to die. They have to decide what they want to do. What do you think of them?"

Surprise widened her eyes. He wanted to take off the mask to receive the full effect. She said, "They're good soldiers. William only ever employed good soldiers."

"Would you want them to stay?"

This time her lips parted too. Adam shifted in his chair.

"In what capacity?" she asked.

He shrugged. "We can give them land. They can farm it or remain soldiers without any other pay. Ross can always use good fighters."

She closed her lips. He watched their changing expressions with fascination. "You would turn them from the King of Scots?"

"They're mercenaries," he said. "They were never 'for' the King of Scots except insofar as Sir William was."

As if becoming aware of the direction of his gaze, she flushed, adding delicious colour to her pale beauty. He wanted to make her whole body flush.

She said in a rush. "Henry might stay. He's a good man."

"Put it to him, if you like. Ask them all to think about it. If they're interested, they can speak to me. But those who want to leave will have to wait. No one can go south just yet."

"Why not?"

"Because no one there knows that Sir William de Lanson no longer holds Tirebeck."

She stared at him. "You're relying on silence to hold off the king's army?"

"For long enough."

"Long enough for what?"

"My father's release."

"Have you ever thought beyond that unlikely eventuality?" she demanded.

"Of course." He could see she didn't believe it would ever happen. He didn't blame her. Kings had come and gone, an entire generation, his own and hers, had grown up while Malcolm mac Aed languished in prison. It had become a background to life, like the sky or the sea. But no one had ever forgotten him. From Orkney to Cumbria, everyone was aware of the prisoner of Roxburgh.

She seemed about to say something, but just then the hall door flew open and Cailean mac Gilleon strode in. The men raised a mocking cheer. "Well done, boy! You missed the best battle since the Isles!"

Cailean, clearly, was furious that things had moved on so quickly without him, but the men's good-natured raillery forced him to smile, however reluctantly, and he remembered his manners well enough to approach the high table and bow to Cairistiona.

"Lady, I rejoice to see you home and well," he managed before turning to Adam with recrimination clear in his face, in his whole stance.

Adam forestalled him. "Our friend went quietly?"

Cailean closed his mouth and swallowed. "Like a lamb in the end. We caught up with the men of Galloway who're all well away from Ross now."

"You did the harder job," Adam said. "And you must have ridden like a demon. Sit and eat."

"I have a message from the lady your mother," Cailean said awkwardly. "She bade me tell you and the lady Cairistiona that she will come tomorrow with priests."

Adam didn't look at Cairistiona. He didn't need to. Whatever fragile armistice had sprung up between them was broken by Cailean's words. She felt rigid and brittle at his side, like some delicate glass that would shatter if you touched it. Which was a problem, in the circumstances.

Not long after, she rose abruptly and said good night as if

she didn't expect to be attended to. Adam, aware since her first movement, stood with her. He wanted to take her hand and kiss it, give her some kind of reassurance or simple affection. But he didn't want the glass to break. This was too public. Instead, he managed to bow, or at least nod his head with respect.

Since it was easier than looking at her, he glanced towards her attendants, who sat together as they had before. Two of them were already on their feet. The third, Lanson's mistress, was staring morosely into her cup until one of the other women seized her by the arm and tugged.

The woman shook herself free, scowling, but at least she rose too and trailed after the others. It must have hurt to see Cairistiona enter the chamber she'd regarded as her own, but Adam spared her no sympathy.

Cairistiona dismissed them at the door, her gesture inviting them to return to their meal. She closed the door firmly behind her. On them, and on him.

No true friends among her women, then. She was alone.

He sat down slowly and poured some more wine into his cup. He wouldn't drink it. He just needed something to do while he adjusted to his next mask. Sitting back in his chair, he raised his cup to Cailean. "It's good to have you back. We missed you in the battle. Without his nurse, Findlaech got a sword in his shoulder."

And so he played his part until it all went on without him. The wounded lay down to sleep; the women and the children cleared off; the able-bodied men drank and told lies and laughed as they should, changing seats and positions the better to join particular conversations.

Which was, he supposed how Findlaech came to be sitting beside him as he stared silently into his swirling wine, keeping his back carefully to the bedchamber door.

Findlaech clinked cups with him. "To victory," he said.

Adam lifted his cup by way of agreement.

"Not drinking," Findlaech observed. "Saving your strength?"

Adam swore at him and reached for the jug, splashing more wine over what was still there.

"Ah. Waiting for the priests," Findlaech said wisely. "Might be best."

Adam looked at him. "There will never be a good time,

will there?"

Findlaech took a large draught from his cup and set it down between his hands. "To begin it? You killed her husband, so no. On the other hand, she hated him and she likes you, for some reason, so there is hope. Myself, I'd get the first over with and move on. But if you think the priest's important to her, wait until tomorrow. What difference will a day make?"

Adam let his lips curve as they wanted to. "What difference did today make?"

Findlaech inclined his head, lifted his cup once more. When Adam rose to his feet, Findlaech said nothing, didn't even look, but Adam was sure he smiled into Lanson's wine.

CHAPTER TWENTY-ONE

She lay in the big bed, tiny and unmoving. The lamp burned low, so perhaps she'd fallen asleep before she'd meant to. Or perhaps she wanted to know who was in her chamber, considering her hall beyond was full of strangers. And him.

Despite his body's raging disappointment, there was relief in her slumber. His wounds ached, and he needed privacy as she did. Besides, everyone had seen him come in here, even if they'd kept talking as if they didn't notice. All he had to do was lie beside her as he'd done before in the open, under the stars. He could pretend it was the same, and perhaps he'd sleep. He needed to sleep. Everything hurt.

By the lamp's glow, he took off his tunic and his shirt and inspected the deep cut across his elbow. It still bled sluggishly through the rough bandage he'd tied onto it in here earlier while Cairistiona tended the other wounded in the hall. He unwrapped it, walking to the washing bowl, and set about cleansing it once more. That done, he tended his other neglected wounds to the best of his ability. Most of his aches, he suspected, were bruises that just needed time to heal. The worst was the sword cut in his thigh, but the old arrow wound that Cairistiona had tended on his last visit looked angry again, as if annoyed by his exertions in battle.

As he began to rewrap the cloth around his thigh, a movement from across the chamber made him turn.

She sat up in the bed, wearing some pale garment that covered her breasts, shoulders, and arms to the elbow. Her hair was night dark, spilling in sleek, straight lines around her face and shoulders. He'd only seen glimpses of her hair before, except in the dreams, and now it fascinated him. She still wore the damned mask, though, even in bed. She'd known he'd come.

"Even Findlaech let me tend his injuries," she said. "And it would hardly be the first time for you."

He forced himself to stillness. "Are you waiting for permission?"

"No." She didn't leave the bed. "If I tend your wounds, will you go?"

He shook his head, holding her gaze steadily.

She bit her lip, as though undecided. Then she sighed. "You'd lose face going back out there after you'd come in."

"I suppose I would."

She lifted the blankets and rose from the bed. The pale garment covered her to her ankles, but at least her feet were bare. Small and slender, and her ankles were so tiny, he could circle them with his finger and thumb. He'd done so, once, waking from a dream the first time he'd captured her...

With quiet deliberation, she lifted the medicine box from the table and laid it on the bed.

"You'd better sit."

His heart was drumming so hard, he couldn't speak. There was something unutterably intimate about sitting on her bed, almost naked, while she bent over him, her hair brushing against his bare shoulder. It smelled of lavender and fresh heather.

"You could leave when it quietens down," she said, unwinding his bandage again. "When everyone's asleep."

"I could," he agreed. "But I won't. I'll stay until morning."

"When you'll be granted absolution by the priest and your mother?" she said bitterly. And yet her hands were gentle, laying aside the bandage, spreading her damned ointment.

He said, "I won't need absolution."

Her gaze flickered up to his eyes as if wondering what he meant by that. He wasn't sure himself; he was still feeling his way. He kept his gaze on her face as she worked, forcing the edges of his anointed wound together, binding it tightly. After which, she turned her attention to his more minor cuts and bruises. As she spread something across the large hurt on his back—he thought it was merely a bruise—her massaging fingers felt all too like those of a lover. He had to hold himself rigid and still, but it was hard to control his breathing. He had to resort to the tricks of his childhood when he'd had to cover his foolish fear of horses and his horror of fighting.

When she touched the old arrow scar, frowning, he could stand no more and seized her hand, drawing it away. "Enough, Cairistiona. I didn't come to be healed." Didn't he? There were more hurts than those inflicted with swords and arrows.

He tugged her hand, forcing her to sit on the bed beside him. It was unfair that she couldn't choose, but he knew she'd never say so; it was too obvious and too irrelevant.

Gazing at their joined hands, she said, "What if you're wrong? What if I'm not descended from Malcolm Canmore at all? You'll have a useless marriage."

"*Useless?*" He stared at her. "You have, I think, a very limited idea of the uses of marriage."

Giving her no time, he pushed her onto her back and leaned over her.

She jeered at him. "You forget. I've been used before."

He reached beneath her, drawing up the annoying garment, pulling it roughly over her head. The mask came with it, and for once, she made no attempt to retrieve it. Instead, she stared at him with defiance, and he saw that she imagined it was her secret weapon, her hidden dagger to repel him.

He stared back, only at her face, at the seamed, blotched scarring, drawing the skin of her cheek and the corner of her eye into unnatural positions. The scar pattern was intricate, interesting in its own right, but there was more, far more of her to see. Her breathing had quickened, her naked breasts rising and falling under him, spreading heat all the way through him.

He couldn't pretend her reaction was desire. He knew fear when he saw it, and it stood out now in Cairistiona's desperate eyes, even though she tried to hide it. But what appalled him more than the fear was the resignation. If she had to, she'd take this punishment as she'd taken William's in the early years. William had raped her.

Adam heard himself swear under his breath and swallowed the rest of his words. He was doubly glad he'd killed William, but he had no wish to frighten her further.

"Ugly, isn't it?" she mocked. "Well, I won't put the lamp

out for you. They're already bedding down in the hall. You'll be able to leave in a few minutes with your manhood unimpugned." She tried to turn away from him, perhaps to pretend to sleep, to curl into a protective ball since he'd stripped her of all her outer defences. Didn't she know those weren't the ones that mattered? Either way, he wouldn't let her.

He held her beneath him, cupping her face, and pressed his parted lips to the damaged skin of her face, kissing his way from her temple to her chin, and then across her mouth to the other side.

She stared at him in bafflement, but at least, realising he wasn't repulsed enough to leave her, she wasn't trying to escape him. Since she was still, he eased his weight off her so that he could finally gaze at her whole, naked body.

He swallowed. "Do you really not know you're beautiful?" It came out as little more than a husky whisper, but words had never been his strong point. He set about showing her, caressing her with slow hands and lips that he had to force to patience because they were too greedy and wanted all of her too quickly.

Touching her, stroking her with ever-increasing intimacy, he lost himself in worship of her body, in a lust more intense than any he could remember. He was no stranger to women. In them, he'd found pleasure, release, comfort, forgetfulness, whatever his need of the moment. But this with Cairistiona was somehow *new*, exciting, blissful, perhaps because it wasn't just her body he wanted. He wanted all of her, *beginning* with her beautiful, silken body…and he was falling far too deep to stop.

Well, perhaps if she begged him to stop, he still could, but as the bafflement in her brilliant eyes changed to confused wonder and her quickened heartbeat no longer felt like fear, he knew she wouldn't.

Slowly, achingly slowly, he trailed his fingers across her soft, warm skin and found the heat between her legs. Found her desire.

For the first time since he'd come into the room, he closed his eyes. He'd found his way. *Thank you, God.*

****

Nothing in Christian's experience had prepared her for

what Adam MacHeth was doing to her. She'd hoped to scare him off by her unsightly scars, but if that didn't work—and it hadn't—she knew she just had to grit her teeth and wait for it to stop.

But he didn't behave like William at all. He *kissed* her scars, kissed her everywhere until the hot, heavy lethargy she'd felt in his arms the night he'd escaped began to grow with more and more intensity. She began to realise this was nothing like her wedding night with William, though exactly what it meant, she had no idea. He didn't climb on her, force himself inside her.

Slowly, her clenched fists unfurled on the sheets. Although she couldn't give in to this, it was good not to hate it. Sweet, even. She held her hands flat on the bed, fighting her curiosity as to how his skin would feel under them. His fingers were rough in texture, and yet they touched her with such gentleness that she was astounded. This wasn't the brutish berserker she'd first met over the bodies of her guards; and yet he was still the man who'd deliberately killed her husband and would marry her for her supposed bloodline.

His wild, tangled hair brushed against her breast, its blackness sharp against her pale skin. It felt curiously soft, although there was little softness anywhere else on his body, not on the powerful arms which held her or the hard chest pressing against her shoulder as he looked down into her face and slid his hand between her thighs.

She gasped, jerking against his fingers in shock. His eyes closed. A smile flickered across his lips as his fingers stirred lethargically and pleasure surged through her, astonishing her more than anything that had gone before.

His eyes opened, blazing into hers. Her heart thundered as his free hand gathered hers and raised it high above her head on the pillow.

"Cairistiona, daughter of Rhuadri," he murmured. "I take you, forsaking all others." Was this a personal promise? Or the words of the ancient handfast that had married people long before the church had come, and still did where the church was too distant to reach.

He waited a moment, but she couldn't speak and didn't want to. That would be giving in...wouldn't it? She barely knew anymore, and in any case, it didn't matter. This had only ever been leading to one thing. She didn't even dread it, since his hand was almost there already and felt so…exciting.

And when he slid his thigh over both of hers and entered her body, there was no pain, only new, shocking fullness and insidious pleasure that deepened with his every move. Maybe because he kept caressing her with his hands, twisting down to kiss her breasts, it all seemed part of the lethargic heat he'd already aroused within her. And when it grew to impossible intensity and shattered astonished joy within her, she turned her face into the pillow to hide whatever it was. She knew instinctively this weakened her, made her vulnerable as nothing else in her life ever had.

But he wouldn't allow it. "Look at me," he whispered, cupping her face between his hands, forcing her to look into his hot, clouded eyes as the strange ecstasy took her. Still he moved above her, in her, trembling now, until he buried his groaning mouth in hers and spent inside her.

Only then did she realise her arms were around him, clutching his neck, his shoulder, maybe in some pointless effort to ground herself.

He lifted his head slowly, trying, she thought, to control his panting breath. She bore his full weight since his good elbow seemed to have collapsed, but he raised himself with unexpected consideration, dragged the blankets up and over them both before he flopped on his stomach beside her instead.

"I took you, Cairistiona," he whispered. "And you took me."

Then his eyelids flickered down, covering his dark, dark eyes, and just like that, with one powerful, naked arm still across her breasts, he fell asleep.

Christian gazed at him, actually brought up her hand and touched his wild hair. A smile rose up, spreading across her lips because it was soft after all. Then she remembered why he was here, why he wanted her, and let her hand fall back on the blanket.

Curiously, she felt those tears in her throat where they'd been lurking most of the day, but they no longer seemed all sad. Adam MacHeth had given her something. It wasn't love, but it wasn't all bad either. She could live with this. She could. Tomorrow, when she was rested, she'd work out how.

****

Gormflaith's memory of Tirebeck was hazy. She knew she'd been here as a child, with her mother, but apart from Tirebeck Hill and the smell of the sea, none of it seemed familiar, least of all Adam being married, and to *her*.

The gates stood open as they approached the hall. Gormflaith hoped Cairistiona would notice how the local people, farmers, fishermen, and their wives hung around to welcome them with smiles and gifts of flowers for her mother and herself. There was only one lady of Ross, and being Adam's wife didn't make her that.

The yard and outbuildings were tidy and well repaired, at least, and servants she didn't recognise, as well as soldiers she did, hurried to meet their horses. Tirebeck was small by Gormflaith's standards and unused to receiving so many distinguished visitors. Gormflaith's anxious eyes picked out her brother at once. He seemed to be discussing building matters, his waving hand moving from a pile of charred wood—presumably all that remained of the Frenchman's castle—to the far side of the enclosure, where he made a pushing gesture.

On the way, he caught sight of his arriving visitors and broke off, striding forward to meet them. At least he looked well, although his happiness was harder to gauge. Dark shadows under his eyes spoke of too little sleep, but she didn't want to think about the reasons for that.

He seemed pleased enough to see them, coming himself to help their mother to dismount.

"How is she?" the lady asked at once, searching Adam's face.

"Judge for yourself," Adam said evasively, standing aside so they could both see Cairistiona coming out of the hall to welcome them. Halfway there, she hesitated, as if wondering if she could make the lady come to her. But Adam held out his hand to her, and she came forward with her head tilted upward, as cold and proud as when Gormflaith had first seen her, and murmured the necessary words of greeting and welcome.

Surely Adam couldn't have bedded this lump of ice already? There was still hope to save him from this marriage.

To Gormflaith's annoyance, her mother closed the distance between them, embracing Cairistiona as if she really accepted this. Worse, she fixed Gormflaith with her sternest glance.

Sighing, Gormflaith went through the motions. Only, when she touched the woman's cold hand did she begin to suspect something deeper was wrong here. Cairistiona felt stiff in her embrace, her cheeks, her lips as cold as her hand. Then she felt the tiny shudder Cairistiona was trying to hide. Shaking. Behind the ice and the pride, the girl was hiding distress. Perhaps she always had been.

Gormflaith's hostility fell away like a discarded cloak. Cairistiona was no older than she and was expected to bury her husband and marry another on the same day. And not any other: her husband's killer. On top of which, to anyone who didn't understand, Adam could be a daunting, not to say terrifying, prospect. She could have sworn that on their last meeting, Cairistiona had shown anger towards Adam, but surely no fear. Because she'd imagined no intimacy then?

Impulsively, Gormflaith held on to her a moment too long so she could whisper in her ear, "It's all right. Everything will be all right."

Another shudder, which, as Gormflaith stepped back, she recognised as suppressed laughter. But it wasn't scornful.

Cairistiona's eyes held a kind of desperate humour. "Your mother said the same thing."

But the formal greetings weren't yet over. Donald bowed to her and kissed her hand and presented the Bishop of Ross and Father Patrick.

Cairistiona's head jerked to face Symeon with new desperation. Her stiffness was back, along with a flush of, surely, shame. A shame she expected Symeon to recognise and share. Cairistiona didn't want this marriage.

Gormflaith's suspicions were confirmed when she realised that even when they walked together, leading their guests into the hall, Cairistiona did not once look at Adam.

****

Adam kept his mind busy with practical problems, namely the building of a new structure within the stockade, which he planned to push outward to make more room. On occasions such as these, the hall was too small to accommodate both his own men and Donald's. A barracks would take care of the overspill, but it would mean enlarging the enclosure.

A new guesthouse might also be in order, although he had not yet had time to speak to Cairistiona about that. She had already made the arrangements for his mother and sister to sleep in her women's house while the women themselves would have to spend a cramped night in the house which had once been hers.

Such plans and calculations of the necessary wood occupied his mind while refreshments were brought to the travellers. Whatever else, Cairistiona ran her household well. And his mother seemed disposed to kindness. Which was a relief, because she'd seemed to like the idea of Cairistiona marrying Donald, although she'd insisted they wait until the earl himself expressed an opinion. There was, after all, still a Galloway marriage to arrange.

Through all these plans, Adam was aware his mother wished to speak to him alone. She made no obvious sign of it, but still he knew. He always had, and generally it was because he'd displeased her. He hoped to avoid this discussion until after the wedding or, preferably, altogether, although he knew his parent too well to hold out much hope for that particular outcome.

In the end, she stymied him by insisting he show her to her sleeping quarters, and then fondly bidding Gormflaith to keep her hostess company until she returned. Cairistiona gave an almost imperceptible, rueful little smile at that. She'd wanted time alone with Symeon, clearly, though whether to confess her sins or plead his help in avoiding the marriage, Adam was unsure.

He wished he'd stayed with her until she'd woken that morning. He wished he'd wakened her in the way he'd wanted so that she'd know...know what exactly, he wasn't sure. He was just aware that he'd woken at dawn curved around her warm, naked body and more than ready to make it his once more. Raising himself on his elbow, he'd gazed down on her sleeping face, and something had constricted his throat. Perhaps her beauty, maskless and open to his gaze. Her vulnerability, which he had shamelessly taken advantage of. And yet he'd brought her pleasure and wanted to again. Not while she slept. The next time, surely, she would come to him willingly. Most certainly not while she slept. She'd been through too much, and she needed to sleep.

And so, after a tense moment, he conquered his lust and

forced himself away from her soft warmth and onto the cold floor, where he hastily dressed and quietly left the chamber.

"Adam." He knew by the way his mother said it and the fact that she had hold of his face that it wasn't the first time she'd spoken to him.

"Sorry," he said, focusing on her. "I was thinking."

"Not dreaming?"

"Thinking," he repeated. In truth, despite the deluge of visions when he'd first encountered Cairistiona, he didn't seem to see much at all around her now, apart from an insistent image of intimacy that was more than half memory. The rest of his mind was fully taken up with the present.

Although his mother didn't release him, his attention would have been caught without her grip, because her eyes looked almost…frightened. He couldn't recall ever seeing her frightened before, except on that distant day when they'd told her his father was taken.

"Adam, did you hurt that girl?"

Adam was aware of the carelessness with which women were often regarded. Especially to soldiers, they could become mere commodities, like wine or gold, to be stolen or consumed. He and Donald, however, had been brought up by their mother, who had more than counteracted other influences until they were old enough to think for themselves. He was no saint, but he'd never taken an unwilling woman.

There were, of course, other hurts. She hadn't wanted to be willing.

Adam said, "I seduced her."

A moment longer, his mother searched his face. "Oh, Adam," she said softly. He wasn't sure what that meant, but at least she didn't appear to be angry. She gave his cheek a last caress and released him.

"It was Donald's idea that *I* marry her," Adam said. "And since we haven't consulted my father, this is probably best."

"Donald's idea. Yes." His mother nodded gravely, although he was fairly sure she was laughing at him. He didn't mind.

"I'll send the women," he said, turning away from her.

Without warning, the door in front of him tilted into another that obscured it. A woman, his mother, stepped over a quite different threshold. She was hazy. He couldn't tell if she was old or young, but he knew the shadowy figure beside her was his father.

When he blinked, the vision was gone. He glanced back over his shoulder in sudden curiosity. "Did you care for my father when you married him?"

She didn't answer. He knew she wouldn't. Instead, she said, "Be kind to Cairistiona, and she will be kind to you."

He went out, closing the door behind him. It wasn't Cairistiona's kindness he wanted.

CHAPTER TWENTY-TWO

She should have known that the lady of Ross wouldn't bring just any priest to marry her son. Christian had been prepared for the family chaplain, but somehow the bishop had never entered her head, and for some reason, the sight of his familiar, kindly, humorous face had almost undone her, and not because she was so overwhelmed by his dignity. Rather, his was a face she couldn't hide her own from.

By the time the lady dragged Adam away with her, Christian knew that Bishop Symeon was the only one who could advise or absolve her. Both. Either.

And yet somehow, she found herself alone not with him but with Gormflaith, in the bedchamber she'd so recently shared with Gormflaith's brother. While Cairistiona sat on the bed trying not to remember what had happened to her there, the other woman rifled the chest containing her clothes.

"You have nothing terribly...*festive*," Gormflaith complained.

"Well, I wasn't really planning a wedding."

Gormflaith gave her a clear look over her shoulder. "You know, I wasn't sure I liked you, or this marriage, but the more I think about it, the more I believe it is a good idea."

"I have the right blood. Maybe."

"There is that," Gormflaith allowed, "but you are...*right* for Adam as you aren't for Donald."

Christian blinked. Although she didn't want to, she asked anyway. "Why do you say that?"

Gormflaith shrugged, shaking out the embroidered green

overgown Christian had worn at court in Perth. "Oh, I don't know. He's always been different about you. Whenever he speaks of you. And you understand the nuances behind everything he says. Most people don't. I think this would do, don't you? What jewellery do you have?"

"None," Christian said vaguely. She'd sold what she had long since to pay William's soldiers in the lean times. In better times, it had never been replaced, although Alys had some pretty trinkets.

Gormflaith frowned over the problem. Then she jumped up. "Of course! My mother brought a wedding gift for you. We meant to give it after the wedding, but now would be best."

"No, please…"

But Gormflaith was already whisking out of the room, leaving Christian to rub her temples with distress. This wedding was becoming like a huge ball of snow, rolling downhill, so fast and growing so big that it was going to crush her. It was becoming impossible to resist.

Could she really do that? Just refuse to make her vow?

Oh yes. If she was brave enough. It would make no difference. Last night had proved that. She would be pronounced married anyway by the MacHeths' tame priest, whatever objections Bishop Symeon might have. But at least Symeon would know the truth. And the MacHeths would know. If they cared.

Adam knew what he'd done to her last night, and she was aware he'd taken time and trouble to do it. Ensuring compliance. But her urge to lash out was all the stronger because of it, because of her own weakness and hurt.

She'd woken this morning with his heat curved around her—hard limbs, hard body. As she'd lain there, she'd been conscious of wonder that he was still with her, and a peculiar comfort that had grown gradually heavy and aroused, just like last night.

When he'd moved, leaning over to look at her, she'd been sure, so sure, he would begin it again. She'd wanted him to do it again. But after a long, tense moment, when she'd kept her eyes defensively closed, he'd slid out of bed and gone.

She'd been wrong last night. She couldn't deal with this. He was…*solving* her, like any other problem.

And now Gormflaith was dressing her for a celebration,

giving her jewels, being kind as she never had been before. So, she was "right" for Adam? She begged to differ. Why did no one ever care what or who was right for her?

Because she was a woman.

Gormflaith herself seemed destined to be married to Fergus of Galloway's son. Would she accept that so willingly?

****

Even during the ceremony, she wouldn't look at him. She'd emerged from the bedchamber wearing a dark green gown heavily embroidered in gold and belted in close to disguise the fact that it was too big and too long for her. A gold disk inlaid with garnets and pearls hung from a heavy gold chain, adorning her pale breast, and the prettier mask was back on her face. A lighter chain with a garnet crescent hung from her veil over her forehead. His mother and Gormflaith had dressed her, and she wasn't happy about it. On the other hand, she did look beautiful and regal, enough to stir his blood just looking at her.

And at least he didn't feel ridiculous in the red silk tunic Donald had brought for him, and which he wore with a gold filigree brooch and the jewelled belt buckle his mother had given him when he'd left Ross to join Somerled.

Everyone, in fact, was dressed for celebration. Only the bride was not celebrating. Like last night, she held herself with rigidity, the delicate glass he'd imagined then, reinforced now with the lead of determination; her eyes were hard, her lips set. As if last night had never been. As if he'd made it worse by bringing her pleasure she'd clearly never known before.

It came to him that the best thing he could do for her was get this over with and leave. Only who would be the best person to stay with her to make sure she didn't send word to the King of Scots?

As earlier with his mother's arrival, he tried to fill his mind with things other than Cairistiona and the fact that she hadn't once looked at him since waking. He felt curiously unstable, and it wasn't until the marriage ceremony had already begun that he began to recognise the feeling.

It had only happened a few times before. Massive visions that went on and on. He'd lost consciousness altogether at least

245

once, and he'd never been able to keep his feet through that kind of vision. He needed to lie down. In the middle of his own wedding.

Inappropriate laughter caught at his breath. Symeon gave him a quick, worried glance but carried on. Symeon took their hands to join them but instead of this forcing the visions back as he'd hoped, they began to surge. Everyone was waiting for his response. He gripped Cairistiona's hand in a feeble effort to keep himself grounded in her, but it was her, her nearness, her touch in this particular situation that had set the dreams off. They were at a crossroads of futures, when their lives could go in so many directions...

"I will," he managed.

For the first time that day, Cairistiona glanced at him. Although he couldn't see her for the flashing images imposed on reality, he felt her head turn and then turn back again to face the bishop. Fearing his grip hurt her, he strove to loosen it, and her fingers curled around his, holding them.

Stunned, he almost let go, almost fell, but she was there beside him, closer now, gripping his hand. Her voice, soft, barely a breath, managed somehow to break through the cacophony in his head.

"Stay with me. Stay with me."

****

Perhaps it was her habit of caring for sick and injured soldiers, but the moment his hand clamped around hers, she caught the fear, the vulnerability emanating from him in waves. A quick glance at him and his blank, unfocused eyes told her he was sunk in dreams, perhaps dreadful ones. Perhaps he just didn't want to disgrace himself at his own wedding. Social fear, however trivial, was something she understood well enough. That moment accomplished what all the bishop's noble words had failed to. The event was no longer solely about her. And Adam, splendid as she'd never seen him in silk and gold, was holding on to her for strength.

Pure instinct caused her to grip his hand. "Stay," she breathed, "Stay with me." She didn't even think, until later, of the possible misconstruction of her words. She just meant stay in the here and now. Didn't she?

She said, "I will" mainly to get it over with. Adam wobbled on his feet, his arm pushing against her shoulder. Somehow, she stayed upright and so did he, but worryingly, each time she glanced at him, his eyes remained wild and unfocused. His breath came quick and short, though somehow he made his responses, and she even fumbled with his hand to help him place the ring of roped gold on her finger.

Dear God, what am I doing?

Perhaps deliberately, Symeon cut his words as far as possible. When it came to the embrace, Adam barely touched her mouth, his cold lips mumbling something that sounded like "Lie down."

His family knew. She saw it in the lady's eyes, in Gormflaith's and Donald's, in their tense posture. She looked no further, just exchanged one glance with the lady of Ross, who embraced them both and pushed them towards the bedchamber before turning to bid everyone sit for the wedding feast.

The fact that their hands and arms were still entwined as they covered the short distance to the bedchamber probably looked more amorous than anything else. She understood his need, his family's need, to hide his weakness.

She opened the door, pulling him inside and kicking it shut much as he'd done yesterday, and stumbled with him to the bed. He fell with relief but still didn't let go of her hand, and she all but fell with him, leaning over him in worry.

"Adam, what is it?" she whispered urgently. "What do I do to help?"

He dragged their joined hands to his cheek, and after a few moments, his eyes closed.

With her free hand, she felt for the pulse at his throat—galloping and warm—and touched his shoulder, his cheek. "Adam."

"You didn't let me fall," he said hoarsely. His eyes opened, clear and brilliant, focusing entirely on her. "You kept me here."

"Were you dreaming? Was it awful?"

He cupped her cheek with his free hand, staring up at her. "God, no, it was beautiful. Mostly. It just wouldn't stop. Images, sounds, fly through me so fast I can barely see them, but you were there—all the yous that have been and will be and might be according to what we choose now. I choose *you*, Cairistiona. I

247

always did. Not for your blood or your land or your husband's Norman soldiers. For you. And you chose me."

She swallowed, gazing down at him as she acknowledged the truth.

"What does it mean?" she whispered.

"That we have something rare and good." Without releasing her gaze, he dragged their joined hands between them. "I take you, Cairistiona."

She'd already made the vow before God, in worry and inattention. She had nothing to lose and everything to gain. And yet with the words came a huge, churning sense of stepping over the dark precipice of the unknown, that after they were spoken, her life, her world, would never be the same again.

"*I take you, Adam.*"

****

"What if that kind of vision took you during battle?" Christian asked as he helped her refasten the gown he'd so recently removed. This had been no slow, coaxing loving like last night. Defences down, she'd welcomed him openly, and they'd come together with swift almost fierce passion that burned too brilliantly to bear for long. Christian, to whom this kind of pleasure was still new and wondrous, still felt dazed as the memory of their wedding guests forced itself into her mind and she tugged at him to make him rise and dress in haste.

Only then did she begin to think of the implications of so debilitating a dream.

He said quite casually, "If it happened in battle, I'd die."

"But even the lesser dreams...it's like reality slips for you, and I'm fairly sure it happens frequently. Doesn't it happen in fights too?"

He hesitated, then shrugged. "Yes. Sometimes. Findlaech watches out for me. Some of the others too. They never talk about it, and neither do I, but I know it happens. Findlaech has saved my life many times over."

She turned to him, pinning her veil in place with the pretty band Gormflaith had lent her. "They think a great deal of you," she observed.

"I'm my father's son."

"It's more than that. You know it is."

His hands fell to his sides, his fingers twisting together uncomfortably. "If they follow me, and I try not to get them killed for no reason, that is enough."

She reached up and smoothed his hair, smiling a little ruefully.

"What?" he asked. "Do I look as if I've just tumbled my wife?"

She blushed and laughed and pushed him towards the door. But as she waited a discreet length of time to join the party, his words echoed in her mind. *"My wife."*

She was Adam MacHeth's *wife*. Daughter-in-law to the prisoner of Roxburgh.

If her loyalties had been divided before between her people and her king, how much more complicated were they now?

CHAPTER TWENTY-THREE

The king's court was in Edinburgh when news of the latest MacHeth raid reached it. Fergus of Galloway was enjoying a convivial evening there with several high-ranking earls who opined gloomily that it would be Perth itself which attracted MacHeth attention soon, that coastal attacks and northern raids would not be enough for them if something wasn't done.

"Don't run me through here," Fergus said with only partially pretended caution, "but couldn't the problem be solved by simply releasing Malcolm MacHeth? He's been captive for twenty years. There can't be much fight left in him."

"There's plenty left in his sons," Ferchar of Strathearn said dryly.

"You don't think they'd stop if their father was freed?"

"When they openly want the downfall of the king and the crown for themselves? No, I don't! And if I were you," the earl added, scowling at Fergus over his cup, "I'd stop suggesting such a course. It could be construed as treason."

Fergus wasn't often surprised, but the last word gave him an unpleasant jolt. "Treason?" he repeated. "I'm only discussing options to prevent any more such depredations by Malcolm MacHeth's sons!"

He saw the look exchanged between several of them and had to fight to maintain his expression of, he hoped, slightly amused surprise.

"There are rumours," Strathearn said, "that you are not long returned from Ross."

Fergus laughed. "You can't rule a country based on

rumour," he said, with just a hint of contempt. "Anyhow, what of Ross? How fares this knight of the king's and his Ross-born lady?"

"The MacHeths seem to have acknowledged the lady's right, for they don't appear to have objected to his presence. On the other hand, I haven't heard he's taken anything from them either, and he clearly hasn't killed the troublesome sons."

Fergus nodded consideringly, as if this was news to him, and moved on to other subjects.

The next morning, it clearly behoved him to visit the king himself in private, which he managed by a request to discuss urgent affairs in Galloway. Since he'd never acknowledged the king's right to interfere in Galloway, he was sure this would produce the audience he wanted, whatever the rumours about himself and Ross—and it did.

On his way through the castle's massive halls, he contrived to run into the lady Mairead.

"More beautiful every time I see you," he exclaimed, kissing her hand. "Tell me, do you still have occasion to visit Roxburgh?"

Although she smiled, her eyes grew wary. "When the court does. And of course, it has a bustling market. You might be interested in the French wine we found there."

"I might have tasted it," Fergus said. "And I believe we may have a mutual friend in the town."

She widened her eyes but didn't back down. "Oh? Who would that be?"

He leaned forward slightly, smiling. An observer—and there were a few—probably imagined he was flirting. "How is he after twenty years? Still angry and bellicose?"

"I don't recognise your description."

She'd been a child when Malcolm MacHeth had been taken. "I expect he's mellowed," Fergus suggested.

Mairead blinked, as if this was very far from the Malcolm MacHeth she knew. A pity, but at least Fergus was aware what he had to work with.

He smiled again and passed on, sure that Mairead wouldn't repeat his questions to anyone for fear of Fergus revealing what he knew of her visits to Malcolm MacHeth in Roxburgh.

The king received him in his private room, and in the circumstances, Fergus decided to get straight to the point. He didn't particularly like what he was about to do, but he could not have his loyalty doubted or his plans thwarted at this stage. There had to be sacrifice, but it wouldn't be him. And the MacHeths *had* foiled his plans to bring Malcolm Canmore's great-great-granddaughter into his family. Whatever the polite fictions Fergus had gone along with, he knew.

"Forgive my half-truth, Your Grace," Fergus said at once. "I'm naturally happy to discuss Galloway with you at any time, but my true reason for this private audience is one that requires rather more discretion."

The king's eyes lit up. He was still young enough to find intrigue exciting rather than dangerous. He sat and waved Fergus eagerly to the chair next to his.

"I recently had an opportunity," Fergus said, seating himself, "of meeting the sons of Malcolm MacHeth."

****

Adam and Donald were with their uncle Somerled in Kintyre when Fergus's messenger reached them. After several raids into the heart of Scotland and a few successful skirmishes with local militia, they'd repaired west for a long-awaited reunion with the Lord of Argyll and the Isles.

Somerled, larger than life and twice as noisy, held his growing territory together with a fist of iron. He had to. The Isles belonged in theory at least, to Norway, and the mainland to Scotland, and he had every intention of being king of both Argyll and the islands himself.

He laughed uproariously at the story of Adam's marriage, which was told him in private after severe warnings on the importance of secrecy.

"I can see the need," Somerled allowed, eyeing Adam with a mixture of pride and curiosity. "Well, by next summer, I should have matters settled in Man. And then I can meet this bride of yours, and together we can throw everything we have at the King of Scots. All the better if Fergus of Galloway joins us."

"Talking of Fergus," Donald said, "He's aware that Mairead is our messenger to my father."

"I know," Somerled replied. "I heard from her too. But I don't believe it matters. To be honest, I'm surprised she wasn't found out before this."

"Perhaps the king knows and is allowing it," Adam interjected.

Somerled frowned at him. "Why would he do that?"

Adam shrugged. "As imprisonment goes, my father's is not the most arduous. Our activities haven't made it worse for him. The king and his advisers, according to both Fergus and Mairead, are looking for alternatives to the current pointless situation."

"Which is?" Somerled enquired with an air of fascination.

"That they don't want the trouble of keeping my father in prison. It's too costly, particularly when they'll have to send the entire royal army against us in the end. Nor can they let him go to be an alternative king to the one who currently sits on the throne of Scone."

"I'm sure you have a solution," Somerled said.

"That in order to be released, my father swears allegiance to the crown, rather than the person of King Malcolm, for the earldom of Ross. In fact, the king is giving nothing away, since we effectively hold Ross in any case. And however the oath is worded, it wouldn't prevent Donald and me continuing the fight."

"You can be sure the king and his advisers are as aware of that as you are," Somerled said dryly. "It won't wash."

"It might if we're troublesome enough. If he has to send an army against Ross, it might as well be against all of us, rather than leaving my father still the focus for discontent. Anyway, none of this may be necessary. Fergus of Galloway claims to have the means to free my father."

Somerled glanced from him to Donald and back, and reached for the ale jug. "How well do you know Fergus?"

"Well enough," Donald said. "We think he wants to use us to topple the king and then seize the crown for himself. Or for his son. He probably even has a claim if you go back far enough."

"He doesn't," Adam said flatly. "Which is why he wanted Cairistiona. And Gormflaith. But he's more than capable of inventing one."

"Then you don't trust him at all," Somerled observed with a worrying shade of relief.

"We trust him to bring about my father's release," Donald said.

"Why? He could never twist Malcolm mac Aed round his

finger, even before."

Donald didn't look at his brother. "Adam's seen it."

Somerled groaned. "Damn it, Adam! I don't doubt your gift—I've seen you right too often. But I can't make policy decisions based on your dreams."

Donald stared at him. "You already have. When you began this rising with us."

Somerled drank a huge draught and banged the empty jug on the table. "Maybe," he said. "Or maybe I just wanted a fight. Come on, let's go and eat with the men—they're delighted to have you back, Adam."

"I'm not back. We leave for Ross in the morning."

His uncle threw his arm around his shoulders. "Do you have to be so bloody literal? So you're back for a night. Enjoy it."

It was as they went into the hall to join Somerled's raucous following that Fergus's messenger arrived, inviting them to Whithorn to finalise arrangements including the position of Malcolm mac Aed, their father.

Over the messenger's head, Adam met Donald's gaze. Somerled sent the messenger into the hall, while they followed more slowly.

"We have to go," Donald said urgently.

"With no following?" Adam returned.

"You said yourself—"

"I never said we should walk into a trap."

Donald cast his eyes upward. "He needs us! Why would he lay a trap for us? If he's to release our father, is this not worth the risk?"

Adam considered. Every instinct was crying out against it. His vision of Fergus with a rope twined around Donald was hard to ignore. And yet... "However many men we take into Galloway, it would never be enough if Fergus wished us ill. We should suggest a different meeting place and a time of our own choosing, and go home to wait for his answer."

Somerled slapped him on the back, hard enough to make him glad he wasn't already eating. "Ha! Desperate to get home to his new—"

"Discretion, my uncle," Donald murmured. "And Adam, there is no point in going home when we're already on this side of the country."

Again, Adam could see his point. But this long-awaited and necessary meeting with Somerled seemed only to make him long for Cairistiona all the more. He wanted to see her face at his first homecoming, read in her eyes if she'd missed him and was glad of his return. For himself, her presence in his hall and in his bed had become a necessity very quickly. Frighteningly quickly. And if he was honest, this feeling was at least partially responsible for his opposition to going farther south now to Galloway.

But Donald was restless, discontented, and as they sat down to feast and drink with Somerled, Adam could understand that too. In the beginning of their rising against the king, their raiding had been full of hope and excitement. And again, when Adam had returned from Somerled in the spring, it had been fun to plan and attack more daring targets together. Even today, they'd still been buoyed up by their success. But where Adam looked forward to his home and his wife, Donald wanted more adventure.

There was, Adam supposed, watching his brother's antics with the pretty serving girl, a certain frustrating sameness to what they were doing. Raid, fight, cause havoc, withdraw. And still their father wasn't released. No messenger from the king to offer terms had ever been sent. A sense of futility was understandable.

"How long are you in Kintyre?" Adam asked his uncle suddenly.

Somerled leaned forward to talk past Donald and the serving girl. "We rest until next week, all being well. Then I return to Man. Why?"

"What if we invite Fergus here?"

Donald pushed the girl to one side, though he didn't let go of her. He looked thoughtful. "You're prepared to wait?"

Adam shook his head. "One of us is enough." And Somerled's protection was far more useful than his own.

Donald grinned and pulled the girl back onto his lap. "I'll send the messenger home in the morning."

Somerled winked. "We'll keep Donald entertained here."

Remembering his own entertainment in Somerled's camps, Adam had no doubt of it.

When he parted from Somerled at dawn the following day, his hand clung to his uncle's in an echo of the same tug of regret he'd felt in the spring.

"Want to stay?" Somerled asked, only half joking.

"Yes," Adam admitted. Another season's campaigning with Somerled was a beguiling prospect in many ways. "Just not enough."

Somerled let out a crack of laughter. "Away and tell my sister to teach you the art of the white lie. Kiss your bride for me, and I'll be up in Ross very soon, hopefully with your father beside me! Do you want me to rouse your brother from whoever's bed he ended up in?"

"No, just kick him when he wakes."

Reluctantly, Adam released his uncle's hand and threw himself into the saddle. He remembered to wave and hoot to the islesmen as he rode through the camp, but his mind, his whole being, was already turning north and east to Ross. To Cairistiona.

****

Henry, his wounds healed, seemed to have become a different person, or at least more of the person Christian had occasionally glimpsed. He walked jauntily up the length of the hall towards the big table where she sat with her women, sewing by the brilliant summer sunlight streaming in the open shutters.

"Might I have a word, lady?" he asked.

Christian glanced around her women. Felicia was blushing.

Christian stood and gestured to him to walk with her. They strolled together towards the open hall door.

"We've been talking," Henry began. "The men and I. About your—and Adam mac Malcolm's—kind offer. Raoul and Gaston are too restless to settle anywhere—true mercenaries—and will head south as soon as they're released. The rest of us would stay."

Christian's spirits rose. She'd been right to work for their acceptance here. "You would need," she warned, "to swear allegiance to Adam mac Malcolm. With all that implies."

"I have no other allegiances to worry about," Henry said simply. He'd given his loyalty to William, but he had no ties, emotional or dutiful, to the King of Scots. Even William's allegiance to the king had been pragmatic, opportunistic. "We'll fight for Adam mac Malcolm. But we'd be happier serving as your house guards the rest of the time."

Touched, Christian said she'd speak to Adam when he

returned. Surely it wouldn't be long now? Findlaech and the men had come home several days ago, laden with booty and animals, which they'd been distributing across Ross on their way home. Tirebeck had some fine new cattle, and a thick purse of trinkets or gold—or both—sat on her table in the bedchamber waiting for Adam. Christian had refused to look at it. She felt uncomfortable enough about the cattle. But Findlaech had been cheerful and full of victorious optimism. Adam mac Malcolm, he'd said, sent his greetings and had gone west with Donald to meet with their uncle Somerled as planned.

How long would he stay? A couple of nights? A week? Perhaps he'd sail with him to Man and it would be months before he came home.

She shouldn't care, shouldn't wait for him, counting the hours, now that she knew he was safe. In truth, she dreaded him coming home, in case she'd been mistaken in his apparent reluctance to leave her, in case she'd read too much into his tenderness. And yet she longed, feeling curiously restless, almost…incomplete.

Oh Adam, what have you done to me?

"There's one other matter," Henry said into her reverie. "I ask your permission to marry Felicia."

Christian, dragged back to the present with a small jolt, blinked and then smiled with genuine pleasure. "You have it, with all my heart."

"It need not even deprive you of an attendant," Henry said eagerly, "if my position is also with you."

"Felicia should have her own household," Christian said, musing aloud. She turned and beckoned Felicia, who was gazing anxiously in their direction. Felicia dropped her sewing and hurried towards them so quickly, she almost tripped over her own feet. "We're discussing where you should live," Christian said with mock gravity, "when you are married to Henry."

Felicia's tense face broke into a huge smile. "Then you've agreed? Oh, thank you, lady! It was nothing either of us intended, only his nursing fell on me after the battle and we grew close. But I have no dowry, as you know, and Henry's position is so insecure…"

"It need not be. We'll sort things out when my—when Adam mac Malcolm returns."

It was odd, but she could never quite bring herself to call Adam "my husband." For so long that term had been used for a man she neither liked nor honoured, for whom she'd accepted continual humiliation and insult. Adam was…her lover. Although married, their relationship still seemed to hold all the guilty pleasures of secrecy, perhaps because her growing feelings for him since their first encounter had always been so secret, mostly even from herself. Besides she had no idea how to marry the duties of a wife with her loyalty to the king. If she didn't say it, she didn't have to think about it.

"My…my choice, if you allow it, would be to live in the little house that was yours before…*before*," she finished more definitely. "That way, I could be of more help to you." She hesitated, then drew in her breath. "I'm aware I…we all…have been poor attendants to you."

"I have been a poor mistress," Christian said ruefully. "I was used to taking care of myself. I didn't need attendants. Sir William thought it would add to my consequence." Or at least to his by implication.

"No," Felicia said emphatically. "You showed us nothing but kindness. We grew so used to ease that I didn't even notice until one day Eua asked me what we were for. I would like to be able to answer that. So would Cecily."

Alys's name was loud in its absence. But it seemed her influence had waned with William's death. Alys, Christian thought with another bout of guilt, seemed to be the only person who truly grieved for him. She sat beside Cecily, her pretty head drooping over her sewing, her hands perfectly still.

"We'll talk more later," Christian said to the happy couple. Then she raised her voice. "Cecily! Felicia has news to share. Go with her and hear it."

As Cecily bounced up with alacrity, Christian made her way back to the table where Alys sat alone. She didn't even look up as Christian sat down.

"It's time," Christian said lightly, "for you to make up your mind what you want to do."

Alys cast her a glance of dislike. "What choice do I have?"

"To stay or go. If you choose to go, it's possible I can arrange some means or a dowry for you. It will not be much, but it will be better than nothing. If you stay, then you must act as my attendant. I have no place for people who use up food and space and contribute nothing."

Alys's eyes flew to her in clear shock. "I'm sewing as you bade me," she said ungraciously.

"Are you?" Christian said dryly. She didn't need to look to know the garment was exactly as it had been when they'd first sat down an hour ago. "So which would you rather do?"

A little frown marred the girl's perfect brow. "Why would *you* do anything at all for *me*?"

Sometimes, Christian had wondered if Alys really understood what she was doing. But this statement left her in no doubt. She wasn't sorry for it, but she knew her behaviour had wronged the woman she called her lady.

Christian sighed. "We're not so different, Alys. Women have very little say in their disposal. My husband wronged you, and I bear the responsibility of that."

Alys's eyes spat as they'd done the day Adam MacHeth had fallen on their bodyguards and defeated them. "He chose me! He did not wrong me!"

Christian held her gaze, almost with pity. "He took you, an orphaned girl of good family, into our household where he might have been expected to hold a position of trust and care for you. And he kept you openly as his mistress. We'll never know whether or not he would have cast you off in time, but the point is, you are ruined for the respectable marriage your parents presumably wished for you. A tiny dowry and my friendship might change that a little. Or you can seek some other form of occupation elsewhere. Go south, go to England or France. If you prefer, the lady of Ross will find you a husband. Or you may stay here and work for me. There are no free places in Tirebeck anymore."

"Since you married Adam MacHeth the day after he killed Sir William."

Christian said nothing, but nor did she lower her gaze. It was Alys who did that.

"You had no choice, did you?" Alys said dully. "I used to tell myself it was all right, what I did with Sir William, because you didn't care for him nor he for you. Because you were a poor thing, disfigured and barren. And he loved *me*."

Maybe. Oddly, Alys's words didn't hurt her, though they might later, and they certainly would have before she came to

Tirebeck and began to realise her worth. And Adam didn't find her disfigured or poor. He called her rare and beautiful and pleasured himself in her every night and many mornings too. He was trying to make heirs, of course, but even Christian recognised there was more to it than that. As she was drawn to him, so was he to her, for however long it lasted. He'd said so on their wedding day, during that brief, urgent interlude between the ceremony and the feast.

"Then think," Christian said, standing up and gathering her work, "what is best for you now. I don't care, either way."

She'd said much the same thing to Adam just a few days after the wedding when his erratic gaze had fallen on Alys, eating at the women's table.

"Do you want her here?" he'd asked abruptly.

"I don't care," she'd replied with truth. She hadn't for a very long time.

"Send her to my mother, if you like. She might be able to find her a husband. Or I'll take her south with me if you prefer."

Something had clawed at her heart then. It felt remarkably like the moment she'd first learned that Alys shared William's bed when she herself did not, only this was both more intense and less certain. But the idea of Alys having the opportunity to take *this* husband was not to be borne.

And yet if not Alys... Men were, by nature, unfaithful. Adam would not insult her as William had, but she didn't delude herself about his celibacy when he left her hall. Like women the world over, she could live with that, though she didn't have to like it.

Dinner was well past, and she was preparing for bed while the extended sunshine of the long, northern summer day still seeped in under the shutters, when she heard the commotion that could only mean one thing. Adam had returned.

Suddenly her heart was galloping, her insides twisting. She hastily redressed with clumsy fingers and hurried out into the hall, which had been cleared for sleep although the men were refastening clothing and weapons as they pushed their way outside to greet their young lord.

A passage miraculously cleared for her, and she stepped outside the hall just as a single horseman rode through the open gate at a gallop. His head uncovered and his wild black hair blowing free in the wind, he wore a familiar red-brown cloak that was looking the worse for wear. But she saw no obvious signs of blood, no stiffness or staggering as he dismounted. But then, he'd learned to cover the signs so that his men never suspected he was ever wounded.

He threw himself off his horse, acknowledging the men with one raised hand while his head turned and his eyes searched and came to rest, finally, on Christian. She might have imagined the relaxing of his shoulders, for the rest of him seemed all restless motion as he strode across the yard to her—or at least to the hall door—expressions flitting across his unquiet face far too fast to be read. And his eyes, when he finally passed in front of her, were wild and intense enough to catch at her breath.

She couldn't move, though at least her mouth automatically formed some formal words of greeting. He took her unsteady hand in his large, rough one and kissed it, before bending and pressing another brief kiss on her lips, making her heart surge.

"Everything is well?" he asked abruptly, fixing her with that gaze that had so terrified her on their first meeting.

She nodded, opening her mouth to ask a thousand questions of her own, but already he was tugging her inside, striding so quickly that she had to trot to keep up with him. Clearly he didn't want to talk, or at least not to her.

She saw him seated and left the hall to find him food and ale, while the men all sat on the floor and demanded to know what had happened since they'd left him. The kitchen maid, who would have slept through a battle in the hall yard unless it was her normal early time to rise, was snoring on the floor. Christian stepped over her and found the cold remains of a chicken, some cheese and oatcakes and sweet, dried fruit and carried them with a jug of ale back to the hall, where she placed the tray in front of her husband.

He murmured thanks but didn't look at her. He was listening to the jointly told tale of the men's return to Ross, suitably embellished, no doubt. Christian sat quietly beside him as she should, not even touching him, and yet his heat seemed to flow into her. For some reason, the man at her side, ignoring her for his men, brought her something very like happiness just by his large, overwhelming presence. And yet amid that happiness and excitement was a churning anticipation, a dread that this now would be all she ever had of him.

For a little, she merely sat, absorbing him as he munched his ravenous way through the food, occasionally pausing for a draught of ale. Part of her wanted to sit there all night, as long as he did, but if Christian had learned anything in her previous marriage, it was when she was de trop.

At least when she rose and murmured good night, he noticed, for he rose with her, though she gave him no time to do more. By the time she closed the bedchamber door, he was seated again with his back to her, hurling an amused question at Cailean.

She undressed once more and climbed between the cool sheets. She closed her eyes and tried to concentrate on that inner part of her that was soothed by his return, ignoring the silly, jangling nerves that didn't matter. It would be a long night if she didn't sleep, and tomorrow would then be twice as difficult.

It took time, but she was finally about to drift off when the bedchamber door opened. Although it wasn't quite dark, she'd left the lamp burning low for him. Its glow shadowed his still figure as he stood just inside the door gazing towards her.

She said, "I'm not asleep. Are you hurt?"

He shook his head, unfastening his belt and dropping it on an open chest as he walked towards her. He sank down on the side of the bed, staring down at her, focused but unreadable, still every inch, it seemed, in his warrior persona.

"I thought you might be injured," she said, mainly to cover his silence. "When you first arrived, you seemed to be looking for me."

His lips parted and closed again as if he'd decided that he wouldn't respond to that either. Then he said, "I thought you might have gone."

"Gone?" she repeated, startled.

He looked away. "You left my mother's hall. I know you didn't want this. Without me here, you could have relied on the king to give you Tirebeck."

Her throat closed up. "That's why you left some of your men here."

"No, I left them to make sure you didn't send any messages to the king. And to make sure the Normans didn't threaten you now that you're my wife."

"But you still weren't sure I'd be here when you returned." She wanted to touch his cheek, to bring back his attention and keep it, but she didn't quite dare; and in any case, it seemed that she'd never lost it.

His gaze came back to her. "I think…I wanted you to have the choice. Before I brought you back."

Deep inside, something was hurting. She said, "When we're apart, I suppose whatever you saw in me, in us, doesn't seem so rare."

A frown flickered across his brow. In one movement, shocking in its swiftness, he swept the mask from her face, as if its concealment irked him. She forced herself not to react, not to snatch it back. It was much too late for that.

"More rare," he said, staring at her, not at her disfigurement, but at her whole face, her eyes, her lips, where he lingered. "I'm travel stained and weary. I haven't washed in three days. I don't suppose you'd accept me into your bed as I am?"

Wordless, she pulled the covers back. A smile chased across his lips, lightening his heavy, dark eyes. He pulled his tunic and shirt up over his head in one movement and dropped them on the floor.

And now, it seemed she could touch him, the dark bruise on his shoulder, his unshaven, hollowed cheek. His eyes widened, as if her gesture startled him. It had been thoughtless, pure instinct, but when she tried to drop her hand, not wishing to intrude if all he wished was to sleep, he turned, caught it in his, and turned his mouth into her palm.

His weight bore her back into the pillows as he lay over her and kissed her mouth as she'd longed for, deep and possessive. Although he took her without even removing all his clothes, it was unhurried, tender, inexorable, a giving and receiving of joy so intense, it made her weep. But finally, it was dark and the lamp had burned out, so she could wipe the tears in secret on the pillow, on her own hair, holding his big, hard body half-slumped across hers, still at last in exhausted sleep.

I love you. God help me, I love you.

CHAPTER TWENTY-FOUR

Emerging from the dairy late the following morning, Christian lifted her face to the sun's warmth. A breeze whipped at her veil, and darker clouds in the distance over the sea threatened the end of the fine weather. Christian didn't mind. The fragile happiness that had been creeping over her since her unsought wedding was settling around her like a warm, comfortable cloak.

Until she lowered her gaze again and saw Adam's tall back, just at the corner of the main hall. A woman's arm snaked around his neck; her body seemed to be draped half across his in a teasing, sensual pose Christian had pretended not to see before when the back had been William's. But the woman was undoubtedly the same.

Stricken, she couldn't move, couldn't breathe, for all the old feelings tumbling over her like a deluge of cold water. *Not this. Not him too. Is this all there ever is?*

She didn't even want to run and hide. She just wondered how she could kill her bright new love for Adam, because even this betrayal didn't seem to be doing the job, judging by the terrible, galloping pain in her heart.

Adam reached up, closing his hand over Alys's on his neck, and yanked it downwards. He brushed her aside like an importunate swarm of midges, and walked on towards the hall. Alys stared after him, her mouth slightly open, as if stunned by her first ever rejection.

Now, it seemed, Christian's knees were inclined not to

hold her up. She allowed herself one moment, leaning against the dairy door, to deal with her easing pain and her relief, and then she straightened and walked on towards Alys's still figure.

As she drew abreast of the other woman, Alys finally turned her head and saw her. "I've thought about it, lady," Alys said in a small, hard voice. "I need to leave this place."

Because she had no chance of being lady here, of supplanting Christian in even the smallest, least important things. Alys must find her own way, as Christian had.

"Very well." Perhaps it was the relief of a sudden, awful suspicion disproved, but Christian wanted to skip across the yard to the hall. Restraining herself, she met Adam in the doorway coming out with her cloak over one arm.

A faint smile lit his face when he saw her. "Walk with me," he suggested, handing her the cloak.

This kind of companionship in aimless wandering was new to her, and she found it rather wonderful. She'd accompanied her half sisters on expeditions, but she'd had the task of looking after them, and, occasionally, her older stepsisters, who'd regarded her as more of a maid. Eua's companionship in visiting some of her people was the closest she'd known to this—and that wasn't very close at all.

Adam seemed to have no purpose except, intoxicatingly, to be with her. He moved easily through the hills and woods, relaxed and apparently at peace, sometimes in silence, sometimes asking her questions about her life before she came home to Scotland.

"My mother told me stories about home," she said. "Traditions, and mythical tales and actual history. I had difficulty telling which was which."

"So do the rest of us," Adam said wryly.

"She never said so, but I know she missed Tirebeck. Despite all that must have happened to her, she used to talk of us coming home as if we really would one day. She told me I was the heir to Tirebeck as my father's only child, but when she died, I had no one else to feed me the tales. I didn't forget them, though, just the language."

"Is that why you came home?" he asked. "Because of your mother? Or was it William's idea?"

"It was my idea," she said. "William married me because

Ranulf told him I had land in Scotland. He didn't tell him it was in a remote and disputed part of the country where the King's word didn't stretch or even count. William found out soon enough, though, added it to his grudges against me and forgot about it until the work began to dry up. I reminded him of Tirebeck, assured him we could get the king's support for him to hold it."

She smiled faintly, pausing to catch her breath as they reached the top of a hill and she could look down on the hall and the village and the sea. "It was the one time we acted in accord. I thought my life would be different if only I could go home, that William and I would reach a better understanding if we were working together."

"Did you?"

She shook her head. "No. We wanted different things for Tirebeck, and it wasn't enough to maintain his mercenaries. He needed to defeat you and receive the earldom the king had promised him. I realised early on that I'd been naive, that he could never defeat you with his handful of knights. But he never saw that."

She glanced up at him. "But then, my new idea of reaching an accord with you and bringing you somehow into the king's fold was equally naive, was it not?"

He put his arm around her shoulders, holding her to his side. "Yes. But I thank you for trying. I was always in accord with you. But never him."

"You don't want foreigners here, and yet you're offering land to Henry and the others."

"I have no objection to foreigners as such, merely those who'd take Ross from us. And keep you from me."

She swayed against him. "Adam. You wanted me for your brother."

"My head said that was how it should go. I could reinterpret the dreams to make that right. Just not my own...wishes." He glanced down, meeting her gaze. "Donald would have been a more...comfortable husband for you."

"Neither of you are comfortable," she retorted. But because she wanted to, she rested her head against his arm, and they stood like that for a long time before they began to walk down the hillside to the wood that ran back down towards the hall.

Here, the sunlight and the birds' song were muffled by the

close growth of the trees. Under the branches of an old spruce, Adam halted and cupped her face, leaning down to kiss her. And when that ended, he kissed her again.

"What are you doing?" she asked breathlessly when she could speak.

"Courting you," he answered. "There was never time before."

And just for a little, it was sweet to reach up to his cheek and kiss him back, even when the black clouds finally caught up with them and rain trickled between their faces and into her mouth. Smiling, she buried her face in his chest, listening to the beat of his heart, and wondered what she'd done to deserve such intense, consuming happiness.

EPILOGUE

Donald wasn't convinced that the monastery at Whithorn was the best place for a discreet meeting, Monks wrote to each other all the time, and the king was bound to hear of it all the quicker. Which meant, he thought with some excitement as he rode through the town on borrowed horses with his two followers and Fergus's messenger, that Fergus's plan to obtain his father's release was surely about to reach fruition.

He wasn't sorry to be the one overseeing it. Since his return from the western isles, Adam had been the one making all the plans. With maturity, Adam had learned to command as well as fight, using rather than hiding his strangeness, and Donald had to admit it sat well on him. Their mother and the men, his own and Adam's, obviously thought so too. Donald loved his brother and had grown up both protecting him and trusting him. It came hard to realise Adam no longer needed that protection. Perhaps he never had. Perhaps it had always been Adam protecting him in his own, weird way.

Whatever, Donald didn't really like the twinges of jealousy that had crept into his thoughts of Adam. Perhaps that was what had changed his mind in Kintyre, and when Adam had ridden north to Ross and his bride, instead of sending Fergus's messenger south to Galloway, Donald had sailed with him.

The messenger, who'd pointed the way, now fell back as they rode up the hill towards the monastery, giving Donald his place. So that when the men erupted from the buildings and the trees, they cut Donald and his two men off from the messenger.

Donald wasn't worried. He'd taken much the same precautions when Fergus's band had entered Ross. Fergus himself strolled across the road on foot, armed to the teeth as always but dressed as the great lord he was.

"Greetings, Donald mac Malcolm!" he called. "Welcome to Galloway, and to Whithorn."

Since Fergus was on foot, Donald dismounted. Which was when the whine of arrows rent the air and both of Donald's men fell to the ground without uttering a sound.

Blood sang in Donald's ears, fury for the death of his friends tore at his heart, along with shame because he'd allowed himself to be betrayed by the man Adam had warned against. He drew his sword free, urging the horses forward with him, to give him cover until they got as far as Fergus's men, when Donald slapped the horses' rumps and lunged, killing one man instantly with his sword through the heart and felling another with his dagger in the stomach.

He'd dealt with four more, dead or incapacitated, before Fergus's men got close enough to disarm him and Fergus himself held a sword point to his throat.

"You'll rot in hell for this, you treacherous bastard," Donald panted.

"Treacherous?" Fergus said, gazing down upon him with curious sympathy. "My dear Donald, you are in my country for unknown reasons, and wanted very badly by the King of Scots. What else could I do but my loyal duty to my royal ally?"

THE END

HISTORICAL NOTE

One of the many mysteries of this shadowy period of Scottish history is the identity of Malcolm MacHeth and the nature of his family's "beef" with the kings of Scots, against whom the MacHeths were in intermittent rebellion from 1124 until 1215.

Most historians agree that the MacHeths' quarrel was dynastic, that they had some kind of genuine claim to the Scottish throne—borne out, perhaps, by the fact that Malcolm MacHeth was imprisoned, not executed or even mutilated, as was the fate of most who took up arms against the Canmore kings. It is possible he was an illegitimate son of King Alexander I, although in this case why would his patronymic be mac Aed?

The suggestion I like best is that he was a descendant of King Lulach, Macbeth's stepson, who was King of Scots for nine months before being killed by Malcolm Canmore who became King Malcolm III.

It was in Malcolm III's reign that the old tradition of alternating the kingship between two branches of the royal family (known as the Cénel Gabrain and the Cénel Loairn), finally died out. In accordance with European customs, Malcolm and his wife Margaret (later Saint) instigated strict primogeniture, which passed the crown directly through the eldest legitimate male line. This may have modernized and stabilized the kinghsip, but it hacked off some powerful families who were thereby excluded from competing for the kinghsip. It seems likely from the dates of their main risings (1124 when King David came to power, 1130 when

Alexander II succeeded, and 1153 when Malcolm IV was crowned) that the MacHeths were fighting for the throne itself.

Malcolm MacHeth has been linked to the earldoms of both Moray and Ross. My own belief (see the genealogical table at the beginning of the book), based on the suggestion of historian R. Andrew McDonald, is that his father was one Aed, Earl of Ross, and that his mother was a granddaughter of King Lulach whose family is historically linked to the earldom of Moray. Malcolm's brother Angus, associated with him in earlier rebellions in the 1130s, inherited Moray from their mother, while Malcolm inherited Ross, which he then lost through his defeat at the Battle of Stracathro in 1130.

We do know that Malcolm MacHeth was married to a sister of Somerled, the Lord of the Isles—although we don't know her name so I gave her the Norse name Halla—and that he had at least three children: the sons who allied with Somerled against the king in 1153, and a daughter, Gormflaith (or Hvarflod).

Historians are fairly sure that one of Malcolm MacHeth's sons was the Donald chronicled as being captured at Whithorn in 1156. We hear no more of Donald, though there is later mention of an Adam son of Donald who was seized by the king in 1186. This Adam may or may not be a MacHeth, but I used his existence to give Donald's brother the name Adam, after whom Donald called his son.

Christian and William de Lanson are entirely made up characters, but there were certainly many "French" knights in Scotland who married Scottish heiresses and settled on their land to found great families such as the Bruces. Lanson, of course, didn't get the chance, but I like to think there were women like Christian whose first care was for her people.

Of the other historical characters in this book, Symeon is documented as Bishop of Ross during this period, and it is possible, although not certain, that the bishopric was still passed on through family inheritance in the old tradition.

Fergus of Galloway most certainly existed, as did his sons Uhtred and Gilbert, although there is no evidence that he ever sought alliance with the MacHeths through marriage or other means. However, since Donald was captured in Whithorn, Galloway, it seems probable that Fergus was responsible, although we can only guess at his motives. Like Donald's life after his capture, and how it affected his family, that is another story...

Please read on for a taste of that story!

If you enjoyed *Rebel of Ross*, and would like to keep up with Mary's new releases and other book news, please sign up to Mary's mailing list to receive her occasional Newsletter: http://eepurl.com/b4Xoif

Now, please read on for an excerpt from the sequel to *Rebel of Ross*, LADY OF ROSS, which will be published towards the end of 2016.

LADY OF ROSS

CHAPTER ONE

"It's done," Fergus of Galloway told the young King of Scots, who was hawking in the Pentland Hills.

King Malcolm, riding with Fergus a little way apart from his courtiers, bestowed a genuine smile upon him. "Excellent! Where *are* the captured MacHeth sons?"

"Well," Fergus confessed, "I only have Donald. Adam didn't come, although with the bait of his brother, I could probably catch him, too. On the other hand, I don't want a war in Galloway if I can help it. Donald is probably enough for our purposes."

The king was still smiling as he gazed into the sky. His hawk had caught a sparrow. He held out his gloved hand and the hawk flew towards it. "Then perhaps it's time I visited Roxburgh. You'd better bring your prisoner there."

"*Your* prisoner, your Grace," Fergus said graciously. He wheeled his horse around and found the lady Mairead of Kingowan almost in front of him, gazing upward at the soaring, hunting hawks.

Damn her, the woman moved like a snake, silent and inconvenient. But he knew how to deal with women, even dangerous ones. Especially when they were as comely as Mairead. Fergus, retreating from the royal presence as the rest of the court advanced, urged his horse even closer to the apparently distracted lady Mairead.

"Lady Mairead," he murmured. "I was just thinking of

you... Can we escape this dullness, do you think?"

Yes, there it was, the betraying blush and flutter that meant a little dalliance would not be unacceptable.

"Slip away into the wood as you pass," she breathed with unmistakable promise.

He watched from the corner of his eye as she began to walk her horse casually in that direction. Fergus's blood heated. She was, in fact, a fine looking woman. Keeping her silent for a few days would be no hardship. He wondered if she did more for his old friend Malcolm mac Aed than carry his messages from prison.

An image of Halla, Malcolm's lady, swam before his eyes. He really was a lucky bastard for a prisoner. To have a pretty, willing woman visiting him in captivity and a beautiful, wise and loyal one to come home to...eventually. Well, the lady of Ross was beyond Fergus's reach, but Mairead, clearly, was not.

Pretending his young hawk had dropped something over the trees—when in fact the stupid bird was probably half way home to Galloway—Fergus rode off to investigate. Although he made a lot of noise clumping about, Mairead didn't immediately appear. He had to search for her, find her tracks. And they led straight through to the other side of the wood, back in the direction of Edinburgh.

****

Mairead was nobody's fool, except perhaps Malcolm MacHeth's. Giving Fergus the slip provided her with the time she needed to ride back to Edinburgh, summon her discreet messenger and send him north to Ross.

That done, she cleansed and anointed her body, put on her best gown and repaired to Fergus's rooms in the city. She'd only just settled herself in his best chair and, making use of the writing materials she found on the table, begun to write a dull letter to her husband, when Fergus came striding in, scowling, no doubt with irritation at being made a fool of. However, his expression when he caught sight of her was almost worth it.

"What-what–what the... " he spluttered.

"Where have you been?" Mairead demanded, throwing down her pen, which spattered ink over her letter. Oh well, it would still do. "I've been waiting here for hours."

"That's funny. I was scouring the wood for hours."

She narrowed her eyes. "Do I look like a woodsman's daughter to you?"

His gaze swept over her person, betraying only too clearly what he'd like to do with it. "No," he said hoarsely. "God, no."

"I thought not," she purred, standing up to let him embrace her exotically scented person before she pulled free and spun around to seize her cloak. "On the other hand, you are too late. My husband misses me. I've been summoned home."

It spoke volumes for Fergus's frustration that it was late in the evening before he even thought to enquire who had left Edinburgh that afternoon while he'd been raking through the woods. And by then, he hadn't a hope of catching them.

****

To counteract the rumours that were already seeping in from Galloway, King Malcolm left Fergus in Edinburgh while he and the Earl of Strathearn travelled in private to Roxburgh.

King Malcolm had met the prisoner in Roxburgh castle once before, when he'd first become king and had gone through curiosity to see what sort of a monster he held that was so frightening even his grandfather King David hadn't had the courage to kill him. Or so young Malcolm had told himself. In reality, he'd been well aware there were other reasons no one would execute Malcolm mac Aed, reasons to do with tradition and honour as well as pragmatism.

The prisoner represented a royal kindred which had been wronged by the king's own. They were cousins, distant but undeniable. Malcolm MacHeth could only be killed in battle, for those reasons...and because a martyr with heirs to his cause was a focus for the swirling discontent in the country, from slighted or greedy nobles to hungry bondsmen and serfs who'd suffered raids or taxation.

The chamber housing Malcolm MacHeth was not uncomfortable. He had a window that allowed in fresh air and light. He had a fireplace for warmth in winter, a bed to sleep in, a bench to sit on, and books to read. He was allowed to exercise in the big inner courtyard, to ride and practice jousting, archery and sword play. He had respectable clothes, books, writing materials and an old harp to strum. He was even allowed an occasional female visitor, although none from his family who would have been instantly seized.

As soon as the guard opened his cell door, Malcolm rose from the bench on which he'd been reading. He would have been warned to expect the king. A beam of sunlight shone from the high window onto the bench, falling partially still on the tall, saturnine prisoner. The other half of his face remained in shadow, and the king wondered if that was deliberate, to hide his true thoughts or to confuse his visitors.

Malcolm MacHeth bowed to the king, but did not kneel. He had a certain stature, a presence that the young king envied because it wasn't haughty or arrogant, just...confident. Which was odd in a man who'd been incarcerated since the age of twenty-three. But then, he'd been in arms against King David since the age of thirteen.

Although now over forty years old, no grey marred the dark head of Malcolm MacHeth, one time Earl of Ross.

"Good day to you, sir," the king said amiably in English. "I see that you are well."

"As are you, sir, by appearance. I'm honoured to receive you in my humble dwelling."

"Actually, you are," the king said, scowling. "But where are my manners? I have brought you another visitor."

The prisoner's eyebrows rose, but he did not move as the guard pushed Donald MacHeth into the room.

Unarmed but unbound and with few hurts apart from those healing after his fight with Fergus of Galloway's men, Donald stood stock still beside the king, his gaze fixed on his father. His Adam's apple wobbled as he swallowed. Tall, dark, lean, with those liquid dark eyes, he was unmistakably a MacHeth

And his father didn't know him.

For the first time, the king felt ashamed, almost guilty. But he'd gone too far to back down at this stage. "I see introductions are required. Malcolm, son of Aed, meet Donald, son of...yourself."

Malcolm's lips parted in shock. Although this was what the king had wanted to provoke in his unflappable prisoner, for some reason the success didn't make him happy.

Without permission, Donald took a stumbling step forward and fell to his knees—as he hadn't before the king.

"Father," Donald whispered, bowing his head. "Forgive me."

As if he couldn't help it, Malcolm's hand reached down, touching the bowed head of the son he hadn't laid eyes on in over twenty years. "Forgive *you*? For what?"

Donald's voice was hoarse, difficult, almost as if he were being strangled. "Being taken, being here. That *you* are still here."

"Well, I can't blame you for either of the latter," Malcolm said with a hint of the humour that must have been his saving grace through his long isolation from the world. "I don't know why you're here, but I can't yet be sorry." He grasped his son's hair, tilting up his head. A smile flickered across his face. Donald's breath caught.

The king couldn't doubt the charged emotion between the two. He'd imagined somehow that there would be more anger, more gnashing of teeth than this silent, curiously helpless staring. He wondered what thoughts filled Donald's head, as he finally beheld his legendary parent, and something almost like jealousy pulled at him. He could never have been king without the death of his own father, whom he missed suddenly with the force of an armoured punch in the chest.

"I see your mother in you," Malcolm said softly to his son.

"I see my brother in you," Donald said. "I never expected that."

"Where is your brother?"

"In Ross." In response to Malcolm's tug, he stumbled to his feet. His father held him by the shoulders in a grip that must have hurt. The man's knuckles were white.

"And Gormflaith? And your mother?"

"Also."

As if forcing himself, Malcolm relaxed his grip without releasing it. Over Donald's shoulder, he addressed the king. "Why have you brought my son here?"

The king smiled. "To take your place. I'm sending you home."

No one moved. The silence rang in the king's ears. Slowly, Malcolm MacHeth's hands fell away from his son's shoulders and back to his own sides.

"Why?" Malcolm asked.

The king shrugged elaborately. "Everyone seems to want

it. I'm told it's unfair to keep you so long, that there's no fight left in you after twenty-two years. That if I let you go, your sons and your brother-in-law will stop attacking my people. On the other hand, I can't have you raising rebellion again as soon as you flex your free muscles. One of your sons is still free to cause havoc. You must exert your fatherly duties and keep him in line."

Malcolm MacHeth regarded him with something like fascination. "Must I?"

"Yes," the king replied. "Because I will have your other son here in your old chamber, hostage to your obedience *and* Adam MacHeth's."

Oddly it was Donald who turned on the king with scorn. "Clearly you have never met my brother Adam."

"It makes no difference," Malcolm MacHeth said abruptly, seating himself once more on the bench. "I will not leave my son here."

Donald blinked rapidly. "No," he said hoarsely. "You *must* go. For everyone's sake. For Ross."

Malcolm shook his head. "I will not compel you to a youth wasted in prison. Mine is over and I'm used to this...half-life."

The king scowled with growing irritation. "By your leave, sir, it is not up to you! If necessary, I will simply have you thrown out of the gates!"

"Then I'll sit there, outside the castle gates," Malcolm MacHeth said stubbornly. "But I will not go home."

This was not going at all the way the king or Fergus had planned. For the first time since he'd ascended the throne, young Malcolm found himself bereft of words. But help came from an unexpected quarter.

Donald threw himself on to the bench beside his father. "No, no, this is right," he said excitedly. "This is the way it's meant to be! Adam *saw* this, sir. That Fergus would bring about your release. Admittedly we didn't expect it *this* way, but that doesn't matter. The gates are open for you and you must go home for everyone's sake." His voice lowered and he murmured something beneath his breath.

The king, however had excellent hearing and to him it sounded like. "It will be all right, I swear. Adam will come for me."

Poor deluded idiot had lived too long in the wilds of Ross. Everyone knew Roxburgh Castle was impregnable. And if no one, not even the notorious Adam, had been able to rescue Malcolm MacHeth, why on earth would he be able to release the son?

Malcolm MacHeth himself seemed to be of a similar mind. He gazed at Donald a moment longer before he said, "No. Keep both of us if you have to, but I will not leave here without my son."

Ungrateful *bastard*. The king knew an urge to run both of them through. Or just to walk away leaving the door open and hope they'd be gone by morning. Instead, he stalked out and slammed the door closed. He hoped the noise would give Malcolm MacHeth second thoughts.

"Now what in the name of all the fiends of hell do I do?" the king raged to Ferchar of Strathearn.

"Send to Malcolm's wife," the earl advised.

The king blinked at him. "And force her to choose between her husband and her son? She hasn't laid eyes on the husband for over twenty years! Why would she choose him?"

The earl gave a wry smile. "Because absence makes the heart grow fonder? No, she is by all accounts a wise lady. And the husband has much more chance of negotiating the release of the son than the other way around. Or so she will imagine."

****

When the messenger was brought in, Halla, the lady of Ross had been enjoying a rare moment of solitude. She sat in the quiet area of her hall, in the little square that had formed around the several short passages that led to the new bed-chambers. A headache had begun to plague her, and the patter of the rain on the hall roof seemed somehow ominous. In the hope of soothing away both headache and groundless fears, she asked Muiredach, her harpist, to play.

As always, he found the music she needed, playing to suit her mood. She should never, she reminded herself, take Muiredach for granted. Leaning her head against the chair's high back, she closed her eyes and let the music in.

It was almost working when the quick footsteps sounded in the main hall, and the rough, peremptory voice of Sweyn, the commander of her house guard, demanded the lady.

Muiredach stopped playing. "Give me the message. I'll

pass it to her when she wakes." Muiredach was not a soldier, but he did everything he could to protect her. He always had, which was sweet. But she was Halla, sister of the turbulent Somerled, Lord of the Isles, lady of the long absent rebel Earl of Ross and mother of the wildest sons in Christendom. There was nothing left for him to protect her from.

She opened her eyes. "Here, Sweyn,"

Muiredach began to play again as Sweyn barged around to her quiet sanctum. He carried a letter sealed with plain wax, and at sight of it, Halla's stomach tightened. She knew the plain seal and she knew the writing on front.

It wasn't yet time for another communication from the lady Mairead.

In truth, Halla's feelings about Mairead's letters had always been confused. When they'd begun, they'd brought Malcolm directly into her life for the first time in almost twenty years. Notes in his handwriting, his words. She'd been able to see him again in her mind, brighter, more intense, even if logic told her he could no longer look like the dashing young man who'd turned the kingdom upside down to win a crown.

Still, Mairead, whom she'd never met, had brought something of him back to her, at no little personal risk. There had always been guilt over that. And jealousy.

None of which she ever had or ever would reveal to another living soul.

Taking the letter, she broke the seal.

It was short. Too short. For an instant, the words danced incomprehensibly before her eyes; a terrible foreboding tried to take hold. But she was the lady of Ross, who'd held the scattered, difficult earldom in peace and prosperity, in the teeth of the King of Scots, for more than twenty years. She could read one more letter.

She did.

The blood sang in her ears, drowning Sweyn's voice and even the music of Muiredach's harp. Her fingers could no longer hold the parchment which fluttered to the floor. Through the ringing of her ears, she heard a voice at last, saying only one word, over and over. "No. No. No. No." It was her own. The burden, at last, was too great.

Gasping, she threw herself from the chair, the habits

twenty years driving her to hide this unbearable grief from her people. Donald, her son was taken. Not just Malcolm, but Donald, too. Would it never end? Why did it never get *better*?

Furious at last with such pathetic whining, she forced her shoulders down and made herself turn to face Sweyn and Muiredach, and the women who were running to her from all over the hall.

"Sweyn, have this taken to Adam in Tirebeck." She didn't tell him to come. She wouldn't need to. They needed to talk, to make plans for this too. And more than that, she needed the comfort of Adam, her remaining free son, under her roof.

Watch out for LADY OF ROSS, available late 2016. To receive immediate word of its release, please sign up to Mary Lancaster's Newsletter: http://eepurl.com/b4Xoif .

Other Books by Mary Lancaster
In e-book and print

A Prince to be Feared: the love story of Vlad Dracula
An Endless Exile
A World to Win

Coming late 2016:
Lady of Ross, a sequel to *Rebel of Ross*

Praise for Mary Lancaster's historical novels:

"An absorbing historical love story... exquisite characterization and storytelling skills... a love story as poignant as Romeo and Juliet... a rich, vibrant historical novel." *TBR Mountain Range*

"Lancaster counters her larger than life male lead with an equally impressive love interest, balancing his vivid energy against her subtle and steady strength... Different yet memorable... a unique perspective." *Flashlight Commentary*

"deep and thought provoking, realistic and exciting... humorous and witty... absolutely stunning." *Love Romances and More*

ABOUT MARY LANCASTER

Mary Lancaster's first love was historical fiction. Her other passions include coffee, chocolate, red wine and black and white films - simultaneously where possible. She hates housework.

As a direct consequence of the first love, she studied history at St. Andrews University. She now writes full time at her seaside home in Scotland, which she shares with her husband, three children and a small, crazy dog.

Connect with Mary on-line:
Email Mary: Mary@MaryLancaster.com
Website: http://www.MaryLancaster.com
Newsletter sign-up: http://eepurl.com/b4Xoif
Facebook: https://www.facebook.com/mary.lancaster.1656